WHERE BLUE BEGINS

JANICE DEANER

WHERE BLUE BEGINS

A DUTTON BOOK

DUTTON
Published by the Penguin Group
Penguin Books USA Inc., 375 Hudson Street,
New York, New York 10014, U.S.A.
Penguin Books Ltd, 27 Wrights Lane,
London W8 5TZ, England
Penguin Books Australia Ltd, Ringwood,
Victoria, Australia
Penguin Books Canada Ltd, 10 Alcorn Avenue,
Toronto, Ontario, Canada M4V 3B2
Penguin Books (N.Z.) Ltd, 182–190 Wairau Road,
Auckland 10, New Zealand

Penguin Books Ltd, Registered Offices:
Harmondsworth, Middlesex, England

First published by Dutton,
an imprint of New American Library,
a division of Penguin Books USA Inc.
Distributed in Canada by McClelland & Stewart Inc.

First Printing, March, 1993
10 9 8 7 6 5 4 3 2 1

Acknowledgment for permission to reprint lyrics on page 378:
"Let's Call the Whole Thing Off" (George Gershwin, Ira Gershwin) © 1936 CHAPPELL & CO.,
(renewed). All rights reserved. Used by permission.

 REGISTERED TRADEMARK—MARCA REGISTRADA

LIBRARY OF CONGRESS CATALOGING-IN-PUBLICATION DATA

Deaner, Janice.
Where blue begins / Janice Deaner.
p.   cm.
ISBN 0-525-93580-0
I. Title.
PS3554.E1743W48   1993
813'.54—dc20   92-18157
                                      CIP

Printed in the United States of America
Set in Cochin
Designed by Steven N. Stathakis

PUBLISHER'S NOTE

For Nik Malvania

I would like to thank the following people for their help and inspiration:

My mother and father, Irving Paul Lazar, Mary Lazar, Alan Nevins, Bruce Kaplan, Peter Mayer, Robert Dreesen, my friends Deborah and Gene Anderson, Helene Leff, and my sister Sandy Deaner.

1

The trouble started when I was ten years old. Actually, it started before that, but it wasn't until I was ten that I really noticed it. My family moved from Detroit that year, in 1967, to a rural town in Upstate New York, and that's when it all came out. It was as if it had been building up all those years only to unfurl in those lush green hills, far away from any place that really mattered.

There was my father, whom we all called Leo, and my mother, who wanted us to call her Mama, though we never did. We called her by her name instead — Lana, or, as Leo called her, La. There was my older sister, Elena, and my younger brother, Harry, and me, Maddie.

Leo was over six feet tall and had arms that seemed too thick and long for the rest of his body. His face had a savagery about it as if he had spent his life sailing Viking ships, and with soft brown hair covering his whole body in some thickness or another, he sometimes looked like a docile ape. One picture comes to mind: Leo standing on Long Island Sound as he strained against a sailboat, looking like an uncoordinated Adonis. He was hunched over, his back arched in a muscled hump, while his bulky arms lumbered through the mechanics of wrestling this thing upright. For a moment I felt sorry for him.

He never seemed completely at ease with his body, as if he were really a smaller man floundering around inside this large frame. I'd sometimes think it would have suited him better to have been born taller and more slender. It was his eyes, though, that flattened any notion that he was filled with the malevolence of apes or Vikings—they were big and soft-edged and cool blue, but more than anything they were as simple as a baby's.

He was a pianist, and he never did look right sitting on that delicate little bench Lana had bought for him, touching those pale keys with his thick fingers. It was always a wonder to me to watch as he set his fingers in motion, running through Bach's Inventions or Clementi's Sonatinas, as if there were no air or gravity around them, as if in the end they had less to do with Leo than they did with God.

His family came from Lansing, Michigan. We went there a few times a year, for holidays and during the summertime, to visit his father and his three sisters and all their children (twelve in all). His mother had died before I was born, but even so I never felt her absence was complete. There were framed photographs of her every-where in that house—on coffee tables, on windowsills, and hanging on the walls. Two large oil paintings of her hung, not over the fire-place, but in the entrance of the house, as if she were hovering there to greet you, and at the top of the second-floor stairs, as if she wanted to tell you good night. Laramie was her name, and they all did what they could to preserve her memory.

Lana, on the other hand, didn't have much of a family, at least not that I knew of. There was her mother, Mimi, who, unlike Laramie, was very much alive and yet rarely mentioned. There were no photo-graphs of Mimi, much less large oil paintings of her, and at the age of ten I could only remember having seen her once at her house on Long Island Sound. As far as I knew she was the only family Lana had. We were told her father had died when she was quite young, and so Mimi was all there was left—Mimi and her summerhouse on Long Island Sound and her apartment in New York City, though I could not remember ever having seen it.

Lana was paler than any woman I've ever seen, and though she was tall, almost as tall as Leo, she was very thin and delicate like a swan, although her shiny black hair made you think more of a china doll. She isn't as easy to describe as Leo, and I don't know anyone who has done it very well, except Mimi when she said, "Lana's a complicated princess."

Lana was a writer, or at least she meant to be, and most of my early memories of her revolve around an overstuffed gray chair in the corner of her bedroom where she read and wrote in thick hardbound notebooks that were completely off-limits to us, Leo included. She kept them locked away in her writing desk, along with the newspaper articles she secretly cut from the *New York Times*. Elena and I would sometimes find the newspapers in the garbage with large holes cut out of the front page, and though we tried more than once to break into the desk to find out what they were, it was always completely and formidably locked. She would be there working in the morning when Elena and I left for school, and when we came back she would be sitting in the gray chair, writing more intensely, it seemed.

She had a slight limp and walked around the house with a dark mahogany cane that had elephants engraved in the handle. It came from New York City, Elena once told me, and whenever it touched us or we touched it small shivers ran through us, as if the cane possessed some dark force of its own. None of us, except Leo, knew why she had to use it, and to ask either of them about it almost constituted a sin.

She sometimes suffered from an illness too, which neither Elena nor I really understood, and like the cane, we couldn't mention it. The illness had certain phases to it, like the moon. Sometimes it would make her hands shake or her breathing deteriorate, and every now and then it would force her to hide in odd places, like in the space downstairs between the boiler and the clammy cold wall. Only when the illness was at its very worst would she stay in the house for days, crying out words of anguish to Leo at night, which we could never understand. She was very sensitive about her condition too, as if it were in some way disfiguring, and what made it worse was that she felt compelled to apologize about it all the time.

Leo was fairly certain that moving to the hills of Upstate New York would help, if not cure her. He even went so far as to promise her stunning mountain views just outside her windows. Of the five of us, it was Lana who couldn't bear the idea of living in those hills. She worried that the bargain she and Leo had struck a long time ago would disintegrate—the bargain that had something to do with Lana's writing and Leo's looking after us. She was afraid too that the isolation of those hills would kill her. Whenever Leo talked about it with enthusiasm, she would say, "Well, won't I have fun up there, sipping tea with the farmers' wives, swapping recipes and housecleaning tips. Gosh, one of them might know how I can brighten my wash." Such was Lana's distaste for housewifery.

Leo was excited about our move, because for him it meant more money and a job he could be proud of. He had been offered a position at Colgate University in Hamilton, teaching music theory and composition, and after five years of teaching piano lessons in our living room, he was ready for a change, the bigger it seemed the better.

His students, mostly girls between the ages of five and fifteen, would come early in the morning and then again after school, the last one leaving sometime after eight o'clock. It drove Lana crazy listening to those girls butchering Mozart and Haydn while she was trying to write, but she didn't say much about it. She would just wear cotton in her ears and a pair of gray earmuffs and play her Mozart records on Elena's record player. Sometimes when I'd go into her room to see her, she'd take the earmuffs off, and if one of the girls was out there plowing through the scales or hacking up a short piece like "Swans on the Lake," she'd close her eyes really tight and ask God for patience. She had to put up with it, though, because without Leo in the house looking after me and Harry and Elena, she couldn't write.

Once, for a little while after Harry was born, Leo went to work building houses, and Lana had to give up writing to cook and clean and look after us. After a couple of weeks, she pretty much stopped talking, and when she did speak it was only to say something like, "Pass me the salt" or "Hang up your clothes." A few more weeks passed and she started shouting things like, "I wash these dishes so I can put them back in the cupboard, so I can take them out and use them, so I can wash them and put them back into the cupboard, so I can take them out and use them, so I . . ."

Leo came back after that and began teaching piano lessons again. I don't think he liked it much either, because after each one of his students left he would play all the songs they had played to clear the air of their discordant notes. He never said so, but I think it hurt his pride to have to pander to a stream of young girls, especially when his heart was bent on composing music. That was what he hoped this new job would bring him—the freedom to compose. A few of his pieces had gotten him the job at Colgate University to begin with, and it was his hope that once he got up there, the music would roll out of him again. He worried, though, that his years of teaching piano lessons had silenced his music forever. One night when I sat alone with him in the living room, he said, "I'm afraid I might have lost my talent, Maddie. I haven't heard music in my head for years."

Harry was four years old at the time, so it made little difference to him that we were moving. When people asked him about it, he would imitate Leo, saying, "We're moving to Back East," as if Back East were the name of some town. He had Leo's nature, gentle and easygoing, and he looked a lot like him too, though he had Lana's white skin and perfect nose.

Elena was on Lana's side about our moving—she couldn't stand the idea of living in the hills either. She was twelve years old and already a real beauty, and it killed her to imagine that she would waste it all up in those hills. She had flower stem legs (which I was envious of) and Lana's black hair, and with the combination of Leo's savage face and Lana's porcelain one, she was exotic-looking, like an Italian sophisticate with pale white skin.

"We'll die of boredom up there, Maddie," she told me one night as we lay side by side in our bed. "Do you know what people do out there?"

I didn't know, though I had an idea they spent a lot of time in the woods.

"They milk cows," she said, "and they shovel manure and go to barn dances with straw on the floor. Can you imagine how boring that will be?"

I asked Leo, and he assured me that we weren't going to live on a farm or milk cows, but he was at least willing to admit that if we were lucky we might all get a chance to go to a barn dance. I worried about Elena getting bored, because whenever she grew disenchanted with our lives, she would speak up very loudly at the dinner table. Then Lana would blame herself and would start her apologetic litany, which never failed to roll around in my mind late at night when I tried to sleep.

Lana had a terrible problem of blaming all our sins, Leo's included, on herself, until the strain got to be too much. Then she would either lose herself in a fugue of grief or a rage so bitter, the sound of it could make even Elena cry. Etched in my mind is the memory of a night when I was nine years old and had to tell Lana why I pulled my pants down in Mitchell Allen's garage. She was sitting in her overstuffed chair, writing in one of her notebooks, dressed in a navy blue dress with small white buttons down the front. It was a little too stylish to sit around in while you wrote, but she had a theory that if you dressed well enough you would eventually begin to feel better; and since we were all for making Lana happy, none of us said anything when she showed up at the dinner table looking like a movie star.

She was smoking one of Leo's cigarettes, and I couldn't help but stare at her as she dragged on it and then blew the smoke from her mouth as if it were something truly lovely. "Come here, Maddie," she said sweetly. "Come and sit next to me." She made room for me on the corner of the chair, and as was always my custom, I sat down and strained my eyes to see what she had been writing. "The wind always blew against their backs," I read, "like some inexorable force—" She snapped the notebook shut before I could read another word.

She stared at me intensely, bearing down on me with gray, mirthful eyes that roved my face with hot affection. Lana had only two real expressions—this playful one that I always hoped for, and another one that burned on her face with such intensity that you couldn't help wondering what was going on inside her head. It was always something far from our lives, something that almost no one else was thinking about, something that consumed her and held her captive for days sometimes. One time when we were sitting on the sand at Lake Huron, watching the waves break, I asked her what she was thinking about, and she told me. "About the sea, Maddie. Just about how it goes on without any concern about you or me. It just keeps going, back and forth, back and forth, just like the sun and the moon, and it doesn't care who's been born or who's died or who's dying. Everything just keeps going, all the time, all the time," she said. There was something very sad about the way she said this, and suddenly I was sorry I had asked.

But now she was regarding me with amiable, mischievous eyes, the eyes that made me feel as if we were somehow the same age. I could smell the pleasant scent of gardenia about her, as if there were a flower perched in her hair, and I felt the strongest urge to tell her something funny. We all loved to make Lana laugh, especially me, because it was an absolutely delicious laugh—spontaneous and runaway, but above all else, true.

"Elena tells me she found you in Mitchell's garage today, Maddie. Is that true?" she asked.

I nodded my head and peered down at my lap as my fingers tugged at one another.

"She said you pulled your pants down. Is that true?"

Though Lana was never anything but frank, I could never get used to it—the way she just came right out and asked you something, as if it weren't delicate at all, as if it were something you could ask someone from across the dining table.

Something quivered in my stomach and threw my heart a little off beat, but finally I answered, "Yes."

"Why?"

I knew it was always best to tell her the truth, no matter how much I didn't want to. Lana could tell the difference between the truth and a lie, as if there were some sort of lie detector embedded in her brain. She wouldn't stand for a lie, no matter how close it was to the truth. She would sit there in silence for long minutes just waiting for you to part with it. So I told her the truth right away. I told her I wanted to see what he looked like, and in order to see that I had to show him what I looked like. It was only fair, I said.

"Were you disappointed?" I could tell by her eyes that she wasn't so angry as she was amused, and that as long as I stuck to the truth I would be all right.

"Some," I admitted, and when she asked me why, I went on to tell her that it was almost as small as Harry's, and that it looked like some kind of a dead, pink turtle.

"They pretty much look alike, Maddie," she said. "So you don't need to ask to see any more of them."

I watched her expression undergo a transformation from one of honest amusement to one of dark intensity, and my heart sank. Her eyes pinched together until I could see those furrows between her eyebrows, and when she said, "Oh, Maddie, I wish you weren't so much like me," I felt truly uncomfortable. In fact, my face burned hot in embarrassment.

"I'm sorry," I said. "I'll try not to be."

"No, sweetheart, I'm sorry I said that. I shouldn't have."

She said it sweetly enough. She even hugged me so tightly she pushed the breath out of me, but her face was all screwed up in lines, and I knew I had upset her again.

She let me go after that. I went straight into the unfinished broom closet just outside her bedroom, where I generally went when I wanted to hide. It was very small in there and barren, like our upstairs, because it had never been finished off. It seemed that the walls could hold me, that in the close darkness I could hide. I pushed the brooms quietly to one side and made my way to the back, where I came to rest on my haunches. There was a small opening between the closet and Lana and Leo's bedroom, and if her stack of boxes hadn't been there, I could have easily crawled through. If I craned my neck down, though, I could look through a gap between them and see the bed.

I heard Lana in there putting her papers away, straightening the tables on either side of her where there were always stacks of books she was reading—fat volumes with long titles like *White Imperialism Through the Nineteenth and Twentieth Centuries*—by men with names like Aaron Von Bernavitz or Dr. Ephraim P. Whitingham. She sat down on the side of the bed after that and stared out the back window. After a while she called for Leo, and when he didn't answer she called for him louder.

He came from the kitchen and stood in front of her so that I couldn't see her anymore.

"What?" he said.

"Do you know what Maddie did today?"

My heart pumped and I hid my face in the palms of my hands.

"Elena found her in the Allens' garage playing show-and-tell with Mitchell," Leo said.

"She said she wanted to see what he looked like, and in order to see that, she had to show herself."

Leo finally moved out of the way and sat down next to her on the bed. "She has a good sense for give and take, Lana," he said. "Don't get so upset about it."

"I'm not upset about *that*," she said. "I'm not upset that she showed him or even that she wanted to see him. I'm upset because—" Her voice broke here and she looked off to the window again.

"What, then?"

She closed her eyes, and though I couldn't really see tears, I watched her fingers gingerly brush them away. "Oh, God," she cried. "She's like me. I look at her and I see myself, and when she explained to me why she did it, I could hear myself. Jesus, Leo," she went on, "when I see how much she's like me, I want to go upstairs when she's asleep and—"

"And *what*?"

"I don't want her to grow up to be like me. Look what happened to me." She closed her eyes and lowered her head to Leo's shoulder, where she sobbed quietly.

"Come on," Leo said, "you're making this—"

"No, I'm not," she asserted. "She's got it. She's got my nature. I always told you one of them would get it. Oh Christ, Leo, the passion she has for boys, and the way she sits at that little tea table, thinking—" She stopped speaking and lurched up. "She's in the broom closet, Leo. I know she's in there. Go and get her."

Before I saw Leo make a start, I heaved up and crashed out of the closet and raced outside to the pine tree at the end of the driveway, which I immediately climbed to the highest branch I dared to climb. I sat there shivering for a long time, knowing that I had been insulted, though I couldn't say about what, until Leo coaxed me down by promising me he would play the piano.

No, I wasn't worried about moving to the hills. In fact, I looked forward to it. Actually it was the best thing that ever happened to me, despite everything. When I was eight, I suffered through an experience that kept me from any kind of real happiness, something I don't think I could have ever lived down had we stayed. I became, by no choice of my own, the lone and loathed cootie bug of my third-grade class, and though the title had fallen out of use by the time we moved, the whole business left some rather nasty marks on my psyche. A cootie bug in those days was the worst thing one could ever be; it was synonymous with being flea-bitten or lice-ridden, and why this title should fall to me, whom Leo bathed every night, puzzled me for a long time.

There were rumors around the elementary school about my family. They said we had ghosts in our upstairs, which I knew to be the truth, and they said we were poor, which was no lie either. Stories about my mother being a lunatic were plentiful, and it was also said that she only came out of the house after dark. The combination of being poor and of having ghosts and a mother who was some sort of nocturnal lunatic was enough to make me a likely candidate, but I think what really put me over the edge were the undersides of my forearms. I had a perpetual rash there from washing the dishes for Leo every night, which no amount of cream would cure. When it got really bad, Leo wrapped gauze around my arms and sent me off to school. Imagine seeing a poor girl who has a lunatic mother and ghosts in her upstairs sitting in your classroom with bandaged arms.

We had ghosts in our upstairs because it was never finished. Leo built our house, and he managed at least to finish off most of the first floor before Harry was born. But when Lana had to have Harry by cesarean section, there went the money they had saved to fix up the upstairs. Elena, Harry, and I had our bedrooms up there in that barren expanse. The walls were made of exposed studs, between which ran strips of yellow insulation covered with shiny silver paper with the words JOHN MASON INSULATION written in blue every foot or so. The floors were plywood, and not being covered up with so much as a rag rug, they were forever handing up splinters.

Elena and I shared a room up there. Harry had a smaller one across the hall. Besides the big iron bed Elena and I slept in, there was only a door leaning against the wall, which we hung our dresses on. The closet was just a bare socket in the wall, which Leo had filled with his personal boxes, one of which was long and wooden and, according to Elena, filled with garter snakes.

The stairwell was a series of raw, wooden steps whose ends weren't flush with walls, and once Harry dropped Leo's alarm clock down there. For the rest of the afternoon the stairwell echoed in eerie ticks. It was as if the ghosts suddenly had heartbeats.

None of us went up there much, save to sleep, because of the ghosts. We politely tiptoed around in our rooms after four o'clock so as not to disturb them, and only when it was impossible to avoid would we go up there alone. They came out just before dark, and though they weren't really mean, they didn't like us coming up there. They lived in the attic. I looked into it a few times when Elena's cat had kittens, but that was from the doorway with a flashlight. It ran along the hallway and along the entire length of our room with an opening at both ends, which made coming up the stairs as frightening an experience as going into the bedroom. Harry's room had a similar horror—it had a huge unfinished closet which dropped into darkness some three feet to its bottom, where Elena told us the ghosts hid just waiting for one of us to step down into it.

It was Elena who let it out about the ghosts. When she was ten and I was eight, Lana said her girlfriend, Georgia, could come and spend the night with us. When it came time to go upstairs to bed, Elena told Leo that she and Georgia would go up alone and change, and then he could bring me and Harry up. She didn't want Georgia to know about the ghosts, so she started up the stairs with her as if our upstairs was ordinary, as if there weren't any ghosts up there, while Harry and I stood down at the bottom and watched her. She tried to walk up normally instead of creeping, but I could tell by her hesitations that it was killing her to disturb the ghosts like that; and when Georgia spoke up in a normal voice and said, "How about if you wear my slippers and I'll wear yours?" Elena turned around quickly and said, "Shh, be quiet." Georgia was silent then, and Elena started moving slower and slower until the two of them were creeping up the stairs like a couple of mummies. When they got to the top, Elena stopped and stared ahead at what I knew was the ghosts' door. That's when Georgia reached up to touch Elena's shoulder. Just as she did, Elena let out the highest, most beautiful scream I'd ever heard, and the two of them whooshed down the steps like a flood of water.

That next week I had the rash quite badly. Leo had to wrap my forearms in white gauze again. If it had been cold out I could have worn a sweater, but it was May and Lana had already packed our sweaters away. I was at least able to wear a dress which had three-quarter-length sleeves, but it wasn't enough—not after Georgia had let it be known that we had ghosts.

By Wednesday afternoon that next week I noticed a group of four boys whispering to each other, while they looked me over. When several of the girls edged away from me in line, I knew Georgia had told everyone about the ghosts. It wasn't until Thursday at recess that the name actually surfaced. After lunch I went outside and headed straight for the merry-go-round. I was attracted to it like no other child's toy; it was whirling quite fast but I leapt on nonetheless and was swept away by the dizzying ride and by the high runaway shrieks of the other children who were happy like me to spin out of control. I threw my head back and watched the blue sky go around and around. I closed my eyes to savor the pleasure and leaned back against someone I wasn't really aware of, and that's when it happened. It started out with a scream that was sharp and edged with fear, as if the merry-go-round had whirled off its track. Someone shoved me, and when I turned around I saw this boy shouting, "Fluberize, sterilize, the cootie bug touched me." I was shoved again from behind and again from somewhere off to my side, and then a panic flooded through them all in a quick wave, one scream turning into two, then four, and then so many I couldn't count anymore. It was when they all began leaping from the merry-go-round as if it had caught fire, tumbling in the dirt, calling out "Cootie bug," that I realized it was I who had inspired the whole thing. The boy who had started it pushed the merry-go-round faster and faster as he called out my new name. I stood alone whirling around while their faces raced past me in a blur of narrowed eyes and moving mouths and ugly sounds. I closed my eyes then and cupped my ears and stood frozen until it all stopped.

The next day wasn't much better. I hung back at the door hoping I could wait out the recess hour there, but a teacher spotted me and flushed me outside. The merry-go-round taunted me, but I thought better of getting on. Instead I tried my luck on the monkey bars. No one seemed to notice me, so I grabbed one of the swings that stood not too far away. As I pumped myself up and flew over the tops of everything, I forgot this whole business. I watched my legs go straight as I reached the highest point, and I got myself going so well that the swing bumped at the top. I felt my dress moving all around me, as if it were outlining me, as if it were beating out something vital about me like the pulse of my heart. I heard someone call out, "Cootie bug," and then I felt something hit me on the back of my skull. There was a kind of dull thromp I heard both from the inside and the outside, a sound which immediately sickened me. I touched the spot, and when I brought my fingers back I saw they were covered with blood. The world wound down after that. My legs lost their rigid strength and dragged back and forth over the dirt until the swing finally stopped. Only then did I turn around to face my assailant—a tall skinny boy whom I'd seen around, but about whom I knew nothing, not even his name. I saw the stick he had hit me with and was filled with rage. I hated him more intensely than I had ever hated anyone, Elena included. I wanted nothing more than to beat his stupid skull with the same stick. I threw the swing off to my right, and seeing the stick lying not more than five feet from his feet, I raced forward and at least managed to scare him away. With all the speed I could muster, I chased this weed of a boy through the middle of the playground, shouting at the top of my lungs, "You skinny shit," cursing myself for not having anything more wounding to yell. It wasn't until later that I realized this chase did little for my cause. A girl who has ghosts in her upstairs and a mother who is thought to be insane should think twice about chasing a boy across the playground, brandishing two bandaged arms and a stick, yelling, "You skinny shit." If someone hadn't heard about the cootie bug, they now knew who she was.

I didn't catch him, nor was I able to get close enough to throw the stick at the back of his skull, but while I sat in the doctor's office an hour later getting six stitches sewn into my scalp, watching Lana growing dimmer and gloomier by the moment, I swore I'd get him back if it killed me.

Of all the things that happened it was Lana's reaction that evening that turned out to be the worst for me. All through dinner I couldn't get away from her vigilant gaze. She kept looking at me, as if she wanted to assure herself that I was still alive. More than once she reached under the table and squeezed my knee in what I could only imagine was the pressure of her own guilt. I kept looking up at her, hoping to find her expression softening, but she was lost in thought, and I worried that it was all going to bring on her illness.

"Come on, La," Leo said at one point. "Tell us a story." We all encouraged her to tell us one, her silence was so painful. After so many "Come on, Lana's," she finally put her fork down.

"You asked for it, Leo," she said, and with all our eyes roving her creased expression, she began. "Once there was a pretty little girl with long black hair, who had this mother who loved her dearly. The mother wasn't wicked or mean—she just wasn't a good mother. She had an ugly ambition, and—"

"Don't, La," Leo interrupted.

She looked at us, first at Leo, then at Elena, then at me, and ever so gently she rose from the table. "I'm sorry, Maddie," she said before she turned around.

We all watched her leave, and afterward Leo tried to cover it up by telling us one of Lana's stories about a boy hyena who was madly in love with a girl hyena, but who couldn't stop laughing long enough to ask her to marry him. I couldn't laugh, not even when Leo did his imitation of the boy hyena, because I couldn't stop hearing Lana's voice saying, "I'm sorry, Maddie."

When Leo got up from the dinner table to go to Lana's room, I quietly slipped into the broom closet and made my way back to the space where I could see their bed through the boxes. Lana was sitting in her chair so I couldn't see her, but Leo sat on the edge of the bed tracing a circle on his pant leg with a ballpoint pen.

"It's true," I heard her say.

"It's not true and even if it were, you don't say it in front of them. They're children, La, young, impressionable children."

"I'm sorry, but I think they should know that they don't have a good mother and that she's sorry as hell she can't be one."

"They love you, La. Did you see their faces when you said you'd tell them a story? Did you see Maddie's face? She'd already forgotten about today," he said. His voice was steady and calming like a seasoned priest's.

"It's my fault that little girl has been called a cootie bug," she said bitterly. "*A cootie bug*, Leo. What a terrible thing to call her. If it weren't for me this house would be finished so that no little girl could tell everyone we have ghosts. You could leave the house and make more money if I could raise those children—if I didn't write. And *if* I were a good writer it might be worth it all, but—"

"Don't say that. It's not true," Leo pleaded. "You're a good writer and you're a good mother to those children. How many times do I have to say that to you, Lana? Jesus . . ."

"She's just like me," she said, as if Leo hadn't spoken at all. "You should have seen her little hands shaking when the doctor started—"

"She was getting stitches. For Christ's sakes, Lana, who wouldn't shake?" He threw the pen across the room and plunged his face into his upturned palms.

"When I think about her going through life only to end up like me, I feel like going upstairs at night to . . . to *smother* her."

Everything went blurry and I plugged my ears up tight with my fingertips and wedged my head between my knees to stopper them even more. I left the closet when I started to make noises. With my ears still plugged I was able to override my most primitive fear of the ghosts and raced up the stairs to my room and crawled into bed with my clothes on. I lay there for a long time staring at the crisscross of beams and insulation overhead, listening to the stabbing sounds of Lana's voice as it drifted up to me through the furnace duct.

After what seemed at least an hour, her voice stopped, as did Leo's. Within a few minutes I heard her climbing the stairs, calling out my name. "I'm in here," I said, worried now that she was going to apologize to me all over again. She stopped in the doorway, a thin, delicate silhouette against the cold light in the hallway. I could tell by the disorder of her hair that she had gone through her anguish again.

"You look so little in that bed, Maddie. Like a little angel. Weren't you afraid of the ghosts?"

"No," I said.

It seemed she floated over to me, her face in darkness until she sat down next to me. I was afraid to see her expression, fearful that it would be grave and etched with lines, but it wasn't—it was soft and calm, and I knew she had shriven herself of whatever demons possessed her. "How are you feeling?" she asked.

I couldn't form a word, but I made a sound, a sort of quiet moan, which conveyed both my relief and sadness.

"How's your head, sweetheart?"

I moaned again and relished her touch as her fingers glided over my cheeks and across my forehead, caressing me as if I were somehow rare.

"You know what?" I said in a small voice.

"What?"

"I'm going to hide behind that big tree outside the school, and when that skinny boy walks by I'm going to hit him in the back of the head with Leo's wrench."

Lana laughed extravagantly, and I felt proud that I had made her laugh when just an hour ago she had been crying. I thought I must be getting better at it, until she quieted down and told me that I couldn't hit the skinny boy with Leo's wrench. "You can't hit anyone with a wrench, Maddie. It's too heavy and it could kill them. What you do is this: whenever you see him, you say hello to him politely and then stare at him with all the energy you have. Just stare right through him so that he knows you're someone to reckon with."

Then something else happened that tore me up all over again and made my escape to those hills even sweeter. In the fall of my ninth year I fell in love with a boy named Andrew Simmons. His family had moved to Detroit during the summer and now lived just four houses down from me. I can't say exactly what attracted me to him other than that he had the whitest face I'd ever seen and a beautiful red flush to his cheeks like Harry had in the winter.

It came as great sorrow to me that his mother was a tight-hearted, religious fanatic. She rarely let him and his older brother, Nathan, come out to play with me and Elena. God only knows why. All we knew was that the Simmons were Jehovah's Witnesses and that Andrew and Nathan weren't allowed to color in coloring books featuring the Easter Bunny or Santa Claus.

I rarely got to see Andrew, so I spent a lot of time lying downstairs in the basement thinking about kissing him. I had seen a movie once with Lana and I was quite impressed with the kissing parts. I watched carefully as the man's and woman's lips touched and their heads moved around for a minute or so, and I wanted to try it. When I couldn't bear lying there thinking about it, I would go down to his house and stand outside hoping he would come to the window. I couldn't help it. It was too big of an emotion for me to control.

Every once in a while his mother would let him and Nathan out, and it seemed one day that it actually might happen—that my lips would touch his. They came over to our yard and we played frozen tag under the pine tree until Elena said we should carve the name of our love in the tree with Leo's pocketknife. She went into the house and got it, and when she came back she gave it to Andrew. As I watched him climb the tree, I imagined that somehow we'd slip into the neighbor's heavy lilac bush to kiss—it was only a matter of time, I thought. When he finally came down Elena handed me the knife, and I climbed up to the branch where he had just been. I saw his carved-out heart, and then darkness passed before my eyes. Inside this crude heart, in bold capitals, was the name ELENA.

I couldn't speak, no matter how many times Elena called my name from below. I just sat there on the branch, the pine sap seeping into my pants, as I stared down at their moving heads. I couldn't move, and after a while the pocketknife slipped from my hand and fell to the ground. I knew something was wrong when Leo appeared below, calling up, "Maddie," and then when Lana showed up. She said, "I'm coming up, sweetheart." As I watched her head and hands coming closer I moved up to the next branch and then the next. Elena's voice floated up to me. "You're going to be just like Lana," she said, and only then did I stop.

Leo slapped Elena across the face and yelled, "That's enough," in a chilly, biting voice. Before he could say another word she tore off across our neighbor's lawn and disappeared behind their house.

I forgot about them when Lana's hands touched my feet and crept up my legs. She crawled up to the branch I was sitting on, and after she arranged her navy blue dress underneath her, she put her arm around me and asked me in the most breathless voice what had happened. I stared down at her stockings where they were ripped at the knees from the rough bark, and touched a spot of sap that stuck to her calf like an invisible, sticky quarter.

"Tell me, sweetheart," she said.

I looked down at the ground and noticed that Nathan and Andrew had drifted out of our yard and were standing across the street throwing stones at a street sign. Harry had wandered over in the meantime, and along with Leo he was craning his neck staring up at me and Lana in that tree.

"Come on, Maddie," she prompted me. "I didn't climb all the way up here just for the view."

She looked at me with those hot eyes of hers and I knew I had to tell her. Lana loved people to tell her things like that and the more details you provided her with the happier it made her. She'd just sit there, her face hanging in front of you, laid out, her eyes big and swallowing, her head nodding eagerly, as if in the movement she could pump it all out of you. It was kind of strange, but you found yourself hoping your story wouldn't disappoint her, that it would be good enough, nourishment for her in fact, because she loved knowing about it so much. So I told her about the knife and how it was Elena's idea to carve the name of our love in the tree. Then I showed her where Andrew had carved Elena's name, instead of mine.

She put her arms around me and hunched forward, looking down through the branches at Andrew and Nathan, who were still chunking stones at that sign. "Maddie," she whispered, "I promise you that in just a few years you will look back on this and wonder how you could have ever been interested in such a sickly white little boy." She waited a moment for that to sink in before she said, "If you promise you won't tell anyone, I'll tell you something."

"A secret?" I asked. I felt something like a whale turn over in my belly. Lana's secrets were the best. They were treasures Elena and I collected, rare bits of knowledge that made us feel as if we owned a piece of her. I had two already—Elena had three.

"Yes, but you have to promise never to tell anyone."

After I promised by crossing my heart and hoping to die, she cleared my hair away from my ear in a slow, loving process like she always did, and put her hands on either side of them. "Men will never be the most important thing to you," she whispered. She paused for a moment, her warm breath spiraling down my ear. "You're going to do something great with your life, Maddie." Something wiggled in my stomach when she said the word *great,* but then again it wasn't the best kind of Lana secret. The best ones were the secrets about her. It was better than no secret at all, and it was nice to think I would one day do something great, but the fact remained that across the street stood my sickly white boyfriend whose heart was bent on Elena.

Lana yanked off her shoes and dropped them for Harry to catch. As he rounded them up, she peeled off her ripped stockings and dropped them on Leo's head. "Catch me, Leo," she yelled. She crawled down to the lowest branch and dropped down on top of him. Then they stood beneath me, their arms outstretched, crying, "Jump, Maddie, jump," with such excitement that I forgot myself and plunged into their arms.

It came back to me after they went into the house—the whole business about Andrew. I watched him for a while from behind the tree until I couldn't stand it anymore and crept down to the cellar where I thought about him some more. He refused to leave my thoughts, even when I forced myself to remember Lana's secret, and seemed to infect my stomach as if a piece of it had fallen down from my brain and was now burning slowly there. I kept going over and over the details, climbing that tree a hundred times to look at that heart with Elena's name gouged into it, as if through sheer exposure it would wear off.

Leo came down after a while and sat next to me on the ratty old sofa we had down there.

"How's Lana?" I asked.

"Not so bad," he said. "She's more worried about you being upset."

"Yes, but Elena said I was like her and that's worse than me finding Elena's name up in that tree." I started worrying about our dinner—what Lana was going to say after she'd spent the rest of the afternoon thinking about it. Things had a way of growing big inside her.

Leo leaned forward and took hold of my chin and then whispered some words into my face. I could feel his warm breath on my lips, and his eyes were so close to mine I saw them swell. "Lana's one hell of a lady," he said, "and I'd be proud if you were like her."

We heard Lana upstairs walking around, so Leo left me there, only to call down a few minutes later that he wanted me to look for Elena. I went upstairs and then outside and wandered back to our fort, where I knew she'd be. She was sitting in her bedroom (we had marked off our bedrooms with white rocks) whacking away at a stick with Leo's pocketknife. I walked through our door and stood in the living room near our fireplace with the pines soaring above me, cutting the light into a thousand shards.

"Hi, Lana," she said, and then she started laughing. It wasn't phoney either; I mean, it really made her laugh to call me Lana. I stood there for a moment watching her, admiring her nerve and the graceful lazy way her legs stretched out in front of her. Even so, I hated her.

"She told me another secret," I said.

As if I had just pushed a button, Elena's face went blank and she stopped laughing altogether. *"She did?"*

I took my time nodding slowly and evenly, the way a person might elongate a bow.

I've always loved Elena's temper. It never took its time and blossomed—it exploded out of her in a sort of convulsion, her arms and legs and mouth moving in violent harmony. She heaved the stick and Leo's pocketknife like a spear-chucker and then jumped to her feet, yelling, "It's not fair," into the quiet, sanctimonious air of those pines. "Shit, Maddie," she yelled. "Shit."

She ran through the imaginary walls of her bedroom, and finally out of our house altogether, with me following behind her yelling, "Look who's Lana now," with a certain amount of uncalculated joy. *Look who's Lana now.*

I raced behind her through the field, through our neighbor's yard, and up the stairs into our kitchen, where Leo was hacking up a chicken. She ran past him and stormed into Lana's room, with me and Leo right behind her. Lana was sitting in her chair writing, or at least she had been, and now she was staring at Elena, her writing hand frozen on the page. "What's going—"

"You told her another secret," Elena screamed. "That's not fair, Lana. Now she has just as many as me."

Though it hardly seemed possible, Elena was on the verge of tears. When Lana's eyes went from her to me I felt the magnitude of my own guilt. I shouldn't have told her, I realized. Saying that you had another secret was almost as bad as telling the secret itself, but in the heat of my anger, I had forgotten. "It's not fair," Elena yelled. While I muttered some lame apology, Lana's restless eyes went straight to Leo's. There was a strange cluster of emotions in her look—amusement, anger, fear, and a kind of helplessness. Until then, I don't think either of them realized how precious Lana's secrets were to us. That we counted and collected them with great enthusiasm I don't think she ever knew. Nor did she realize how fiercely we guarded them, holding onto them as if they were our most prized possessions.

Lana closed her eyes tightly for a moment and then stood up. When she bent down and picked up her cane from the side of the chair, Elena and I moved back in respect and tried not to watch her limp. When she took one step forward and winced, we both went cold.

"Did you hurt your hip?" Elena asked.

"What happened?" I echoed.

"When I climbed the tree." She winced again and moved between me and Elena, glancing over at Leo with hot, pained eyes. "Now go on, Leo, and take Maddie with you. I want to talk to Elena."

Her hand fell on top of Elena's head. As I watched it slide gracefully down her black hair, Leo steered me out of there. I tried to duck into the closet so I could hear what they said, to see if Lana would tell her another secret, but Leo wouldn't let me. I went down to the cellar instead and sat at my tea table drinking stagnant water from a teacup, worrying about Lana and her cane.

That night Elena and I lay side by side in bed and listened separately and quietly to the sound of Lana's mournful, unintelligible voice as it drifted up to us through the furnace duct. Leo's voice, like a soft necessary refrain, came every so often, washing over us like water over a hot wound.

"It's that cane," I whispered.

"It's not just the cane. It was you getting upset about a boy and what I said and then you telling me about the secret and *then* the cane." She was quiet for a moment, and I felt a small shudder pass through her. "I think she's getting worse, Maddie. I really do."

I considered that for a moment, but it was as unbearable a thought as any I'd ever had, so I thrust it out of my mind. "Did she tell you another secret?"

"I can't tell."

"I know," I said. "I'm sorry I asked."

She squeezed my hand under the sheets and then said something that kept me awake for a long time after she fell asleep. "If you think about it," she said, "Lana is a whole secret herself."

I went over and over in my mind what I knew about Lana, and only then did I realize how right Elena was. The only thing I really knew about her was that she had been born in 1927 and had grown up in New York City. It was then, I think, that my curiosity took on a terrible edge and I was invaded with the desire to know what had happened to her, to know why she carried a cane and why she was sometimes swept away by an illness no one could name.

2

We moved to Upstate New York two weeks later. Lana was still sick about it, and what made it worse was that her hip was aching so much she had to depend more heavily on her cane. Leo had to do most of the packing, and he did so with such an old woman's fastidiousness that Lana started calling him Ethel. Elena was suddenly doting on Lana, bringing her tea in the special bone china teacups Mimi had given Lana, so much so that my suspicions were instantly aroused. Either Elena wanted something or Lana had told her a secret so delicious and provocative that it had the power to transform her.

My guess was that after Leo steered me out of her room that afternoon, Lana had told Elena the secret about her cane, or at least some part of it. When I asked Elena why she was all of a sudden Lana's slave, she looked at me like I was a fool and said, "She's in pain, Maddie. Do you know what it's like to be in pain?" I didn't know exactly, but I knew then that Lana had told her something about the cane. When it became intolerable watching Elena carrying those china teacups into Lana's room, I went and asked Lana myself.

She was upstairs sitting on Harry's twin bed, folding his clothes and putting them into a brown suitcase. With the light spilling in through the window, illuminating the barren shabby ribs and bones of our unfinished house, she looked like a rose, a misplaced rose.

"Hi," she said quietly, reaching up to touch my face. "Have you been helping Ethel?" (She meant Leo.)

I muttered an "Uh-huh," and my eyes fell on her cane. It was lying straight across the bed, cutting it in half. I couldn't resist the temptation to touch it. I ran my fingers down the body of it, and very slowly I made my way around to the handle where the engraved elephants stood out in touchable relief. I skirted around her legs and eased myself up on Harry's bed, next to the cane. It was touching my knee on one side and hers on the other. "I wish I knew about your cane," I said carefully. I touched it with the tips of my fingers.

She laid Harry's little pants across her legs and looked at me with quiet, solemn eyes. "What do you want to know about it?" she asked me. The mere mention of it deflated her. The smile faded from her lips, but even so I pressed closer to her.

"I want to know why you have it," I said quietly. When I saw the sadness crawl into her eyes, I looked away, down at the naked floorboards where a puddle of warm light fell.

She touched my hand that couldn't stop touching the cane and said, "Sweetheart, I know you're curious, and it's good to be curious, but you can't always know everything right away. It's very personal and you just have to respect that. Everyone has the right to keep things personal —"

"But I won't tell anyone," I interrupted. I knew it was in bad taste to press her about the cane, but it was painful to be shut out like that.

"I know you won't. It's not that I don't trust you. It's just that you're too young to understand." She brushed my cheek with the backs of her fingers, as if doing that would make my curiosity go away.

When the pressure built up inside me, when my heart started thrumming against my rib cage like a lost bird, I asked her, "When will you tell me, then?" I realized I was clutching the cane, and when the tears backed up behind my eyes, she hastily said, "When you're thirteen. Now go on."

That was an eternity to me, a time too far in the future to do me any good. I couldn't wait that long, but life has a strange way of accommodating you—a few nights later in our motel room I found something out about that cane.

We had driven through Canada all day, Leo in a moving van and Lana driving steadily behind him in our station wagon. We all took turns riding with Leo high up in the cab, me and Harry arguing about it mostly, Elena content now to sit in the front seat with Lana to look over road maps and pour her tea from a thermos. That night we got a little roadside motel room and ate the picnic dinner Leo had packed for us. We took our baths, and afterward Lana invited us onto her bed to swap tall tales. Since she had never allowed a television set in our house, this had become our only family pastime. Harry told one about a whale who could talk to people. Elena told one about a snapping turtle who had lived for over three hundred years in a pond and had watched this one family for centuries, until he knew the great, great, great, great, great grandchildren of the original settlers. Mine was about a girl who got married when she was ten years old. Leo started telling one about an American officer who could read the minds of the Nazis, but Lana kept teasing him so much, tickling him and saying, "Well, if it isn't Ethel telling tall tales," that he never really finished it.

Lana's story was the to-be-continued-tomorrow kind. She lay down on the bed, and with the four of us propped up by her side, she told us this really good one about a bear and a sparrow.

The bear was the biggest one in the woods, she said, *but he was so softhearted that none of the other bears would have anything to do with him. One day a sick little sparrow flew into his cave by mistake. She had a broken wing and was terrified when she found herself inside the bear's cave. She was sure she would be eaten, but the bear picked her up and washed her off and tried to fix her wing. He got so taken up with looking after her that he forgot to hibernate. He finally remembered, but then he couldn't fall asleep, no matter how hard he tried. The sparrow tried to sing him to sleep; she lay by his side for hours, singing, but the bear never even dozed off. He couldn't because he knew if he slept the sparrow would die, but the sparrow knew that if he didn't hibernate he would die too. So the sparrow secretly practiced making her wing better. When the bear went out to find food, she exercised it, flapping it up and down, making it stronger and stronger. She practiced every day, until one day she could fly again. She told the bear he could finally hibernate. "I can fly again," she said. The bear rejoiced, but then he was sad—she would fly away and he would be lonely again. But she promised him she would return in the spring so they could be together again, and after she sang him to sleep, she flew away.*

Lana ended the story here and told us to stay tuned for the next episode. Elena and Harry fell asleep not too long afterward, but I couldn't sleep. I kept seeing the bear hibernating peacefully, thinking the sparrow would return, while the sparrow flew further and further away. I don't know why, but it bothered me.

I was still awake after Lana took her bath and came to bed. When she and Leo started speaking softly, I wanted to switch places with Harry because he was nearest their bed, but his mouth was already hanging open, so I raised myself a little on my elbow to get my ears away from the covers.

"It hurts," Lana said, hobbling over to him.

"I was afraid it would. Come here and I'll rub it for you."

Lana lay down on her side, her back to me, her right hip up, and ever so slowly she pulled her blue nightgown up her legs and her thighs, until I saw the swell of her soft, white buttock. I realized two things at once: that I had never seen Lana's naked body, much less her buttock, and that I was intruding upon something private, something that wasn't meant for my eyes. I couldn't help myself, though. I watched on in fascination as Leo's thick fingers pulled that blue gown away from her body, revealing to me the first great section of a woman's body I had ever seen. The way that hip swelled gracefully from the thigh and then gradually tapered off to a perfect valley of white waist was so beautiful I forgot for a moment what Leo was doing. But when my eyes fell upon the skin beneath his kneading fingertips, I saw something I would never be able to forget. There was a thick, purple scar that stood out in relief on her soft skin like a piece of dark hemp—a touchable squiggle, a zigzag of at least six inches, which Leo palpitated with ease, as if he'd done so a hundred times before.

I became aware then of my arm. It was fast asleep beneath me, and I had to shift my weight to relieve the uncomfortable sensation of pins and needles. I swear that I made almost no sound, that the movement was so slight Lana couldn't possibly have heard, but in the next moment she pulled her nightgown down and her voice came to me.

"Maddie," she said, without so much as turning her head. "The sparrow went back to the bear in the spring."

My head fell quietly back to my pillow, and I closed my eyes tightly as if that would prove I had been sleeping. Her voice drifted out from behind her back again, over Harry, and came straight to me, filling me with dread. "I can feel your eyes on me," she said. She turned over to look at me, and no matter how hard I tried to keep my eyes closed, I couldn't. "I know you, Maddie." When our eyes locked for a brief moment I had the eeriest feeling that she was right, that she knew me completely, better even than I knew myself. As if a light or something equally intangible and mysterious had passed through me, I knew that Lana was a powerful woman.

I lay still between Harry and Elena, barely breathing, and felt for the first time a sensation that would descend on me time after time, making it impossible for me to sleep. It was an electric feeling, as if my limbs were wired with small circuits that were suddenly turned on without any real warning. It was a restless, uncomfortable feeling—the sort of feeling a runner would get if you bound his legs and tied him in a wheelchair.

I couldn't get that scar out of my mind. I was fascinated by scars, I always had been, and without a doubt, I knew the one on Lana's hip was the best one I'd ever seen. I liked knowing how a person got one. I liked staring at it in leisure, and if possible, I liked running my fingers over it. One of the neighbor ladies in Detroit had a good one on the side of her knee; it was white and thin and had little dots on the side of it, and she let me touch it and ask her questions about it whenever I liked.

I wanted very badly to get close to Lana's scar, to look at it, to touch it, but I knew I could no more ask to see it than I could ask how she had acquired it. I couldn't stop thinking about it though, and that's what started the electricity flowing through my limbs. Acts of violence hacked through my mind, one after the other. I saw butcher's knives and big axes careening off Lana's white hip. I saw cars and then bulldozers smashing into it. I saw Lana walking alone at night on a dark, rainy road, wailing, when all of a sudden a speeding truck plowed into her. I saw Lana running down a dark, moonless street in New York City, being chased by a huge man with a hacksaw. And then I saw Lana falling from a high tower and being swept away by the powerful undertow on Long Island Sound.

I strained against these thoughts until the wire circuits in my limbs bore so much electricity I couldn't keep still. As I moved them back and forth under the covers to spend their energy, it occurred to me what this electricity was—nerves. Plain and simple nerves. I had them, I realized in horror. God help me but I had Lana's nerves. This was the first recognizable symptom, I understood. As I lay there feeling them jump under my skin—a whole battalion of them thrusting and writhing about—I knew I was in trouble. I could just see them— little black insects pounding their small fists against the ceiling of my skin, their little mouths screaming in high pitches, while their six booted feet stomped impassively on my veins.

I never slept that night, my first truly sleepless night. I watched Leo fall off and later Lana, and I lay awake worrying about what these nerves were going to do to me, or rather what they were going to make me do. I couldn't imagine exactly, but I knew whatever it was it would be awful.

It soothed me the next day to ride with Leo in the moving van, because he didn't have any nerves—none that I could detect anyway. He talked mostly about this little town we were driving to, filling my mind with so many warm images that my nerves finally fell asleep. I couldn't wait to see this place that was surrounded by so much grass and trees and stocked with friendly people who were nice enough to inquire about your health all the time. He talked it up so much that when we finally got there I was disappointed. I had imagined a whole community nestled in the woods; I was kind of shocked to discover cars like ours driving on paved streets. What was even more disappointing was the size of this place. It was minuscule.

Leo pulled up to a stoplight and announced, "Here we are, Maddie," and while we waited for the light to turn green, I took in this small town. There was a bank on my left. The Blue Bird Restaurant stood next door, its front window filled with shelves of pastries. Across the street was a drugstore, which had a mortar and pestle hanging above the door, and next to it was a movie theater whose marquee read, THE GRADUATE.

The light turned green, and Leo drove straight, past another row of stores and a small green park. That was it, though—just two blocks. There was no more.

"What do you think, Maddie?" He turned toward me and smiled, his cool blue eyes radiating wonder, as if he had just shown me something marvelous.

"That's all?" I said. I was beginning to wonder if Leo had led us astray, if it were really going to be as horrible as Lana and Elena feared.

"Ah, come on, Maddie," he said, "don't be like Elena. I was counting on you to like it here. That was just the downtown. You haven't seen the campus yet, and wait until you see our house." I watched as his hands gripped the steering wheel and a dark crease settled on his brow.

I kept quiet and waited because I didn't want to hurt Leo's feelings. I felt a little sorry for him, knowing already what Lana and Elena were saying behind us. "Are they still in back of us?" I asked. I was worried that Lana had turned around when she saw the two measly blocks and was already heading back to Detroit.

"Sure, they're still behind us. You wait, Maddie. You wait until you see our house." He drove down a block lined with trees and large houses, mainly white with black shutters. I had to admit it was very pretty. In the late afternoon, in the June heat, it looked rather inviting, almost perfect. All the houses had big windows and front porches with flower boxes of petunias and pansies and marigolds. The lawns were a healthy green, and I could smell in the air the pleasant scent of sun-warmed, freshly mown grass. There were plenty of bikes dotting these lawns, promising me other children, and huge lawns in the back offering me kickball and frozen tag and camping out.

"Okay, Maddie, this is it," Leo said, and he swung into the driveway of this great old gray house with long, thin black shutters. It was two stories tall, and a huge screened-in porch jutted out from the front and wrapped itself around the left side. I stared straight ahead, my mouth hanging open. I couldn't imagine this sprawling gray wonder to be our house. Leo pulled in further, and I saw it had a garage and a back lawn that stared out at the distant, green hills and seemed to go on forever.

It was really huge inside. We walked up the back steps and went into the kitchen first. It was long and narrow, and through the doorway was a big dining room with three great bay windows. The living room was just to the left of it and had the same bay windows, only it was bigger, with a small bedroom lying just beyond it. Off the dining room was a long narrow hallway which opened onto the screened-in porch, and to the right of it was a nice open stairway with a dark mahogany banister.

It was a little run-down inside—the wallpaper was old and unattractive, and the floors were scuffed and a bit dull looking—but Elena and Harry and I were so glad that we had real walls and real floors that we didn't mind. We hardly even noticed until Lana called our attention to it.

The four of us followed behind her as she clomped from one room to the next, telling Leo what had to be done to make it more livable. He was so happy to finally be here, he agreed to wallpaper all the rooms and strip the floors down, but that didn't cheer her up. The size of Hamilton was more of a disappointment to her than it was to me, and this house, so big and broken down, overwhelmed her.

She got worse when we started picking our rooms. There were two sets of adjoining bedrooms on either side of the hall upstairs, which meant you had to go through the front room to get to the back one. What Elena first proposed was this: she would have two adjoining bedrooms to herself, I could have the room off Lana and Leo's front room, and Harry could sleep downstairs. Harry didn't like the idea of being alone downstairs, and Lana hardly wanted me in the room off their bedroom. "She'd never get any sleep, Elena," Lana said. "She'd be up all night listening at the door." What I wanted was never voiced—between Harry crying and Lana and Elena yelling, there was no more air.

Leo stepped in between them and said something about going downtown for hot fudge sundaes. I think he understood that they weren't fighting over the bedrooms really, that instead, they were fighting their own anger at having ended up, as Lana put it, in a jerkwater town. No one cared about hot fudge sundaes, though, and Lana stomped off down the dim hallway with her cane. When we started to follow her, she turned around and yelled, "I want to be alone."

No one meant to leave Lana alone in the house after that, but it happened. Elena ran off somewhere, and Leo went looking for her. Then Harry and I went looking for Leo. We walked up and down four blocks, staring at all the unfamiliar houses, half listening to the sound of a softball game somewhere. Above us the sky was a gorgeous blue, with only the tiniest breath of white clouds floating untouchably high. In the distance we could see the lazy, green hills, as if they were soft, padded walls which were wrapped around this little town to keep it safe and warm.

We didn't find either Elena or Leo, so we drifted home. We walked across the back lawn and came into the kitchen, me first, with Harry scrambling after me. I took one look at Lana whirling around in the empty room and froze.

"Where were you? I've been looking all over for you!" Her voice bordered on a scream, and when she raised her cane above her head I was suddenly terrified. Her hair was loose and wild, the top buttons of her beige dress gaping open. I'd never seen quite the same eyes, so hard-edged and bitter, and when she charged forward I didn't know what to do. "Where have you been?" she shouted again. I pointed a skinny finger in the general direction of outside and watched in amazement the effect my dumb silence had on her.

She wheeled around the ill-lit, empty kitchen and stabbed at the air with her cane. I think more than anything she wanted to be back in Detroit with all her things around her. It seemed she was looking for them. She turned abruptly away from us, cracking down on the countertop with her cane. "I won't have you running away from me!" she shouted. *"Do you hear me?* I'm not in this house for fifteen minutes and you all run away." An anguished moan came out of her, a wounded sound which emanated from some small dark place, as if it were being squeezed out of her by strong, invisible hands.

She fled the room, and Harry and I found her sitting out on the porch steps in the faint, diffused light of the street lamp. She looked small and girlish holding her knees up against her chest. If the cane hadn't been lying next to her, I would have thrown my arms around her neck. But there it was, silently marking off her place from ours, the tips of our dusty shoes touching its hook.

"Where's Elena?" she asked. I could tell by her smooth voice that she had shriven herself of her anger.

"We don't know," I said carefully, kneeling down on my side of the cane. "We went looking for her."

Her hands drifted up to the sides of my face, her fingers touching my cheeks as if she were blind and was trying to recognize me. "I'm sorry about the fit, Maddie. Leo went off to look for Elena, and then I was looking for you and Harry, and that *kitchen* . . ." She paused and shuddered. "Say you'll forgive me."

The way she took things and twisted them around until the blame fell on her, always aroused in me a feeling of guilt. It was a strange feeling—the kind you'd get if you accidentally burned someone's house down and they apologized to you for having left the matches out.

"Come here Harry-berry," she said, opening her arms to him. "I scared you in there, didn't I? Stomping around like Godzilla." He fell into her arms and sank his face into the hollow of her neck. "I'll bet you thought, 'Oh no, Lana has turned into a gorilla. Oh no, what'll we do with a gorilla mother?'"

She stood up on the porch and did some gorilla imitations, snorting and scratching and whacking us over the heads with her swinging arms, excusing herself with a gorilla voice, doing such a great job that I forgot about what had happened in the kitchen. Lana was good that way—she could really make it up to you.

Leo showed up a few minutes later with Elena tucked under his arm and ruined it all. Her hair was tangled and sweaty, the wet front of her navy blue shirt sticking to her rib cage. "I found her down at the college track jumping the hurdles," Leo said. Elena kept eyeballing the ground, twitching her neck, as if she were calculating her next escape.

"I've thought about it, Elena," Lana said, "and the best I can do is to give you a choice. You can choose whichever room you like of the two adjoining rooms upstairs, or you can take the bedroom downstairs and have all the privacy you want."

We all followed Elena and Lana through the house, first to the bedroom downstairs, then to the two adjoining rooms upstairs, and waited patiently for her to decide. Of all of us, I was especially anxious about her decision, because of its bearing on my own small fate. Her reject was my option.

The bedroom downstairs was not to Elena's liking—it didn't have enough windows—so we all tromped upstairs and stood in the two adjoining rooms, waiting for her to choose. There was a small door between them that didn't close—something that worried us both. The floor in the back bedroom had warped and shifted so much that it stood permanently ajar. The front room was a little smaller than the back room, but there was a door in the back room which opened into an attic Elena didn't even want to see. Because of her lingering fear of ghosts that room was out of the question.

She took the front bedroom, and I was then given the next choice—

either the back bedroom with the attic or the nearly windowless room downstairs. At my request, Leo opened the attic door very slowly, and we all stood gaping in at it, Harry, Elena, and I scrutinizing it for the telltale signs of ghosts. It was a hot room, smelling pleasantly musty, with dusty wooden eaves, under which the roof pitched together, so low near the walls that even a dwarf would have had a hard time standing. The floors were made of old wooden planks with wide cracks between them, and at the far end was a small window that opened onto our backyard. An old overstuffed red chair stood near it, and as for the ghosts—I sensed not a one. I didn't let on to Elena that I actually liked the attic, but rather I feigned a bit of apprehension and yet a certain bravery to put up with the ghosts nonetheless, which made her believe she had won.

Harry had to be persuaded that he had gotten a deal on the bedroom downstairs. Leo and Lana ran him down the steps and presented him with this dark little room, promising him that out of all the rooms this one was really the best. When he worried that it was too faraway, Lana had him race up the stairs to her room to show him how little time it took to get there.

"Not even a minute," I heard her yell. "It was only forty seconds, Harry. See if you can make it faster. See if you can make it in thirty seconds." By that time we were all crowded at the top of the stairs, cheering Harry on as he made a mad dash from his bedroom to Lana's, making it this time in thirty-two seconds.

I ran down the stairs with him, pulling him outside, closing the door behind me. Above us was the blue sky, fading into the dusk, with a reddish sun set into it like a resplendent bauble. The air was pickled with the scent of marigolds and lilacs, and it was so warm and fresh it seemed to draw me in, as if I were some fleshy extension of it all. It really was a paradise, I thought, and as if the sight of all those green lawns and potted flowers and old elms presaged it, I knew somehow I would thrive here.

We settled into our new house and got to know the town, which didn't take us long—there was only one supermarket, one shoe store, one clothing store, one bank, and one post office. There were maybe fifteen streets in the whole town, and by the end of June we knew them all.

We got to know the Colgate campus too, which was almost like a separate town. It was a few blocks from the park and just one street away from where we lived. It began gracefully at the curb as a green lawn anchored by old elms and awash in a huge pond on which a dozen or so white swans floated. It rode up an enormous hill, as steep as any I'd ever seen, with great old stone buildings perched here and there on the steppes, looking ancient and regal under their old ivy skins. I knew no matter what else was wrong with this small town, Lana could never find fault with this place.

Not knowing anyone else, Elena and I got to be pretty good friends. We pedaled our bikes together through the balmy days, and just before the sun set, we went down to the track and jumped the hurdles. We took turns timing each other with Leo's stopwatch, and by the end of June she had shaved three seconds off her time, while I had only managed one. After a while I became her coach, goading her on from the side of the track at the top of my lungs—*Go, Elena, go*—while she ran and jumped like a beautiful gazelle.

We camped out in the backyard some nights and tried to decide what we were going to tell people about ourselves, in case we ever met any. I thought we should stick to our real story and just leave the worst parts out—like about Lana being crazy and me being a cootie bug—but Elena liked the idea of making one up. She wanted to say we came from the East, where we spent our summers on Long Island Sound and our winters in New York, as Mimi did.

I had only the vaguest memory of the Sound and none at all of New York City. The only thing I could remember about those days was a small house in a suburban New Jersey town and a fat babysitter named Babs. It was so distant and sketchy in my mind it meant almost nothing.

"We were rich too," she said in the darkness of our tent. "Very rich."

However much I preferred this story to our own, I knew we couldn't tell it. "It's too much of a lie."

"It's not a lie, Maddie. You and I did come from the East. We did live in New York. We weren't born in New Jersey or Detroit, you idiot. We were born in New York. Only Harry was born in Detroit."

The idea that she spoke the truth raised the cold-headed goose bumps on my arms. I had never really known I was born in New York City, the very place where Lana's mysterious life had unfolded and then collapsed for all I knew. To think I had been part of her vast, unknown secret without having come away from it with the slightest knowledge was maddening.

Elena didn't tell this story, though. She opted instead to say that our father was a composer and our mother a writer, and that we had moved from Chicago for the peace and quiet of the hills. When she said the part about Chicago, I didn't say anything. I didn't begrudge her this one lie. I understood she had to tell one, and just so long as she left out the awful parts, I didn't care.

We swam in the Colgate pool in the mornings and followed Leo around campus until lunchtime. He was undergoing a lovely metamorphosis that none of us could fail to notice. It had him singing and telling stories and bounding in and out of the doors, happy both to be coming and to be going. None of us really understood how much he hated teaching those piano students until we saw how happy he was to be rid of them. "The music didn't die inside me, Maddie," he told me. "It's still there, thank God. The sap's still there."

He kept his word to Lana too—he worked at the college only mornings. During the afternoons he came home and sat at the piano, composing a piece he named "Meiling," the first song of the musical he said he was going to write.

It wasn't the same with Lana. It was obvious that she wasn't undergoing any kind of metamorphosis like Leo was. She didn't warm up to the place like he hoped she would. She really didn't like it here, and though she pretty much kept it to herself, I could tell she longed to be someplace else by the way her eyes would drift off when we were in the backyard.

When her dresses began to hang on her and her hands to shake, Elena and I started watching her, to see if the illness had followed her. She didn't do anything really unusual right away, although we found her stretched out on the grass near the picnic table quite a few times—twice in the dark—where she lay staring up at the sky. Elena said it wasn't that strange, but even so I knew there was something a little odd about it, that Lana didn't lie in the grass quite like anyone else. Maybe it was the way her arms were outstretched and her hands clamped the grass.

When she took me down to the Blue Bird Restaurant one morning and told me something I know she never meant to tell me, I couldn't help but think there was something about living in these lazy hills that had a way of wearing her down. She ordered eggs and I ordered pancakes, and while we waited for them to come, we overheard a young couple in the next booth arguing about someone who had run away.

"She don't have any money," the girl said. "She ain't going to get very far, believe me." She pushed her red hair off her shoulders and straightened her back.

"She won't come back, though," the boy said. "This time I know she won't come back. She's run away for good this time, Lindy."

The waitress finally brought our eggs and pancakes, and while Lana poured cream into her coffee, I watched her eyes grow distant. "My very first memory is of running away," she said. "I ran away when I was two years old. Me and Teddy walked down to the market on Second Avenue to buy some candy, and while he was inside, I decide to run away."

"Who's Teddy?" I asked. I hated to interrupt her, but she had never mentioned Teddy before.

She looked at me strangely, and a flush raced up her throat and spread across her face. "He was my older brother."

"I didn't know you had a brother."

When she fidgeted with her coffeecup, I knew she wished she hadn't said this. It came as quite a shock to me. In fact, I couldn't fathom Lana's having a brother. It was like my never telling anyone about Harry, and somehow my whole image of her underwent a drastic shift. Suddenly I envisioned her differently—instead of seeing her and Mimi standing alone against Long Island Sound, I saw her sitting on a porch swing with her brother.

Lana looked up at me for a moment, her eyes wandering across my face. "His name was Theodore," she said, "but we called him Teddy." She dropped her eyes down to her plate again and toyed nervously with the tiny buttons on her pearl white blouse.

"How come I've never met him?"

When the flush retreated from her face, I felt instantly sick. "Ah, sweetheart," she breathed, "Teddy was killed in the war."

"What war?" I didn't know why, but my heart began to hammer inside my chest.

"World War Two, Maddie—the worst war ever." She went silent and put her fork down, and as if the reminder of this awful war had wiped out her appetite forever, she spat a bite of egg from her mouth into a napkin and stuffed it under her plate. I stared across the table at her, wishing to God I'd never asked her.

"Some things in this life are too terrible," she said. Her eyes left my face, and her gaze drifted out the window, where she stared vacantly at the passing cars. I thought of telling her I was sorry. I even considered telling her a joke, but I couldn't think of any.

Later that night I sat outside in our backyard and stared at the distant hills, which were still and enduring like great lazy elephants, and puzzled over this latest mystery. I tried to imagine what Teddy might have looked like. I wondered how he'd been killed and how they'd all found out. Where was he buried? I thought, but more than anything I wondered why Lana had never told us about him. I could sort of understand why she might not have wanted to tell us about her cane, but why she couldn't tell us she had a brother named Teddy, I could not fathom. It worried me too the way it had just slipped out of her so easily. I thought that she was losing her grip or that maybe the illness was beginning to eat up her mind.

When she gave us the next installment of the Bear and Sparrow story, I was almost certain it was true. It was weeks before she got around to telling it, but when she finally did, I couldn't sleep afterward.

We crowded onto her mattress, and she immediately told us that the sparrow flew back to the bear's cave and was waiting for him when he woke up in the spring. *He was so happy to find her there, but after a few minutes he realized there was something wrong with her. She was so quiet, and when he asked her what had happened, she couldn't find the words to tell him. He gave her some tree sap to drink and put a few leaves over her shoulders and lit a small fire in the back of the cave to warm her.*

Days went by and she wouldn't speak. She wouldn't eat either, and when the bear noticed how thin she was, he went out and found her favorite worms. He warmed them over the fire and fed them to her slowly. After a few more days, she finally found the strength to tell him what had happened.

Even though her wing was better, she said, it wasn't strong enough for her to fly south with the other birds. From the beginning she fell behind, and no one but a scrawny sparrow would wait for her. After a while the scrawny sparrow got tired of resting and waiting, so the sparrow told her to catch up with the others before it was too late. She flew off and left the sparrow alone in a snowy field. The sparrow tried to fly by herself, but the winds were too strong. For two weeks she struggled to make some headway, but she couldn't fly for very long before the wind overpowered her. Her wing hadn't quite healed, and she began to favor it more and more until it was impossible to fly at all. When a big gust of wind came, she tucked it under her belly and lost all the height she had struggled to gain. Finally, she gave up hope of ever flying south and decided she would have to find some way to stay alive until she could get back to the bear.

The first night was awful—she sang mournfully, hoping someone would hear her, but she was completely alone. She fell asleep in exhaustion. When she awoke in the morning to a snowstorm, she sang all day, hoping someone would help her, but no one came. For weeks, she walked across long fields and through the woods on her way back to the bear, singing mournfully, until she couldn't stand to hear the sound of her own voice. She stopped singing completely, growing weaker and weaker by the day. A month went by, and finally on a warm afternoon when she felt a little better, she tried to sing, but when she opened up her mouth nothing came out but a horrible noise.

She told this to the bear, and she tried to sing for him, but the only sound that came out was a shrill squawk. It was bad enough she couldn't fly, she said, but now she couldn't sing.

All spring and summer the bear helped her fly again, practicing with her for hours until she was flying around the cave. He fed her the best worms and rubbed her wing for hours every night to make it stronger. He took her out into the wind and made her fly against it, until she could do it without favoring her wing. But still she couldn't sing and the bear didn't know how to help her. He tried, but it wasn't quite the same thing as helping her fly. The more he tried the worse the squawk became.

Finally, the winter descended and the bear couldn't hibernate. He was too worried about the sparrow's flying away again, and though she tried to convince him she would be all right, flying valiantly around the cave to prove it, he couldn't fall asleep. He needed her to sing him to sleep, but she couldn't. The sparrow knew she would live—she could fly again. She didn't need to sing to survive, but she knew if she left without singing the bear to sleep, he would die. She had to learn how to sing again, but she didn't know how.

That was as much as Lana would tell us. "Stay tuned for the next episode," she said, and she sent us off to bed.

I couldn't fall asleep. I felt Lana's story under my skin, swimming around like something queasy. I lay in my bed, blinking at the walls, and felt my nerves rise up. I didn't know much about them yet, but I was beginning to understand that they got up at night when I was supposed to sleep. Maybe they were like cats, I thought, or vampires. Whatever they were, they were rude, and though I hated to think about it, I knew they were getting worse.

I glanced at Elena through the door between our rooms. Leo had never fixed it. It was stuck fast and permanently open, and I could see her perfectly. She was lying on her back, her hands folded on top of her stomach, while the light from the street lamp fell gently across her face, bathing it in a soft, white glow.

"Elena," I whispered across the darkness, "do you think Lana's the sparrow?"

She lay there quietly for a long time, the silence swimming between us like a moat. "I don't know, Maddie," she whispered back. "I thought about that too, but I doubt she would just tell us something about herself like that."

"Why?"

"Because she's not that dumb."

"Maybe the illness is eating up her mind," I whispered.

"I doubt it, Maddie." She turned over, as if that were the end of it, but I still couldn't sleep. I was too worried that something awful was going to happen to Lana.

It wasn't long before we started to notice how her hands shook when they were just lying in her lap and how she sometimes ran out of breath when she was just sitting down. It was the illness, we worried, but it wasn't until I dragged her up the hill to see Miss Thomas that I realized it had come back.

Harry and I had found Miss Thomas one afternoon when Leo was gone and Elena and Lana were taking naps. Her old brown house sat up on a hill, just beyond our backyard. It was tantalizing, the way it peeked out from the woods, and without thinking twice about it, I pulled Harry up with me. It was a very old, clapboard house with a yard that barely emerged from the woods. The lawn was made up of great clumps of wildflowers, and there were bird feeders everywhere. They hung from trees and special orange poles and sat on old stumps and buckets and little red sawhorses. There were little statues dotting the lawn too—stone statues of men with fat bellies and long dangling earlobes, sitting with twisted legs.

The house itself had wide, upwardly sloping eaves, under which hung a variety of fascinating objects that were all in perpetual motion—metal and wooden wind chimes that moved languidly in the

June air and sang in high, peaceful notes; lanterns of all shapes, most of which were orange with strange black markings; and delicate paper airplanes that drifted up and down on strings.

I never considered who might live here until we heard wild rapping on the window above us. We looked up in fear and discovered an old woman struggling to get the window open. Harry suddenly clutched me, and I clutched him back. The window flew open, and the woman thrust her head out, like I had never seen anyone do, like a horse almost. She looked old and wrinkled with gray hair like steel wool. She wore glasses that were as thick as windshields and magnified her eyes to the size of great black olives. They were terrifying, but she smiled hugely, and something warm and wonderful radiated from her.

"Hey, you cuckoo birds, I've got something magnificent to show you," she called out. Her enthusiasm was so immense, it seemed it reached out and touched me. "You won't believe it. I tell you, you just won't believe it." Harry and I stood there and stared up at her, amazed by the sheer energy that flooded out of her.

"Come on in," she said, and then her arm came out of the window, big and baggy, and she began motioning to us in great exaggeration, as if the stronger she made the gesture, the more believable her invitation would become. "Come round to the door. I'll meet you there." As quickly as she had flung the window open, she threw it shut. Then as Harry and I stared at her, she bent forward, near to the glass, and there was her arm again, inviting us in like I'd never been invited anywhere.

By the look on her face and that tremendous arm, I knew she had something good to show us. For the moment I forgot all that Lana and Leo had ever told me about accepting things from strangers. I was going to see what it was, no matter, so I grabbed Harry's hand and towed him through the clumps of wildflowers up to her door.

It opened immediately, and there she stood. I'd never seen anything like her in my life. I couldn't take my eyes off her arms. The old flesh dangled off the backs of them, wagging back and forth like huge turkey wattles. I couldn't get rid of the idea of taking a scissors to them. Her legs, though—they were even more arresting. They stuck out of her pale gray dress and were, without exaggeration, the skinniest, longest legs I'd ever seen on a grown woman. They looked like the legs of a starving Biafran, stretched out to stiltish proportions, baked and then aged to a wrinkled, crepey gooseflesh. I couldn't imagine how she got around on them or how she had gotten them to begin with, but I didn't have much time to think about it. As soon as she flung the door open, she began gesturing wildly, the sheer force of which drew both Harry and me in immediately.

"Oh, you two are going to love this," she said excitedly. Her voice was full of something, something that I couldn't name. I only knew I wanted to hear more of it; there was promise to it, as if it were going to tell me thrilling things. It wasn't a beautiful voice—it was old and thin and wavered a great deal, but even so it was singular, like a simple string of notes Leo sometimes played on the piano with his right hand.

The sight of her making off across the room on her legs was so absorbing I forgot for the moment to follow her. They didn't move like any legs I'd ever seen. My first impression was that of an ostrich I had once seen racing across a zoo yard. They locked backward, and how she was able to build up the sort of speed at which she was moving, I couldn't quite understand.

"Come on, you cuckoo birds," she called out, her arm beckoning us forward. I had a weakness for people like her—for people who had arms and legs like hers and didn't try to hide them, for people who called you *cuckoo* before they knew your name.

We followed her down a beautiful hallway filled with small colored windows, through which the light poured in a combination of soft, diffused colors. She was ahead of us, plowing steadily forward in a series of awkward, jerking motions, as if some invisible force impelled her. She finally stopped at a set of double wooden doors and turned to us. "Oh, it will be like nothing you've ever seen before," she said. "You just wait, you cuckoo birds." Her eyes, magnified by those windshield lenses, were huge beyond belief. "It'll take your breath away." She raised her arms high above her head, like she was about to conduct an orchestra, and then lowered them, throwing the doors open.

What I saw next was more than I could have ever hoped for. We were inside an enclosed porch, which had many long windows with lacy white curtains that blew lazily in the stingy breeze. From the ceiling hung over a hundred bird cages, with all different kinds of birds perched inside. She closed the doors, and with great enthusiasm she picked up a black stick and announced, "Now, you watch this."

She raised the stick above her head, and with amazing speed she went from cage to cage opening all the doors, as if she had spent her life doing just this, the birds rushing out into the still air.

She didn't do it silently either—she did it with a crazy noisy abandon, cawing loudly and calling out their names in what I could only imagine was her own bird voice. She looked mad running around on her stilt legs, racing to open those cages, her baggy arms swinging violently over her head, as she crowed and whistled and cawed, all the while whipping those birds into a beautiful frenzy. They flew over our heads, soaring and dipping and gliding, shrieking along with her, filling the air with the silken sound of their beating wings. There were doves and sparrows, thrushes and whippoorwills, finches and parrots. They came in dozens of colors and sizes, their sounds as variable as human voices, some of them fighting, some of them chasing, some of them mating. But they all flew above us and swooped down, over and over again.

Harry forgot himself completely and ran after her screaming while she opened the cages, but I couldn't move. I stood frozen and watched her, marveling over the power of her decrepit limbs and her voice as she stirred us all into a wonderful frenzy.

"Isn't it grand?" she screamed. *"Isn't it grand?"* She was out of breath, and I could see small beads of perspiration on her forehead and upper lip. "Look how many there are. Aren't they something? *Aren't they just the living end?"* I didn't know what she meant by the living end—all I knew was that it was very magical and that it made my heart beat very fast. Time stood still too in a way I would search for again and again. I liked that feeling more than any I'd ever known, and I wished just then that it would never leave me.

This is what I wanted to give Lana. I wanted to make her heart beat really fast, to make time stand still for her in a way she would never forget. I couldn't tell her what I wanted to show her, because that would have ruined it, so it took me a few days to convince her to go. Her hip was still hurting her, and when we first looked up the hill, I worried that we weren't going, but she told Harry to get up front and pull her. She put me in charge of pushing her from behind. "Okay, when I say, 'Heave,' you pull, Harry. You push, Maddie, and when I say, 'Ho,' you stop. All right?" We took up our positions, and as soon as Lana said, "Heave," I pushed, Harry pulled, and we took a nice stride forward.

I was in back of her long enough to learn something more about her body, for beneath the thin cotton of her dress, I felt the bumpy line of her scar. It was only for a brief moment that my fingers chanced to fall on it, but it was long enough for me to discover that beyond this scar lay something else—something flat and hard and very unlike bone. I remembered the images I had conjured before— the truck plowing into her hip, the madman with the hacksaw, the undertow on Long Island Sound—and I wondered if perhaps a piece of the truck or hacksaw or maybe even a bit of sunken hull was forever embedded in Lana's hip.

I didn't get to touch it for very long before Lana told me to stop. She moved my hands to her waist, and while I waited for her command of "Heave," I felt how thin she was. I could feel her shaking; she was breathing hard, as if she had just raced up the hill. When we finally got to the woods and she had to lean up against a tree to catch her breath, I knew she was getting sick again.

When we got to the house I wanted Miss Thomas to plow down her light-hazy hallway, exclaiming that we'd never seen anything like this in all our lives, for Lana's sake. It wouldn't be good otherwise, and when she didn't do it I stopped her. I had to. She was about to ruin it all, and if not that, then to diminish its greatness.

"Do it like you did before," I said.

She understood. She turned to us and with great enthusiasm she said, "This will take your breath away." Then she raised her huge, pendulous arms into the air and lowered them dramatically, throwing open the doors. We rushed inside, and she closed the doors behind us. Then just like before, she said, "You watch," and suddenly the black stick was in her hands and she was off on those legs of hers, freeing her birds, cawing and screaming, whipping them into a wonderful havoc. Harry ran after her again, squealing and cawing, and I stood frozen, my heart beating just as wildly, just as fast. It was all perfect, and just when the birds began soaring overhead, their wings beating in time to my own heart, I turned to Lana.

She wasn't by my side like she had been when it began, and for a moment I thought she had run out. I turned around and found her leaning against the doors, struggling to breathe. Her head was bent, and she clutched her throat, and when she wiped her brow, I saw her hand tremble. Her eyes twitched back and forth nervously, and when she looked from the birds to me, I knew they terrified her. I rushed back to her, and she clutched me under her arm, as if I could possibly hold her up. Her legs wobbled so much, I worried they would buckle.

"Oh, Maddie," she breathed, "could we sit down?" Her voice was so high and pitifully thin that it went right through me.

I noticed a wicker chair in the corner. We struggled over to it, me mashed against her side, as if we were Siamese twins who shared a leg. It was covered with bird droppings, some of which were fresh, but she didn't care. She slumped down, doubling over in her lap, and gasped for air. Harry saw her and ran over to us, and when he found his way into her arms, she seemed to find herself again. She pulled him close to her and buried her nose in his hair. As if the clean, baby scent of his head were like smelling salts, she started to come around.

I found her out in the backyard later that night, sitting at our picnic table, writing in the meager light of Leo's kerosene lamp. Leo had told me she was out there, and when I remembered the attic and the small window that overlooked the backyard, I crept inside it and walked slowly back to the overstuffed chair, losing my foot down a crack only once. I kept the light off so I wouldn't be noticed and left the door open just in case I discovered any ghosts and had to run out. I climbed into the red chair and pulled the window open until I could see her perfectly. She was bent over a pad of white paper, writing furiously. Her hair was pulled back in a makeshift bun, and a black sweater fell across her shoulders. Before I spoke, I watched her pen scratch noisily across a whole page.

"Hi, Lana," I finally said. I dropped down to the dusty floor on my bare knees.

She let out a scream as high and beautiful as Elena's. "Where are you, Maddie?" Her hand flew to her heart, as if to keep it from beating through.

"Up here, in the attic," I said, pressing my face closer to the screen.

Her eyes shot up so quickly it scared me. "What are you doing?" The pen slipped from her fingers, and the light from the kerosene lamp flickered gently across her face.

"Just sitting here." She stared up at the window, and though I knew she couldn't see me very well, I felt her eyes as if they had tiny microscopic feelers. "I'm sorry," I said quietly.

"For what, sweetheart?" She was faraway from me, but even so I saw a dark crease settle across her brow.

"I'm sorry the birds didn't make you happy." I hadn't counted on saying that. It just came out of the black of my mind.

"They did, sweetheart," she said softly. "Please don't say that. They were wonderful, and your friend, Miss Thomas, was very sweet."

"But they didn't make your heart beat really fast." I shifted my weight from one aching knee to the other and pressed my face against the dirty window screen, as if that would take me closer to her.

"Oh, but they did," she argued. "They made it beat so fast I almost fell down."

Silence fell between us then. I knew she was waiting for me to tell her something else, leveraging the silence, counting on it to pump me of all my small confessions, but I didn't know what else to say. I listened to the luscious sound of the crickets instead and watched the fireflies flickering.

"I'm sorry, Maddie," she said. "I'm sorry I wasn't myself this afternoon. I was feeling, well . . . There were too many things flying at me, and then—they were magnificent, though. That was the discovery of a lifetime. Really. I'm very proud of you. You know something good when you see it." She smiled, but when she pushed the hair off her forehead, I saw her hand shake.

Later that night, after she went to bed, I listened for the sound of her voice. It came to me, not through the furnace ducts as it had in Detroit, but through the floor registers. It was high and lacerating and wordless, and I knew then that the illness had followed her.

3

Lana didn't go down that dark drain like Elena and I worried she would. Barbara Lamb hosted a welcoming party for us in her sumptuous backyard, and somehow that changed things for Lana.

Barbara was a very visible member of the Hamilton community, active in all the usual ways—a trustee for the United Church, a school board member, one of the leaders of the DAR—but what really gave her distinction was her presence on the WDRA radio show in Utica as the voice for "Women Speak Up."

She went to great lengths putting together this afternoon lunch. She borrowed tables from the United Church and dressed them with white tablecloths and scarlet napkins. In the center of each table was a huge vase of pink gladiolas handpicked from her garden, and on the back of each chair she tied white balloons with the word WEL-COME written in deep red. She invited eight of her closest friends, most of whom were the wives of Colgate professors, and a woman named Garta, who didn't for a moment pretend to belong.

We crunched down Barbara Lamb's gravel driveway, Harry and I flanking Lana, Elena bringing up the rear. Lana was wearing her pearl white blouse and a long tan skirt, and her hair was carefully done in a French bun. She wasn't the least bit interested in coming to this party, but she realized she had to—it was too small a town to snub people and expect to get along. Her hands were shaking, but even if she'd felt better, I doubt she would have wanted to come. Potluck lunches with borrowed church tables did not interest Lana.

The drive finally ended and we were suddenly face to face with Barbara Lamb. She was tall, almost six feet tall, and so thin she was gangly. She tried to take Lana's arm, but Lana held tight to me and Harry, so the three of us crossed Barbara Lamb's festooned lawn in a long row, Barbara at the head, Elena bringing up the rear. I felt Lana shaking, and when she spoke I knew she was feeling especially bad—her voice was smaller than normal and edged upward a note too high. I'm sure she wanted to turn around and vanish.

Barbara Lamb eased us over to a cluster of lawn chairs where a group of women sat. They were all about Lana's age, in their late thirties, early forties, and I knew just by looking at them that none of them would become Lana's friend. There was Ester Hill, a sweet old gray-haired woman, and Charlene Parks, a woman so thick-limbed and strapping, she reminded me more of a man than a woman. Patty Shepard sat next to her. She had an acrid Southern accent, so munchy and crackling it sounded like she was kidding. Then there was Joan Thayer—she wasn't the wife of a Colgate professor, but rather the wife of a man who owned a trucking business, and I suppose this gave her special license to be less of a lady. "What in the hell are you wearing those high heels for, Barb?" she said. "They're sticking in the grass, for Christ's sake."

As Barbara Lamb steered us over to another woman, the back door banged open and disgorged a large woman. She was young, younger than anyone else there, and distinctly different. She was big, not so much fat as just big, and the way she stood in the doorway attracted our attention. She wore a pair of gigantic blue thongs and an over-sized man's shirt, the tails of which hung down over a pair of blue denim cut-off shorts. Her short brown hair had a dry straw fuzziness about it as if it had fallen victim to too many permanents; her face was marred by six large boils, and a downy layer of dark hair covered her cheeks, whiskers springing stubbornly from her chin.

She wasn't normal. She had something wrong with her. I could tell that right away. It was nothing physical—there wasn't anything protruding from her body or anything. It was something else, which she presented to us immediately.

"GODDAMN IT, JIMMY!" she shrieked over our heads. It wasn't just a yell—it was a scream, a full-volumed, uninhibited scream, which one would only use in case of great danger. We all turned around and looked at the sandbox, where a four-year-old boy was standing stark-naked in terror.

She stormed down the stairs in her blue plastic thongs, oblivious to us. She marched across the lawn, a tank in motion, her eyes locked on that poor naked boy.

"GODDAMN IT, JIMMY, WHAT DID I TELL YOU?" The air, as if something sonic had roared past, reverberated with her voice, and the little boy slapped his hands to his ears. He was speechless. All he could do was stand in the sandbox and brace himself.

When one of her large thonged feet slammed down in the sandbox, Barbara Lamb tried to dissuade us from watching by offering around a tray of crackers. No one wanted any. We were completely transfixed by this woman in the sandbox.

"WHAT DID I TELL YOU, JIMMY?" she screamed again. Her voice had not dwindled in the least. In fact it was louder—it was driven not by any rules of distance but by her unfathomable rage. She yanked his hands from his ears, and in one violent movement she strung him up in the air by his arm, leaving only his toes to touch the ground. Then she beat him with a savage loss of self-control. The only sound louder than her brutal thwacks was Jimmy's plaintive wail.

"YOU TAKE YOUR CLOTHES OFF AGAIN AND I'LL CUT YOUR WIENER OFF. DO YOU HEAR ME?" she yelled.

This was too much for Barbara Lamb, who fled gracelessly across the lawn to the boy's rescue, her bone-colored high heels sticking in the grass.

"Garta," she implored. "Garta!" She stopped just short of the sandbox and laid her delicate hand on Garta's arm. The boy was dangling from Garta's grip, and only after Barbara Lamb succeeded in calming her down was he finally lowered to his feet, where he fell to his knees and doubled over in a knot of sorrow. Barbara hurriedly gathered up his strewn clothes and began dressing him, but Garta stopped her.

"Let Lizzy do it," she barked. "It's her fault. She was supposed to watch him." The venom filled in her eyes again. "LIZZY," she yelled, scanning Barbara Lamb's lawn. "LIZZY, COME AND PUT YOUR BROTHER'S CLOTHES ON." Her voice was still completely unrestrained, like she was alone in her own backyard. *"LIZZY!"* When this last failed to produce anyone, Barbara Lamb began dressing the little boy.

"That little shit probably went downtown to buy that asinine thing," Garta said bitterly. "She wanted that jackknife in the bubble gum machine. Gus gave her a quarter even though I told her she don't deserve it."

Barbara Lamb mentioned something about how it was only a quarter and continued dressing the boy. Garta huffed across the lawn, stiffly acknowledging the warm hellos which emanated from Ester Hill, Charlene Parks, and Patty Shepard, and disappeared into the house, slamming the door behind her.

I hurried back to the women and waited to hear what they all had to say about Garta. Charlene Parks spoke up first. "Well," she said, straightening herself in the chair, "the wrath of God hath descendeth," which sent Patty Shepard into a convulsion of hee-haw laughter. Ester Hill shook her gray head as if to dispel the hold Garta had on us all, and Barbara Lamb began plying her tray of small crackers. "I know, I know," she said, shaking her blond head. "I've got myself into this thing with Garta—" She stopped there as if she couldn't possibly tell us what this thing was and then added, "She needs our help."

Barbara Lamb disappeared into the house, and the women graciously turned their attention to Lana, asking all the questions you usually ask a newcomer. I waited for someone to ask about her cane; I knew it was only a matter of time. There it was, at her side, her hand resting languidly on the carved handle, as if it were part of her, as important to her as her own leg. It was Joan Thayer, with her air of bored nonchalance, who finally asked. "What's the cane for?" she said, as if it were a gimmick Lana had picked up, a prop of no more importance than a hat or a pair of gloves.

I felt Elena behind me immediately. Lana smiled and repositioned the cane slightly. "I'm getting old," she said, and when she laughed, no one said another word about it.

"As if she would have told them," Elena whispered in my ear.

It wasn't long afterward that Lana got around to asking about Garta. I knew it had to be coming. Someone like Garta couldn't come charging out of a house like a blue-thonged bull without Lana having to know why, so while Barbara Lamb was still in the house, Lana turned to Charlene Parks and asked, "Is Garta related to Barbara?"

Charlene Parks shook her head, and as Lana struggled to formulate the next question, Barbara Lamb and Garta came out of the house.

"Garta," she said, gracefully steering her toward Lana. "This is Lana. Lana, this is Garta."

Lana extended her hand, and Garta, obviously unused to this practice, wiped her hand off on the back of her shorts with a quick slap-slap.

"It's good to meet you," she said awkwardly.

Lana mentioned the same, and as soon as they dropped hands, Garta slumped heavily into a chair and extracted a cigarette from a red leather, rhinestone case.

"Garta is our newest member at the United Church," Barbara told Lana.

Lana nodded politely and Garta rolled her eyes. "Yeah," she said. "If you could call it that." She nervously shuffled her blue-thonged feet in the grass. "Me, a member of a church. Ain't that a laugh. And you can believe there are a few people who don't like it much too." She rolled her eyes again, crossed her legs, and with the tip of her cigarette, she became intent on burning down a hair which jutted out from a large mole on the side of her knee.

"That's not true," Barbara Lamb said. "We're very pleased you've joined us."

A moment passed while Garta burned that hair down, and when Barbara Lamb felt certain nothing was forthcoming she asked Lana a deadly question.

"Which church do you belong to, Lana?"

Elena made me push over on the footstool.

"We don't belong to any church," Lana said. It was true, we didn't, and as far as Lana cared we never would. She didn't believe in Christianity much.

"No?" was all Barbara Lamb said.

"Not really," Lana said, and I knew right then and there that that was the end of Lana and Barbara Lamb.

The back door opened again, and an old Negro woman walked out carrying an enormous tray. She wore a neatly pressed and starched white uniform with a small white hat perched ridiculously in her hair.

She looked miserable, and when Lana saw her she dropped her cane and rushed up the steps to relieve her. Just as she was about to take the tray away, Barbara Lamb dashed up the stairs and stopped her. Another awkward moment ensued. "No, no, Lana," she implored. "Gus has got it. Now you sit down. You can't be carrying that." Everyone's eyes fell on Lana's cane, lying in the grass not too far from Garta's blue thongs.

Gus moved slowly and methodically down the stairs, saying nothing, looking at no one. She passed lightly between Lana and Patty Shepard and lowered the tray onto the table. "Lordy," she groaned quietly, and with practiced hands she unloaded it.

No one paid any attention to her, except Lana, and of course me and Elena. We had never seen a real maid, much less a Negro one, and it was with great curiosity that I observed the white uniform against her dark brown skin.

"Gus," I heard Barbara say, "I told you I wanted those nice red tomatoes cut up in small sections and put around the edge of the bowl." Barbara smiled patiently, and I struggled to figure out what was wrong with the exchange. She had said it nicely, but even so there was something deadly cold about it.

Gus took the salad bowl without saying a word and padded up the stairs in her white-soled shoes.

"GUS," Garta called out. "YOU GIVE LIZZY A QUARTER?"

Gus nodded. "She helped me clean the corn when she come."

"DON'T GIVE HER NO MORE QUARTERS, GUS. SHE JUST BLOWS IT ON THAT GUMBALL MACHINE AT THE DRUGSTORE."

Gus started to say something, but on second thought she turned around and walked into the house.

It was after she disappeared that I noticed Lana. Elena noticed her at the same time and pinched my arm. It came as quite a shock to see her face—just moments ago she had been perfectly composed, but now her face was red and her eyes were hot. It had something to do with Gus—what, we couldn't imagine—but something about Gus had done it.

Very shortly we sat down at the tables to eat lunch. Lana seemed to regain her composure, but whenever Gus walked by, carrying a tray or taking one away, I noticed Lana watched her. In fact, she couldn't take her eyes off her.

The lunch was quite nice, and it seemed all would go off quite peacefully, until Garta spotted Lizzy lurking over by the garage.

"LIZZY!" she yelled. We all turned around to look. I didn't see her right away, but whoever she was, I already felt sorry for her.

"LIZZY," Garta yelled again. A young girl of about ten or twelve years old stepped out of the shadows, away from the garage. Her head was hanging and her hands were stuffed deep in the pockets of her sea green shorts. She didn't look like anyone else I had ever seen. Her hair was jet black and curly, and her skin was brown, only slightly lighter than Gus's.

Garta rose up and huffed across the lawn, her blue thongs snapping furiously at her heels. Lizzy didn't move—she stood her ground, as Jimmy had, and waited for Garta's onslaught. When Garta reached her, she pulled her hand back as if she were going to strike her, but on second thought (we were all there, after all) she grabbed her by the arm and shook her violently.

"I TOLD YOU YOU COULDN'T LEAVE," she yelled, the boils on her face reddening.

Lizzy looked up, and for the first time since she had appeared I saw her face. I noticed her eyes first. They were black and enormous, but more than anything they were fearless. It seemed she only hung her head in deference to Garta's rage, as a matter of habit, of simple decorum.

"WHERE WERE YOU?" she yelled, digging her fingers into Lizzy's arm.

"I went down to the drugstore," she said. I was startled by her voice—it was so clear and strong for a girl her age, singular you might even say. It had a certain power to it, as though God might use it to speak the truth.

"I TOLD YOU NOT TO GO DOWN THERE, SHITHEAD. I TOLD YOU TO WATCH JIMMY. WHO DO YOU THINK YOU ARE?"

Garta's voice reached such a pitch, I felt the hairs on the back of my neck stand up. Barbara Lamb, fearing a public beating, jumped up from the table and hurried over to them. As if the situation required reinforcements, Gus put down her tray and moved across the lawn at a pace I didn't think her capable of. Barbara Lamb went for Garta, and Gus made a move for Lizzy. Within moments, Lizzy was safely tucked under Gus's arm, and Garta was struggling against Barbara

Lamb. I glanced over at Lana—she was so thoroughly absorbed by this little drama that her mouth hung open.

"DON'T BABY HER, GUS," Garta yelled. "SHE DON'T GET ANY LUNCH."

"She'll have lunch," Gus yelled back. Her voice, though it wavered with emotion, was final.

"Of course she'll have lunch," Barbara Lamb said.

Garta stomped off in the direction of the house with Barbara Lamb trailing after her in those bone-colored high heels. Gus kept Lizzy stowed under her arm and steered her over to the tables, where, with the exception of Lana, Elena, and me, everyone was bent over their plates eating.

Not content to let Barbara Lamb have the last word, Garta turned around and yelled, "YOU LITTLE SHITHEAD. WHEN WE GET HOME I'M GONNA *KILL* YOU."

It sent a shiver through us all, for coming from Garta it seemed entirely possible.

Lizzy quietly slipped into the chair next to mine. Gus took her plate away to fill it up, and while she waited, she stuck her hand into her pocket and fished something out. She did it with a graceful, practiced stealth, and it wasn't until I saw what she had that I understood why. In the palm of her hand lay the prize—the jackknife she wanted so much she had risked her mother's wrath to get it. It was nothing really, a red plastic jackknife, a poor imitation of Leo's, but the way she held it and stared down at it made it seem like no other jackknife in the world.

Gus came back shortly with a plate of food and wrapped her arms around Lizzy's neck. Only then did I notice how much more Lizzy looked like Gus than she did Garta. Their skin was similar in its glossy brown sheen, their hair was the same color, even their nostrils flared in the same exotic way. I wondered if Gus were her real mother and if for some strange reason Garta had adopted her.

"Honey," I heard Gus whisper, "you come see me when you're through."

When Gus left, Lizzy picked up her fork and began very slowly and quietly to eat her lunch. Elena and I couldn't keep our eyes off her—neither could Lana. She was utterly transfixed by her.

Lizzy left the table after eating half of her sandwich. I didn't see her again until Lana took me and Harry into Barbara Lamb's house to use the bathroom. She was inside with Gus, in a small room off the kitchen where Barbara Lamb kept her washer and dryer. There Gus sat at a card table eating her lunch, listening to Lizzy tell her the great feats her new jackknife was capable of.

"This part can open a bottle," she said. "This part can cut finger-nails, but probably only baby ones. And this part is a spoon."

Lana stepped into the hot, stuffy room, where only a small metal fan whirred to cool it, and thrust her hand out to Gus.

"Hello, I'm Lana," she said. "We were never introduced."

Gus looked up at her with a mixture of surprise and fear, and only after Lana repeated herself did Gus offer her hand. "Pleased to know you, Lana," she said. "I'm Gus." She paused for a moment to smile, her eyes searching Lana's face. "Do I know you?"

"I don't think so," Lana said. She looked down after that, as if to hide her face from Gus's eyes, and then Gus looked away politely. The two of them hung there awkwardly for a good minute, something unspoken passing between them.

I watched Lizzy as she fingered her jackknife, the silence finally forcing me to speak up. "How old are you?" I asked her. I always had to know that about children—that way I knew if they were meant for me or for Elena.

"Ten and a half," she said, which meant she was mine.

It came as quite a shock to Barbara Lamb when she heard that out of all her luncheon guests, it was Garta whom Lana invited over first. We never really found out very much about Garta that afternoon at Barbara Lamb's party. Lana had asked her a few questions, such as, "Are Gus and Lizzy related?" but Barbara didn't know that there was no better or safer repository for secrets than Lana—she simply ignored Lana and steered the conversation to less murky waters.

So Garta came to lunch and the seven of us sat down at our old picnic table in the backyard, while the sky stretched out above us in perfect, unblemished blue. Garta wore her big blue thongs and an-other oversized man's shirt, which hung down over a pair of black cutoff shorts. Her hair was pulled away from her face in a short ponytail, which jutted out from the back of her head like a small bundle of straw. Lana had on her long, navy blue dress with the tiny buttons, and all afternoon it blew gently around her in the June breeze like a trace of swirling smoke.

While Lana passed around plates of sandwiches and potato chips, we ate and Garta talked. Lana got her started, but it didn't take much. "Are Lizzy and Gus related?" was all Lana needed to ask, and Garta repositioned herself on the picnic bench, as if to prepare herself for a long discourse. "Gus is Lizzy's grandma," she said. "Course, Barbara don't like to acknowledge that too openly. Gus has been with her ever since she come here, and she thinks of her as family, though she don't always treat Gus so good, huh, Lizzy?"

Lizzy looked up from her plate, but she was no help to Garta—she just shrugged her shoulders and went back to her bologna sandwich.

"Barbara never says Gus is Lizzy's grandma," Garta went on, "because that would make Lizzy a Negro, and it don't sit well with Barbara for anyone to be white and a Negro, which Lizzy is." She held her sandwich aloft in her large hands and took a huge bite. "She's a mulatto," she said with a mouth full of bologna and bread. "Her daddy was nigger Joe. That's what a lot of people here called him. He's Gus's son. They run him off eleven years ago when he got me pregnant. And now I got a mulatto daughter." Garta shoved a few potato chips into her mouth. "Joe and me was going to get married, but my father wouldn't let us," she crunched. "They run him out of town not too long after that—my brothers and their friends. Gus was brokenhearted, you know. He was her baby, and her only son. She's never been the same since then."

"So where's Joe now?" Lana asked.

"Oh, he's in New York somewhere, living with Gus's sister. He writes every so often, and he has snuck up here a couple of times to see Lizzy and Gus. She said maybe he'll come back this summer, but I doubt it. Gus is always saying he's gonna come and he don't. I don't care—he never sent me so much as a penny for Lizzy. He's always threatening to come up here and bust up my marriage with Don. I tell him to put his money where his mouth is, but he don't ever come through. Don, he pays for Lizzy."

She glanced over at Lizzy only to discover Lizzy whispering in Jimmy's ear.

"QUIT WHISPERING, LIZZY. I'M TALKING. CAN'T YOU SEE THAT?"

"I'm sorry," Lizzy said. She bowed her head in that same deferential way she had when she first appeared by Barbara Lamb's garage. I watched her, her head locked down in obedience, and when she glanced up at me, she rolled her eyes and fluttered her eyelashes, as if to say Garta was full of shit. I liked her for that.

Garta told us about her family after that. She told us almost everything, and if Lizzy suffered from any embarrassment, I couldn't tell. If anything she looked bored, as if Garta had trouped their lives out so many times, in so many backyards, that she was sick of hearing it. Elena and I were spellbound, though. In fact, we forgot all about eating. To hear a mother speak so openly and truthfully about her family and her life amazed us.

During the time it took us to eat our lunch, Garta told us every detail she could remember about her family—her mother, her four half-sisters, her two half-brothers, her grandmother, her great-grandmother, and all five of her aunts. She said that her great-grandmother on her father's side had three illegitimate children, was married two times, and never had any children while she was married. Her two half-brothers had each been in prison, the older one twice, the younger one only once. One of her aunts had had an affair with another aunt's husband, and two of them were divorced. Her middle sister had run away recently, for the third time, and her youngest sister was having an affair with a forty-year-old married man. All of which caused her grandmother, Esther Hodges, to spend most of her days and nights on her knees in prayer.

As I listened to Garta pour out her life, I realized for the first time just how strange it really was that we didn't know anything about Lana. In one hour's time I knew more about Garta than I did about Lana, whom I had lived with for ten years. I felt the sting and frustration all over again of being so thoroughly shut out of Lana's life. That more than anything else is what prompted me to tell Lizzy as much as I did that late afternoon.

When Garta finished her story, Elena, Lizzy, and I got up from the table. For a while we hung around the yard, tossing a baseball, eavesdropping on Lana and Garta's conversation. "You don't want to say bad things about her father, Garta," we heard Lana say. "You must have thought something of him at one time. You almost married him once. It's not nice to call him a nigger. You don't want her growing up thinking she's less because she's mulatto."

When it got too uncomfortable for Lizzy to listen, she secretly flashed me a glimpse of her jackknife, and told me she knew where we could get all the ice cream we wanted. After Elena went into the house, I followed her out of the backyard and down the street, where we stole across the Colgate lawns. We climbed a steep hill—Heart Attack Hill, she called it—and crept quietly along the back wall of one of the dining halls, slipping in through the large service entry. We sneaked back to a huge walk-in refrigerator, where we were surrounded by at least fifty tubs of ice cream—chocolate, vanilla, and strawberry. The cardboard tops were too hard to pry off, so Lizzy cut squares in them with the scissors of her jackknife, and we used the spoon to eat it. That's why she had wanted the jackknife.

Garta worked there, she told me, as we lolled on the side of a greened hill, baking the chill out of our bones. That's how she knew about it in the first place. Occasionally they got in candy bars, she said. They were generally good for potato chips and Fritos; there was almost always a stockpile of Cokes and root beer, and sometimes they got in sweet baby gherkins and black olives—two things which, oddly enough, we both loved.

"She would kill me if she knew we went in there," she said. I noticed her eyes again. They were huge and clear and wholly untroubled. They reminded me of the kind of eyes God might use when he looked out across great vistas. "My mom is really mean sometimes. Lana's nice, though. You're lucky."

I nodded—it was true. Garta was mean, Lana was nice, and I was very lucky. At the moment, however, I felt luckier that Garta wasn't my mother than that Lana was. At the thought of Garta's life spilling so effortlessly from her tongue, I was annoyed all over again by Lana's secrecy.

"Lana's not so perfect," I said almost bitterly. I leaned back on my elbows and stared up at the unmarred sky. "She's very secretive, you know. I hardly know anything about her family. I met her mother only once that I can remember, and I didn't even know she had a—" I stopped myself, or rather panic stopped me from saying the word *brother*. The thought that I had almost let that secret slip out into the air made me sick.

"You know that cane she has?" I said instead, though it wasn't much better. I squinted my eyes and stared down at the pond below and at the ivy-skinned backs of the university buildings.

Lizzy nodded and drifted back on her elbows.

"None of us knows why she has it, you know." I went on to tell her about Lana's scar, supplying her with all the details as only a true lover of scars would. I said it was deep purple, that it lay on her hip like a piece of rope, and that beneath it lay something hard, perhaps metal, from the hull of a ship.

My eyes drifted down the hill. We were so high up that the swans looked like white dots floating on the water. "She might have been taken by the undertow on Long Island Sound," I said. "Maybe she got sucked out and a piece of a ship or something on the bottom of the ocean got stuck in her hip." I could tell by Lizzy's eyes that she was intensely interested, so I went on. "Then sometimes I think maybe she was walking along a dark road and a Mack truck hit her. Or else, maybe a man from New York City hit her in the hip with an axe or something, and maybe the blade is still in her hip." Despite the hot sun we both shivered at the thought of any one of these gruesome fates.

"What if somebody tried to bury her alive," Lizzy whispered, rolling onto her side, "and they stabbed her with a shovel and that's what's in there now? Or what if somebody pushed her out a window and it's glass she's got in her hip?" Her eyes grew huge at the thought of it.

Oh, how I relished her enthusiasm. I relaxed back in the warm, lush grass, shivering at the thought of finding a friend. I had never had a friend before, and it seemed it would be wonderful. She leaned back on her elbows next to me, and in the silence we gazed out at the green hills.

"You know what else she does?" I said. We heard the distant sound of a lawn mower starting up, and somewhere in the back of my mind I worried that the mention of Lana's secret had summoned it.

"What?" She turned her head, and I felt her eyes on my face.

"She cuts articles out of the newspaper and then locks them in her desk drawer." It seemed I couldn't speak fast enough. "Then she throws the newspaper away. Elena and I went through the trash a couple of times and found them, but it didn't help because she cut the whole article out."

"Just get another newspaper and see which articles are gone," Lizzy said. "That's easy."

"But it's a special one. She orders it. It never came to Detroit. It was a New York newspaper, and they don't get them in Detroit."

"What's the paper?"

"The *New York Times*," I said. As if the mention of Lana's newspaper had triggered it, I heard a lone woodpecker start hammering in a nearby tree. It made me a little nervous, but even so I couldn't stop myself from going on.

"Maybe they have it here."

"No, they don't, because it still comes in the mail. But you know what else?" I said, inching closer to her.

"What?" She stared into my eyes and her breath caught in the back of her throat.

I looked over my shoulder before I said anything, just to make sure Elena hadn't turned up anywhere. "I think those articles have something to do with that scar," I whispered. "I'm almost positive." A shiver raced down my spine after I said it. For one thing, I had never uttered anything out loud about Lana's secrets, and for another thing I had never really considered the connection between the newspaper articles and her scar until this very moment. But now that I had, it seemed true.

"Really?" she said. She was fascinated.

"Really."

I lay back in the warm grass and felt a certain satisfaction at having captivated her imagination. Even so I felt a little sick—not sick for telling the secrets themselves, for I didn't know what they were, but for confessing the existence of them. Still, I wanted to go on, to tell her about Teddy and the illness Lana sometimes suffered from—the one I couldn't name. I relished seeing her eyes blaze with the same hot, unquenched curiosity as mine, sensing in her something of a partner in this business of Lana's secrecy. For the same reason I preferred Garta's honesty, she preferred Lana's secrecy. To have a mother whose life was a mystery and who could be trusted to keep yours a mystery as well seemed like heaven to her.

She had an affinity for secrecy, Lizzy did.

4

It amazed me how quickly Lizzy became part of my family, the ease with which she walked our hallways and sat at our dinner table and slept in our beds. Lana embraced her and Garta entirely, like I had never seen her embrace anyone before; and while Garta was on summer vacation from her job at the dining hall, we spent many afternoons together out in our backyard or down at Lake Morraine, Lana trying to work her magic on her.

She spent hours with Garta, giving up whole afternoons of writing, listening patiently while Garta wept and screamed about all her problems, throwing her snarled-up mind in Lana's lap so that Lana could untangle it and hand it back. There was never enough money, Garta was always complaining. Her husband, Don, drank it up most of the time, and then in drunken rages he'd beat her up. Garta would then push up her sleeve or pull up her pant leg to show Lana the latest bruise, and Lana would either get misty-eyed or she'd apply cold compresses.

Garta despised her job at the dining hall, and hours would go by as she told Lana about every last person who worked there. They were all assholes, according to Garta, that no one, not even Florence Nightingale, could get along with. She wanted to be a registered nurse, she told Lana, and she would have been if it hadn't been for Lizzy.

It seemed Lizzy was always the problem—she wasn't Don's real daughter, for one, Garta said, and for another, she was a mulatto. "It makes no difference what color she is, Garta," Lana would say firmly. "Black, yellow, green, pink—I don't care. She's a human being, Garta, and don't you ever forget that."

Lana adored Lizzy, sometimes to the point of making me and Elena jealous, and whenever Garta so much as raised her voice against her, Lana wasn't shy about rescuing her. "Garta," she'd say, "now, this is what I'm talking about. Lizzy was just standing there breathing, and you're yelling at her."

Lana often gave Garta lists of things to do to help her overcome whatever monstrous thing made her Garta. Lizzy was always finding them in the garbage, and in the privacy of my attic, we studied them to find some hint of Lana.

1. *Whenever you find yourself getting angry with Lizzy and Jimmy, watch yourself. See what you do and why.*
2. *For each good behavior shown by Lizzy and Jimmy (and there are many) give them praise. This will encourage their goodness.*
3. *Try not to say negative things to them. This only encourages a poor self-image and increases the possibility of continued badness, which only increases your anger. You must break this negative cycle—it goes nowhere but round and round.*

Lana gave her these lists often, and as Lizzy collected them we began to notice that they each had the same message: break the negative cycle your life has fallen into, Garta.

With Garta around, Lana's illness seemed a safe distance away, and whenever it threatened to descend, another visit from Garta would send it into remission.

Things began to change between Lana and Leo because of Garta and all her afternoon visits. Lana still wrote in the mornings when Leo went over to the school to work on his teaching plans. He came home in the afternoons for a while, like he always did. He tried to work at the piano, writing the songs for his musical, while we were all running through the house or screaming out in the backyard. It was hard for him to concentrate, and when it was raining outside it was he who got in our way. Little by little he started going up to the theater, which sat halfway up Heart Attack Hill, where he would compose in peace on the grand piano that stood on the empty stage.

Elena wondered about their bargain, but since neither of them seemed to notice that bit by bit it was being broken, we didn't say anything. They were happy together, as happy as they ever were when Lana was well. They took long walks in the evening, holding hands, and they often sat outside together in the backyard and watched as we played tag in the fading light.

Leo took us out to the movies sometimes, and at least twice a week we all traipsed down to the Blue Bird Restaurant for hot fudge sundaes, often including Garta, Lizzy, and Jimmy. Leo didn't think too much of Garta, but he never said anything when Lana invited her. He understood Garta's value.

With Lana so thoroughly absorbed and Leo as happy as I'd ever seen him, my nerves seemed to vanish into the warm summer air. For a while anyway, the sting of Lana's secrecy faded from my thoughts. Lizzy showed me and Elena the town in a way we hadn't yet seen it, and helped us feel more at home in these Upstate New York hills. She took us into the woods, where water fell some forty feet from a cliff. She pulled us up to her favorite field on top of a hill, where it seemed you could see the whole world. She showed us how to get into the back of the Catholic church just in case we ever wanted any sacrificial wine or wafers, and she introduced us to the chapel on the campus, which stood on top of Heart Attack Hill. It was open twenty-four hours a day, she said, in case we ever needed to run away.

We hung around Shorty's gas station downtown some afternoons, skulking around in the corners, watching the teenage boys smoking cigarettes and playing pool. A couple of times we stole up to their fort in back and snooped through their beer cans and wine bottles and thumbed, fascinated, through their *Playboy* magazines. Lizzy lived downtown in an apartment above the movie theater, so we went to the movies quite a bit too, using the free passes she was always getting from the old man up in the projection booth. By the end of July, we'd seen *The Graduate* five times.

She knew her way around the Colgate library too. We stole down the steps to the basement a couple of times, where in the back, Lizzy showed us some of the World War II artifacts they kept down there in glass cases.

She was fascinated by Nazis, and one day she and I spent the whole afternoon looking through books with gruesome photographs of the concentration camps. She pulled me back to the stacks at the far end of the second floor. After I gave her a boost, she crawled up to the top shelf and grabbed a thick book entitled *Nazi Germany: World War II*. She carried it over to a big table near a window and slapped it down. I sat down next to her, and before she opened the book, she whispered, "These Nazis were murderers, Maddie. They killed Jews, lots of them." The way she said it, with such icy seriousness, sent a cold wave down my spine. She opened the book and turned the pages slowly and deliberately, revealing photographs of naked men and women standing in gang showers.

"They told them they were going to take showers," she whispered. "Then they made them take off their clothes and led them into these showers. Poison gas came out instead of water and killed them all."

Whack—she turned the page and covered it with her hands.

"They sometimes put them in ovens." She spoke with such fierce devotion, it awed me. Her hands flew from the page and there they were—photographs of naked, emaciated bodies being loaded into huge ovens.

Whack—she turned the page again.

"They'd pile them outside, all dead and naked, and some of them they'd burn and some of them they'd push into the ground." Her hands slowly receded from the page, until what faced me were the most horrifying photographs I would ever see: emaciated human beings, thrown one on top of the other in huge piles, mounds, lying lifeless in inhuman poses, arms and legs and heads twisted and intertwined until it seemed impossible that they were actually people.

My mouth hung open—I had never imagined anything so terrible.

"The Nazis did this," she whispered. There were no more photographs, so she closed the book and rested her hands on top of it. A few moments passed in silence, as if we were paying our respect to these long-dead Jews. When she felt the time was right, she turned to me and told me the most fantastic thing I had ever heard. "We have a Nazi living in this town," she whispered. Her eyes flashed like lights. It was as if she had spent the last few weeks and these last hours indoctrinating me, preparing me for just this moment when she would tell me this.

"Really?" I said. I couldn't imagine.

She took me down to see Minnie Harp, a woman, who as rumor had it, was harboring a Nazi. I followed her down Heart Attack Hill, across three streets, and down another hill, into some woods where an old wooden sign was nailed to a tree decades ago, with the words NO TRESPASSING written in red by a shaky hand.

"She wrote it in blood," Lizzy said. The woods were so quiet when she said it that it gave me the creeps. She steered me past the sign over to a small knoll where you could see the side of Minnie Harp's ruined house. It had lost all its paint and stood there huge and naked, like something skinned. Her lawn had turned to weeds and was at least waist-high. Huge, stray bushes had sprung up here and there too, like monsters, some of them more than ten feet tall.

"She might be on the other side of her house," Lizzy whispered. "She comes out sometimes to plant flowers."

I couldn't fathom why or where she would plant flowers. Her lawn was a disaster, and had she planted flowers no one could have seen them. I understood, though, that Minnie Harp, whoever she was, was not a regular person.

We ran through the rest of the woods and headed for a large tree on the edge of her lawn, where we hid until Lizzy felt it was safe to move out again. We ran from this tree to another one, the tall grass brushing at our elbows, and finally to a great elm that anchored her front yard. We concealed ourselves behind it, and very slowly we eased our eyes around it and stared at the front of her house. It looked like a rotten tooth poking out of the grass.

"This place used to be a parsonage," Lizzy whispered. "Minnie Harp's father used to be a preacher. They say he never let her out of the house. He died a long time ago, and now she only comes outside once in a while. She never leaves here. A grocery boy from the Victory brings her groceries, but that's all. No one *ever* comes here."

I shuddered at the thought.

Minnie Harp's lawn was thick with insects, which kept crawling up our bare legs, and the July sun was so bright I had to squint. Beyond the drone of the insects and the beat of my heart, I couldn't hear anything—it was so quiet, it was eerie.

"Look at the windows," Lizzy whispered.

There was a great bay window that jutted out from the front of the house on the left, and a large porch on the right which was made entirely of windows. The front entrance had long windows on either side of a dark wooden door, and above, on the second floor, there were more sets of windows. The place was full of them, but it wasn't their abundance that struck you—it was the fact that every single solitary one of them had been meticulously covered with old, yellowed newspaper. In her obsession for privacy, Minnie Harp had sealed them all up.

"That's so no one can see the Nazi," Lizzy whispered.

Just then, one of the rickety hatch doors on the right side of the house was thrown open, and a gray head popped out and surveyed the lawn. Lizzy and I pulled back behind the tree, and Minnie Harp, seeing no one, threw open the other hatch. It landed on top of the tall grass in a clattery heap. Almost immediately a broom came sailing forth, and suddenly the air was saturated with the unadorned sound of Minnie Harp's humming.

"She's a spinster," Lizzy whispered. "And she only went away once in her life, to Germany during the war. She was a nurse there."

Minnie emerged slowly from the cellar, dragging something which was obviously heavy and yet out of our sight. Through the whole process she hummed loudly, and though it was hard to believe, her voice wasn't completely terrible. At one time she might have even been a decent singer. It was untrained, though, wild and overdone— perhaps the voice of Garta, I couldn't help but think, if Garta were ever to sing.

She emerged from the cellar after what looked like quite a struggle, and we finally discovered what she was hauling out. It was an old mattress, the kind with black pinstripes, which was so stained that we could see the old yellow pee spots from behind the tree. She lugged it out to the tall grass and started looking around for the broom.

She wasn't more than five-four. She wasn't fat either, but nonetheless there was something imposing about her: she loomed over the grass. She was agile and strong, strapping even, and she wore her hair in a haphazard bun at the back of her head. Her dress was old faded black cotton, and despite the heat, she wore a brown sweater with holes in it and a pair of thick hose with seams down the back.

Her movements were large and jerky. She seemed to stomp instead of walk, perhaps because the grass was so tall, and she looked at things strangely as if she were half-blind or seeing them for the first time. When she discovered her broom, she snatched it from the grass and began whacking the mattress in great, bold strikes while huge clouds of dust billowed up and enveloped her. To this, she appeared oblivious. Instead she hummed louder, marking the time with her broom swats. Hm, hm, hm, smack. Hm, hm, hm, smack, smack.

"When she came back from the war," Lizzy whispered in my ear, "she never spoke again. They say she was a traitor and that her tongue was cut out as punishment."

"Really?" I was fascinated.

She nodded. "She can't sing. She has to hum, because she doesn't have a tongue."

It was an arresting thought, one I wouldn't be able to get out of my mind for quite some time.

"And she's hiding a Nazi in her house."

I shivered, remembering the gruesome photographs I'd just seen, and something huge turned over in my belly.

Lizzy's grandmother, Esther Hodges, sent her to Bible school in the Poconos that next week, which meant that I had to fend for myself. Garta came by in the afternoons, and Lana listened and advised her and wrote those lists, but without Lizzy around it wasn't the same. Elena and I got tired of listening to them and started following Leo around in the afternoons when he ran his errands around campus. One day he took us up to the theater to show us the grand piano. I know he never meant to, but he leaked something out about Lana up there.

He opened the door slowly and we stepped inside. He whispered reverently, "This is the theater," as if it were one of God's special havens. His voice and the quiet solemn way he moved down the aisle awed me. The silence in there breathed all around us, like I'd only heard in empty churches. The air was so cool and moist, it seemed a spring ran beneath it. Long thin windows lined either side of it, and rows of red velvet chairs stood like soldiers. The red velvet curtains on the stage were pulled back, and a few shafts of light escaped from the draped windows and pierced the darkness like lightning rods. There was nothing on it besides the grand piano and a long table.

We moved down the aisle behind Leo, none of us saying a word. We followed him up the side steps onto the stage and waited near the edge while he went behind the curtain to do something. We heard a few clicks and then suddenly three great circles of light appeared on the stage—two in the center, side by side, and one illuminating the piano. A shiver bumped through me, and I knew something was going to happen. I could feel it, like it was growing on top of my skin. Harry wandered into one of the light spots and started stomping at its edges, and though I wanted to rush into the other one, I waited next to Elena for Leo to come back. He brushed through the heavy red curtain, and for the first time since we'd entered this sanctuary, he spoke.

"You guys want to hear something?" he said.

"Yes." It was eerie how we all spoke at once.

"Come here, then." He walked over to the piano and sat down on the bench. I was there in an instant, Elena coming in a close second.

"This has to be a secret," he said, and I shivered.

For all I knew, none of us had any secrets from Leo. At least I didn't, and for a moment it saddened me to know that my first secret would be a collective one, jointly owned by all three of us.

"You can never tell anyone," he said, "especially Lana." The wind stirred the drapes, and I saw a nervousness shoot through his eyes. It only lasted a moment, though. When the breeze ceased, it went away.

"We won't," I said before he took another breath. "I swear."

Elena swore too, and Harry made a lopsided cross over his heart. After that Leo rolled up his white shirt sleeves and positioned himself on the bench. He raised his hands in the air, poising them high above the keys, and looked at us with rapt, excited eyes.

"Ready, guys?" he said.

We nodded our heads, and as I held my breath waiting for his thick fingers to touch down on those pale white keys, Elena edged up next to me and pinched my arm. Leo's fingers began their descent, and then in mid-air, they stopped. "I forgot to tell you. I wrote this for Elena before she was born." He hoisted his arms back up, and just before they made the plunge, I looked over at Elena—she was incandescent.

His fingers made contact with those keys, and honest to God we were paralyzed by this new sound. It was crazy and bold and so downright snappy that it invaded me instantly. I'd never heard anything like it before, and from the look on Elena's face I knew she hadn't either. Leo's fingers raced up and down the keyboard, his eyes fluttering, his head rolling back and forth as if his shoulders were a liquid seesaw. His feet tapped wildly on the floor, pounding it almost, yet I had never seen him move with such ease. What lumbered and jerked in him normally was now so completely smooth and fluid it didn't figure. For the first time he seemed the right size for himself, as if he needed all that mass and physical bulk to play this music.

Harry was the first one to come out of the paralysis. His little feet started moving in a hyper-shuffle, his head rolling around like Leo's as he played the air like it was a piano. My feet and legs and arms just started working. I couldn't stop them from moving. The music made me, and it wasn't long before it infected Elena too, who, unlike me and Harry, had a sense for it and started to dance, to really dance. Elena moved us out to those circles of light. She looked so good that Harry and I let her have one all to herself and took the other one for ourselves, where we jumped around as if we were on fire.

The music was in my spine. I could feel it moving up and down, creating such an electrical storm that I felt dizzy. It was as much fun as watching Miss Thomas's birds, if not more, and I wished it would never end. I wanted Leo to play that music forever. I wanted Elena to dance around on her perfect legs, and for me and Harry to stomp around in that spotlight forever.

What is this? I wondered. What is this crazy music that flew into your ears and went straight to your feet, washing your insides with a kind of red mania?

"What is it, Leo?" I shouted. "What is this?"

"It's jazz," he hollered back. "It's wonderful, crazy jazz!"

Almost as soon as Leo spoke the word *jazz*, Elena stopped dancing. A panic washed over her, and she raced off the stage and ran down the aisle, the heels of her shoes clacking loudly against the wooden floors. The music stopped abruptly, and Leo was on his feet immediately, hurrying to the edge of the stage.

"Elena!" he cried. "Please, Elena!" but she was already out the door.

"Go get her, Maddie," he told me, and within moments I was in motion, tearing through the theater after her.

She was flying down Heart Attack Hill when I spotted her. I

chased after her, my mind reeling with confusion. Why hadn't Leo ever played that music before? Especially since it was as old as Elena? And why was it a secret? And why—*why*—did Elena run out as soon as she heard the word *jazz*? The word buzzed in my mind like a bee, and I remembered the afternoon when Lana had told Elena another secret. The jazz must have had something to do with that secret, I couldn't help but think, but even so I couldn't imagine what. I could feel Lana in it though, as if she radiated from the center of it all.

Elena ran down to the track, and though it nearly killed me, I caught up with her just as she was about to round the bend on her second turn. My sides ached, and I was so out of breath I could barely speak.

"Why did you leave?" I asked her, my chest heaving. I tried to keep up with her, but I couldn't. I watched her black hair swing violently from side to side, her feet pounding down on the sweltering black track. "You were having fun, Elena." She clenched her fists and poured on more steam. "Was it because of Lana's last secret?" I yelled after her.

"No," she said so fast I didn't know what to think.

She sprinted ahead of me, her calf muscles riding up and down under her skin like small, tightfisted knots. She was slipping away from me with each graceful stride. The world of green trees and grinding asphalt pounded by, and with each rocky step I became more and more desperate to know, if not the whole story, then at least some small part of it.

"I'll tell you all my Lana secrets, if you tell me yours." I could scarcely believe I had said that until Elena wheeled around and stopped. She stopped so suddenly that I almost knocked into her.

"What?" she yelled. Her chest heaved like a racehorse's, her breathing so labored she could hardly speak.

"I'll tell you my Lana secrets if you tell me yours," I panted.

Elena bent over at the waist to catch her breath, and when she came back up she said, "All yours for one of mine."

"That's not fair—" I gasped.

"I've got four, Maddie, and you've only got three. That wouldn't be fair either." She threw her head back and gulped in the hot, humid air.

"Then three for three," I said. I pulled my damp shirt off my back where it was sticking and squatted down on the hot track.

"No, one for three."

"The last one then." That was the one I really wanted to know, and I wanted to know it so badly I was willing to give up all my secrets.

"Okay, then," she said. She turned around and began running slowly, as if that slight, steady motion would help pull it out of us. I caught up to her, and we padded lightly over the track, our elbows rocking slowly by our sides, touching. "You go first."

"Why do I have to go first?" I protested. "I've got to tell you three and go first at the same time! That's not fair, Elena. *You go first, and then I'll tell you.*"

We jogged along in silence for a few moments, Elena trying to leverage the silence to force me to speak first. I really wanted to know Lana's last secret to her, but at the same time I didn't want to part with all of mine. They were the only things I had. I worried too that something bad would happen were I to tell them. Pressure built up in my skull, until I felt my head throb. It scared me to imagine Lana's secrets escaping from my tongue, one after the other, stealing off into the sweet summer air, never to be retrieved. Who knew what they would do if they were suddenly released into the air where they could float for centuries.

"I can't, Elena," I said. A few drops of sweat rolled down my back like itches. "I can't." It seemed I could no more part with Lana's secrets than I could my own skin.

"I can't either," she said, and then she sped up. I kept up with her, the silence riding back and forth between us like a rope, tying us together.

We looked up and saw Leo and Harry racing across the field toward us, Harry dangling from Leo's right hand, his little feet pedling through the grass. The sight of Leo running like that, like he was rushing to ward off some catastrophe, made both Elena and me stop dead. I had never really seen him run so fast, and to watch him now crashing forward, his legs moving with the grace of unearthed tree trunks, absorbed me completely. He looked wounded, and when I finally saw his face, my heart stopped. It was broken up by deep lines—a couple slashed across his forehead and two cut across his cheeks near his eyes. His face looked like it was made of six tense pieces, welded together on those furrows.

"Where have you guys been?" he yelled from the edge of the field.

"Right here," Elena yelled back. She shielded her eyes against the sun and watched him crash forward.

He bounded onto the track, Harry stumbling behind him. "We couldn't find you," he said nervously. He bent over to catch his breath. When he came back up for air, he looked scared, like he'd done something terrible. "Where were you?"

"Right here," I said. "We were always here." The sun overhead was so hot I felt myself baking.

"You didn't go home?" The sweat poured out from his hairline, as if there were a faucet hidden somewhere under his curls.

We both shook our heads, and it occurred to me that he was afraid we'd gone home and told Lana about the jazz. It bothered me to see Leo so nervous like that. I was used to seeing it in Lana, but not Leo.

We walked back through the campus, making a special pass by the pond so Harry could see the swans. While he stomped on the edges, scaring the swans away, Leo and Elena started walking ahead of us, talking so quietly I could barely hear them.

"I'm sorry, Elena," I heard him say. "I didn't know." It was all I could do to hear those words, he spoke them so softly.

"Didn't know what?" she said. She swung her damp hair over her shoulders, and as if she wanted to get away from him she began walking faster.

I caught up to him and grabbed ahold of his shirt. "What didn't you know about Elena?" My voice sounded kind of desperate. "What did Elena know, and how come I can't know? I want to know too, Leo."

Leo dropped to his knees on the sidewalk and drew me into his big arms. "I know you do, sweetheart. I know you do." I felt him shake, as if the power of my hunger scared him.

"Why can't I know?" I demanded. It seemed like there was a huge, black world out there, a world which was being kept from me, as if whenever I was around the door slammed shut.

"Know what, sweetheart?" he said. A whole stream of sweat spilled from his hairline and rolled down his face.

"Know what Elena knows," I said, stomping my feet on the boiling hot sidewalk.

"What does she know?"

"I don't know," I yelled. As if the sound of my loud voice woke them, my nerves woke up and fled to my thighs where they loped back and forth across my muscles.

"I'm sorry, Maddie," he said. "I'm sorry." He squinted his blue eyes against the sun. "Lana doesn't like me to play the jazz."

"Why not?"

"I'm sorry, Maddie. I can't tell you why."

Elena suddenly picked Harry up and started running. Before I could say another word, Leo grabbed my hand and pulled me along with him. He didn't want Elena to get home before he did. He wanted to make sure that she didn't say anything to Lana. We walked hurriedly in silence, Leo towing me along, and every so often I looked up at his face to see if it was all right, but it was still in pieces.

When we got home Elena took Harry out in the backyard; I ran straight up to the bathroom to douse my nerves with hot water. They were still aching in my thighs, and some of them had begun migrating to the backs of my arms. I didn't know what to do, so I alternated between pouring hot water over their heads and punching them.

I saw Leo pass the bathroom, and after he stepped into his room and closed the door quietly, I made one of my greatest discoveries. I turned off the water to listen; I could hear him perfectly. It was as if I were in the same room with him. There was something immediately intriguing about the tone of his voice. It was liquid and importuning — the same voice that had nervously apologized to me on the sidewalk. I looked around for a door or a phony wall or whatever it was that afforded me such good reception, and traced his voice to a small metal grate about the size of a large cereal box, just to the right of the sink. When I hunched down to look at it, I discovered that not only could I hear through it, I could see through it as well — straight into their bedroom. It was a heat vent, and it was better than the old broom closet, much better.

I saw Leo sitting on the edge of the bed, slumped over in an apelike pose, while Lana sat on the floor plowing through a pile of photographs. The way she handled them, I could tell she was mad.

"Which one did you play?" Her voice was aggressive, almost bitter.

"Elena's," he said quietly, his thick fingers raking through his hair.

"How many more?" She slammed down two photographs.

"No more, La. Just that one," he whispered.

Her hands stopped, and she stared unblinkingly down at her photographs. "Why did you do it, Leo?"

She glanced over her shoulder at him, and Leo slumped forward even further. "Because I love that music, La. And Elena needed cheering up. You should have seen them dancing on that—"

"Yes, I should have," she said sharply, cutting him off. She stood up and moved across the room, toward the open windows where a small breeze blew. Within a matter of moments Leo was behind her, the sweat rolling down his face, dripping onto the front of his white shirt.

"I'm sorry, La. I don't know why—I thought—"

"Did you tell them anything more?" Her voice was bitter, and when she yanked the lacy curtains back, I could almost see the storm clouds forming above her head.

"No," he said. "Nothing."

Her back was to him, and he stood for the longest time behind her, struggling between the desire to touch her or not. His hands inched upward and then fell, rose again and dropped. Finally he reached up and laid his fingers gently on her shoulders, much the same way he touched those pale white keys when he played something lovely. All awkwardness left him; in a series of slow motions he turned her to him, and then very gracefully, he descended to his knees, his thick arms wrapping around her small waist so carefully and delicately that it looked like a slow, mournful dance. Then he buried his face into her belly, and I heard him whisper, "I had to tell you, La. I'm sorry. Say you'll forgive me."

Her hand rested motionless on top of his head, but within moments she began moving her fingers through his hair, like she had a thousand times before. I knew then that she had forgiven him.

All was right between them again, but that didn't make any difference to my nerves. They hung around all day, dragging their hot, sticky weight from one muscle to the other, and by nighttime, they rose up beneath my skin, as if in protest, and stung me. Why couldn't

Leo play the jazz, I wondered, and what did Lana mean when she said, "Did you tell them anything more?" I couldn't stop thinking about it. I kept turning it over and over in my thoughts, as if through sheer exposure it would come clear. I felt a darkness in my mind instead, a big wad of black through which steams and vapors passed like the wind.

I made a great discovery not too long after this that—at least nominally—gave me some hope. It was my greatest discovery, bigger and better even than the metal grate in the bathroom. It happened a few days after Lizzy came back from the Poconos, on a hot afternoon just after it had rained, when Elena and I brought home a sick baby robin to show Lana. Elena, Leo, and I were on our way back from his office when we found it floundering on the sidewalk. Its wings were sticky and wet, and we guessed that either a dog or a cat had gotten it. Elena picked it up and laid it carefully in the hammock of my white shirt, and we took it home to show Lana.

When I opened the door, I heard Lana cry out Leo's name. She sounded so bereft I couldn't imagine what had happened. Before Leo was even inside, she appeared in the hallway and raced toward us, her cane working furiously at her side.

"Leo," she cried again, when she saw him in the doorway. She looked deranged, as if she had just witnessed a murder, and it seemed she was flying loose, as if bits and pieces of her were strewn through the hallway, fluttering down to the floor. All thoughts of the robin vanished from my mind, and when I turned to look at Leo I saw his face break into those terrible lines. He rushed past us to catch her in his arms, as if that would keep her from flying apart anymore.

"What happened?"

"All my journals, Leo," she cried. "They're all lost. Those old boxes—they're gone, and all my journals—every one of them. We lost them." Her face was red and blotchy and eaten up with panic.

"They're in the attic," Leo raced to say. "I put them in the attic when we unpacked, La." His fingers worked her shoulders furiously as if they were the valves to her steam.

"All of them?" she asked.

"Yes, La, all of them. Every single one of them." When he brushed the hair out of her eyes, I could almost see the tension rise from her.

"The journals? Everything?"

He nodded, and her arms drifted down to her sides. She hadn't really realized we were there until now, and when she looked up at us I knew she was embarrassed. We waited to see what she would do. After a few moments she started ramming into Leo, dancing around him like a boxer, hitting him in the chest with her fists, releasing the tension in all of us with each dull thud.

"So you put them in the attic, eh?" she said, knocking into him. "You put them up there to fool me, didn't you? Eh? You did it on purpose, didn't you, LEE-OO? Didn't he, Harry?"

She could be funny, like now, the way she shuffled around Leo like a boxer, flattening him with her low, deep voice. But even so, I couldn't forget about her journals. I couldn't stop thinking about them. "They're in my attic," I kept telling myself, but it terrified me. They were Lana's journals, after all, and I feared they were guarded by gaseous spirits night and day.

When I tried to sleep that night I felt them in the attic. It was the same nerve-wracking attraction I had felt standing outside Andrew's house when his mother wouldn't let him come out, only it was much stronger, much worse. It put my nerves under such great pressure that I felt them swell and then vibrate, and I had the scariest feeling I was going to explode or go beserk. To make matters worse, the baby robin I had found in the afternoon was thrashing around in the box next to my bed, the dried grass scratching endlessly against the cardboard as it writhed back and forth. When I couldn't stand it anymore, I got out of bed and started pacing around my room, jumping every few steps, moving my arms around like windmills, until my nerves finally brought me to the attic door.

They had numbed my conscience, and my hands fell easily to the door latch. I opened it and snapped the light on. Sure enough, there were Lana's boxes. Leo had piled a lot of junk inside, but I could see her boxes standing one on top of the other against the dusty eaves. I walked quietly over to them and laid my hand on the top one, as if that would cool me off. They weren't sealed up, but rather the flaps were tucked under each other. I stared at them for a long time, stopped by the thought that they contained Lana's secrets. It was the closest I had ever gotten to her, and the sudden realization that the answers might lie inches from my hot fingers drove my heart like a piston. I forgot about the gaseous spirits and pried loose the flaps, my hands falling on top of one of her bound journals. I lifted it out delicately, as if it were a newborn baby, and when I looked at it closely it terrified me.

I sat down and very carefully laid the journal on the wooden floor, where I stared at it for a long time half expecting it to do something— what, I don't know. After a while, I realized I was shaking and that little streams of sweat had collected at my hairline. I wiped my forehead with the back of my hand, and then very gingerly I opened the journal to the first page.

Lana's bold handwriting leapt out at me, and I remembered all the times I had struggled to catch small glimpses of it. Now here it was, all mine, but for the rush of my heart and the panic in my mind, it was incomprehensible to me. Very slowly, I edged forward until I was hanging over the page, my face not more than four inches from her words. I experienced both an attraction and a repulsion so strong it crushed me. The world began to compress, until it consisted of my trembling hands on the edges of her journal and her dark, inky words.

June 5, 1947

A sizable portion of my past descended upon me this morning, when I awoke from a dream I have had numerous times. It was the same dream, the same damned one, and when I awoke with it fresh in my mind, not only did I feel my past descend, I felt immersed in it. My emotions plunged back four years in time; all my senses were in tune with the happenings of that lost summer, that lost home, my lost lover. I am in bed with him. We are kissing passionately, our clothes slipping from our bodies one by one. I am in a vulnerable state of absolute desire that is so strong, it is as deep as hunger. I am so far gone on him, so entangled that I can think of nothing else but to have him nearer, closer, closer, inside. I want to eat him up, I want to devour him. I am starved, nearly stark ravingly so, to be as close to him as possible, merging into one flesh. We are kissing. Our lips are melting, smearing together —

I heard someone in my room and I knew it was Lana. I had forgotten how powerful she was, how she could feel someone reading her journals, and I wanted nothing more than to vanish. I looked around the attic but I was powerless to move. Instead, I froze, my heart pounding in my chest. The door creaked openly slowly and painfully, yawning on its old hinges, and I waited for her cane to come into the light. I saw a bare foot first and then suddenly she appeared. Her dark hair fell across her shoulders, and when she stepped into the light I realized it wasn't Lana. It was Elena.

"What are you doing, Maddie?" she said, squinting her eyes in the light. I looked down at the journal and then back up at her. In that brief moment she made the connection. *"Maddie!"* she yelled, in a voice that stung my conscience.

I tried to pick the journal up to put it back, but she was across the attic already, pulling it out of my hands.

"How much did you read?" she demanded to know.

"Only just a little. Only a paragraph on the first page." I felt drenched and muscleless and sick at heart.

"Show me."

I showed her, and while I watched her read it, I realized how bad it looked to be reading Lana's journal, to be trespassing on Lana's life. "We shouldn't be reading it," I said, pulling it out of her hands.

"No kidding, Maddie." She yanked it back and went on reading, her eyes racing across the words.

"Just read what I read and then we'll be even." I put my hand over the portion I hadn't read, and when she didn't object I knew she felt as bad as I did.

When she finished the paragraph, we carefully lowered the journal down into the box like it was a coffin descending into a grave and struggled to put those flaps back the way they had been. When a few cars passed, and the neighbor's dog barked loudly, we held our breath to make sure it hadn't woken Lana up. We could only hear the soft chorus of crickets and the sound of our old house settling on its haunches.

When the dog stopped barking I moved closer to Elena and laid my sweaty hand on her arm. "What did it mean?" I asked. I could feel Lana's strong words coursing through my body, as if they had a force all their own.

"It has something to do with why men and women sleep in the same bed." She stared at me for a moment in the weak, yellow light, and I saw fear in her eyes. "We shouldn't have read it, Maddie," she whispered. A deep furrow settled on her pale forehead, and she clutched my hand. She pulled me into my room and dragged me over to the window, where we stood like two ghosts in our white nightgowns. She was so nervous she started shaking, and when the baby robin began to thrash in the box next to us, my heart filled with dread.

"Look at the moon, Maddie," she whispered loudly, yanking my wrist. It appeared in the black sky, a small white crescent, clouds stalking past it like willowy puffs of anger. "We have to swear on the moon that we will never do it again."

"You first," I said.

I watched her eyes as they hardened around the sliver of moon. "I swear on the moon, I'll never read Lana's journals again," she whispered fiercely.

The baby robin writhed in its bed of dried grass and thumped its maimed wing against the side of the box, and Elena pinched my arm. "Come on, Maddie," she said, as if the moon had no time.

"I swear on the moon," I whispered, "I will never read Lana's journals again."

I hardly knew what I was saying.

I had a small breakdown in Miss Thomas's bird shed the next morning. I awoke very early to the most pitiful cries. It was the baby robin. It was still in the box next to my bed, crying. Its little head writhed back and forth on its neck, and the rest of it lay in the dried grass damp, heavy, and inert.

I picked up the box and ran across the hall to Lana's room, but when I saw her and Leo asleep in one another's arms, I stopped. I remembered Elena's words last night—"It has something to do with why men and women sleep in the same bed"—and a sense of shame stole through me for looking at them. I wondered if they had smeared lips and eaten each other up. I wondered too what it would look like to see two people do that. However it was done, I imagined, it had to be reversible because they were still two people, completely intact and uneaten, breathing their own air. Even so, I couldn't wake them. They were somehow untouchable, their warm togetherness in that bed impenetrable and sacred.

While the robin thumped urgently in the box, I dressed quickly. As fast as I could I climbed the hill to Miss Thomas's in the baby morning and scrambled through the woods. When I cleared the trees and stepped into Miss Thomas's yard, I froze. She was sitting on the lawn dressed in a carmine red dress with white tassles, sitting in a pose of—of what I couldn't say. She was partially kneeling (if you could call it that), her legs halfway tucked underneath her, the other half sort of jutting out on either side of her as if they couldn't quite bend. She was seated among those statues, facing the one with the fat belly, muttering something that was completely incomprehensible to me. She said it over and over again, this string of sounds—something like Na-Mo-Ari-Hun-Tanun—in a voice I had never heard. It was rhythmic and smooth, but mostly it was flat and devoid of any inflection. I thought she'd lost her mind, and just as I turned around to creep back through the woods, never to visit her again, she saw me.

"Is that you, Maddie?"

I looked up at her. She looked like herself again, and when she raised her baggy arm over her head and waved to me, I knew whatever madness had possessed her had miraculously vanished into the foggy morning.

"Good morning," she said. "How come I'm so lucky to see you?"

That was all I needed. I was by her side in an instant showing her my bird. When she picked it up and put it to her ear, I felt the world come back together again.

"You've come to the right place," she said. She rose up on her amazing legs and steamed across her lawn with me and my bird following behind, my eyes transfixed by her moving form. Her arms pumped through the air as if they were making up for what her legs couldn't quite do, and I noticed then that she had no rear end to speak of. It was as if someone had gone under her dress one night and sawed it off.

"We'll feed him some of Miss Thomas's Amazing Life-Saving Potion," she said. The way she said "amazing life-saving potion"—it was as if she were in the circus telling everyone she was going to attempt a death-defying feat. It made my heart beat fast just to hear her.

She led me back to a small shed that was connected to her huge bird room. It was a tiny, warm room with plenty of light. Shelves lined the walls, stocked with all sorts of glass jars filled with food and herbs and medicines. A pile of old bird cages stood in one corner, just heaped there like a mound of discarded clam shells. Bird nests were stacked neatly on the floor, and along the windowsills stood these huge glass boxes that looked like sea aquariums.

She cleared a place on the table and put on a pair of white gloves. She took the bird out and laid it down and started examining it like a doctor would. I really liked her for this, for the way she didn't stop to chitchat, for the way she got right down to work, like the most important thing in the world was this poor bird. I edged up to her so I could see what she was doing and watched as she cleaned the robin off with a wet cloth. She kept talking to it, saying that it was going to be fine, just fine, and in the middle of it she asked me, "What's her name?"

I felt embarrassed that I hadn't given it a name. Here I'd brought it to her like it was my most precious possession and I hadn't even named it.

"Howard."

"Howard!" she exclaimed. "But it's a girl. It's a baby girl. You've got to give her a better name than Howard. How about something like Venus or Aphrodite?"

I opted for Aphrodite, and while Miss Thomas nodded in approval, she took down a jar of white ashes and pulled a clean glass test tube from a small drawer. She picked up a small tin bucket and asked me to get her a pail of water from her rain barrel. "We've got to mix the potion," she said.

I crossed her lawn, half listening to the lullaby she sang Aphrodite, and found her rain barrel on the side of the house, beneath a small wooden plane that hung from the eave and drifted up and down on a string. I dipped the pail in, pulled up a bucketful of water, and when I turned around I saw something I had never expected to see. Across the street, in a yard of tall elms, stood a boy. His hair was as black as mine, and though I couldn't see his face very well I could tell he had nice straight, tanned legs.

I realized I was staring at him. I was about to look away when he threw his arm over his head and proceeded to wave to me as if he'd been waving to me for years. I was shocked but I waved back. We both stood there for a moment, staring across the cluttered expanse of Miss Thomas's lawn, half expecting something to happen. It finally became so awkward I broke it off and headed back to the shed.

When I stepped inside, Miss Thomas wrenched my attention away. She was lying flat on her stomach on the floor, muttering something, her head beneath a shelf, her legs floundering like two drunken snakes. She was muttering those alien words, and the only thing I could think to do was utter her name. "Miss Thomas," I whispered.

She turned around quickly and somewhere underneath her displaced hair I saw her mouth moving. "Oh, Maddie — thank goodness," she said. She worked her way backward, the whole length of her body moving down the floor toward me, until her head cleared that shelf. Then with great effort she pulled herself up. I had never seen anything quite like that, and when she handed me the end of a black cord I didn't understand.

"You plug it in," she said.

It was the plug to one of those glass boxes, she finally explained. It was an incubator she used to keep the bird warm. I understood, at least, that finding her on the floor like this had nothing to do with finding her on the lawn as I had earlier, but nonetheless I was shaken. I plugged it in and then stood by her side watching as she mixed the white ashes and the water together in the test tube, keeping my eye on her the whole time lest something go wrong.

"Who's the boy across the street?" I asked.

"Oh, that's Louis Bartalucci. He's a nice boy."

I was afraid to know but I asked her anyway. "How old is he?"

"I think he's twelve," she said, and my heart floundered in my chest. Elena was twelve, exactly twelve.

The bird started screeching again, and when Miss Thomas began to cluck in her strange bird voice, the world inside the shed suddenly squeezed in around me. It seemed I understood nothing, that there was a whole world to which I was uninvited, and that for reasons I could not fathom, I was not permitted to know anything. Lana had a cane and a scar, and I didn't know why. She'd eaten a man once, and now I couldn't read her journal anymore because I'd sworn on the moon. Jazz was poisonous, and Leo couldn't play it for reasons I doubted I'd ever know. Minnie Harp had a cut-out tongue and a Nazi, Louis Bartalucci was Elena's age, and now I had discovered that Miss Thomas sometimes lost her mind. I tried to stay still by her side but I couldn't. I started to jump up and down, and when that didn't help I moved over to the door and finally ran outside.

"What's the matter, Maddie?" Miss Thomas asked, rushing after me.

I felt the presence of a sticky black knot in my mind, and suddenly tears backed up in my eyes. I knew I couldn't ask her what she'd been doing on the lawn. The words were struggling on my tongue, beating against my teeth to be let out—*What were you doing on the lawn this morning, Miss Thomas?*—but I kept my jaw clamped down and squeezed my eyes shut.

"What's the matter?" she asked again.

I made an awful sound, one that embarrassed me it was so low and mournful, but if nothing else it communicated to her the snarl of my thoughts. She dropped to her knees, and suddenly her kind, misshapen face hung before me. "Tell me what's the matter," she whispered.

I stared into her big black eyes, and judging them to be as honest and as uncomplicated as any I'd ever seen, I uttered the whole basic truth in one sentence. "I don't understand."

"What don't you understand, cuckoo bird?" she asked, wiping my cheeks with the flats of her big crooked thumbs. "You tell me what you don't understand."

I stood there for a moment, thinking crookedly about the whole tangle of Lana and Leo and all that was maddeningly absent from my knowledge of them, remembering in the end the most recent and puzzling question, which I now put to her. "Why do people eat other people?"

If she looked shocked, it didn't show. In fact, she didn't even take in a second breath or widen her already huge eyes. She simply returned my gaze and said very calmly, "Oh, they don't, Maddie. Only cannibals eat people, but we don't have any cannibals here. In all my life I've never seen it happen, and I've known a lot of people."

I stared into her face, stifling the awful urge I had to tell her about Lana's journal, to explain how Lana once ate a man. A wave of fear passed through me at the thought that I had sworn on the moon never to read her journals again. How was I going to do that? How in God's name was I going to keep that vow?

"Miss Thomas, is the moon powerful?"

"Oh, yes," she whispered, drawing her yes out, as if to let me know just how powerful it was. "It pulls the ocean from one side of the world to the other once a day, and when it's full it makes people fall in love."

"What if you swore on the moon about something and made a promise?" I asked her, snuffling into my sleeve.

"You'd have to keep it, cuckoo bird. You should keep all your promises, especially the ones you make to the moon."

5

It was as if our eyes on Lana's journal started all the trouble, because after we read it something terrible happened. Lana and I were on our way home from shopping on a warm humid afternoon when dark clouds hung overhead, threatening to crack open and spill. We'd walked downtown to buy Elena new socks and Leo more underwear, and on our way back it started to drizzle. Lana opened her black umbrella, and we walked underneath it together, relishing our privacy.

She was happy that day and full of the energy I was so attracted to. She began teasing me and knocking into me underneath the umbrella. "Quit bumping into me, lady," she cried. "Can't you see I'm handicapped?" She laughed and bumped into me again. "Have some respect, for crying out loud."

"But you're bumping into me."

"But, but, but, but," she said, and then she knocked into me again.

When we were underway again, swinging our hands in the warm, muggy air, I felt close to her. She was warm and accessible, and it seemed if there were ever a time to ask her something it was while we walked underneath this umbrella, drawn together by the rain. I knew I couldn't ask her about her cane—that was too big a question—but it seemed I could ask her something about Mimi, at least.

"Lana," I said, watching my feet move forward, "how come we don't know Mimi?"

"She lives so far away, sweetheart."

"How come you don't call her or write her letters?" I finally looked up, straight into her balmy eyes. The look she returned was so odd it prompted me to say, "You don't like her?"

She struggled not to smile, but I saw it on the corners of her mouth. "Maddie, you shouldn't say that." Then the smile spread across her lips and she started laughing.

"You don't like her?" I said again. I was confused. It seemed it was the case, but then why was she laughing? Disliking your mother was one thing—laughing about it was another.

"I'll tell you a secret about Mimi," she said.

When I stopped and cleared the hair from my ear, a crack of thunder sounded in the gray, leaky sky, and she said she'd have to tell me when we got to the porch. It was only a half block away, but it seemed longer, and when the skies opened and the rain came in torrents, I worried that she would lose interest in telling me, or worse yet forget.

"Come on," I said, tugging at her hand. A streak of lightning carved up the sky, and another crack of thunder rattled the quiet air. As I towed her along the wet sidewalk, cars drove slowly past us, their windshield wipers thumping fiercely against the rain. I heard the distant sound of music, of children screaming happily, of something lovely going on somewhere, but I couldn't think of anything but Lana's secret. When we reached the driveway she stopped abruptly and listened, and suddenly I heard it too. Underneath the sound of the rumbling skies and the beating rain was the jazz. It was coming from our living room, and I could hear Harry squealing and laughing inside. Lana pulled away from me and started down the drive, her soaked black shoes pounding down on the gravel, the rain pelting her umbrella. I watched my secret vanish with each swift step.

When lightning split open the sky again and another clap of thunder sounded, I raced after her. I wanted to stop her from looking in the open window, or more importantly, from hearing the jazz spilling out. She was already there, staring inside, her umbrella forgotten and tipped back, while the rain drenched her dark hair and her pale blue dress. I saw the illness fall over her in an instant. She couldn't breath all of a sudden, and her hands started trembling, one of them flying to her heart and then to her throat.

I stood on my tiptoes and stared through the living room window at what I knew, in her eyes, was a spectacle. Leo was rocking back and forth on the piano bench, his eyes tipped heavenward, his shoulders rocking to the beat of the jazz. It wasn't the same song as before, I realized, but one just as enlivening, as invigorating, as absolutely foot-stomping as the first one. My eyes fell next on Elena—she was in the middle of the floor kicking her perfect legs up and down like a cancan girl, while Harry screamed and stomped around in circles, his head charging back and forth like a wild, hooting Indian's.

When she'd seen enough, Lana threw the umbrella down, picked up her cane, and ran down the driveway to our garage. I ran after her, but before I could reach her she was already backing the car out, and no amount of my voice could stop her.

"Lana," I yelled. *"Lana!"*

She backed out quickly, racing past me, leaving me on the side of the driveway. The rain poured down fiercely, drenching me, and streamed down the windshield where the wipers swished back and forth rapidly in a rubbery flap, flap sound that only heightened my anxiety. I ran after the car, hitting the hood with my fist. *"Lana, stop!"*

She thrust her head out of the window. "Go inside, Maddie," she yelled over the sound of the rain. She backed over the umbrella and kept going. I called out for her to stop again, but she backed into the street and then switched gears and shot forward. I ran to the end of the driveway, but it was no use—she tore off down the rain-slicked street and disappeared around the corner. When I turned around, I saw Leo, Elena, and Harry standing on the porch, looking white and speechless. As if they had committed some grave, unpardonable sin, I glared at them, especially Leo, and in my rage I shouted loud enough for the whole neighborhood to hear, "You ruined everything, you . . . you . . . you *pigs.*"

I turned around and raced away. I didn't have anyplace to go, but I had the vague idea of running onto the velvety green lawns of the university, as if they might cool me down. I ran across the street and headed swiftly toward the pond, where the swans floated gaily in the rain. I bent my head and plowed up Heart Attack Hill in the downpour, the lightning cutting open the sky just above the treetops. When

I reached the theater I rested against the building near one of the tall open windows and listened to the sound of my heavy breath. I stared inside, down at the puddle that lay on the wooden floor beneath the window, and then up at the stage where Leo had taken us not so long ago and transformed us in a matter of moments. What was this jazz? I wondered. *What was it!*

I heard someone coming and turned around to see Elena storming up the hill, her head bent in concentration, her legs moving with great strength. She was soaking wet, and her long hair was plastered against her arms and shoulders, the front of her white blouse sticking to her ribs. There was no place to hide, and since I couldn't just shoot out onto the sidewalk and start running (she would catch me in a matter of seconds), I hoisted myself up to the low windowsill and scrambled inside.

It was wet in there too—the first few seats were drenched and the puddle on the floor had gotten bigger. I was afraid to move anywhere, so I crouched down near the edge of it and closed my eyes. When I heard her shoes squeaking outside I held my breath. The next thing I felt were her knuckles on the top of my skull.

"Come on, Maddie," she gasped. "You shouldn't be in there."

I looked up at her. Her chest was heaving under her wet blouse, and her face was so twisted I knew she had been crying. "Someone will find you in there," she struggled to say.

"I don't care." I tucked my head down and blew air through my knees.

She climbed in the window and collapsed in the wet chair next to me, falling forward in her lap where I heard a high, shrill voice emanate from her. "What if she never comes back?"

That stabbing thought had crossed my mind too, but it was such a horrible one I couldn't hold onto it for long.

"Why'd you do it, Elena?"

She turned to me and spoke through a veil of guilty tears. "He just started playing and I couldn't help it, Maddie. I just started and Harry, the way he gets all—"

"I know," I said. And I did know. I remembered how the music had pulled at me too, and I understood exactly how it could have happened.

"How come you ran out of here before, Elena?"

She wiped her face off with the back of her hand and sat up

straight. "I can't just tell you without knowing one of your secrets," she said.

"Then I'll tell you one, but it's only one for one, Elena. Not two for one." I was firm about that. I meant it with all my heart, and she knew it.

"All right," she said, "but you have to go first."

I had the quasi secret Lana had told me about Teddy. She had said it was just between me and her, but even so it wouldn't be exactly like giving away a secret if I told it. I listened to the rain for a moment, letting the silence hang. When the wind stirred the red curtains, I decided it would be better if we whispered the secrets into each other's ears, out of respect for Lana. At least that way the air wouldn't hear it, and somehow that made it better, or rather less bad.

She cleared her hair away from her ear, and I pressed my lips to it. "She had an older brother named Teddy."

Elena turned to me with her mouth wide open. "She did?" The look on her face was precious—it made it worth telling her the secret.

I pressed forward to her ear and divulged the rest. "He was killed in a war."

"He was?" She was stunned. "In World War Two?"

I nodded and she shivered.

"God, Maddie! I can't believe it." I knew exactly how she felt. I had felt the same way, so I let her sit there for a long time so she could think about it. She stared up at the tall ceiling for a long while, listening to the rain pelting down on the rooftop. "Why do you think she never told us?" she finally said.

"Maybe because he died in disgrace."

"No, it's not that, I don't think." She paused for a moment. "She doesn't want us to know anything about her. Nothing, because Lana's a freak, Maddie. She's a real freak."

A crack of thunder split the air and rattled the windows, reminding me of Elena's secret. "It's your turn," I said to her.

She looked at me for a moment and bowed her head, and then tortured me with a long silence. I understood how much it would have killed me if I had to part with one of Lana's real secrets, so I let her take her time to work up to it. She communicated her anguish to me through the rasp of her fingernails on the back of the seat ahead of her.

"Okay, Maddie," she finally whispered. Her lips touched the rim of my ear, and as soon as she took a deep breath I closed my eyes. "Lana doesn't like jazz music," she whispered. She moved away from my ear, as if that were the sum total of her confession.

"That was it?" I whispered loudly.

She didn't say anything. She didn't even move.

"No kidding, Elena," I yelled. "You think I didn't know that? You think I didn't?"

"All right, Maddie. Just shut up." I felt her lips again and her breath and then her hand as it touched down lightly on my shoulder. "She hates jazz music because it makes her remember something awful that happened to her." Her voice was tense and full of tears. "That jazz music has something to do with why she has that cane. And I don't know the rest. But I'll tell you something. That song Leo was playing today—it was a song he wrote for her."

After that she pulled away from me and immediately dropped her head into her lap where she cried the muffled sounds of the guilty. I felt so many things at once that all I could do was stroke her wet hair and promise her that I'd never tell Lana anything, no matter what.

Lana didn't come home that night. We ate dinner in silence—me, Elena, Harry, and Leo. We worried that she never would, though none of us dared to say it. Leo was beside himself. His face, instead of being carved up into pieces, was so flat and drawn it looked muscleless. He was morbidly silent, intent on listening to every car that drove past our house. Twice I found him staring forlornly out the front window, watching for her. I wanted to ask him why he'd played the jazz when he knew she'd be coming back, but it would have been like asking someone why they struck the match that burned the house down. I wondered, though, if he might have actually wanted her to catch him. Why else would he have played that song, her song, when he knew she would be coming home? That's when I really started to wonder about Leo.

Elena was still upset about having told me the secret, because after dinner she disappeared. When I saw her heading out the back door I slipped into the kitchen and called Lizzy on the phone.

"Lana left," I whispered. "She took off in the car this afternoon, and she hasn't come back."

Lizzy told me to hold on for a moment while she slipped into the closet. I heard the door squeak open and then some thrashing sounds. "What happened?" she finally said.

I thought about what had happened and realized it was not such a simple question to answer. To tell the truth, which was to say, "Leo played the jazz," wasn't much of an answer. It required certain explanations, so I told her to meet me down at the swan pond at dusk.

It had stopped raining, but the sky was still gray and swirling with black clouds. We met up on the bridge and walked down to the banks of the pond, concealing ourselves behind a thicket of rushes. I didn't know how much I was going to tell her. I had a vague idea I would tell her about the jazz, but I decided against telling her Elena's secret. It was too close to telling her one of Lana's, and I was not so depraved as to do that. I wanted her to know about the jazz, at least. It was time for her to know that.

"Leo played the jazz," I whispered, digging my heels into the wet earth.

"What?" She didn't have the slightest idea what I was talking about.

"He plays this music called jazz. It's the kind of music that forces people to dance." I shuffled my feet in the wet grass, as if that would bring it to life for her, but it didn't.

I told her about how I'd first heard it in the theater when Leo played the song he'd written for Elena, and about how much it had upset Lana when she found out. "Then he played it again today," I said. I glanced up at the gray sky and a shudder passed through me. "Me and Lana went to the store, and when we came back she heard it coming from the living room. That's when she got in the car and left."

"She never called?" Lizzy asked.

I shook my head and threw a couple of pebbles into the pond and watched them sink.

"That's weird," Lizzy whispered.

"See what I mean about Lana?"

She nodded.

"It's been like this my whole life." I picked up a twig and heaved it out to the middle of the pond, where it floated near a pair of swans.

"Maybe she went to her mother's," Lizzy said. "Maybe she's going to get a job there."

"Lana doesn't like jobs," I reminded her. "She writes, and besides Mimi's her mother, and she never talks to her. We don't know anything about her. Remember?" I recalled Lana's face when I asked her if she didn't like her mother. "I think Lana hates her."

Lizzy stared out through the rushes at some unfixed point in the distance. "She didn't go there, then," she said. If anyone understood that, it was Lizzy.

I didn't need to, it wasn't even the next obvious point in our conversation, but I told Lizzy about Teddy. It wasn't really a secret, not in the truest sense of the word, not in the way Lana had taught us, but even so I made her swear to God she would never tell anyone.

"Cross my heart, hope to die," she said, crossing her heart.

"She had a brother named Teddy who was killed in World War Two," I said. "We never knew she even had a brother. She never told us." My throat suddenly pinched off, and it felt like something elephantine squatted on my chest. I had let this semi-secret out in the air where I could never take it back. If only I had whispered it in her ear, but I had forgotten. I leaned back on my elbows in the wet grass and clenched my eyes shut.

"Maybe that jazz has something to do with what happened to her," Lizzy whispered a few moments later. "Maybe it reminds her of what happened."

My ears rang and my stomach floated sour. This was Elena's secret. She had guessed Elena's secret.

"Maybe that jazz was playing when Mimi told her Teddy died," she said, "and now she can't stand to hear the music because it reminds her that Teddy is dead."

"But what about her hip and that cane?" I asked.

"Maybe she went crazy when she heard that Teddy died and jumped out the window and broke her hip."

"What about the metal in her hip, though?" I whispered.

"Maybe Mimi's car was down below and Lana fell on it. Maybe it's part of a fender."

"I don't know," I said, though I highly doubted it.

"Maybe she was standing on a dock on Long Island Sound when Mimi told her, and maybe she fainted and fell in the water and got sucked up in the undertow. Maybe she hit into a sunken ship."

"But what about the jazz? How could she hear the jazz if she was down at the dock?" I asked.

"Maybe they brought a record player down there."

"How could they plug it in?"

"With an extension cord."

"I don't think they had extension cords back in those days," I said. "It was a long time ago."

"Oh yeah."

It had gotten dark, and when Lizzy told me she had left Garta's apartment without telling her where she was going, I made her go home. I walked downtown with her to the movie theater, where one flight up, Garta had her apartment. We hung around outside for about a half hour trying to dry the seats of our shorts. We had big wet spots on them from sitting on the soaked grass near the pond, and Lizzy was afraid if Garta saw it, she would accuse her of pissing in her pants. "And she'd get me for that," she said.

When I got home Lana still hadn't come back. Elena's guilt must have worn her out, because she was already in bed, asleep. Leo was sitting out in the backyard, at the picnic table, gazing up at the sky. I watched him for a while from the attic window, until Lana's boxes drove me out of there. I was sorry I had sworn on the moon not to ever touch her journals again. I was even sorrier that I had asked Miss Thomas how powerful the moon was. I wished I hadn't known.

When I finally lay down in bed and remembered what I had done at the swan pond, my nerves came out in force. I had spoken out loud about Lana and the jazz and Teddy. I hadn't whispered it into Lizzy's ear like I should have. It was out in the air where it now had the power to fly, to drift, to grow—to hurt Lana. She could be driving along and it could come out of the dark like a boomerang and knock her in the head. I worried too that the words Elena and I had spoken in the theater had sprouted black hands which now pushed her deeper and deeper into the night.

I awoke early the next morning to the sound of Lana climbing the stairs. It was a sound that was unmistakably hers. I would have known it anywhere—two brisk footsteps mixed with the punctual clomp of her cane. I threw my covers off and tiptoed through Elena's room (she was sound asleep), where I watched Lana through a crack in the door. She still wore the blue linen dress, which was now utterly rumpled and water-stained, and her hair was haphazardly braided in one long braid that hung down her back. She passed quickly through the hallway and slipped into her bedroom, slamming the door behind her. I knew then that whatever anger had fueled her rage yesterday was still very much with her. It edged up my spine with cold and heavy fingers, and in the early morning heat I shivered.

I waited, frozen, behind the door, listening for the sound of her angry voice or for Leo's placating one, but I heard nothing—only the distant sound of a sleepy lawn mower. It was as if she had closed the door behind her and then had vanished into the morning air.

I stole down the hallway into the bathroom and crouched down by the grate. The gray morning light sifted through their open windows, falling across Leo as he lay asleep on top of the covers, yet dressed in his black pants and white shirt. I couldn't see Lana, though. I contorted myself to see if she were in her writing room, but she wasn't in there either. My small knowledge of the physical world told me she had to be in the room somewhere, but even so I couldn't find her. There wasn't a sound either, not so much as a rustle. The silence hung heavy in the air—even the lawn mower had ceased.

I waited, crouched down and motionless, my thighs aching, until out of the silence came a shoe, a flying black shoe, which hit solidly against Leo's back. He lurched up, a slumbering giant roused, and the first word out of his mouth was a gasped and pitiful *"Lana."*

She was sitting in the chair in the corner, completely out of my view.

"How could you sleep?" she said. Her voice was strange to me. It was devoid of all lyricism; instead, it was harsh and biting. It was a voice I had never heard.

Leo was sitting up, wiping the sleep out of his eyes, speaking in the quick, short replies of the guilty. "I didn't mean . . . I was waiting up, but—I thought you'd—"

"Left?" Lana shot back. Before he got a chance to answer her, she rose up and steamed across the room toward him. Her face was red and twisted and full of grief. "How could you, Leo?" she yelled, holding her voice back. "You promised me you wouldn't. You promised me, and then you play it like it's nothing. I hear it coming out of the window, and then I see Elena and Harry in there dancing. Of all the songs, Leo—you have no respect for me, goddamn you," she yelled a little louder. "Why that one? *Why that one?*"

"I love that song," he whispered loudly. He pushed his rolled sleeves up past his elbows and slammed his feet into his shoes.

"Then play it far away from me. Don't play it, or any of them, in my house around my children. I've asked one thing of you, Leo— I've asked you never to play—"

"It's my music, Lana. It's mine, and it's beautiful, and the children love it."

At this last, Lana picked up her cane and heaved it against the wall. It fell to the floor in a dull thud, and she pressed closer to the bed. "I won't have it in my house, Leo. I won't have my children—"

"They're not just your children, La—"

She leaned close to him until their eyes were not more than ten inches apart. "I knew this would happen. I told you you couldn't leave it alone. I knew it in New York. I knew we couldn't get past it. I told you then, goddamn it—I shouldn't have listened to you, because now—"

"It hasn't come back, La," Leo whispered fiercely. "You're blowing this out of proportion." His thick fingers stabbed through his brown hair and his face broke apart again.

"You've begun it, Leo, and now that you have there's no stopping it. I'm not stupid, I know human nature, but I won't have it, Leo. I won't allow it to *haunt* me." This last was a scream, and in a matter of moments her body began to shake in rage. She grabbed her cane off the floor and whirled around, slamming it down on the wooden footboard, just inches from where Leo sat.

"I will not have it. Do you hear me?" She slammed her cane down once again, as if to underscore her words, and then she rushed at Leo. Her fury was towering, and it seemed if she didn't calm down she would fly loose in a hundred different directions. Her voice was hoarse and her body so tense, I felt my shoulders crawl up my neck. I'd never seen her like this—she was almost unrecognizable.

"Calm down, La," Leo yelled. He jumped to his feet and reached for her, as if his touch could keep her intact, but she darted away.

"What did you tell them?" she yelled.

"Nothing, La, only that it was a song I wrote for—"

"What else?"

"Nothing—I swear to you." He raked his fingers through his hair again.

"I don't believe you," she shouted. "You can't stand for them not to know. If it were up to you, you'd tell them the whole fucking story, wouldn't you?"

"No, I wouldn't, but they're curious, La. They want to know you. I think—"

"I don't care what you think." She whirled around, her eyes narrowed, her hands clenched. "You promised me we'd never talk about it, that we'd never tell them. That's the only reason I went along with you. I knew this would happen. *I told you it would.*" This last ended in a shrill wail, and she rushed toward the windows as if she might throw herself through them.

Leo raced after her and caught her in his arms, shushing her and working his hands over her face. "I didn't tell them anything. I swear to you, I only played the song."

"You will, though. I know you will, and then what will I do?" she cried, her voice breaking.

"I won't, La. I promise. For Christ's sake, I won't tell them, and I won't play the music. All right?"

Her face was pressed between Leo's hands. They stared at one another for a long moment, as if to make sure they were still the same people. Then Lana sank to her knees in a puddle of graceful form and exploded in tears. Leo knelt down beside her and delicately laid his hands on her, gently working her face and neck as if to cure her.

"Where'd you go last night?" he asked her. His voice was gentle again, shriven of his anger. "Did you go back?"

"Almost," she choked out. "I got to the George Washington Bridge, but—"

Leo shuddered visibly, and I wondered, where was back? Where was the George Washington Bridge? But maddeningly there was no more mention of it. Instead, Lana sobbed bitterly at the thought of whatever it was, and Leo gathered her into his arms to pull her back from wherever she had gone.

I was completely lost. It seemed I didn't know these two people who knelt before me in this pose of—of what, I wondered? I had no idea what they spoke of, or where Lana had gone, or why she was crying so hopelessly. Where did it all come from? Only yesterday she was tickling me on the sidewalk.

"I'm afraid it's going to happen again, Leo. I can feel it all starting to happen again." Her voice was panicked and her fingers grasping, and suddenly Leo pushed her back and shook her.

"Fight it, La. Beat it back."

Fight what? was my question. Beat what back? But no sooner had those questions sprung into my mind than something altogether new and fascinating began to happen. Lana let out a terrible cry, and Leo picked her up in his arms and held her like a baby. She lay there like that, crushed against him, while he rocked her in his arms, shushing her over and over again, like a mother shushes a crying child.

"It's going to happen," she gasped. "I can feel it. When I was driving I had to pull over. When I got to the bridge it came over me in a huge wave." The thought of it reduced her to tears again, and Leo repeated his soothing, practiced litany. It was the illness, I understood, the illness which Lana could never name, not even now in front of Leo.

I can't tell you what it did to me to see Lana like this. I had never really seen her fears. I had only heard them, muffled and unintelligible, as they floated up to me through the furnace duct in our house in Detroit. Is this what went on, though? And if so, what on earth was it?

I couldn't think about it for very long, because something else altogether different began to happen. Leo stood up and carried her to the bed, where he laid her down as if she were gossamer. He held her for a few minutes, staring at the side of her face with eyes so liquid and soft they were like inky, blue ponds. Then it happened, and so fast it didn't figure. They raced from this moment of devotion, to one of frenzy. Leo sought her mouth, she sought his, and there was a fusion of lips and tongues, an intermingling of breath, a strange twisting of bodies, as if they were trying to wriggle out of their skins. The way their mouths kissed and their bodies yearned forward reminded me of two hungry people, intent on nourishment, beating back starvation. That's when I remembered Lana's journal. The words, *I want to eat him up, I want to devour him,* flew into my mind, and for one stark moment I was terrified. What would they do? Would they start eating one another? Would their bodies collapse into one, or worse yet, disintegrate?

Perhaps it was best that Elena stumbled into the bathroom. I wasn't ready to see such a thing. I stood up immediately and retreated to the edge of the bathtub, where I sat trembling while she peed.

"Lana's back," I whispered. My hands were shaking, so I slipped them under my legs and gripped the cold porcelain.

"She is?" Her eyes dropped the sleep immediately. "How do you know?"

"I heard her come up the stairs."

Leo came out shortly and found us sitting in the bathroom. Then Lana appeared in the doorway just moments later. Her eyes were deep and churning like the center of a clean, fathomless river, and I couldn't look at them for very long. She edged up against the door, and before she even said, "Good morning," she slumped over and held her sides, as if she might vomit. Leo quickly ushered her back to their room and closed the door behind him, and then all we heard was the low muffle of his voice. Elena braced herself against the wall and closed her eyes. "Oh, God," she breathed quietly. "Now she'll be in there for *days*. Come on, Maddie, let's get the hell out of here."

She stormed out, her white nightgown sailing after her, and as I heard her crash down the front stairs, I quickly squatted down by the grate and watched. Lana lay in bed, under a beige afghan, the shoulders of her blue linen dress poking up near her ears. Her hair had fallen out of the braid and was now spread across the pillow, and Leo was sitting next to her, his back to me, his hand smoothing her face.

"I should go down and make breakfast for them," Lana said. Her voice was high and thin, and she draped her arm over her forehead.

"I'll make it, La," Leo said. "Don't worry, just—"

"I should—they're going to want to know," she struggled to say. "I should at least put in an appearance." A moment of silence passed, and in that time she must have thought of something terrible because when she spoke again her voice was in worse shape. "Oh God, Leo," she said, "what kind of mother—"

"You're a wonderful mother," he interrupted. He touched her face with the tips of his fingers, drawing warm circles on her cheeks. "You rest now, La, and when you feel better—"

"What are you going to tell them?"

"I'll tell them you're not feeling—"

"What are they going to think, for God's sake—that their mother is falling apart at the seams?"

I heard the telephone ring in the kitchen. Elena answered it and then came to the foot of the stairs and screamed my name. *"Maddd-dieeeee."* I ran downstairs to get it—it was Lizzy.

"Did she come home?" she whispered. She was in the closet again. I could hear her punching out a space for herself.

"Yes, she's upstairs in bed." I turned my back on Elena. She was sitting at the dining room table, staring out the window, twisting her hair around her fingers.

Lizzy cupped her hand to the phone. "I figured out a way to find out which articles Lana cuts from the paper."

There was silence on my end. I shuddered to think of Lana languishing up in her room, fighting off something dreaded while Lizzy and I secretly discussed solving the mystery of her newspaper articles. Even so I wanted to know.

"How?" I said. I clenched my eyes shut, as if that would insure that her words and their effect went no further than me.

"We'll wait for the mailman and get the newspaper before she does. Then we'll copy it so that after she cuts the article out we'll know which one it was."

I felt embarrassed I hadn't thought of this. It was so simple, so obvious a solution that I should have discovered it long ago. Still, I felt relieved to know that I had an opening, no matter how small it was, into Lana's secrecy. I worried, though, about what our discovery might do to Lana. Elena and I had read her journal and Leo had played a jazz song on the piano, and now she lay in a terrible state up in her bed. What would happen to her if I discovered the articles she so meticulously cut out and hid? I remembered her rage and her collapse into Leo's arms where he rocked her like a baby. Did those articles possess a power that great? I could only guess that they did. She hid them, after all, didn't she?

I told Lizzy to meet me down at the swan pond in fifteen minutes. We met at the bridge, and in the foggy morning haze we walked down to the banks of the swan pond and sat down in the dewy grass. The sky was overcast in an unbroken blanket of yellow-gray, through which we could see the dulled and diffused brilliance of the sun. It was already hot out, so we took off our shoes and sank our feet into the cool water at the pond's edge. We sat in silence for a few moments, watching the water ripple over our feet, and though I knew I shouldn't have, that it might make Lana worse, I told Lizzy what had happened. I whispered it into her ear this time and not into the air, which I hoped would help. When I finished I looked over at her—her eyes were so large and moist, I felt I could slip into them.

"God, Maddie," she breathed. "I can't believe Lana would scream like that."

I thought about the part where Lana had broken down sobbing and had sunk to the floor, and decided it was best not to tell her that yet. Instead, I told her the part about how they started to eat each other up, and she tried to straighten it out for me.

"They weren't really eating each other, Maddie. They were probably going to do the nasty thing."

"What nasty thing?"

"The *nasty* thing," she whispered delicately.

"I don't know what it is."

She leaned closer to me and whispered in my ear. "It's making babies."

"Lana and Leo were trying to make a baby?" When I considered the circumstances of their embrace, I knew it was out of the question. It wasn't even in the realm of possibility.

"They don't make babies every time they do it, Maddie," she said. She switched her thick hair from the right side of her shoulder to the left.

"Do what? What do they do?"

"You don't know?"

"No, I don't." I had never heard of it before.

"They take their clothes off and the man puts his thing inside the lady, and that's how babies are made." She plucked a cattail out of the water and stirred the pebbles on the edge of the pond.

"How do you know?"

"I've seen it lots of times."

"When?"

"When I used to sleep in the same room with my mom and Don." She heaved the cattail out to the center of the pond like a spear chucker, and pushed her feet deeper under the water.

Without question I believed her. If there was ever a mother who could take a private act like that and make it a public event for her children, it was Garta. There was no doubt in my mind that Lizzy knew exactly what she was talking about, and from that moment on, she was my sole source and authority on the subject.

We both lay back in the grass and stared up at the blank gray sky, half listening to the early morning traffic, to the faraway sound of lawn mowers. The sun shimmered beyond the dull, lead coating, and a breeze stirred the cattails nearby, cooling our sweaty skin.

"What about the newspaper, Maddie?" she asked me.

"It's a good idea," I said, "but she's sick now and I doubt she'll cut out any articles. The jazz made her sickness come back. You'll see," I told her. "The next time you come over you'll see what I mean."

6

Lana was more or less incapacitated for the next couple of weeks. She came out of her room and looked after Harry and helped Leo with dinner, but she wasn't herself. She hardly spoke at all, and when she did it was with a voice so high and choked, so unlike her own, it pained me to hear it. She was shaky too, and since she had reinjured her hip racing down the drive, she was more dependent upon her cane. She hobbled around the house apologizing for herself.

Elena and I speculated as to what the illness might be, Elena imagining Parkinson's disease, which would account for the shaking, but I held out for the theory that she had an acute case of old, mature nerves.

"Nerves don't make people shake, Maddie," she said.

She had no idea about nerves. She didn't know what they could make you do, shaking being the lesser of their terrible effects. Elena didn't have nerves—not like I did, so it was impossible for her to detect the symptoms.

When we found Lana doubled over in her lap in her writing room, Elena worried that she had stomach cancer. Lizzy had a few theories too, the most worthy one being that Lana had a heart condition. Her grandmother, Esther Hodges, had one, she said, and she was always walking around the house shaking and breathing hard. When she overdid herself carrying things up and down the cellar stairs, she had to sit down in a chair and double over to catch her breath.

Whatever it was it was serious enough that Lizzy and I postponed our plans to copy the *New York Times*. Neither one of us had the heart for such stealth when Lana was so obviously ill. She wasn't reading the newspaper anyway, much less cutting articles out of it. Instead we watched her through the grate in the bathroom. It became our job—the sole purpose of our afternoons together—to sit on the cool bathroom tiles and watch over Lana.

She couldn't always disappear into her writing room, though. Leo had pretty much stopped coming home in the afternoons, so she had to take care of Harry and get us breakfast and lunch, not to mention doing the laundry. He'd gotten used to Garta taking up all of Lana's time, but more than that, he'd gotten used to working on that grand piano alone, on that empty stage. He still cooked us dinner and kept up with the dusting and held Lana in his arms at night, but he refused to give up to her either his mornings or his afternoons, even when she was shaking the most.

Lizzy and I heard them in their bedroom yelling about it one night not too long after she'd come back. Lizzy didn't know anything about their bargain, but she could tell that something was starting to break between them.

"You won't come home in the afternoons? Is that what you're telling me?" she asked him. She was staring out the tall window in their bedroom, as the evening shadows stole across our side lawn. She pulled at the curtain, the lace trembling in her hand.

Leo was sitting on the edge of their bed taking off his shoes. "I've gotten used to the piano up there, La, and the silence too."

He stared at her back, but she didn't so much as move.

"So I'm on my own, then," we heard her say. She said it quietly, like it was a fact. She turned to him, and in the fading light her eyes seemed darker, more penetrating. "You promised me it would be the same here, and it isn't," she said sharply. It sounded like a knife had gotten stuck in her voice.

Leo shoved his shoes under the bed. "I like it up there in the theater. It's a dream come true and I'm not giving it up. I sat in that fucking living room for five years, Lana—"

When she turned her back on him he stopped speaking. "I know,

Leo," she said faintly. "I understand that, but you're forgetting about me." The words seemed to grind out of her.

"I'm not forgetting about you. I'm living, goddamn it. Is that so terrible?"

Lana turned around again and thrust her shaking hands out for him to see, holding them out long enough so he could really get a good look at them. "You're lucky," she whispered fiercely. She dropped her hands down to her side and walked out of the room, leaving Leo sitting alone on the bed. When she was gone he clenched his eyes shut, and I knew somehow Lana's illness was getting harder and harder for him to bear.

Lizzy turned to me in the semi-darkness of the bathroom and whispered, "He'll still hold her at night, won't he?"

"I think so."

"If he doesn't, then we'll have to," she said.

Lizzy had attached herself to me so completely by now and had taken to the story of Lana so greedily it became almost impossible for me to cut her out. As time went by I felt an obligation, a responsibility, to give her all my confidences, bit by bit, leaking out to her the facts of Lana's life—those I knew anyway. We shared all the worrying about Lana, and in the privacy of the attic we speculated as to what Lana had been writing or thinking or feeling while we watched her through the bathroom grate.

"I bet she was thinking about what happened to her," Lizzy would say. "Did you see the way she kept touching her cane? And I bet she was thinking about Mimi too. Did you see the way she kept rubbing her eyes? I read somewhere that people rub their eyes when they think about their mothers."

Near the end of July Lizzy thought she had it figured out. We were up in the attic, sitting near the open window, Lizzy slumped in the red chair, me stretched out on the dusty floorboards. Elena was out in the backyard pushing Harry on the swing, while Lana sat in the shade, in a wicker chair, with her dark sunglasses on.

"This is it, Maddie," she said. She swung one lazy leg over the other and put her arm behind her head. "I bet Mimi was very nosy, and I bet she read Lana's diaries when she was a girl, and that drove Lana crazy. Suppose she read Lana's diary, and then Lana got so mad she ran away. Then Mimi ran after her, and maybe that's how Lana's hip got broken. Mimi chased her across the street in New

York—just in case that's where they were—and Lana got hit by a car. Or maybe they were out on Long Island Sound, and when Lana ran away, Mimi got in her car to find her, and then Mimi ran her over. Maybe that's what happened, and now Lana won't speak to her."

"I doubt it," I said, rolling over onto my stomach. "Try again."

Lizzy was absolutely tireless when it came to speculating about Lana. She could spend an entire afternoon hidden away in that hot, stuffy attic trying to figure out what had happened to her. It drove my nerves crazy to see Lana's boxes standing in the attic just beyond the red chair where Lizzy usually sat, knowing that I had vowed not to touch them, and knowing that they were probably filled with what *really* happened to Lana. I couldn't tell Lizzy about them, though. That was one thing I could not do. To tell her would invite disaster, because even though she loved Lana, she did not yet appreciate the intensity of her privacy.

When Lizzy went home every night after dark, I was left alone with Lana's illness and her boxes and all my thoughts. After a while it became almost impossible to sleep. There were too many pieces missing for my life to be quiet. It seemed the world was very black and sketchy, vaporous even and floating around without the slightest semblance of order. My nerves came out in droves and charged under my skin, night after night, butting their heads against the ceiling. What if Leo played the jazz again? I would wonder. And what if Lana was right—that he had begun it now and couldn't stop? But stop what?

I would listen for the sound of her anguished voice at night. When it didn't come to me through the floor registers, I would go into the bathroom and peer through the grate. Most of the time she and Leo were lying on top of the covers, fully clothed, Lana lying tightly curled in his arms. Her eyes were usually shut like doors, as if she were in silent and heated battle. She was beating it back, I would think, whatever it was.

The last night in July I crept downstairs, and in a pool of moonlight, I pulled out the W volume of Leo's *Encyclopedia Britannica* and looked up the George Washington Bridge. It said it was constructed in 1931 and connected the state of New Jersey to the island of Manhattan, also known as New York City. I leaned back against the bookshelf and stared down at my outstretched legs. *Back there* was New York City, I realized. Lana had almost gone back to New York City. But why? Mimi, I thought. She had gone back to see Mimi, but something had made her change her mind. I remembered the secret she hadn't told me yet, the one about Mimi, and though I knew it was impossible, I wanted to know it.

I stretched out on the living room floor and put my hands behind my head. I wondered whether or not I had the nerve to go up and ask her and what she would do if I did. I listened to Harry's long, sleepy breathing in the next room and watched the passing car lights spread out on the walls and then disappear. It was just one question, I thought. What's one question in this life? The wooden floor cooled my hot skin, and something about the utter quiet gave me the courage. I put the W volume of the encyclopedia back in the bookshelf and drifted quietly up the stairs, stopping in front of Lana's door. I was polite about it. I knocked.

"Who's there?" Lana asked.

"It's me."

She told me to come in, so I pushed the door open slowly and stepped inside. Leo was sleeping on his stomach. A white sheet covered his back, and the small gooseneck lamp burned on the table beside their bed. Lana kept it on all night when she was sick—the dark frightened her and made whatever demon she wrestled with seem bigger. She was sitting up in bed, reading a book by Eudora Welty, while the radio played softly.

"What do you want, Maddie?" she whispered. She looked feverish, and when she touched my face I felt her hand shake.

"I want to ask you something, Lana."

She moved over in the bed to make room for me. She was shivering, but when I felt how warm it was, how muggy, I realized it couldn't be that. She was trembling instead—not just her hands, but her whole body. It seemed I shouldn't ask her, that it would be rude of me, but I asked her anyway. I'd already spent too many nights aching.

"You were going to tell me a secret about Mimi." I mouthed the word *secret* and pulled the sheet up under my chin.

She stared at me in disbelief. "Oh, Maddie. You still remember that?"

I nodded, and the breeze blew a lock of hair across her face. "It was nothing, sweetheart," she whispered. "Really. We were playing, and I was just kidding around."

"No, you weren't," I said. The radio began to play a march, whose dirgelike beat depressed me. "You said did I want to know a secret about Mimi." I pressed my finger to my lips as if to silence myself.

"Not tonight, Maddie. It's late, and I don't want to think about Mimi. I'm not myself right now." Her voice broke, and her face made a grievous twist. "I wasn't always this way. I used to be very different than I am now." She turned away from me so I wouldn't see her face. "I'm sorry, Maddie," she whispered. She squeezed my hand, as if that was all that was left of her, and I knew it was time for me to go.

I found out the secret about Mimi anyway. Lana told me a few days later when I got upset and hid behind a barrel at the bottom of the cellar steps.

Elena and I had ridden our bikes down to the school to look at the class lists posted on the front doors. I was afraid she and Louis Bartalucci were in the same class, but even so I wanted to know. We laid our bikes down in the grass and climbed the concrete steps to the front doors, where, on the glass, six class lists were taped. I looked around to make sure no one else was there.

"I've got Mr. Laraway," Elena said, "whoever the hell that is. You've got Mrs. Devonshire, Maddie. Mrs. Devonshit." Since Lana had gotten ill, Elena had taken up swearing in a big way.

I pushed ahead of her, and before I looked at my list, I looked at hers. My eye didn't go very far, because at the top of her list was Louis Bartalucci, second on the list, below Robert Anderson.

"Goddamn it," I said quietly.

"What'd you say?"

"I said goddamn it!" I shouted.

"Why?"

I didn't answer her. I stormed down the stairs and took off on my bike, leaving her behind. She was completely mystified, and it wasn't long before she was peddling behind me, shouting into the hazy, dusk air, "What's wrong, Maddie? Is it because of Mrs. Devonshire? Because you've got Mrs. Devonshit?"

I raced blindly through the summer streets feeling unjustly robbed and forsaken. She would take him away from me. Before the first day of school was over he would be hers. He would never even know who I was. Envy ate up my reason, and I threw my bike down on the back lawn and fled down the cellar steps, where I hid myself between an old barrel and the outer wall. I crouched down and wedged myself into the darkest corner, where I felt the wet dirt seep through my shorts.

Elena slammed her bike down in the yard and raced over to the cellar steps, where I could see her perfect legs framed against the vanishing blue sky. "What in the hell is wrong with you?"

I couldn't speak. My chest tightened, and I heard my heart in my ears.

She shuffled her feet, and then there was silence for a few moments. "There's ghosts down there, Maddie." She screamed a convincing, shrill scream that shot terror through my heart. "I just saw one running down there," she yelled. She screamed again, even louder, and threw a stone at it.

I couldn't move. I just sat there behind the barrel, a spider crawling up my leg, the wet dirt soaking through my underwear. I couldn't speak either, no matter how many times Elena asked me what was wrong. I knew something had happened to me again when I saw Lana's legs at the top of the stairs, and then Leo's.

"I'm coming down, Maddie," she said.

She beamed a flashlight down, but the light didn't touch me. I watched her climb down, her cane coming first, while the light shimmied all over the place. I pushed myself deeper into the corner, until I felt the rough cement scrape against my bare shoulder. I don't know if it was the light or if it was seeing Lana's face just beyond it that did it to me, but all of a sudden I started shivering. As if someone had just thrown open the doors to the North Pole, I shivered violently.

Lana slid the barrel aside and shone the flashlight down on me.

"Maddie, what happened to you?" She looked like a giant standing above me in the dark like that.

I threw my arms around myself and hid my face in my knees. She shoved the barrel out of the way, and then scrambled down next to me. I loved Lana for that—for the way she'd forget about herself when someone else was in trouble and sit down in the dirt if that's where you happened to be.

"What's wrong, Maddie? You're shaking." She thrust the flashlight between her knees and pulled me close to her.

I couldn't answer because Elena was still standing up at the top of the stairs. I could see her legs next to Leo's.

"Tell me, Maddie."

"Not until Elena's gone," I managed to say. My voice was shaking too.

Lana shone the flashlight up the steps, illuminating their legs. "Leo, take Elena inside and don't let her come back out."

We watched their legs move away, and just before they disappeared Elena yelled out, "You're just like Lana, Maddie. You really are." I could tell by the way she said it that she had to. It was killing her that I was down there like that.

"I'll get you for that, Elena," Lana yelled back. We heard the back door open and slam really hard, and then it was quiet again.

"You tell me, sweetheart. I have to know, so you tell me." If she was disturbed by Elena's words, she didn't show it, because her voice was sweet and even and hers again.

I stared up at the circle of light cast by her flashlight and fixed my eyes on the dark splinters of wood and the ripped-up cobwebs. "I saw Louis's name on the list with Elena's," I said weakly. "He's a boy I saw up at Miss Thomas's. And she'll take him away. I know she will. She took Andrew away from me." That wound, already a year old, had not even begun to close.

As I struggled against the tears building up behind my eyes, Lana pulled me closer to her chest. She smoothed the hair from the side of my face, and I felt the warm touch of her lips on my ear. "Remember the secret I told you," she whispered. "Men will never be the most important thing to you. You're going to do something great with your life, Maddie. Remember?"

I remembered, but it did little to soothe me. It was too far away, and I couldn't imagine it anyway.

"The truth is they may come to like one another and they may not," she whispered. "Only time will tell, and either way there's nothing you can do about it. That's one of the ways life is. That's the truth, sweetheart, and that's all I know to tell you."

I leaned my head against her chest, where beneath the thin silk of her navy blue dress I could not only hear but feel the rapid beat of her heart. It was so quick and strong, so much like Aphrodite's heart, that I worried something awful was going to happen. I touched my hand to my own to see if it was racing as fast as hers, but it wasn't. I wondered if that's what her sickness was, if perhaps she did have a bad heart, as Lizzy had speculated.

"Lana, is your heart bad?"

"No, sweetheart," she said. She even laughed. "Not that I know of." I don't know why, but I believed her.

I glanced up the stairs. The sun had set behind the faraway hills, and night had descended completely. I stared up at the beam of light above us, noticing a few fly wings hanging delicately from a shredded cobweb. The crickets sounded loudly from somewhere in the cellar, and I heard someone yell, "Roy," out a window, and then silence.

"What was the secret about Mimi you were going to tell me?" I quietly asked her. All thoughts of Louis and Elena faded into the darkness.

"Oh, Maddie," she sighed. She shifted her weight, and the flashlight slipped a little, the light falling forward across the steps.

"But Lana, you said—"

"I know, but—"

"But I've been waiting. I've been waiting all this time." I clambered up on my knees.

"Sweetheart, I can't hardly remember."

"It was about Mimi," I raced to say. "You were going to tell me a secret about Mimi."

Lana remained silent for a minute or two, during which time my desperation welled to uncomfortable levels. If I let her go without telling me the secret, I knew my nerves would rise up and revolt and I would never sleep.

I pressed forward. "Please, Lana. I've been waiting all this time."

"All right," she finally said. "I'll tell you a secret about Mimi."

I never knew for sure if she told me the same secret she had planned on telling me that day, or if she decided upon a different one that night. It was a secret, though. Any way you looked at it, it was a secret, and one I would puzzle over for a long time to come. I never knew why either, out of her multitude of secrets, she had chosen to tell me this one.

I pushed my hair away from my ear and fitted it against her mouth, where I felt her lips struggling to form the first word.

"Maddie," she whispered, and then she stopped and took a deep breath. She shifted her weight and straightened the flashlight, until the light shot straight up again. Her lips returned to my ear, and I felt her warm breath spiral down. "Maddie," she breathed, "Mimi was a *terrible* woman."

I was stunned. A *terrible* woman? Her mother was a terrible woman? As if the word *terrible* had conjured it, I remembered something which until this very moment I had never remembered. I was sitting on the beach between Lana and Mimi, digging holes around their feet and burying them in the sand. Leo and Elena were down by the shore, Elena running back and forth with the waves, Leo struggling with a sailboat. I couldn't recall a word of what they said, but I remembered something strange Mimi did. Out of nowhere it seemed, she wrenched her foot out of the little grave I'd dug for it and kicked sand all over Lana and me. She was angry about something, and I remembered she stalked off across the sand, her form wavering in the piping hot heat. The door to my memory slammed shut then, and I couldn't remember another thing.

"Lana," I said, inching forward on my breath. "I remember when we were on the beach and Mimi got mad about something and kicked sand at us. What was she mad about?"

"Oh, sweetheart. I don't know. It could have been anything. Maybe she didn't like the dress I was wearing, or maybe she thought I'd eaten too much lunch, or maybe I wasn't sitting up properly. Who knows?"

"Why was Mimi so terrible?"

Lana turned to me so quickly it scared me.

"Oh, Maddie, don't say that. Don't ever say that out loud."

I had slipped again—I had let another secret out into the air.

Her eyes were wild, and she quickly pressed her finger to my lips as if to silence me forever. "It's our secret, Maddie," she whispered. "And let's never speak of it again." Her breathing had become gusty, and when she pulled me to her chest for a moment, I noticed again how fast her heart raced—faster even than before.

"I promise, Lana. Cross my heart and hope to die. Cross my heart," I said again, which I promptly did with my right hand.

She shuddered enormously at the thought of something, something which I had a feeling I'd never know, and then suddenly she rose up and pulled me up with her.

I followed behind her, holding the flashlight, while she struggled up those steep cellar stairs with her cane. I followed her into the kitchen, through the house, past Leo, Elena, and Harry, and up the stairs to the threshold of her room. I would have followed her inside except she turned to me and said, "I'm sorry, Maddie." That horrible look of apology invaded her expression, and I knew she couldn't let me in.

I let her go and crept into the bathroom, where from behind the grate I watched her. She doubled over in her chair and gasped for air, saying something which at first I could not understand. "God help me," I finally understood her to say. "God help me."

Elena and I went down to the track the next day, and after I wore her out on the hurdles, we walked up Heart Attack Hill, and I asked her what she remembered about Mimi. I sat down next to her in the cool grass under the shade of an elm tree and waited for her to remember something. The sky overhead fluctuated between brilliance and cloudiness, the light under the tree flickering on and off.

Elena lay back in the grass and wiped her sweaty forehead with the back of her hand. "Why do you want to know?"

I had to keep myself from appearing too eager, because that would have made her ask me in return for something greater than I was willing to give, so I answered as casually as possible. "Because I'm curious about her. Because she's Lana's mother and I can't hardly remember her."

She lay still for a few moments, squinting up at the sun. "I remember something, Maddie, and I'll tell you, but first you have to tell me why you ran down the cellar steps last night."

The possibility of telling her the truth was out of the question. No matter how much I wanted to know her memory of Mimi, I couldn't tell her about Louis. It would only pave her way to him, and I didn't want to do that to myself.

"Because I don't want to go to school," I lied.

She looked pleased to hear that. It put us in the same boat that way, and made her feel less lonely.

"Why?" she asked.

"Because I'm afraid that the kids will tease me again. Maybe they won't call me a cootie bug, but something else, something worse."

"I'll beat the crap out of whoever calls you a name," she said. "If anyone calls you anything, I promise you, Maddie, I'll pound the shit out of them." She stared at me for a moment, the corners of her mouth turning up—the idea of it thrilled her.

"What do you remember about Mimi?" I said.

She turned over on her side. "I was only three, I think," she said. "I don't remember the whole thing, Maddie, but I remember I was playing with alphabet blocks in Mimi's apartment in New York. You were sleeping on the floor on a blanket. I remember because I kept dropping the blocks on your butt so you'd wake up. Mimi and Lana started yelling at each other, I remember, but I don't remember what they said. I remember, though, when Lana jumped up on the radiator under the window and started screaming, 'You want me to jump? You want me to jump?' Mimi was hitting her legs with a broom, screaming for her to get down, and Lana just kept yelling, 'You want me to jump?' " She closed her mouth and looked up at me, one eye squinted against the sun. "That's all I remember."

She rolled over on her back and stared up at the shifting sky. I was stunned by her memory. Had I seen something like that, I'm sure I would have told her before now. "How come you never told me? I mean, how come you never did?"

"I don't know, Maddie. I never really remembered it until now. Besides, it was a long time ago, and it doesn't make any sense anyway."

Just hearing Elena speak of Mimi's apartment in New York made my nerves itch. It killed me to know I had once lain on the floor of that apartment when Lana and Mimi were having a fight and could not remember a thing about it. I closed my eyes and strained against time, trying to transport myself back to that day when I was all of one year old, but it was no use. I might as well have been in Lana's womb, for all I could remember.

I realized, however, that Elena most likely knew more and that with a little more coaxing she might remember it. The time wasn't now, not while we were baking on the side of a hill in the August heat, but at nighttime when she lay in her bed and I lay in mine. I'd ask her then, when it was quiet and dark and she could close her eyes and fish through her memory banks for any more shards of Mimi.

I waited until after dinner when no one was in the kitchen before I called Lizzy to tell her what Elena had remembered about Mimi.

Harry was asleep, and Lana had gone upstairs to her writing room, where she was huddled over her desk, scrawling something secret on white paper. Leo was sitting in the living room, pouring over some music scores, plunking out a string of notes every so often with his right hand, and I could see Elena out in the backyard catching fireflies in an old jar.

I clambered up to the kitchen stool and dialed Lizzy's number. When she answered, I cupped my hand over the phone. "Lizzy," I whispered, "I found something out about Mimi."

"There's a big fight here," she whispered back. "Gus is here, and my mom and Don are fighting. I'm in the closet."

"What happened?"

"I don't know. Can you hear them?" She opened the closet door a crack and stuck the telephone out. "Listen," she whispered loudly.

I pressed the phone hard against my ear, though I didn't need to. "GODDAMN IT," I heard Garta yell. "GOD DAMN YOU TO HELL." The sound and pitch of her voice were harrowing, more overdone than usual.

Lizzy brought the phone back into the closet and closed the door. "What did you find out about Mimi?" she whispered. I heard thrashing and a stampede of feet, and then more of Garta's voice.

"I'll have to tell you tomorrow." Elena had come in from the backyard and was ferreting through the refrigerator looking for something to eat. She had put her jar of fireflies on the top shelf, next to a carton of milk, while she looked through the fruit drawer. There were seven of them glowing inside, flickering on and off like lights.

"Tell me now," Lizzy said.

"I can't," I whispered. I heard another burst from Garta, "YOU FUCKER," and something else which I missed, and then I heard the crash of something large being knocked over.

"Why not? Is Elena there?"

"Yes," I said. Elena, through no choice of her own, had become our adversary.

I heard a dull thud outside Lizzy's closet door. It could have been Garta going down, I thought. "It sounds bad over there," I said.

"I know. I've got to go. I'll call you later."

"Do you want me to come over?"

I heard Garta's voice. "LIZZY," she yelled, and then Lizzy hung up.

I sat out on the back porch, staring up at a perfect night sky, and asked the moon to intervene on Lizzy's behalf, though I didn't know if the moon's powers extended that far. I sat there for a good ten minutes, my eyes sunk into the moon's flesh. I didn't know what to do with myself after that, so I went upstairs and checked on Lana through the bathroom grate. She was lying in bed next to Leo, on top of the covers, curled up on her right side. Every so often a shudder passed through her like a wave, and when she clutched her sides, I worried that she had stomach cancer, like Elena had said. I thought about telling her that Garta and Don were fighting in Garta's apartment, but she looked too sick.

I passed through Elena's room and crept into my bed. She was lying under a sheet, holding her jar of fireflies, watching them flicker on and off. I lay there a long time, unable to fall asleep. My nerves were more riled up than usual—they were scraping at my veins. The thought of Lizzy hiding deep in the closet while Garta and Don and Gus went at it produced in me a feeling of dread. Whenever Garta was involved, a thing got to be too big—it always leapt out of control. There was no stopping a thing once Garta was involved. I could just see her storming through her apartment in her gigantic blue thongs, hurtling vases and china plates against the wall.

"Garta and Don were having a big fight when I called Lizzy," I whispered to Elena. I turned over on my side so I could see her through the doorway.

"Did you tell Lana?"

"No, she looks really sick tonight." I kicked my blanket off—it was too hot.

"I know. I saw her in there. She looks like she's dying, Maddie." She shook her jar of fireflies and watched them scatter.

"Maybe she does have stomach cancer, Elena," I said. "She was holding her sides again."

We heard Garta's voice outside our opened windows. Elena and I jumped out of bed and hurried over to the windows. As if she were forging her way through a great storm, she plowed across our side lawn, dragging Lizzy behind her. Her shirt was ripped halfway off her body, exposing part of her breast, and her hair was twisted as if she had come from a windstorm.

She descended upon our house, both she and Lizzy laying siege, once again, to Lana's heart. In a matter of moments Lana took charge, cleaning Garta up, ministering to her wounds, finally sitting down at the dining room table to listen to her story as it came out—wet and mangled with sobs. It had all started over a letter Gus had brought over from Joe, one he'd written to Lizzy and Garta, in which he had told them he loved them. When Don overheard it being read, he stormed into the kitchen where they were sitting, and like a truculent bear he overturned the table, grabbing Gus's neck as he pushed her out the door. "Get out you shit-stirring nigger," he had said. *"Get out."*

As Garta told Lana every last detail, Elena, Lizzy, and I watched in amazement as her illness fell away. With each word uttered, it seemed Lana sat up taller, her eyes growing steadier. When Garta admitted that Don had knocked Lizzy over, Lana stopped Garta's story to check every inch of Lizzy's body to make certain that she wasn't hurt, finally holding her in her arms for such a long time that I felt a pang of jealousy. When Garta resumed her story again, we all noticed Lana's hands lying on top of the table, stilled. Then Gus came over, and after Lana sent Elena, Lizzy, and me to bed, we listened to the sound of her voice as she talked to Gus and Garta late into the night—it was sure and strong, powerful even.

None of us knew exactly what it was about Garta's story and her undoing that had the power to switch the gears of Lana's illness, to turn it back, but when we woke the next morning, Lana was herself once again. She had stopped shaking, and her voice was her own. For whatever mystifying reason, it seemed she was ours again. We could only be grateful.

After Garta and Lizzy left early that morning, escaping to a friend of Garta's in Binghamton, Lana pulled Elena and Leo out into the hallway, and from the top of the stairs, she called Harry, inviting him to break his previous record of thirty-one seconds flat. He took a few steps two at a time in his haste to get to her, and when he finally made it to the top, he flew into her arms. She enveloped him, and it seemed their embrace purged us all of our heartache of losing her. Through Harry we could all welcome her back.

She made us go into her bedroom and climb into her bed, and then she vanished down the staircase, promising us she'd be back soon. She returned fifteen minutes later with Mimi's silver tray filled with teacups of hot cocoa, plates of toast, bowls of peeled fruit, and a big platter of scrambled eggs. She set the tray down on her dresser and made a long, elegant bow. "This breakfast is in honor of all of you," she said. She looked graceful and beautiful in the morning light, and when Leo clapped, she laughed and then bowed again.

We watched her carefully as she hobbled toward us with the tray. I winced when I saw the weight fall to her bad hip, but if it hurt she didn't show it. Her face was radiant, and her power spread through the room. She set the tray in the middle of the bed and climbed on, sitting opposite from us. Then she uncovered a bowl with five wet, rolled-up washcloths, and like a magician she unfurled them one by one and washed our hands.

"I'm sorry that I sometimes misplace my mind," she said. "Sometimes I lose it, but I want you to know that I think the world of all of you." I felt her sadness just then, as if it were my own, but even more than that, I felt her helplessness in the face of—of what, I thought? Whatever it was that took hold of her from time to time, I finally understood, was something she was powerless against.

She propelled our breakfast forward, making it one of the most memorable of my childhood. She felt terrible for having "left" us these past few weeks, and when she began apologizing all over again, Leo stopped her. Her guilt was killing him, and he said he thought it was high time for some tall tales. He hadn't heard one in a long time, and he needed one. So Harry started us off with his favorite one, about a horse who had a pet boy. I followed with one about a young girl who could read peoples' minds just by looking at them. Elena told a pretty good one about a teenager who could run faster than anyone else in the world, so fast that when she really got going she was just a blur. And Leo made one up about a musician who had grown enough hands and mouths to play a whole orchestra by himself.

Then Lana gave us the next installment of the Bear and Sparrow story—one of the last, though we didn't know it at the time. She lay down in the middle of the bed, and while Leo lay next to her, Elena, Harry, and I stretched out along their sides. The world outside our windows barely stirred. A few birds sang in the trees, a couple of cars drove past slowly, and we heard a dog bark a few houses away. Other than that it was quiet, and the sun streamed in the open windows in wide, unbroken beams.

The sparrow couldn't sing, Lana told us, *and the harder she tried, the worse the squawk became, until the bear forbid her to try anymore. The bear was growing weaker and weaker by the day. He needed to hibernate, and the sparrow knew she had to do something; otherwise the bear would die.*

So the sparrow devised a plan. Instead of going out every afternoon with the bear to practice flying, she went out alone. She needed to learn to fly without him, she told him, and instead of practicing her flying she went to a tree on the edge of the forest, where in the quiet privacy she tried to sing. She thought she was alone, but above her in the tree was a man sparrow who watched her with great curiosity.

"What's happened to you that you can't sing anymore?" he said.

His voice was low and gentle, and when she looked at him, his eyes were so soft and friendly she found herself answering him.

"I cried so sadly for so long that I couldn't stand to hear myself sing anymore," she said. "And now I can't sing at all." The man sparrow flew down to her branch and sat next to her. "The bear will die if I can't learn to sing again. He's getting weaker and weaker by the day, and I must sing again. I must."

"I have a solution," the man sparrow said. "Tell the bear you can sing again, and when he lies down to sleep, you open your mouth, and I will sing from a hiding place behind a rock."

The sparrow thought this was a great idea, and the two of them flew back to the bear's cave to save his life. They got there before the bear came back from hunting, and the sparrow hid her new friend behind a rock next to where the bear slept. When he came home, she told him she had learned to sing again. When he asked to hear her, she made him lie down and close his eyes.

"I will miss you very much," she said. "I promise you I will be back in the spring, and now I am going to sing you to sleep."

The bear closed his eyes. Then she opened her mouth, and the man sparrow began to sing beautifully from behind the rock. It took a while, but the bear finally fell into a deep sleep.

The sparrow was worried she wouldn't be able to fly south — her wing had stiffened in those few weeks she hadn't practiced flying, and the winter had grown more advanced. The whole prospect terrified her, she told the man sparrow. He never flew south in the winter, he said. He hadn't done so in years, and she didn't have to either. "You can be my guest this winter," he said, and he took her to his tree.

It was warm and cozy in his nest, and for a few weeks they had a wonderful time together. They ate the man sparrow's pile of acorns and drank tea sap by the gallons. He told her good stories and flattered her with compliments, and little by little she began to fall in love with him. She gave up practicing her flying completely, as he told her she didn't need to worry about it anymore. It was too cold now, he said, and it was much nicer to stay in the warm nest together. So her wing grew stiffer and stiffer, until all the bear's work had vanished.

All might have worked out had there been enough food to last them the winter, but not more than a month passed before it was all gone. The man sparrow said not to worry, and they ventured out into the deep snow with shovels he had fashioned out of acorn shells and tree bark. He showed her how to dig down deep into the earth to extract roots and worms, and for a few days he worked vigorously by her side. It was hard work, especially since her wing wasn't strong, but if she kept at it, eventually the shovel penetrated the frozen earth, and she would find a nice clump of root.

A week passed and the man sparrow stopped going out with her. He said he was feeling ill and asked her to go out for him. He promised when he was feeling better he would go out for her, and then she could stay home and rest. The sparrow loved him deeply, so she gladly went out and searched for their food alone. It went on like this for a few weeks, the sparrow working out in the cold all day, the man sparrow sleeping peacefully in his nest, until the sparrow began to grow ill.

She became thinner and thinner, and her lungs developed a deep cold, almost like pneumonia. She hoped the man sparrow would notice on his own and make good on his promise to relieve her, but he never mentioned it. Then one day she collapsed in the forest under a great elm tree not too far from the bear's cave, where he was deep in hibernation.

She struggled against the snow which kept falling on her, but she had so little strength left. She cried out in her weak voice for the man sparrow to rescue her, but he didn't hear her. She lay there for hours, crying out and fighting the snow off, until her voice and strength were completely gone. Just before nightfall, the cold numbed her and she drifted off painlessly into unconsciousness. There she lay, completely and totally unaware, the snow falling on top of her until you couldn't see so much as a feather on her wing.

7

Lizzy and Garta came back from Binghamton a few days later, and against Lana's advice, they moved back in with Don. Garta came over the next day with Lizzy and Jimmy, and while she and Lana talked, Lizzy and I vanished to the attic, where we could speak in private.

"Lana got a lot better," I said. I sat down in the red chair while Lizzy stretched out on the dusty floor under the opened window. Lana and Garta were out in the backyard with Harry and Jimmy, and every few moments Garta's full-tongued voice thundered up to us. "You should see her. She writes all the time. Not like before either, but really fast like she can't get it down quick enough. And when she's done she takes me and Elena swimming at Lake Morraine."

"Just when I'm away she gets better," Lizzy said sadly. She was disappointed that she had missed the transformation. She rolled over on her side and pushed the window open further with the tip of her big toe so that she could get a better look at Lana. She and Garta were sitting in the shade, in a couple of wicker chairs, drinking lemonade, their feet up on the wobbly seat of our old picnic table. Lana was wearing her dark sunglasses and a white dress, while Garta sat there in a man's blue shirt and chain-smoked one Kool cigarette after another.

"She does look good," Lizzy said. "I can see she's got more color in her face, and she's not shaking anymore." I crouched down next to her at the window, and for a few minutes we gazed down at Lana contentedly, as if she were our child who had outgrown a particularly bad phase.

Lizzy pushed the window half shut after that and leaned up against the rough wall. "Now that she's better, I think it's time for operation newspaper." She turned to me, and her eyes flashed like lights.

I moved away from her and sat in the chair. All week I had been expecting this, and I dreaded it. I knew when she found out how much better Lana was, she would insist we go ahead with operation newspaper. Still, I wasn't prepared to feel as queasy about it as I did. I told myself that it was only a newspaper, that copying the words wasn't exactly a direct violation of Lana's privacy—it wasn't like going through her journals—but even so I felt squeamish.

I thought we should wait until we were sure Lana was really better, but Lizzy felt that we should strike while Lana was hot. I wasn't completely convinced, but I followed her down the front stairs nonetheless and waited out on the front porch for the mailman to come. When he handed us the August 5th copy of the *New York Times* my heart rode up to my throat, while Lizzy's eyes glowed like two dark moons.

We had to decide where we were going to copy it, and furthermore where we were going to keep the copies. It had to be some place good and safe, a place we could slip in and out of with ease. Lizzy thought we should just do it up in the attic, but I disagreed.

"But we do everything up there," she said.

"We just talk. We've never really done anything besides talk, Lizzy. This is different." It seemed it would be like stealing someone's food and then sitting down at their dining table to eat it. "It's Lana's attic," I emphasized, "and what would happen if she found the copies? It could make her sick. Look what happened when Leo played the jazz."

"Oh, yeah," she said.

I was in favor of some place neutral, like the woods, but Lizzy decided we should go to Garta's apartment.

"I can just hide it under my mattress, and if my mom found it, it wouldn't matter anyway. She wouldn't know what it was. I could just tell her it was a game or something."

"What if we need it and Garta's there?" I asked, envisioning Garta standing on top of Lizzy's bed, blue thongs and all.

"We'll just go and get it. She's mean, Maddie, but she lets me in the apartment." She narrowed her eyes and looked at me sideways. I shut up about Garta after that. Surely it was true—Garta was mean, but Lizzy had the right to keep a piece of paper under her mattress, didn't she?

She tucked the newspaper down the front of her shorts, and we raced out the front door and ran downtown to Garta's apartment over the movie theater. Lizzy had pointed it out to me from the street a couple of times, but I had never actually been up there. *Bonnie and Clyde* was playing in the theater, and when we climbed the filthy, decrepit stairs, we heard the faint sound of movie voices.

The old man who was always giving Lizzy free movie passes came out of the projection room with a gray mug of coffee, and met us at the top of the stairs. He was somewhere in his sixties, a thick, heavy-set man with sloped shoulders and droopy pants. He had a silver brushcut and two gold front teeth. I noticed too that the index finger on his right hand was permanently bent. His name was Art, and after Lizzy introduced me to him, he offered me his crooked-finger hand. I didn't know what to do, so I shook it.

He slipped us a few more movie passes, and while he shuffled down the stairs, Lizzy unlocked the door to Garta's apartment. When I stepped inside I didn't say anything, but I was shocked. Lana and Leo were poor, but even so I had never seen such squalor. The crusty lime-green wallpaper was old and peeling and dirty plasterboard the color of grease lay exposed. In some places you could see the old, crumbling lathing. The kitchen sink was stained charcoal gray; the bathroom had a tin shower stall that had so many rusted holes, it was polka-dotted, and the toilet bowl was the color of a flowerpot.

Garta and Don had the only bedroom in the place—a tiny, windowless room wholly usurped by a double bed, and more suitable for a dwarf. But at least they had a bedroom, which was more than Lizzy or Jimmy had—a fact which worried me some. How safe was it going to be to hide our copies of the *New York Times* under Lizzy's mattress (she had no bed) when it lay in the corner of the living room next to Jimmy's?

"Where's the closet?" I asked her. Besides it being the closet where Lizzy always used the telephone, I had a morbid interest in it—it was the place where Lizzy had hidden when Don kicked Garta around the apartment.

Lizzy opened it—it was a dark, cramped area of say four-by-four dimensions, which held in its every inch the wardrobes of four people, and which smelled as if a dozen sweating people spent most of their time in there.

We hoisted her mattress up, and Lizzy pulled out our tools—a stack of white typing paper, three felt tip pens, and a thick wooden ruler with both inches and centimeters inscribed in red, raised numbers. It made me realize how much she had prepared for this day, and it scared me a little.

We sat down on the mattress and opened up the newspaper, spreading it out in front of us on the scarred wooden floor. Only then did we realize how daunting our task was. We understood instantly that it would be impossible to literally copy the newspaper, so we settled on copying only the headlines on the front page and their first sentence.

"Red pen for the headline," she said, holding up the red felt tip pen, "green for the first sentence, and black for the outline." I didn't think it was necessary to go that far, but I didn't say anything. It gave her such a thrill to use those pens.

"August fifth, nineteen sixty-seven," I read, which Lizzy neatly copied in the righthand corner, just above her bold, block-lettered *New York Times*. There were eleven articles on the front page: KERNER PLEDGES THOROUGH STUDY OF URBAN RIOTING; NATIONAL GUARD LEAVING DETROIT; RAIN AND SOME UNHAPPY TEENAGERS SPOIL CITY'S HARLEM SPRAY PARTY . . .

Because Lizzy was such a perfectionist, it took us nearly an hour. She insisted on using those felt tip pens and on drawing all the lines with the ruler, although I thought we could do without them. When we were finished we had a beautiful dummy of the front page of the *New York Times*.

We looked in every wastebasket in the house the next morning, but Lana hadn't cut any articles out of the August 5 issue of the *New York Times*, nor did she cut any from the next six issues, which Lizzy and I so meticulously copied. She was too busy writing and taking us to the lake and talking to Garta to ever read the newspaper. Most of them didn't even end up in the trash; they lay on top of the hutch in the dining room folded and unread. This came as a big disappointment to us, especially Lizzy, and after so many days went by with no luck, Lizzy wasn't sure we should keep doing it.

"It takes so long and it hurts my hand," she complained.

"We might find out something big, though," I said, to which she replied, "You copy it, then."

With me copying and Lizzy doing the reading and the spelling, it took us only fifteen minutes, compared with her plodding hour. I simply dispensed with the felt tip pens, the ruler, and the neat handwriting, arguing that so long as we could read it what did it matter. She came to see it my way after a while, and what was once a long chore became now a simple task. Even so, we didn't have any luck.

Elena and I had some good luck remembering something about Mimi, though. I had succeeded in interesting her in the cause, and at nighttime when we lay in our beds, we went fishing through our memory banks in search of Mimi. It became our bedtime sport. We'd close our eyes in the semi-darkness and transport ourselves back to our earlier days, to a time that was, at least in my mind, murky. I never had much hope that I'd come up with anything good. I could only vaguely remember a small house in a suburban New Jersey town, and a fat, cheerful babysitter named Babs. It was Elena I was counting on, and she didn't let me down. She remembered the time when we had lived with Lana and Leo in an apartment in New York City. She remembered bits and pieces of their two-room flat—an elevator, a window with grating over it, a ceiling fan that hovered and rotated incessantly. These facts meant almost nothing to me— what interested me was that the apartment had been in New York City.

She remembered other things too, small, inconsequential things which interested her more than me, like someone's little poodle dog, or the little doorman with the green suit. I liked hearing about them, but I was most interested in Mimi. Then finally one night in the middle of August she remembered something I knew was important.

I watched her through the doorway between our rooms. She was lying on her back with her eyes closed, her hands folded peacefully on her stomach. The light from the street lamp touched her face and turned it a pale shade of white. She said she saw windows with grating or something on them, and I told her she'd already told me about those windows.

"No, Maddie," she whispered. "They're not the same ones. They're different ones." Her legs twitched underneath her white sheets, and she pressed her hands against her temples, as if that would force it out.

"Is it about Mimi?" I asked, because if it wasn't, I wasn't interested in pursuing it.

"I think so. I'm not exactly positive but I keep seeing these windows. I keep seeing them, Maddie."

I could tell from the urgent sound of her voice that she was onto something, so I kept quiet and sent her my support via this mental telepathy I'd taken up lately. I lay still as a statue under my sheets, and in my mind I repeated Mimi's name over and over, as if that would conjure her up in Elena's mind.

A few minutes passed in silence, and I began to feel something happening. I felt it forming on Elena's side. As if it were made of hands which reached over and touched me, I swear I felt it.

"Oh, my God, Maddie," she whispered loudly. She lurched up in bed and clasped the sheet to her chest.

"What?" I bolted up too, and my heart began pounding like a hammer.

"Come here," she said. I scrambled across my room and slipped into her bed. Perhaps it was the darkness or the way the small bit of light from the hallway leaked onto her face, but she looked possessed. Her eyes were huge and her mouth hung open, and before I even settled myself, she groped under the sheets for my hand and squeezed it hard. "Mimi's face is on the other side," she announced. Something tactile rippled through the air and brushed across our skin.

"What do you mean?" A strange, surrealistic image of Mimi's head floating bodiless outside a grated window, with a maniacal smile frozen on her mouth, fled through my mind.

"I don't know. That's all I can see—just Mimi's face on the other side of that window. I don't know what it is, but it feels cold or something, and musty and kind of dark like there aren't any windows." She dug herself under the sheets, and despite the August heat she pulled the blanket up to her chin. "It's weird, Maddie. It's like Mimi's face just appeared like the answer does in one of those eight balls." A small shudder passed through her, and I pressed her for more.

"What's her face look like? Does it look"—I stopped myself for a moment—"terrible?"

"Yes, it looks terrible." I rolled my head on the pillow and looked at her. Her fingers were pressed into each eyelid, probing and pushing restlessly against her eyeballs, as if they were stalking the memory.

"Why does she look terrible? Is she crying or something?"

"No, she's not crying. She looks old and sad, but really sad like someone just told her she was going to die."

"Where is she?" I asked, feeling a strange chill. I looked at her again. She lay frozen in concentration, little beads of sweat accumulating on her upper lip. "You said it was someplace dark," I whispered. "You said there weren't any windows." I turned on my side and moved closer to her.

"I don't know, Maddie," Elena snapped. "Shut up for a minute, will you. Jesus Christ, how can you expect me to remember anything if you keep talking."

I rolled over onto my back and lay there quietly. While I watched the passing car lights wander across the ugly pink wallpaper, it struck me. "How can Mimi be on the other side of a window if there aren't any windows in the place?"

There was a long pause on her end. "You're right," she said. "There aren't any windows, and Mimi is behind a window. I don't know how that can be, Maddie, but that's what I see. Don't talk, though. Just shut up."

She clenched her eyes shut again and pressed the tips of her index fingers into them as if that would unclog her memory. I stared at the side of her face and sent her my mental telepathy—*Mimi behind a window, Mimi behind a window*—hoping that that would clear up her vision.

Time passed and I became maddeningly aware of every sound around me—of Elena's labored breathing, of Leo's muffled cough across the hallway, the sound of Lana's Underwood as she pecked away at it in her writing room. I heard the short bark of a dog down the block. Three cars passed in succession, and somewhere very far away I heard the canned laughter of a television show.

"Oh my God," Elena finally said. Her eyes were still clenched shut, her fingers yet pressed against them.

"What?"

"Oh, Maddie, you're not going to believe this." She rolled her head back and forth on top of the pillow.

"*What?*"

Elena jerked her head to my side, and suddenly we were eye to eye, with not more than an inch separating our noses. "Mimi was in jail."

"You're kidding?" My mouth fell open and something with long, cold legs crawled up my spine.

"No, I'm not, Maddie. The window with the grating on it. It was one of those windows in a waiting room. That's where me and Lana were—in a prison waiting room, visiting Mimi in jail."

It was hard to believe her, but her eyes, so close to mine, told me that she was telling the truth, or at least she thought she was telling the truth.

"Why was she in jail?" I whispered, digging myself deeper under her covers.

"How in the hell would I know?" she said. "She must have done something pretty terrible, though," and with the word *terrible*, something icy shot through my heart.

"Did you go just once?"

"I think I went a couple of times," she whispered. "I don't know why, but I get this feeling that I went there a few times. I remember Lana had a wicker purse. I remember opening and closing it while Lana and Mimi talked, and then looking up and seeing Mimi's face behind the glass." She paused and drew closer to me. "It's hard to remember. It's like it was a hundred years ago, like it's coming to me from a grave." I felt her shudder, she was so spooked.

We lay in the plush silence, each separately appreciating the gift of Elena's memory, relishing the idea that we had unearthed a noteworthy fact about Lana's life. Mimi had been in prison. We didn't know why, but for whatever reason she had been in prison. At the thought of what she might have done, a fear passed through us and pulled us closer together. We were onto something, we knew, something more complicated than we had ever imagined. It felt weighty and enormous, and the idea of it hung in our thoughts like fog.

When I told Lizzy about it the next day in the sanctuary of the attic, I watched the goose bumps race up her arms.

"God, Maddie," she breathed, "it's worse than we thought. Mimi was a criminal." Her eyes shone in the dim light, and her jaw dropped.

This led to hours of speculation, most of which was done by Lizzy. It was my job, I was beginning to realize, to rule out her wildest speculations, to pull her back when she went out too far.

"Maybe Mimi was a thief," she said. Her eyes drifted out through the opened window and settled on the rolling hills. "Maybe she stole something big, like a bunch of diamonds or something. And maybe when the police came to get her, she pulled Lana in front of herself for protection, and when the police went to shoot Mimi they shot Lana instead."

"I don't know," I said.

"Maybe Mimi had a gun herself," Lizzy went on. "Maybe she was going to shoot Lana if the police didn't go away. Maybe that's how it happened."

"The police wouldn't be such bad shooters. They would have shot Mimi, not Lana, and they would have been pretty far off to shoot Lana in the hip. Besides, it's not a bullet in her hip," I said. I turned over and glanced out the window. Lana was kneeling in grass along the edge of the garage, pulling the weeds out of her flowerbeds, while Harry pushed the lawn mower back and forth behind her.

"What if Mimi was a murderer?" Lizzy said. I could tell by the way her eyes filled up that she preferred this explanation to the other ones. "What if she really murdered her son, Teddy? Maybe he really didn't get killed in the war. Maybe she murdered him and maybe she tried to murder Lana. Remember how Elena told you Mimi was hitting Lana with that broom. She was probably trying to kill her. And maybe Lana fell from the window, and there was something down there, like a kid's bike or a sled, or maybe even an axe, and Lana fell on it. Or maybe Mimi tried to shoot Lana with a gun. Maybe it's a bullet in her hip."

"It was flat, Lizzy," I reminded her. "And bullets aren't flat. They're round."

"Maybe once it was in her body it flattened out. Maybe the heat from her body melted it, like when you put a penny on the train track. The train goes over it and flattens it out. Maybe that's what happened to Mimi's bullet."

That was only the beginning of Lizzy's speculations. They went on unceasingly, in bed at night, in the attic, up in the woods, inside the movie theater, in the Colgate Library, at Lake Morraine when we were swimming. "Maybe Mimi was a communist," she said to me under the dock. "Maybe Mimi was a drunk and she drank too much and tried to hurt Lana," she whispered in bed. And so on until one day it seemed Lizzy had imagined Mimi to be every subversive, criminal, depraved, aberrant type of being that ever existed.

"I think we need more information," I finally told her one night. "We just don't know enough to be sure."

I tried to pry more from Elena's memory, but it seemed there was no more. As quickly as her mind had opened and disgorged this last great one, it closed down, and nothing of the same magnitude ever surfaced again.

Elena and I worried that discovering this fact about Mimi had somehow affected Lana, because after that her illness came back. If nothing else it kept us both away from her journals. They stood in the attic, day after day, free and unfettered, kept from violation only by my conscience. Lizzy and I brushed past them on our way to the attic window. We even rested our backs against them, but I never once opened them or confessed their existence. Lana's condition was too unstable, and I worried that were I to read so much as a page of her journal, it would tip the scales against her.

She just couldn't steady herself. She'd go along for a week being her old self, giving us tea parties and making us tents, but then she'd wake up one morning and something wouldn't be right. We would have no real warning either—sometimes her hands shook and sometimes they didn't. Even her breathing wasn't really a signal to us anymore. It wasn't quite like the days in Detroit when one phase followed the other. I told Elena I thought there was something about the hills which had changed the progression, but Elena said it was a combination of Leo not being around much and her just getting worse. "She's deteriorating, Maddie," she whispered to me one night. "When someone starts to deteriorate they just go like that—they just go haywire."

So Lizzy and I watched her more. Once we found her stretched out on the tiles in the bathroom. She said it was because they were so cool and it was hot out, but we didn't believe her completely. Another time we found her perched out in a tree in the backyard. She never really completely disappeared into her room, like she had in Detroit. She couldn't really now that Leo was gone, so she was forced to spend her day with us shaking or breathing hard, her voice sometimes as high as a girl's.

Under the circumstances I didn't think it was a good idea, but Lizzy and I continued with operation newspaper. We considered dropping the effort until I discovered a discarded *New York Times* in the wastebasket with an article cut from its front page. I was in the kitchen cleaning up after lunch, scraping leftover macaroni and cheese off Harry's plate, when I noticed it lying underneath some half-eaten melon slices. I pulled it out and cleaned it off, and as soon as I finished washing the dishes, I raced outside and tore down Broad Street to Garta's apartment. I bounded up those decrepit steps, the newspaper hidden down my shorts, while I listened vacantly to the sound of the movie matinee. Only when I reached Garta's grimy, fist-worn door did it occur to me that she might be there. Ordinarily I wouldn't have cared. Garta didn't bother me—she never yelled at me or complained about me—but today, when Lizzy and I could finally share our first success, I didn't want her around.

"DOOR'S OPEN," I heard her yell. I opened it and found her sitting at the kitchen table in an aqua bathrobe, listening to Barbara Lamb's radio show. Her hair was pulled up in a ponytail on the top of her head, and her face lay under one of Lana's homemade blue beauty masks, making her cheeks look like moonscapes. Lizzy was folding the clothes in the living room, while Jimmy ran a little red truck around the rungs of Garta's chair.

I made my way across the living room to Lizzy. When Garta wasn't looking I mouthed the word *newspaper*, and pulled my shorts down enough for her to see it. When she realized why I had it her eyes swelled, not around the edges, but from the inside. She waited until Garta wasn't paying attention, and then made her move for the mattress. It made me nervous to see the stealth in her posture and hands. It was too much, and it drew more attention to her than it would have had she just gone over and pulled out our copy, like it was nothing. She felt the need to be stealthy because Garta was always catching her, and Garta was always catching her because her stealth was too obvious. It was another one of those bad cycles Lana had warned Garta about.

When she raised the mattress she looked over her shoulder so much that Garta couldn't help but notice. The whole apartment wasn't longer than twenty feet—it was so small you could *feel* the stealth. The mattress wasn't up for more than thirty seconds when Garta's voice sounded from the kitchen. "WHAT'S THAT, LIZZY?"

Even though I told myself we were in no danger—what could Garta possibly do to Lizzy for copying down the headlines to the *New York Times*?—my heart raced ahead anyway.

"Nothing," Lizzy said. She should have said, "It's just our papers," but she wasn't thinking. Garta's voice had the power to fog up her thoughts.

"WHAT'S THE RED RULER?"

Lizzy's hand made the mistake of pushing the red ruler deeper under the mattress.

"WHERE'D YOU GET THAT?" she yelled, stamping her foot on the floor. Her face twisted so much that cracks began to appear in her blue beauty mask.

"I bought it," she said. I watched her quick, stealthy fingers grip the three felt tip pens and thrust them back with the ruler.

"I TOLD YOU YOU COULDN'T HAVE THAT RULER," Garta yelled. "WHERE'D YOU GET THE MONEY?"

Lizzy remained silent for one moment too long, and her fingers, in desperation, strained to push those pens deeper into oblivion.

Garta charged across the living room, the blue thongs harping after her in counterpoint, her aqua robe falling open enough so I was given my first glimpse of Garta's naked breast—a drooping physical manifestation the size of a kickball. I moved out of the way, but Lizzy stayed where she was and guarded the end of the mattress. Garta gave her a side kick and hoisted the end of the mattress up with one of her tree-thick arms. There, amid a variety of Lizzy's secret treasures, lay the ruler and the three felt tip pens.

"I TOLD YOU YOU COULDN'T HAVE THESE," she yelled. Her free hand swooped down and snatched them up. "YOU STOLE THEM, LIZZY. YOU STOLE THEM FROM THAT STORE IN BINGHAMTON, YOU SHITHEAD."

Garta didn't bother to lower the mattress. She dropped it from where it was raised in the air, and in the whoosh of air some of our copies fluttered out, one falling on top of Garta's big foot. She bent down and grabbed it.

"WHAT THE HELL IS THIS?" she yelled.

Unfortunately, it was one of our first copies—one of the ones we had used the ruler and the felt tip pens on. Lizzy was at a loss for words, so she looked to me to rescue her.

"We copied down the headlines in the newspaper," I said. It sounded ridiculous but harmless, and so Garta let the paper drop to the floor.

"YOU STOLE THESE, LIZZY," she roared.

"No, I didn't," Lizzy said quietly. She was on her knees, her chin plastered against her chest.

"DO YOU KNOW HOW MUCH THESE COST? THEY COST ONE DOLLAR EACH. THAT'S FOUR DOLLARS, YOU SHIT-ASS LIAR."

It was after this that Garta went after Lizzy with the red ruler. She chased her around the apartment in her blue thongs, beating Lizzy on her arms, her legs, her butt, while I stood there with my mouth hanging open. I had never seen such violence. For a few moments I was paralyzed, but when the ruler cracked down on Lizzy's skull, I let out the loudest yell of my lifetime.

"GARTA," I yelled. It was a reprimand, plain and simple—just "GARTA," but it stopped her long enough for Lizzy to make her escape. She ran out the door, and the room went silent, Garta turning to me as if I had more to say, but I didn't. We stood and gaped at each other.

"GET THE HELL OUT OF HERE, MADDIE."

I fled the apartment. I was about to race down the stairs when Art quietly stepped out of the projection room and motioned me inside. Lizzy was huddled beneath a table, her knees drawn up to her chest, her hair wild and tangled and covering one dark eye.

"Come here," she whispered.

I crawled under the table and crouched down next to her, while Art rewound a roll of film above us. I thought for sure she would be crying, but she wasn't. I admired her for that. I know if Lana had beaten me with a wooden ruler, I would have sobbed myself sick.

I huddled closer to Lizzy, and in the distance we heard Garta's monstrous feet pounding down the hallway. It sounded like she was wearing a pair of snowshoes. When she banged loudly on Art's door with her fist, Lizzy and I backed ourselves into the deepest corner. Art finally got up and opened the door just wide enough so he could see out.

"LIZZY, GET OUT HERE," she yelled.

"She's not in here," Art said. "I haven't seen her all day."

Garta slapped the side of the door with her palm and exhaled like a snorting horse. "YOU'RE LYING, ART." She tried to push the door open, but he wouldn't let her. "I KNOW YOU'RE IN THERE, SHITHEAD."

Without a word Art closed the door in her face and, though we couldn't believe it, we watched as he calmly walked back over to the table and started rewinding his film. "Give it a minute," he whispered. Then we heard Garta's door shut.

A few minutes later he opened the door wide enough for us to slip through. After we whispered our thanks, we stole down the stairs and raced out into the soft, summer air. I followed Lizzy up Broad Street, across it, and onto the campus, where at the bottom of Heart Attack Hill we finally stopped. We threw ourselves down in the grass and tried to catch our breath.

"We should tell Lana," I struggled to say, staring at the red welts which had swollen up on her arms and face.

"No," Lizzy said, "because then Lana will say something to my mom, and I'll get it worse." She doubled over and held her sides.

"We could tell her not to," I said, but I realized that wouldn't work either. Lana would have to say something to Garta, and then the lists would start up again.

"Forget it," she said, and she pulled our copy out of her shorts. After all that, she had managed to slip our copy down her shorts. "Get yours out."

I stared at her in amazement. I couldn't believe she could just forget about it, but her eyes begged me to drop it, so I took the newspaper out of my shorts and spread it out on the grass. We leaned over it, and almost immediately we noticed something was wrong. The shapes of the articles in the newspaper weren't the same shapes as in our copy.

"Oh no," Lizzy said. "They're different dates." It was true—the newspaper was an older issue, July 30, and our copy was dated August 15.

"Oh, shit," I said, falling backward in the grass. There was no going back to Garta's now.

"God damn," she said, falling backward too. "I'll have to find it tonight."

We lay in the grass not speaking, staring up at the white sky.

Swirls of purple dimpled it and made it look like cold, pale flesh. A trail of black birds flew across it like a dotted line, and somewhere in the distance I heard the rhythmic peck of a woodpecker.

"Lizzy," I said a few moments later.

"What?"

"Did you steal those things?"

She shook her head, no, but I knew by the way her eyes angled away from me that she had.

We didn't know what to do with ourselves after that, so we went down to Minnie Harp's. We wanted some kind of revenge, and since Minnie was the nearest person at hand, we marched across the street and charged down the hill to her creepy house. We wanted to see her cut-out tongue, and if not that, then we wanted to scare the shit out of her. When we reached her dense, overgrown woods, we saw her stomping across her side lawn, coming toward us, carrying an old wrinkled brown paper bag filled with something lumpy. She whacked at the waist-high grass with her left hand, as if to clear her path, and stared straight ahead at something in the woods. Locks of gray hair fell from her haphazard bun and blew in the lazy breeze. We crouched down and crept over to a small grassy knoll, where we quietly dropped down to our knees and flattened ourselves out. We peered over the top and watched as she came closer. She had a leash around her wrist, which was attached to something that alternately stopped and trailed behind her, though we couldn't tell what it was. The grass was too high to see it, but when she came into the woods we saw that it was a cat, a bony white cat with great patches of fur missing. It didn't like being dragged around on a leash either, and every so often it would sit down and dig its claws into the earth, but Minnie kept on walking. Half the time it rode over the ground on its butt.

She went directly over to a rotted log, and bent down stiffly, pulling up a rusty shovel. She had on a pair of old black shoes with thick, stacked heels and a navy blue dress that was ripped at least a foot along one side, revealing to us a pink threadbare slip, through which, when she moved right, you could see a dirty white garter. When she straightened up, she pressed her fingers into the small of her back and scoured the woods with her fierce, black eyes. I think she sensed she was not alone.

She hurried over to a spot on top of the knoll not more than twenty feet away from us, and started prodding the earth with the toe of her shoe to see where it was softest. We shimmied down a little in the grass and kept our heads low so she wouldn't see us. When she found a spot of earth that was loose, she carefully pinched the top of the bag closed and put it down on the ground. The cat bucked and lurched, but Minnie was oblivious to it. She took the shovel and started digging a hole instead. She did it so quickly and easily, with such mannish skill, that it seemed she had done it hundreds of times before.

"What's she doing?" I whispered to Lizzy.

"Maybe the Nazi died and she chopped him up and put him in that bag."

Our eyes were now riveted to this bag. They edged along its bumpy contours, and despite the muggy August heat, we shuddered to think that the butchered-up remains of a Nazi were inside it.

When Minnie finished digging the hole, she pulled the bag toward her, her eyes growing thick with fear. She scanned the woods in all directions to make certain that no one was around before she stuck her hand into the bag and quickly pulled something out and thrust it into the hole. She did it so fast we didn't see it.

"What was it?" I asked Lizzy.

"Probably the neck."

She plunged her hand into the bag and extracted yet another neck and thrust it into the ground. Only it wasn't a neck—it was an empty Johnny Walker bottle. There were a dozen of them that she placed rapidly, one after the other, into the hole, looking up every so often with insatiable eyes to make certain no one was watching her. When the bag was empty she began to fiercely fill the hole, raking the dirt in with her hands and forearms, small beads of sweat breaking out on her forehead. In the midst of it she started humming another opera. She never opened her mouth, though. Not even once, and I watched her carefully too, because I wanted to see her cut-out tongue, but her lips did not so much as move. The song came through her nose.

She stamped the newly covered hole down with her black shoes, humming steadily with an abandon I found moving. She returned the shovel to the side of the rotting log, and then she and her mangy white cat retraced their steps, crossing through the tall grass on her back lawn. She never stopped humming. Through her whole exit she hummed wildly, missing only one really high note. It was nice, the way she hummed this opera. She could have been an opera singer. We watched her until she disappeared around the corner of her skinned house, the cat riding over the grass on its butt.

Only then did we feel it safe to breathe.

"Oh my God," Lizzy whispered. "Those are the Nazi's bottles." We looked at each other, and thrill surged through us. "She buries them because she doesn't want anyone to know the Nazi is still alive and living in her house." She looked at me again, and for the first time since we'd begun speculating, I thought Lizzy was right.

I rolled over on my side and stared through the grass at her barren house. "We didn't get to see her cut-out tongue," I said. I couldn't stop thinking about that. We hadn't scared the shit out of her either, nor had we disturbed her in any remarkable way. We had only watched her.

"Come on," I said. "I know how we can get her to open her mouth."

She followed me out of the woods and up the hill to the back of my garage where an old woodpile stood, filled with dried-out logs and steel-gray boards. I picked out two boards, one three feet long, the other two, and after searching the garage for a hammer and some nails, Lizzy and I nailed the two pieces together in the shape of a cross. I found a black pen on top of Leo's workbench, and told Lizzy to write, HERE LIES ONE HUNDRED DRUNK SOLDIERS.

Her eyes swam and a smile settled slowly on her lips. "We're going to put it where she dug that hole," she whispered, and I nodded. "Like a grave for those booze bottles."

I nodded again. "She'll be so shocked to see it there, that she'll either scream or drop her jaw, and then we'll see her cut-out tongue."

"I bet she'll scream," Lizzy said. "It will kill her that someone knows about those bottles." I hoped she would only drop her jaw. A scream from Minnie Harp might do horrible things to us, like permanently damage our hearing or linger in our psyches forever.

Lizzy etched the words with the black pen, taking so much time making the letters thick and outlined, I was sorry I'd asked her to do it. By the time she was done I had no doubt that if Minnie looked through a crack in her newspaper-covered windows, she would be able to read it.

I carried the cross, and we raced down the hill and plunged into

Minnie Harp's tangled woods. We took a couple of heavy rocks from her fire pit; while Lizzy held the cross I pounded it into the ground on top of her newly dug grave. We threw ourselves down in the grass on the side of the knoll after that and stared at it. The sight of it jabbed into the raw ground like a knife in a wound quenched me. It wasn't perfect revenge, but it was sweet, and it eased my nerves.

I lay back in the grass and closed my eyes and drifted. It was lush in Minnie's woods, like a jungle. The heat was muggy and the air seethed with the sound of a thousand insects. We couldn't hear another sound—not a car, not a person, not even a dog barking in the distance—only the insects and the sound of our breath. The trees spread across the blue sky above us like beautiful green lacework, and every so often the breeze blew softly and rearranged their patterns.

"We're going to have to come here every day and wait for her," Lizzy said. "Or else she'll come out when we're not here and drop her jaw, and we won't get to see her cut-out tongue. Then it will have been a waste." I rolled over onto my stomach and glanced up at the cross stuck in the ground. The sight of it, so stark and lonely, sent a thrill through me. "I just hope Lana doesn't get really sick again," she whispered.

I hated to think about it, but she hadn't been very good. Just this morning we had found her leaning up against the shimmying washing machine, crying.

I waited all night for Lizzy's call. I was worried sick about what Garta had done to her, for one thing. For another thing, I wanted her to meet me at the swan pond with our August fifteenth copy so we could finally find out which article Lana had cut out. I sat near the phone after dinner and stared out the back door at the green hills, watching the fireflies lilt through the darkness. When she hadn't called by seven o'clock, I called her, but the line was busy. It was busy for the next hour, and when it stopped being busy, no one answered.

Garta had killed her, I feared. I felt feverish, and when I lay down in my bed, my nerves reared up and raced around in my thighs like wild horses.

When the telephone rang at about eleven o'clock, I knew it was Lizzy. The sound of it ripped through the dark silence and unnerved me. I raced downstairs to answer it before it woke everyone up.

"Hello," I whispered. The wind chimes on the neighbor's back porch tinkled, as if an angel had just passed them.

"Maddie," Lizzy whispered.

"What happened? Did you get it?" I fixed my eyes on the white wicker chairs out in the backyard. They looked like small, squat ghosts.

"She said I can't go out or talk on the phone for two weeks." Her voice quavered as if she were standing naked in a deep freezer.

"Did she hit you again?"

"No," she said, but she took so long to answer I knew Garta had hit her. I wondered if she'd done it with the red ruler again, or if she'd used her bare hand, or maybe even one of her gigantic blue thongs. I didn't ask her, though, because I knew it was something she hated to talk about.

"She threw them away, Maddie," she whispered bitterly.

"Threw what away?"

"Our copies. I came back and looked under the mattress and she'd already taken them."

"All of them?" A couple of white moths bumped into the screen on the kitchen window, their wings beating furiously.

"Yes."

My heart sank. Garta had thrown all our copies away. All that hard, diligent work, and just when it was about to pay off, Garta had thrown them all away.

"Did she throw them in the trash like Lana's lists?" I asked loudly. I felt desperate, like Garta had stolen all my money or something. "Maybe they're —"

"She ripped them up into tiny pieces, and then she burned them." I heard the phone jerk on her end, and then it sounded like she knocked into something.

"Maybe she was lying," I said, though I doubted it.

"She showed me the ashes. She put them in a shoe box and showed me." She sniffled and took a deep breath. "Don't you hate her, Maddie?"

"Yes," I said. I hated her guts.

"We should burn something of hers," she whispered fiercely. "Like her old love letters."

"Garta has love letters?" I gasped. I couldn't imagine.

"She's got a whole stack of them in her closet. They're all tied up in a box that Don doesn't know about. I could get them."

There was a long pause on Lizzy's end. I heard her shuddered breath, and as I gazed out the back door at the fireflies flashing on and off, I realized how much she meant to me. She was the only friend I'd ever had, and it was killing me that she had to live with Garta.

"We'll get her back," I whispered. "As soon as she lets you out, we'll get her back."

Lizzy made it out of Garta's in three days. She said she cleaned the whole apartment, she did all the wash, cooked breakfast, lunch, and dinner, and put a perm in Garta's hair. Somehow I didn't believe that was all Garta made her do, but whatever else it was Lizzy never said.

The first thing we did was go into the woods up near the waterfalls with a box of kitchen matches Lizzy brought from Garta's apartment. We rode our bikes up a dirt path, across the street from Miss Thomas's house, and dropped them in a field just outside the pine woods. We hiked in a ways, walking quietly and solemnly as if we were on our way to a funeral, and stopped just before the waterfalls. We couldn't see them very well from where we stood, but we heard the roar of the water and a fine spray drifted over to us, cooling our hot skin. It was only morning, but the sun cut through the pine trees in long shafts and heated the woods up like a greenhouse. Flies buzzed in the air, and in the distant field we heard the rumble of a combine and the rhythmic cut, cut of a wheat thrasher. Above us, perched high up in the pine boughs, the sparrows sang loudly.

We cleared away a spot on the ground about three feet wide, pushing the pine needles out of the circle with our shoes, until we exposed the damp, black earth underneath. When we finished, we stood on either side of it and gazed down at it, imagining Garta's prized possessions blackening in a fire. Lizzy solemnly pulled a photograph of Garta out of her aqua green shorts and handed it over to me. It was a good one. Garta was posing in front of a lake, in a pink bathing suit, smiling, her mouth painted a lurid red. Her head was cocked to one side alluringly, and one of her tanned legs was poised in front of the other, the way women stand in bathing suit pageants. It had been taken so long ago she was almost unrecognizable. She was much thinner, her hair was long and straight and hung down her shoulders, and her face was clear of those boils. She looked so good I was almost reluctant to burn it.

Lizzy pulled out the last copy of Garta's *True Confessions* from the back of her shorts, assuring me that Garta hadn't read very much of it, and then she revealed what she thought was the best revenge of all—two of Garta's love letters. One was from Joe and one was from a boy named Paul Horton. They were both over ten years old.

"One for you and one for me." She handed me the one from Paul. She kept the one from Joe for herself. Since he was her father, I imagined it had more revenge value.

She just wanted to burn them, but I thought we should read them first and then burn them. I didn't think we should miss the opportunity to stick it to Garta one more time. Lizzy was all for that, so we both took out our letters and flapped them open in the warm, muggy air. Mine was short and unmemorable, and as we both agreed, stupid, but nonetheless I stood on the edge of our fireplace and read it out loud, the tall pines swallowing my words.

> *Dear Garta,*
> *You said you loved me and I was fool enough to believe you then why did you go off with Dean and Eddie M. to the shale bed last night and then tell them you didn't love me you only used me for a ride to school? I thought we were going steady Garta I thought you loved me.*

If I hadn't seen that photograph of Garta, I wouldn't have believed this letter possible. Nonetheless, it was still hard to imagine. Lizzy and I stared at each other across the fireplace for a few moments in disbelief, and then we burst out laughing. I threw my head back and laughed up at the blue sky, and Lizzy bent over and held her sides.

"He sounds like a retard," she said between snorts.

I then did a deft imitation of Garta, which brought Lizzy down to her knees. "GET OVER HERE SHITHEAD," I thundered into the pines, "AND KISS ME BEFORE I CUT YOUR WIENER OFF."

Lizzy straightened up after a while, and once she calmed down she shifted her weight from one hip to the other and raised her own letter. I saw her eyes skim quickly over the words, as if she worried about what they might say, and when she glanced up at me, I could tell something about them had moved her.

The letter from Joe was very unlike Paul's. Lizzy read it in a halting, shaky voice, stopping every so often to look up at me with stranded black eyes, which begged something from me—secrecy, understanding, the promise that I'd never tell anyone about Joe. I didn't know.

> *Dear Garta,*
>
> *I'm in my uncle's barn writing you this letter. I hope they didn't do anything to you. I'm all right so don't worry about me.*
>
> *The worst thing they did was taking you away from me. They think because I'm a Negro I didn't love you, that cause you're white I wanted to hurt you and ruin you. I love you just the same as a white man loves a white woman, and when we were in Esther's attic making our love, I meant what I said. I want to marry you, and if you want to marry me we'll go someplace where a white woman and a Negro can live together in peace. I want us to raise up our baby. If it's a boy let's call him Jimmy, after my grampa, he was a good man. If it's a girl, let's name her Lizzy after my gramma, she was a saint.*
>
> *I'm gonna come back and get you in a month when things cool down. Don't let them poison you against me. Remember what we said in Esther's attic. Our hearts are the same and our souls are colorless. I love you.*
>
> *Love forever, Joe.*

Lizzy stared down at the letter for a few moments before she folded it up and put it back in the envelope. I could tell it meant something to her by the way she handled it, gently and carefully.

"Let's burn this stuff," she said quietly.

We lighted the magazine and dropped it to the ground where it went up in flames bigger and higher than we expected. We had to keep stomping the ground around it to make sure it didn't spread. That's all we needed, to burn the woods down, Lizzy said. I dropped the letter from Paul into the fire and waited for Lizzy to follow with Joe's letter, but in the end she quietly slipped it down her shorts.

We solemnly watched the fire consume Garta's latest issue of *True Confessions*, Paul's ill-written letter, and the photograph, while we stamped around the edges of our fireplace to contain it. The heat from the flames combined with the warm, muggy morning to make our faces sweat. It didn't seem like enough to burn, considering Garta had burned all our copies of the *New York Times*, but there was no more. As we watched the fire die out completely, we had to content ourselves with the small pile of black ashes.

We went down to Minnie Harp's afterward to see what had become of our cross. It was still there, sticking out of the ground, yet unseen and untouched. We lay down on our bellies on the side of the knoll and waited for her to come out to bury some more bottles. Her house was still—it lay beyond the woods, shrouded in silence and neglect, its eyes blanked out with newspapers.

"We shouldn't be here when she comes out, Lizzy," I said. "If we want to see her cut-out tongue we should be above her, like up in a tree."

"Good thinking," she said.

We quietly hunted for a tree with a vantage point—one that would give us the best possible view of Minnie Harp's cut-out tongue. We finally found one near the round fire pit Minnie had made out of red bricks. We climbed it as high as we dared, high enough anyway to discover Minnie kneeling on some old newspapers, planting marigolds along the edge of her naked house. She was quite a ways away from us, but if we listened carefully and if the wind blew in the right direction, we could hear her humming another opera.

While we sat up in the knotty branches and waited for her to give up on the marigolds and bury some more bottles, we tried to figure out where we were going to copy the *New York Times*, and where were we going to hide them. Garta's apartment was out of the question now, both for copying and for hiding, and it couldn't be in Lana's attic either. I was absolutely firm about that.

When we couldn't think of anything we agreed, at least, that we would copy it up in the attic just this once. We spent the early afternoon catching up on the newspapers we'd missed while Lizzy was grounded in Garta's apartment. We opened the window to let the breeze infiltrate the stifling, closed-up heat, and while Lizzy sat in the chair and read, I knelt down on the dusty floor and copied. China downed two U.S. Navy planes and seized one pilot, while U.S. planes bombed Hanoi suburbs. Stokely Carmichael called for a black revolution in the United States, and Thurgood Marshall was the first Negro to be appointed to the Supreme Court.

The day ended without our finding anywhere to hide our copies. I could think of no other place besides the attic, so I agreed to keep them hidden under the cushion of the red chair overnight, provided we found another place for them, tomorrow, early. It bothered me, though, and my nerves came out in droves. I hardly ate dinner, and late into the night I lay in my bed unable to sleep, feeling our copies in the attic as if they were radioactive. I was afraid somehow that hiding those copies in there would make Lana worse.

Lizzy came over early like she'd promised, and we climbed the hill to Miss Thomas's thinking perhaps we could hide our copies in her bird shed. By the time we reached the woods I knew we could no more hide those copies in Miss Thomas's bird shed than we could in Lana's writing room.

"She might be on her lawn losing her mind," I said, remembering Miss Thomas's early morning madness. "It's really early." Lizzy nodded, and we pressed quietly forward through her woods, me hoping she wasn't, Lizzy hoping she was. Watching Miss Thomas lose her mind out on the side lawn was almost as bad as watching Lana double over in her writing room.

She was out there, though. Before we reached the edge of the woods we saw her. She was sitting crookedly on her screwy legs, half speaking, half moaning those incomprehensible words, her face yearning toward the sun.

"What's she doing?" Lizzy whispered. She was fascinated. We ducked behind a tree and watched her for a few moments.

"She's losing her mind," I said quietly. "It happens to her in the early morning, but it goes away. In a few hours she'll be all right again."

"Maybe she's having an epileptic fit."

"I doubt it, Lizzy. She's probably got a rare kind of mental problem." I was the expert on Miss Thomas. She was the expert on Minnie Harp.

It was Lizzy's idea that Miss Thomas needed help, so to our growing list of jobs, we added Miss Thomas. We would watch her in the morning before we went to see Minnie Harp, before we copied the newspaper and kept our watch over Lana.

8

We never did find a place to hide our copies, so we kept them under the cushion of the red chair in the attic. We were always on the lookout for another place, searching for possible replacements when we weren't busy doing something else. After a while the copies seemed to lose their radioactivity, and when Lana didn't fall apart I began to think I had overestimated their power. Perhaps it was not so great. I stopped worrying about them, and my nerves quit pacing at night, and slowly I got used to the idea of them being there.

Our summer came to an end without our seeing Minnie Harp's cut-out tongue, without our discovering either an article or the root of Miss Thomas's strange morning madness, and without our finding out anything more about Lana.

When school began we had to reconsider everything. When were we going to do our work now, especially the work we did in the morning? And how were we going to keep our vigil over Lana? She was alone now, without Garta, since she had gone back to work at the dining hall, without me and Lizzy and Elena, and without Leo since his classes had begun. She had only Harry, and Lizzy and I worried that he wouldn't be enough to absorb her.

None of us were looking forward to school, especially Elena. She had been waiting in dread all summer for it to start and had bit by bit, though I hadn't realized it, infected my image of it. At night while we lay in our beds talking, she spoke lowly of dirty, dark hallways along which farm children, dulled almost to retardation by generations of inbreeding, groped and lagged. The teachers were these children grown up, so dulled and addle-brained that Elena worried she might have to teach the class.

"Most of them will be morons, Maddie," she said. "They live out on these poor farms with broken-down cars and old washing machines out on their lawns. They marry their brothers and sisters and their first cousins, and it makes their kids morons."

I asked Lizzy if this were true, and she said it wasn't completely, although she admitted there were children who smelled like piss and came to school with cow shit on their shoes. She thought Elena was exaggerating, which I knew was true, but still her anxieties about school became my own. Whenever I thought of it, my nerves jumped into my stomach.

Lizzy wasn't very fond of school either. When our first day rolled around, we walked quietly down the warm, shady blocks, each harboring her own private dread. A lot of children were walking down the tree-lined blocks too—children I had never seen before, dressed in starchy new clothes, walking as stiffly as Elena, Lizzy, and I. It was as if they had just materialized from the sidewalk cracks.

When we reached the school, Elena, Lizzy, and I stopped on the edge of the front lawns and stared at it. It was a two-story redbrick building with white pillars on either side of double black doors, and tall, wide windows running in rows, on both floors. A one-story white-bricked addition jutted out of the right side of the building like a deformed, inferior arm. Elena was lucky enough to be in a class on the top floor of the old building, but Lizzy and I were relegated to the ugly, squat wing.

Elena left us without a word, only a dreaded look, and climbed the stairs to the second floor, trailing behind a whole knot of girls who all knew each other and talked at once. Lizzy and I walked down the hallway side by side, she looking straight ahead, me shooting nervous glances at the other children.

Her classroom came first, and after she disappeared inside, I was left to walk the last stretch alone. It was a twenty-foot plank, which ended at the door marked MRS. DEVONSHIRE, and when I looked inside my heart filled with dread all over again. I crept in and quietly sat down at the first empty desk, three desks from the front in the second aisle. I was surrounded completely by strangers, most of whom I suspected were retarded, and who were all staring at me. For a moment I could not breathe. I had forgotten about my days in school. I had forgotten completely about Detroit. It was like another lifetime altogether, but now it all came back to me, and I began scanning my classmates, while they looked me up and down. Which one would call me a cootie bug? Which one would throw me off the merry-go-round? Which one would split my head open? They were no longer dim-witted imbeciles. They were the enemy.

Mrs. Devonshire walked into the classroom and everyone went silent. Mrs. Devonshit, I thought. She was old and her hair was short-cropped and gray. She was tall and rakish, and she looked strung together, knotted at the elbows and knees, like a female Icha-bod Crane. Her face was thin and pinched and she had no lips to speak of. Her mouth looked like a faded red line, a slot, and she had the tiniest brown eyes I'd ever seen. They were the size of two plain M&M's.

"We have a new girl in class," she said quietly, looking up at me. "This is Madeline," she announced, pointing me out with her skinny finger. "Why don't you tell us something about yourself, Madeline?"

She had to be kidding, I thought. She couldn't be serious. She was, though—she repeated herself, but I was powerless to speak. My nerves smashed into my skin and then crashed down on my veins. I almost passed out. My whole body convulsed in a shudder, and I worried about what cruel nicknames might surface from that visible tremor. I thanked God that my arms weren't bandaged with gauze at least, and that our upstairs was normal and finished off and com-pletely empty of ghosts. That gave me courage, and so did the fact that no one thought Lana was crazy. She had friends here—Garta, Gus, and, by a stretch, even Barbara Lamb—and a lot of people had seen her at Lake Morraine in her bathing suit, looking like a model with a cane, but a model nonetheless.

"Madeline," Mrs. Devonshit said. Her thin voice invaded my con-sciousness like a scratch. "Do you have anything to say?"

I looked around the classroom and discovered that my classmates were all staring at me, especially the red-haired girl who sat in front of me. She had turned around in her chair and sat gaping at me, breathing loudly through her mouth. A lump formed in my throat, but I managed to talk past it. "Just that I'd rather to be called Maddie," I said, and Mrs. Devonshit let it go at that. She left me alone to ride out my first day wrapped in silence.

It took me a few long weeks to understand that this was not truly the end, but rather an extension. I slowly got used to my classmates and they to me, and no one called me a cootie bug, nor did any other debilitating nicknames surface. It helped too that Elena emerged as something of a maverick. Word traveled fast about this new girl who threw fits and cursed, and it served to bring me some notoriety as well. As far as I could tell she and Louis hadn't become friends either. I watched her out on the playground and waited for her after school, but she never met up with him. She didn't seem the least bit interested in him, and when I asked her about him once, she just wrinkled up her nose.

Lizzy and I figured out how to keep up with our morning work. We woke up early and climbed the foggy hill to Miss Thomas's, where, from behind a tree, we watched her lose her mind, trying to understand what it might be, though we couldn't imagine. Then we plunged into Minnie Harp's woods and flattened ourselves against the grassy knoll, where we waited for her to come out and discover our cross. It stood there untouched like a gray sword, thrust in the belly of the dying woods. We walked over to school after that, where we parted for the morning and met by the dugouts on the playground at noon. We joined forces once school let out, and now that Garta was working and her sister babysat for Jimmy, Lizzy was free to have dinner with us and to stay over two or three times a week. Elena even began to warm up to her, considering her at times a second sister.

The days got colder and the skies grayer, and the air began to smell clean and crisp. The insects died off, and only a handful of crickets survived in the cellar, their thin chorus soothing me at night when I mourned the loss of summer. Lizzy, Elena, and I still managed to spend some time outside. We hiked up to Lizzy's favorite field and lay down in the stubbly grass, and afterward we sat on top of the cliff and watched the cold waterfalls, huddled in our fall jackets. We spent some time in the boys' fort out in the back of Shorty's gas station, thumbing through their girlie magazines and tasting the dregs in the bottom of their wine bottles; and when we felt brave, we edged into Shorty's and stood in the corners watching the older boys shoot pool and smoke cigarettes. Art gave us a lot of free passes to the late afternoon matinees, where three rows from the front, we watched *Bonnie and Clyde* more times than I can say.

When we noticed that Lana had really begun to slip in the weeks since school had started, Lizzy and I began watching her all the time again. If she wrote anymore, it was while we were all gone, because we rarely saw her working when we came home. She pretty much watched Harry all the time, and it seemed all the cooking and cleaning and looking after fell on her. She didn't say much about it, but we could tell she didn't like it.

Her hands shook a lot, and her breathing wasn't all that good some days, but nonetheless she took us to the lake as long as the weather stayed warm and hosted a couple of fashion shows out on the back lawn. We didn't find her in odd places anymore, but we noticed that her dresses started to hang on her again and that she was much quieter than usual. Her silence unnerved me at times—it made me worry that she was dying.

Elena said it was because Leo wasn't around very much, which was true. He'd come home to eat the dinner Lana had cooked, and then a lot of times he'd turn around and go back to the theater, where he and the head of the Theater Department, Bob Hendrix, continued to work on their musical. (Bob was writing the lyrics, while Leo wrote the music.) This upset Lana, but she never said anything about it to us. Sometimes at night when Lizzy and I watched her through the bathroom grate, we saw her open the curtains every ten minutes to see if he were coming.

He was still undergoing that metamorphosis, getting stronger and stronger, it seemed, while Lana slowly but surely sank. The more power he took for himself, the less she had, until it seemed she was always struggling to get through the day, the next hour even. He was so busy, he didn't even notice—a fact which Elena started to hold against him.

"He doesn't give a shit, Maddie," she'd whisper to me at night. "If we all just died he'd probably be happy."

It wasn't completely true. He still took us out for hot fudge sundaes, and he always made sure to kiss us good night, but he wasn't really ours anymore, not like he was in Detroit.

He and Lana had an argument about it out in the backyard one evening. Half of her petunias had died one night in a freeze, and he was helping her take the baskets down from the branches. A few times she lost her breath and had to lean up against one of the trees, but it wasn't until she sat down in the wicker chair that he finally said anything.

"You're not feeling well," he said quietly. We watched his hand slip gently from his lap to her knee.

"I'm all right," she said, though even Lizzy and I could see the hectic rise and fall of her chest. She started to say something else, but when Leo glanced down at his watch we saw her close her mouth.

"What can I do, La?"

She looked at him for a long time, his eyes alternating between her face and his lap, until her hand rose slowly from her lap and delicately touched the side of his face. "I miss you," she said softly.

"It's only until December." There was something steely in his voice, as if it angered him to have to keep reminding her of this.

"Can't I miss you, Leo?" she said.

"It's only until December," he yelled.

"I'm not an idiot, Leo," she whispered fiercely. "I may only clean the floors and cook the meals, but I am not an idiot. It's not a matter of only until December, and you know it. It's more than that you're trying to get away with, and you know that too." She leaned closer to him, pressing her face near him so that he couldn't miss seeing her eyes. "When we were in that lousy hospital room this is exactly what I told you I didn't want, what you promised me I would never have."

Leo stared at her for a few long moments, and then without a word, he stood up and walked out of our backyard, leaving Lana completely alone.

Lizzy and I looked at one another—it was the bargain they were talking about, the bargain that was slowly but surely disintegrating.

After this we noticed that Lana pretty much stopped telling him things. She'd lie in his arms at night, and I sometimes saw them start to eat one another up, but she didn't really tell him her thoughts anymore, not like she used to. We never heard her voice anymore through the floor registers. It just seemed she got quieter and quieter.

Elena and I didn't know quite what to make of her silence. It had never happened this way in Detroit. "I think there's a bomb ticking inside her," Elena whispered one night, "and we don't know when it's going to go off." I worried that it was just a signal that death wasn't far off, but Elena said no.

"You watch, Maddie. She's going to blow up one of these days. You just watch."

So Lizzy and I watched harder and prepared ourselves for the worst.

Around October, things started happening—two good things, and one really bad one. We thought we saw Minnie Harp's cut-out tongue, for one thing. She never came out to bury the bottles—we had either overestimated the Nazi's degree of alcoholism, or else Minnie was behind in her burying. Whatever, the cross stood ever vigilant in the woods waiting to be discovered.

We started going onto her lawn and hiding behind her trees so we could get a better look at her. She was planting tulip bulbs around the edge of her house, moving closer and closer to the front screen porch that had a huge crawl space underneath it. The steps were gone and there was a gaping hole there, big enough for even Garta to crawl through. When she finally got around to planting her tulips there, Lizzy and I made our plan.

We hurried down the misty hill early one morning before she came out, and crept through her thinning woods and across her dying lawn and crawled underneath the porch. It was filled with dried leaves and cat shit and cold sharp stones, but we crawled in on our hands and knees nonetheless and then flattened out on our stomachs behind the old, decayed lattice.

She came out about a half hour later with the cat leashed to her wrist and dropped down to her knees right in front of our eyes. Finally, I thought. She wore a faded red scarf on her head, and instead of her black shoes with the stacked heels, she had on a pair of brown rubber boots that flapped around her thick ankles. We had never been so close to her, and now that we were we saw the dark whiskers on her chin and the big mole just to the left of her nose, out of which three long, black hairs sprouted.

She laid out her bulbs on some old newspaper, then took her trowel out of her coat pocket and began digging with a clean, urgent power. She started humming an opera almost immediately, conducting every few measures with her trowel. We were hoping that she would abandon herself to it so fully that her jaw would drop without her even knowing it. When she started throwing stones over her shoulder in time with the opera—hum, hum, hum, *heave*, hum, hum, hum, *heave*— Lizzy and I made the mistake of looking at one another. She gave into it first, and after that there was no stopping our laughter. It came out of us in piggish snorts, which we tried to suppress by covering our mouths, but it rolled out our noses instead.

It took Minnie a few moments to find us. She looked to her right and then to her left. When she finally spotted us under her porch, she stared at us oddly like people do when they see something unfathomable. When we moved backward on our hands and knees through the dried, crackling leaves, she started banging her trowel violently against the old latticework, making a bizarre sound. "Nnung, nnung," she yelled fiercely. Her white breath came out of her nose in cloudy snorts. *"Nnung, nnunnnnnnnngggggggg."*

I struggled to see inside her mouth, but everything happened so quickly I couldn't be sure I had really seen it. I had at least seen the darkness where it wasn't, I later told Lizzy. She claimed she got a better look. She said it was completely cut out, down to the root. We couldn't be sure, though, because as soon as Minnie started banging her trowel against the lattice, we fled the crawl space under the porch and raced through her tall, dead grass. Just before I plunged into the woods I looked over my shoulder and saw her standing in her yard, her hand held aloft like the Statue of Liberty, wielding not a torch, but a trowel, repeating the strange sound of "nnung, nnung," as if it had the power to chase us away.

In the middle of October we had some more good luck. I was in the bathroom late one night pouring hot water over my nerves when my eyes fell on the wastebasket. Inside, the *New York Times* lay amid empty toilet paper rolls and used razor blades, minus one front-page article. I clambered down from the sink and checked the grate to make certain neither Lana nor Leo was awake. They weren't, so I pulled my white nightgown up and shoved the newspaper down my underwear and hurried down to the dark kitchen. I knew I had it this time. There was no Garta now, no mattress in a public living room, no stolen rulers or felt tip pens.

I called Lizzy. She always slept with the phone by her bed just in case something like this happened, so it only rang once before she answered it.

"She cut out an article," I said, shivering in the cold. I leaned up against the wall and closed my eyes, savoring the pleasure.

"I'll be right over."

I waited outside on the porch, bracing myself against the cold wind. She was there in a matter of ten minutes, wearing her pale pink pajama top, her red pants, and Garta's enormous blue thongs.

"Why are you wearing Garta's thongs?" I said, a chill zipping down my spine.

"Mine were in her room. Hers were in the kitchen," she said.

I made her take them off. "They're bad luck," I said. "She was wearing them when she found our copies under your mattress. Remember?"

She kicked them off and held them out as if they were contaminated. "Where should I put them?" I thought we could just leave them outside on the front porch, but Lizzy didn't think that was good enough. She thrust them deep under the steps, and as if they possessed a spirit of their own, she placed a big rock on top of them.

We crept up the front stairs and tiptoed through Elena's room, into mine, and quietly opened the attic door, slipping inside. We made our way back to the red chair, where underneath the cushion we kept all our copies. Lizzy knelt down on the dusty floor and lifted it up, pulling out our thick stack of papers, while I yanked the *New York Times* out of my underwear and spread it open on the floor. A thrill surged through us at the sight of the gaping hole on the front page.

"What's the date?" she asked.

"October sixteenth," I said. While she flipped through our copies, I leaned my back against the chair and listened to the wind blowing through the trees and to the soft rustle of the falling leaves. This is it, I thought. We're finally going to find out about Lana. Something effervescent bubbled just beneath my skin.

Lizzy pulled out our October 16 copy, her dark eyes flashing like fireflies. She laid the copy down on the floor next to the *New York Times,* and when we bent over it, we spotted it right away. It was the main center article; the headline ran: LAG IN NEGRO JOBS IS SEEN FOR SOUTH, *Study Predicts Wide Growth in Region's Economy Will*

Mainly Benefit Whites. We had only the first sentence: *A team of economists and educators commissioned by the Twentieth Century Fund to study the employment outlook of the Southern Negro has reported that it is "a discouraging one."*

We stared down at the empty socket on the front page of the *New York Times* and then over at our copy.

"Why would Lana cut *that* out?" Lizzy asked. She looked at me with stranded, black eyes, but I could only shrug my shoulders.

"I wish we had the whole article." I stretched my legs out in front of me and stared up at the cold, dusty eaves. "If we had the whole article we could probably tell," I said, though for some reason I doubted it.

We looked down at the newspaper and our copy again, and then shoved them back under the red cushion in case Lana walked in. We leaned against the chair in the cold air, thoroughly disappointed that our find did not illuminate the whole mystery.

We heard a couple of dogs fighting in the neighbor's yard, and then a man's voice yelling, "Get out of here, you mangy fucking dog." He threw something hard which hit in a solid thwack, and then there was silence.

"What if they are all about Negroes?" I said. "What do Negroes have to do with Lana?"

"I don't know," Lizzy said. She couldn't even speculate, it was that hard to imagine.

A week later, the worst happened. When Lizzy and I walked home from school, I sensed something cold and alien in the air. The weather had begun to change for the worse. The wind was stiff, and the gray, bruised clouds overhead swirled viciously. Leaves raced down the street, and the cold seeped through our fall coats and headed straight for our bones.

As soon as Lizzy and I opened the back door and stepped inside, I knew something was wrong. Harry didn't come running out to meet us, and all the breakfast dishes were still in the sink, the faucet dripping into a bowl of leftover cereal and milk. We looked for Lana downstairs, calling out her name, but there was no answer, and when we went upstairs to her bedroom and found it empty, I knew she was gone.

"She left us again," I said. Goosebumps rose up under my skin like small anthills, and blood rushed so swiftly through my heart, it made my nerves sick.

"Maybe she only went down to the store. Or maybe she took Harry for a drive," Lizzy said.

She knew as well as I did it was more than that. The cold, empty house whispered that to us.

Lana didn't come home for dinner, so Leo, Lizzy, Elena, and I ate a macaroni dish Garta had taught Lizzy to make. Lana hadn't been there in the afternoon to turn up the heat, so the house was still cold. The wind blew outside and drafts of air leaked in through the bay windows, making us shiver. We all bent over our plates and took small, forced bites, while Lizzy, Elena, and I glanced up at Leo suspiciously every now and then, as if Lana's absence were his fault. He swore to us he hadn't done anything.

"Then why did she leave?" Elena asked. She pushed her half-eaten plate of macaroni away and gaped at him.

"I don't know," he said defensively. "I honestly don't know." He shook his head a few times and swallowed hard, his Adam's apple riding up his throat like a golf ball.

It occurred to me that he had played the jazz, that he'd come home for lunch and had played the jazz for Harry while Lana was outside or down in the cellar.

"Did you play the jazz?" I said quietly.

Leo laid his fork down heavily on top of the table. I had insulted him. "No, I did not play the jazz, Maddie." The wind blew, and a few brittle twigs from the lilac bush outside scratched against the window like cold claws.

"What was she like when you came home for lunch?" Elena asked him.

He stared at us for a few moments and then picked up his fork again. "I didn't make it home for lunch," he said quietly. He cast his eyes down to his plate and speared a few macaronis with his fork.

"Then that's it," Elena said loudly. "She was hurt you didn't come home for lunch."

I remembered how Lana pulled the curtains back at night when he hadn't come home, to see if he were on his way.

"Lana is made of tougher stuff than that," Leo argued. He speared a few green beans from his plate and shoved them into his mouth.

"Yeah, but how many lunches have you missed?" Elena yelled. She heaved her wadded-up napkin across the table, where it dropped in the cold pan of macaroni and cheese.

Leo stared across the table at her, his eyes narrowing. "Listen, young lady, I have a job to do over at the university. I am not over there playing hoops, so don't accuse me." His face broke into those six gouged-out pieces, and within moments he shoved his chair back and left the table. He grabbed his black coat from the dining room hutch and stormed down the hallway, the front door slamming loudly behind him. We ran out to the porch, and through the steamy windows we watched him course down the street and cross over to the dark campus lawns, where he was swallowed up by the night.

When he disappeared completely, Elena threw one of her beautiful fits. She exploded right there on the porch, her arms and legs and mouth moving in violent harmony. She swept through it, knocking over the wicker chairs, heaving magazines like boomerangs, and shouting, "Goddamn, Leo," with such high, perfect anger that Lizzy's mouth hung open. If only Minnie Harp could have seen her, I thought—she'd have dropped her jaw for sure.

The three of us went into the living room and sat huddled on the sofa in our coats and watched the passing cars' lights flicker across the dark wall. "She's gone for good this time," Elena whispered, and we all shuddered. "This is how it's going to be from now on. Just like this." She meant cold and dark and lonely, and when the branches clawed at our house with bony fingers, we all shivered.

The phone rang—it was Garta. "SEND LIZZY HOME," she yelled. She wouldn't let her stay overnight with us, even after I got on the phone and begged her. To elicit her sympathy, I even told her that Lana had left us, but Garta wasn't a regular person really. She offered to send her sister over, but she said Lizzy had to go home right now.

Lizzy left, and Elena and I were left alone to worry about Lana and Leo and Harry. The house was so cold and empty that we climbed into Elena's bed at eight o'clock with our coats on. There was nothing to hold onto except Elena's cold hand and nothing to look at besides the ugly pink wallpaper on her walls. Everything felt odd, even the way the light filtered into the room. Harry wasn't asleep downstairs, Lana wasn't across the hall clacking away at the typewriter, and Leo wasn't snoring in his bed. They were all floating around in the darkness, lost to the night.

"If you think about it, Maddie," Elena said, "it's all Leo's fault." She dug herself deeper under the covers and pulled the blankets up to her chin.

"How?" I whispered.

"He's the one who made her come here. And now that she's here he leaves her all the time, and she has to do all the things she hates to do. She has to clean and wash the clothes and take care of Harry. She doesn't have time to write anymore."

I rolled my head on the pillow and stared into Elena's mournful eyes. "I thought maybe she wrote while we were at school."

"Not really," Elena said. "She watches Harry all the time now. She has to—we're not here anymore and Leo's never here and Garta's working, so what else is she supposed to do?"

I remembered then what had happened when Leo had quit teaching piano lessons in Detroit and had taken another job. Lana had stopped talking and had started throwing the dishes and slamming the cupboard doors. "I wash these dishes so I can put them back in the cupboard, so I can take them out and use them, so I can wash them and put them back in the cupboard, so I can take them out and use them," she had said. Leo came back and started teaching piano lessons in our living room again, but something told me that would never happen again.

He came home at ten o'clock that night, an hour earlier than usual, but that didn't appease Elena.

"You shouldn't have left," she said when he sat down next to us on her bed.

"Your mother shouldn't have left, Elena," he said less than gently. "I had an obligation to be there tonight, so I was there." He wasn't feeling any better—his face looked especially bad in the ugly yellow light.

"Yeah, so what about us?" Elena yelled. "And what about Lana and Harry? They could be in a ditch somewhere for all you care." The sound of the brisk, chill wind outside sent a shiver down our spines.

"What can I do, Elena?" Leo said quietly. "Lana has the car, for one thing, and where would I go looking for her? It's a big dark world out there." He bent over in his lap and sank his tired face into the palms of his hands.

"You could have stayed here with us." Her legs thrashed under the covers, and I felt the air grow colder. "Maddie is still a little girl, you know," she said bitterly. "You don't even give her baths anymore.

You don't do anything anymore." At the thought of Leo's absence, of his irreversible change, Elena's voice broke.

Leo looked down at me—his expression was anything but bitter. "You want a bath, Maddie. I'll give you a bath. Come on." He started to pick me up, but I clung to the warm bed. I didn't want a bath.

"Garta wanted to send her creepy sister over here, you know," Elena said. She hiked herself up on her elbows and tossed her head back. "Even Garta wouldn't leave us home all alone."

"You might tell your mother the same thing," he whispered. He tried to touch her cheek with his fingertips, but she turned away from him.

He didn't know what to do, so he picked me up and carried me to my room and helped me into my pajamas.

"You know what, Maddie?" he said, loud enough for Elena to hear. "What?"

"This is the first time in ten years that I've written some decent music. Guys my age have usually made it by now. A man from New York came to see what Bob and I are doing, and you know what? He really liked it, Maddie." He smiled and pushed my hair off my shoulders and then touched my face softly with the tips of his fingers.

I remembered about Leo, then—how he'd play the pieces his students had just played to rid the air of their fumbled notes, how he'd sit at the piano nights and tell me he hadn't heard music in his head for years, and how he worried that it was gone forever. He used to play a lot back then, Mozart and Bach and Clementi. Our house was always filled with music, if not Leo's then Lana's records. We hadn't heard music in a long time—not since he had played the jazz.

He hugged me and tucked me into bed, and when he left he made a point of pulling the covers over Elena and kissing her on the ear. She ignored him, but he said good night anyway.

Elena fell asleep after that, but I couldn't. My nerves were up thrashing around, denting my muscles. I lay awake for a long time in the cold darkness fighting them, listening to Leo's sounds across the hallway. I thought he was pacing back and forth, until I finally got up to check on him. He was cleaning their room. He had taken everything off Lana's dresser and was dusting it off with one of his T-shirts. I went back to bed and listened to him as he cleaned the bathroom sink and then the bathtub.

When he went downstairs to clean the kitchen, I realized what had really happened, what had *really* driven Lana away. She knew we

had discovered her article. Just like I had suspected, and as soon as
we discovered her article she had felt it. She knew, just as she had
known I was watching her in that motel room, and that's why she
left. It all began to make such horrible sense to me, panic swept
through me like a hurricane.

I crawled out of bed and staggered down the stairs on rubbery legs
to call Lizzy, my heart fluttering like a moth. The wind knocked up
against the house, and when my dark shadow stretched out mon-
strously on the wall, the telephone rang in the kitchen, ripping a hole
in the cold silence. What if it was Lana? I thought. I ran down the
rest of the stairs and raced through the hallway, into the dimly lit
kitchen, where I grabbed the phone off the hook and slammed it
against my ear.

"Hello," I gasped, jamming my back against the wall.

"Maddie, it's me," I heard Lana say. Her voice was high and
sickly—as thin as ever.

"Where are you?" I breathed. I closed my eyes and braced myself,
pressing my back against the wall until I felt my spine crunch. I
could just see her standing in a muddy ditch, the cold wind blowing
all over her.

"I'm in Syracuse, sweetheart," she said. "Harry and I are staying
in the Syracuse Hotel." As if someone had their hands around her
neck, her voice sounded strained. Leo appeared in the kitchen, and
then Elena drifted in. They hovered next to me, breathing down my
back, the warmth of their bodies radiating in the cold air. "Could
you put Leo on?" she said.

I handed the phone to Leo, and while he listened to her, Elena
and I hung at his elbows, pressing around him, trying to hear what
stabbing thing had taken her away. It was no use, though—her voice
was too weak to carry, and Leo's side of the conversation did little
to illuminate us.

"Why, La?" he said, and then he paused for a long time. "No, I
don't understand." Then another silence rolled in. "Where?" he asked,
pausing again—this time for over three minutes.

"Yes, Lana," he said bitingly, and then he turned his back on us.
"You might think of your children, Lana," he yelled under his breath.
"This world isn't made up of just you. What am I supposed to do,
goddamn it?" He started toying with the phone cord, twisting it in
his fingers until it couldn't be twisted anymore. "Get a hold of your-

self, Lana, for God's sake!" he yelled. "Does this *never* end?" He slammed his eyes shut, and I watched him clench his fist.

He stood there for a long time listening, and then finally he said, "Good night," and he hung up.

"Why'd she leave?" Elena asked him, accusing him with her eyes. She stood in the doorway, framed against the black night like a thin, white wraith.

"Because she needed to get away," he yelled. "Okay? Because she needed to goddamn get away."

It was killing him that she was gone, that she couldn't pull herself together, that whatever it was that was wrong with her would never end. It had such a terrible effect on him, he couldn't say anymore. He didn't even defend himself when Elena accused him again. He grabbed his coat and stumbled out of the house, the front door banging behind him.

"She left because you're never here anymore," Elena screamed to his disappearing back. She ran out to the back porch after that and threw on Lana's long black coat and slammed her feet into Lana's old boots.

"Where are you going?" I said, but my voice was legless.

"The hell out of here," she yelled. She turned around and lurched out the door, and all I could do was watch her. I stood frozen as she raced across the back lawn, Lana's coat flapping wildly in the wind, her dark hair flying loose behind her. I turned around and faced the empty kitchen, shivering under my nightgown. I was alone, I realized, and my life had just fallen down around my ankles.

I moved through the dark kitchen on feet that felt like chunks of ice. I sat down on the kitchen stool and stared out the back window, hoping to see Elena bent against the wind, on her way home. I would straighten myself out after this, I told myself. I wouldn't read Lana's journals ever again as I had promised the moon, and I'd stop looking for her newspaper articles. I'd never look in the wastebasket for as long as I lived, and I'd quit watching her through the grate; and when her secrecy drove my nerves wild, I'd punch them until my skin bruised. From now on, I would be good. I would even leave Minnie Harp alone.

I picked up the phone and dialed Lizzy's number, and then stretched the cord out into the dining room, where I squatted down on the floor register and felt the heat blow up my nightgown.

"Lana just called a few minutes ago," I whispered. A lump the size of a doorknob had formed in my throat, and I could hardly speak. "She only talked to Leo, but I know why she left." The lump swelled in my throat and I felt my eyes sting.

"Why?"

I looked around the dining room to make sure Elena hadn't slipped back in. There was no one in there—there was just a shabby piece of light striking the dining room table in two.

"Because we found her article," I struggled to say. There was silence on Lizzy's end. "She knew we cut it out. She knows things like that, Lizzy. I don't know how, but she does. It's just like the jazz. I knew we shouldn't have put those copies up there." When I heard Lizzy's breathless silence, warm salty tears fled from my eyes and dripped off my chin. By not speaking, but not arguing back, she confirmed my worst fears.

I couldn't talk anymore, so I hung up and went upstairs to see if Leo had come home. He wasn't there. I looked through all the rooms, including the attic, and called for him loudly, my voice skinny in the emptiness, but there was no answer. It seemed the house held its breath, it was so quiet. He had gone to look for Elena, I reasoned, or he had borrowed someone's car and was on his way to the Syracuse Hotel. I knew it was his job to do these things, but he should have told me. I couldn't bear being left alone in this dead, unbreathing house.

I went back to my room and crept under the covers. My nerves were clinging to my bones, their teeth chattering so much it sent small tremors through me. Everyone was floating out in the darkness—Lana, Leo, Elena, and Harry. I worried that they would never come back, that I'd have to live in this stilled house alone. I thought about Lana's journals in the attic. If they never came back they would rightfully be mine. Nothing would matter anymore. I could look at them freely, unfettered by my conscience; I could bring them into my room and read them at leisure on my bed, with a couple of cookies and a glass of milk. Or I could read them on Lana's bed if I felt like it.

I worried about what these acts might do to Lana. I feared they would affect her even if she weren't here. Was it true? Would my trespassing thrust her deeper into darkness? Would it push her further and further away, out to Ohio, through Utah, past California, to the Pacific Ocean and whatever strange lands lay beyond that?

9

When I woke up the next morning I was still alone. Leo wasn't in his room—he hadn't even slept there. Elena hadn't come home either. Her bed, completely undisturbed, bore testimony to that. I didn't know what to do, so I walked up and down the stairs a few times, then sat down on the edge of my bed and stared out the window. The sky was still grisly, and the wind hadn't died down much either. It ripped the metal lid off our garbage can and blew it around the backyard, where it knocked against the tree and then smashed into the metal rungs on the picnic table. It stopped for a moment before the wind sent it across the yard and threw it up against the garage. The clattery metallic sound of it made the neighbor's dog nervous, and he started howling. I stared down at my bare feet, where small cold dots of purple swirled like marble in the whiteness. It didn't seem possible that just two days ago a family had inhabited this house, acting and functioning like one, getting up in the morning, taking baths and making breakfast, talking, hurrying not to be late. The house now felt like cold wet skins I wanted to cast off.

I thought maybe I should get dressed and eat my breakfast. I didn't know what else to do, so I pulled on a pair of wool pants and a sweater, and then wandered down to the dining room, where I sat alone at the table in Lana's chair. I couldn't eat, though. I could only sit there like I was supposed to and wait.

Elena came in after a while. She was silent as a snake, the way she slipped in the back door. She was still wearing Lana's coat and boots, and when she didn't take them off I knew she needed to wear them.

"Where were you?" I asked her.

"I slept in a barn," she said, sliding into her chair.

She must have been very upset to have slept in a barn, considering the way she felt about farms in general. I would even venture to guess that given a choice between a ghost-ridden attic and a barn, Elena would have chosen the ghost-ridden attic.

"Where's Leo?" I asked her. I stared across the table at her red, chapped cheeks.

Her eyes bolted open in shock. "He's not here?"

"No. He left before you left last night," I said, noticing the small, swollen cuts on her knuckles.

"He didn't come home?" I could see the fit underneath her eyes.

"I don't think so."

Elena was appalled. "I can't believe he just left you here, Maddie. I can't believe it." She got up and walked down to the end of the table and knocked one of the chairs over. It slammed against the hutch and then fell over sideways on the floor in a loud thwack. "He doesn't give a shit about us anymore, Maddie. He could care less now, now that he's got that job. That's all he cares about, that fucking job." She slammed her fist down on the hutch and hurled all the mail across the room, where it fell in a white shower all over the living room floor. "He didn't even look for me either." She knocked another chair over, and when she kicked it against the wall, I knew she was most hurt about that—that Leo hadn't looked for her.

She stormed over to the drafty window and stared angrily out at the vile day, across our shriveled lawn, to the deflated, brown hills in the distance. "Where the hell is he, Maddie?" Her breath was so warm, it fogged up the glass.

"I don't know. Maybe he went up to the Syracuse Hotel to get Lana." Somehow I knew that wasn't true, but I wanted to spare Elena another fit.

"I bet you he's up at the theater, Maddie," she said. Her eyes narrowed, and I could feel her mind turning. "I bet you he is." She stared at me for a few moments and then stormed out of the dining room, Lana's black coat trailing after her.

I followed her across the campus. She was like a steamroller, plowing forward in Lana's stylish boots, her eyes fixed straight ahead. She said one sentence the whole way up Heart Attack Hill. "He better not be up here, Maddie." I trailed along in her wake, hoping to God he wasn't. If I felt any anger toward Lana or Leo, it was submerged under the weight of my own corrosive guilt. Somewhere in the back of my mind I kept hearing, "It's your fault, Maddie. It's your fault," but I couldn't really think about it.

When we got to the theater, she put her hand on the doorknob and looked over at me. "It better not be open." I watched her hand as it turned the doorknob and held my breath as she pushed the door slowly, agonizingly open until we could finally see inside.

Leo was in there. Sadly, he was standing at the foot of the stage next to Bob Hendrix, wearing the same rumpled white shirt and black pants he'd worn last night, talking with seven students who were clustered up on the stage in a few round spots of light — six young women and one young man who stood in the center. They were all dressed in black tights and sweatshirts. We couldn't hear what they were saying, but at one point the man did a series of dance steps, the women following, their shiny black tap shoes clacking in unison on the wooden floor.

I looked at Elena to see what she was going to do. She pulled me into the open doorway and clutched my hand. Hers was cold and trembling, and I heard her ragged breath at my ear. "Get ready to run, Maddie."

"Okay, I'm ready."

Then she did it. She screamed in a voice that was too loud, a voice that was unstrung — a voice Garta would have used. "THANKS A LOT, LEO," she yelled. "THANKS A FUCKING LOT." She waited for them to stop speaking, to turn around and gape at us in the doorway — Leo's children, one dressed in a large coat and big boots, the other shivering without a coat. When she was sure Leo had seen us perfectly well, she whispered, "Okay, Maddie, run like hell."

I heard Leo call, not Elena's name, but my own, and for a moment I considered staying. He was here, though, I remembered. He wasn't in Syracuse with Lana, nor at home with us — he was on a stage, directing a group of tap dancers. I turned and fled the theater, trying in vain to catch up to Elena, throwing myself down Heart Attack Hill, but I couldn't close the distance between us. When she was near the bottom, I heard her unhinged voice sting the morning silence. "FUCK YOU, LEO," she cried out. "FUCK YOU."

She really thought it was all Leo's fault, but I didn't. It was partly my fault (though I couldn't tell her that), it was partly Leo's, and though it pained me to admit it, it was partly Lana's fault too. No matter how I looked at it, I couldn't deny that she had just up and left us. She hadn't even said good-bye or left us so much as a note. Elena thought if Leo hadn't taken the job, if he'd just stayed in Detroit and taught piano lessons in our living room, everything would have been all right. But I knew that wasn't completely true. Maybe Lana and Elena would have been happier, but what about Leo?

"He hated teaching piano lessons," I reminded her.

I watched her shed her dirty clothes and slip into a warm pair of wool pants. "Yeah, and now everyone else is unhappy, except Leo. Think about that, Maddie." She jammed her feet down into Lana's boots and threw on Lana's black coat again.

We looked out her bedroom window and saw Leo charging down the street, his gait long and loose, his arms flailing apelike at his sides. He looked too big for himself again, as if there was just too much of him to haul down a cold street. Neither one of us felt like seeing him, so we ran downstairs and escaped through the back door, racing across six neighboring lawns, until we felt it safe to reemerge on the street, on our way to school.

I didn't listen to Mrs. Devonshit the whole morning. I looked out the window and watched the wind rip the leaves off the trees and then push them across the playground, heaving them against the wooden dugouts at the end of the field. Lizzy and I met there after lunch and stabbed the ground with the toes of our shoes, not knowing quite what to say. She mentioned Minnie Harp a few times as a diversion, but Minnie's cut-out tongue was very far from my mind.

I spent the afternoon drawing in the palm of my hand with a black pen, losing myself so completely in the maze of lines and crosshatches that Mrs. Devonshit caught me and sent me into the bathroom with a can of Comet and a sponge. I stayed in there for a long time, filling the sink with water and letting it out, filling it again, until my fingertips looked like bleached prunes.

"I bet he's not home," Elena said when we climbed the porch steps after school. We stood outside in the cold wind for a few minutes, heaving small stones at the street sign, not wanting to open the door to find out.

When we finally went inside, Leo wasn't there. It was completely still and quiet, as if death had settled in. The house was warmer now that the furnace had been running all afternoon, but there was such an empty, ghostly feeling inside that it gave us the creeps. A gray air seemed to waft through the rooms and settle in the pits of our stomachs.

We drifted up to Lana's writing room, where we sat in her chair and stared out the window at the darkening brown hills. "No wonder she left, Maddie," Elena whispered. "This is what she looked at all day. It's so fucking ugly." I couldn't deny it. It was. It was depressingly desolate. The trees had lost most of their leaves and stood against the greasy yellow-gray sky like spindly skeletons. The hills were bald now, and the grass was no longer green. It was dried and brown and looked deathly ill, and the sound of the wind outside beating everything up only made it all worse. It was only four o'clock too, and it looked like it was half-night already.

By the time Leo got home Elena and I were sitting in the dining room in the pitch dark. In fact, the whole house was pitch dark. I wouldn't let Elena turn any of the lights on. I liked the idea of floating around in the darkness. It soothed me somehow.

When Leo flipped the light switch and found us eating our bologna sandwiches, his face fell. The skin just sort of slid down to his throat. He apologized three times and insisted on making us tomato soup and grilled cheese sandwiches, even though we told him we didn't want any. Or rather I told him—Elena wouldn't speak to him. She left the table almost immediately and went up to Lana's writing room, where she listened to one of Lana's Mozart records, full blast. All the while Leo ate his sticky grilled cheese sandwich and lumpy tomato soup, Mozart's dark, racing music filled our airless house. It was Elena's voice, I couldn't help but think.

As I watched him bolt down this meager supper, I knew that the Leo who sat across from me now was a very different Leo from the one who used to give us baths and make us dinner in Detroit. He was more his and less ours, I realized. I feared that the other Leo, the one Elena so desperately wanted back, was gone forever.

He looked up from his tomato soup and caught me staring at him. "I'm sorry, Maddie," he said, letting his spoon slide down the side of his bowl. "That guy from New York—he's very interested in what we're doing." He stopped and stared at me, waiting for me to say something, but I didn't know what to say. "He's produced shows on Broadway, sweetheart. He's got some pull down in New York." I nodded and he smiled thinly, and I noticed how deep and red the lines in his face were, how worried and haggard he looked.

I went upstairs not too long afterward and found Elena sitting in the chair in Lana's writing room, wearing Lana's white silk robe. She was bent over a notebook writing furiously, a torrent of words, which flowed smoothly from Lana's favorite Cross pen. The arm of the record player rocked in the last grooves—Mozart had ceased his melancholic dirge.

"What are you doing?" I asked her. I tried to look over her shoulder, but she crowded the page with her hands.

"Writing the bastard a letter." She hunched over even further, until I could only see the very top of the white paper.

I went over to the window and looked out at our backyard. It looked better at night. The dark covered up all the brown and gray, all the winter scars. "Leo said the guy from New York really likes his music."

"So?" She didn't even look up, that's how absorbed she was.

"Maybe he'll make a lot of money and get famous."

"I wouldn't count on it, Maddie. He's not that good." As if she had said it about me, a pang shot through my chest.

The phone rang downstairs. It only rang twice before Leo answered it. I ran out of the room, Elena dropping the notebook on the floor, following behind me in Lana's white silk robe. When we got there, Leo was standing in the dark kitchen, his fingers nervously twisting the cord again, while he stared vacantly out the kitchen window at the bush, which swayed and scratched against the glass. Elena and I slipped quietly into our chairs at the dining room table and listened to every word he uttered.

"When are you coming back?" he asked her. While he paused, those awful lines crept onto his face like worms. "This is the worst time, La," he complained. "Bob and I have a lot of work ahead of us if we're going to get this thing done by Christmas." Another long silence ensued, and then Leo spoke up boldly. "Lana, I want you to come home. You have two daughters who are wondering what the hell is going on."

He turned then and glanced over his shoulder at us. For a long time he didn't say anything. When he spoke again, he was yelling. "I don't care, Lana. I just don't care. I don't have the time now to be responsible for everything. I can't be doing *everything* now. I want you to come home tomorrow. You're not the only one *suffering*." He listened to her for a few more minutes and then glanced over his shoulder at us again. "Your daughters are waiting to talk to you," he said. And though I couldn't believe it, he told her again, "Just say hello to them."

She must have said no again, because Leo whispered, "Jesus Christ, La."

Elena rose up from the table and knocked her chair over. "TELL HER I DON'T WANT TO TALK TO HER EITHER." It was the same voice that had said, "Fuck you, Leo," at the bottom of Heart Attack Hill. She ran out of the dining room and pounded up the front stairs.

Leo hung up the phone and just stood there. "Why didn't she want to talk with us?" I said. I felt that lump materialize in my throat again. He started to say something, but on second thought he closed his mouth, and I got up and left too.

"You know, Maddie," Elena said bitterly from her bed, "it's going to be like this for the rest of our lives. Do you know that?" She was stretched out on top of the covers, the small light from the hallway falling gently on her face. We heard Leo climb the stairs. Then he appeared in Elena's doorway, a huge, dark silhouette. He sat down on the edge of Elena's bed and tried to lay his hand on her arm, but she shook him off like a fly.

"You two will have to forgive Lana," he said softly. "She's not herself right now."

"What is her self?" Elena wanted to know. The more I thought about it, the more I wondered what Lana's real self was too. Was it the woman I had seen collapse in Leo's arms like a baby, or was it the woman who'd made us breakfast and fed us fruit? Was it the woman who apologized for every transgression, minor or otherwise, or was it the one who had just now forgotten to talk to her children?

Leo lowered his face into the palms of his hands. At last he looked up, first at Elena, then at me. "A lot of things happened in Lana's life," he said. "Some of them bad, some of them horrible."

"Like what?" Elena said. *"Like what?"*

"It's up to Lana to tell you that. I can't tell you," he yelled.

He stared at us helplessly, and then Elena spoke up. "Then we'll never know, because she'll never tell us. For the rest of her life, she won't tell us."

"I wish I could tell you. If I could I would. It's her story, goddamn it. Don't you understand?"

When neither of us said anything, he left the room and went downstairs. When we couldn't hear his footsteps anymore, Elena heaved up and flopped down on her back in disgust. "She won't ever tell us, Maddie," she said bitingly. "This will go on for the rest of our lives, and it will only get worse. Then one day she'll end up in an *insane* asylum."

That word *insane* hung in the air as I stared at her and continued to sting the silence long after I turned away. Was Lana insane? I wondered. Was that what was wrong with her? Insanity? It had nothing to do with her heart or her stomach? It was her mind? I worried that nerves somehow led to insanity, and the more I considered it the more paralyzing the thought became. Was that what Lana meant when she told Leo she was afraid I was just like her? Was she afraid I was going to grow up to be insane? Spears stuck in my heart at the thought of it, and as if my life were about to veer off the face of the earth, I clutched the mattress.

"Maddie," Elena whispered. "Are you asleep?"

I couldn't answer her, and a long time passed in silence. I heard Leo come upstairs and go into Lana's writing room, where he pecked something out slowly on her typewriter. Elena tossed and turned in her bed, as if she suddenly possessed nerves, and quite a few cars passed in succession, their lights parading across our walls. Leo went into the bathroom after a while and took a long bath, and when he was done he came in and looked at us. He didn't say anything, nor did he touch us—he just stared at us across the darkness. I couldn't move, though. I held fast to the mattress, fearing that if I let go I might very well be hurtled out into the dark, seething universe.

Elena thought I was asleep. I hadn't moved in almost an hour by the time she got up and tiptoed into my room. I thought she was going to crawl in bed with me because Lana had deserted us and she needed to be near me, but then I heard the attic door yawn open slowly. I turned my head quietly and saw her standing on the threshold, bracing herself against the ghosts she feared lurked inside. She'd come prepared—she wore her coat and a pair of heavy white socks. After a few tense moments she stepped in and pulled the door closed behind her, although not completely—just in case.

I knew exactly what she was after. Lana's journals. With her loyalty to Lana flagging, she felt the courage to sail past those fierce wolves who guarded her conscience. All thoughts of insanity, mine or Lana's, dissolved instantly when I heard the sound of Elena's hands opening the cardboard box. I drifted quietly over to the door and watched her through the crack. The box was opened, and she was staring down inside it. I saw the indecision play across her brow; I saw it in her hands as they descended into the box twice and then drifted back to her sides. Do it, Elena, I thought anxiously. Do it, do it, do it. Finally, she reached down and grabbed the notebook. Her hands trembled, and for a moment she stared at it, as if it might speak to her or bite her or scream bloody murder. She opened it then, not to the first page as I had done, but to somewhere in the middle. She read a few sentences, and judging it to be worthy of her attention, she crept back to my red chair and sat down. I couldn't stand it any longer—I burst in, and without meaning to I scared the shit out of her.

"Jesus, Maddie," she panted. Her hand flew to her heart as if to keep it from pounding out of her chest.

I closed the door behind me and hurried back to the red chair, tripping over the rusty bedsprings. "You're reading one of Lana's journals." My breath came out in white gusts, and my feet were already turning blue in the cold.

"It's the same one you read."

I stepped over the board with the biggest crack and somehow collided with an old cobweb which hung down from the eave. "You read it too," I reminded her.

"Not until after you did, though," she said, as if that made it less of a crime.

I finally made it over to her and squatted down on the dusty floor at her feet, pulling my nightgown over my knees to preserve what little warmth I had left. "You have to let me read what you've already read," I said. Fair was fair and she knew it. Without a word she moved over in the chair, and after I crawled up next to her, she was good enough to take off her coat and spread it over both of us. I took hold of Lana's journal and pressed it open in our laps. The sprawling, loopy handwriting jumped out at me again, and I couldn't help but think, Lana is in these pages. There was more of her in here than either Elena or I had ever known.

"This is where I started," Elena said, touching the old inky date with her fingertip.

July 12, 1947.

"Lana was only twenty years old," Elena whispered. "That's only about seven years older than I am now."

We stared down at the pockmarked page and tried to imagine Lana so young. I conjured an image of her sitting on the shore on Long Island Sound, wearing her straw hat, her notebook perched on her knees as she alternately wrote and then stared out across the choppy water.

The wind picked up outside a little and rattled the window. I longed for the summer, for the breeze to wander in to cool our brows, for the insects to keep us company as we bent over Lana's journal. It was cold, though—the light was weak and yellow, and we had to huddle together under Elena's coat just to stay warm.

She read it softly to me, her index finger tracing a path through Lana's crooked scrawl.

I did what Effy told me. I went up to 125th St., near the Audubon Ballroom, and waited for Sticks outside the drugstore. It was hotter than hell and he was late, and all the Negroes were staring at me. Sticks finally came ambling up the street. He was six feet tall and skinny; he wore a black cap and a scrawny goatee. His eyes looked glassy, like he was loaded up on something, and his fingernails were lady long. He was pissed off that she'd sent me. "What the fuck it gonna look like, me standing here with you?" he said out of the side of his mouth. "I can't give you this." He spit and then looked up and down the street and spit again. "You tell Effy don't she never do this again."

He made me walk up the street alone and drop Effy's envelope in the trash can on the corner. I waited across the street near the bus stop while he walked up to the trash can, took the envelope, and dropped Effy's snow. I had to stand there until he was out of sight before I could go back to the trash can and pick it up.

I shoved it down my bra and went up to Mimi's and snuck up the back stairs. It was still early enough—hardly anyone was up. I could hear Mimi on the first floor, though, yelling at Leonard about something that had happened last night. I walked as softly as I could, but the old stairs groaned, and I was afraid Mimi would hear me. I crept down the dim wooden hallway past Delors's and Charette's rooms on tiptoe and stopped in front of Effy's door. She was waiting for me inside. The shades were pulled and Billy was singing on the radio, "I'll Never Be the Same." The morning sun shone through them and bathed her room in a soft, yellow light. It was a beautiful room, considering—the dark sleigh bed, the rose red satin cover, the tall lamps with the white fringe shades, even the wallpaper with the white background and the tiny, pink rosebuds. I love the big windows too, the way the breeze comes through.

Effy was sitting at her dressing table in her white silk robe and froufrou slippers. I handed her the snow and watched her dark eyes flash.

"Thanks, La," she said. There's no one who says my name better than Effy.

I watched her like I always do, though I found it disturbing. She put the snow on top of the dresser, broke it up with the Ace of Spades, and then took it up her right nostril. Her left one is no good anymore. It is starting to work on her. I can see it's starting to eat her up, like it ate up Yvette and Charisse. She is still the most beautiful woman I have ever known, but her bones are starting to rattle around under her skin. I still love her, though. I love her better than anyone.

"You gonna go down to that club and talk to Sammy?" she asked me, rubbing some of the powder on her upper gums. "You're too good for Mimi's," she said. "You know that, La."

I nodded my head and watched her wrap her head in a red taffeta scarf. I'll go tomorrow maybe.

We heard someone out in the hallway. The steps were loud and heavy, and I thought it was Leonard until I looked down at my watch. It was too early for anyone.

"It ain't time yet," Effy said, glancing over at the little clock on the windowsill.

Sticks barged through the door and scared the shit out of us. He must have followed me up the back stairs. Mimi would never have let him in. He closed the door behind him and leaned up against it hard. "Nigger bitch," he yelled. "Where's the rest?" He held up the envelope with Effy's money. "You twenty dollars short. Give it over, or I'll have to do you, Effy, and you know I don't want nothing to do with that." Effy stood up and told him she'd give it to him in a few days, but he wanted it now. "Nobody stiffs me. You hear?"

They started to scream at each other, Effy cursing him out, Sticks yelling at her like she was a dog, and I knew Mimi was going to hear them. She was going to kill us all.

"I've got twenty bucks," I said, digging down into my purse for it.

He looked at me and then at Effy. "Some stupid hole you are—sending this white bitch down in the morning."

He forgot about guarding the door and stormed over to Effy and grabbed her by the shoulders. I thought he was going to kill her, his eyes were so crazed, so I rushed over to him and tried to give him the money. He threw Effy down on the bed, and the damn thing broke. It went down and the whole house shook. Then I heard Mimi's hell-bent footsteps on the front stairs.

He wheeled around and grabbed the money from my hand, and Mimi lurched into the room. Her eyes went from Effy, to Sticks, and then landed on me. They filled with her usual cheap rage. "Leonard," she screamed. "Leonard." Sticks pushed past her and fled the room, crashing down the back stairs. Charette and Delors stumbled out of their rooms, rubbing the sleep out of their eyes, and drifted into the doorway. "Go down to the office," Mimi yelled at me. "Go down there right now." She gave me her vile eyes, and I took one last look at Effy. She was sprawled on the collapsed bed, rubbing her chin with her hands. When I see her like this, it does bad things to me. I can't ever get it out of my mind. When I try to sleep at night, it surfaces in my thoughts like a phosphorescent movie screen that plays over and over and over again. Then it falls down to my heart and burns there.

I quietly closed the door behind me and stood outside for a few moments while Mimi screamed at Effy.

"I keep this place clean. I protect you better than any other place in Harlem. I pay you more than anyone else. And you reward me with this shit!" Blah, blah, blah.

Mimi doesn't begin to understand her part in this sordidness. She doesn't realize it all starts with her.

I went down to her office and told Leonard to make sure Sticks wasn't in the house and waited for Mimi to come down. I sat down on the edge of her big mahogany desk and stared out the window. The sidewalk was baking in the morning sun. I could hear the sound of a hundred fans beating out their *madrigals in the heat-stroked air. I glanced around Mimi's office. You would think she was a business tycoon—the huge desk, the velvety drapes, the bookshelves filled with books she's never read. She can't even pronounce half the titles. Her paintings too—as if Mimi really understands high art.*

I toyed with the idea of going back to our apartment, but she would only follow me down there. Besides, she came down with Leonard a few minutes later, and I heard them checking the downstairs parlor for Sticks. He wasn't there, though. He just wanted his $20.00—he didn't give a shit about Mimi's place.

She stormed into the office after that and slammed the door and then stood there and glared at me. I hovered over by the window and screwed my eyes up so everything went blurry.

"I told you I don't want you going up there," she yelled. "What in the hell do I have to do to keep you out of there? Everytime I turn around you're up there with Effy or Delors, or crazy Ummy. And now you bring scum and drugs into my house. What in the hell is wrong with you?"

Paper is not a good medium to communicate the sound of Mimi's voice. The pitch alone would send big dogs running for cover. I turned around and stared at her dyed black hair, coiffed to such starchy perfection that if a tornado blew through the room, it would not have moved. Her eyes, loaded down with blue eye shadow, fixed on me again.

"Answer me, goddamn it. What in the hell is wrong with you?"

She really thinks there is something wrong with me. How can I tell her it is her fault? She can't understand this. Who did she think raised me? Her? Don't make me laugh. I couldn't answer her, though, because all I wanted to say was, "Fuck you, Mimi. Fuck you."

"I send you to the best damn schools and you seek out niggers."

"Don't call them that," I yelled. "You make your living off them."

She came after me. I moved away from the window, toward the door, but she caught me. Her fingers bit down into my shoulders. "I make a better life for you, and what do you do—you run out and buy drugs from a Harlem nigger." It enraged her so much she slapped me.

"I don't want a better life," I yelled.

She slapped the other side of my face. Bravo, Mimi. Bravo and fuck you.

"You're going to have a better life," she yelled. "You're going to forget Effy and the rest of them. They're animals and you're better than they are."

"They are not animals," I screamed. They are not animals. I repeat, They . . . are . . . not . . . animals.

Mimi stared at me for quite a while, and then her eyes shifted down to my red dress. She pinched the thin cotton of the sleeve between her fingers. *"This is cheap,"* she said lowly. *"Why aren't you wearing your Chanel suit?"*

"It's one hundred degrees out, Mimi. Nobody wears a Chanel suit in the summer."

"It's Sunday. You should be wearing your Chanel suit, I don't care how hot it is."

This is what I live with day in and day out.

The phone rang. It was one of her steerers, probably Greer. The after-church crowd is starting up — that disgusting tide of paunch-bellied hypocrites. It was Mr. Larkin. He wants Ummy again. Has to have Ummy — the blackest and the craziest. I saw him once through the keyhole, cringing on his hands and knees, with Ummy, greased up and looming over him, slapping his pink white ass. Another image I can't get rid of. It floats up in my mind at the strangest times — when I'm walking through a crowd of white people, when I'm folding the clothes, when I'm eating Chinese food with chopsticks.

I slipped upstairs to see how Effy was doing. She said Sticks knocked two of her teeth loose. The bastard. She was sitting on the window ledge crying. I sat down next to her and held her hand.

"Mimi said she's going to fire me, La," she sobbed. *Louis Armstrong was playing on the radio. "Ain't Misbehavin' " — one of Effy's favorites.*

"She won't," I said. *"She always says that. Anyway, I won't let her."*

She put her arms around me, and I felt torn up inside again. How can I tell Mimi not to fire her when I think she ought to walk out of Mimi's house forever? She shouldn't have to do this, and people like Mimi should be put away.

What's wrong with this fucking world anyway? White men skulking around these dimly lit hallways, fucking Negro whores in smelly closed-off rooms, and then calling them animals behind their backs. Things are so dead wrong, I don't understand. If Negroes are so inferior, why are white men always coming around asking for the blackest, and if they're so much less, why do white people stand in line to hear them sing?

If some guy came into the room with a gun and told me I had to decide whether he was going to shoot Effy or Mimi, I would tell him to shoot Mimi. I have no preference for white. Some of the worst people I know are white.

Effy asked me once if I wished I were a Negro. I told her I felt like I was partly Negro. I grew up in Effy's arms — I listened to Effy's stories, I learned Effy's songs. I ate her food, I slept in her bed, I touched her skin. That was before Mimi put her in the house — back when Effy still had some dignity. When I asked her if she wished she were white, she said, "No, child. Never."

"You go over to Sammy's," Effy whispered in my ear. "I don't want you working at Mimi's anymore. You're too good for Mimi. You've got something to do with your life that doesn't include sticking around with Mimi. You're somebody, La."

The way she said it scared me. The words seemed to come from a grave. They wavered in the air, and it gave me a creeping chill. It reminded me of the time Effy predicted James Irving would be killed, and a week later he was.

She kissed my forehead and hugged me close to her bones. "You got to leave this ugly place, child. You hear?"

Leonard knocked on the door. Mr. Larkin was standing nervously behind him, a fat creepy man with a bald pate and a lot of money. He was wearing a blue seersucker suit and a pair of shiny black shoes. He'd just come from church. When he saw me he lowered his eyes in shame. Ummy was sick, Leonard said, so Effy had to take him. Mimi did it to be mean, because Effy hates crazy shit. Leonard gave her a few minutes to pull herself together. I helped her fix her hair, and we greased up her arms and legs with mineral oil, so she would shine. I knew he wouldn't touch her, but it bothered me to grease her up like that. It made me sick, and I knew it wouldn't leave my thoughts for months. I can't see things like this. It makes me do crazy things.

If a genie came to me and granted me three wishes, I'd take Effy out of the house and give her back her dignity, I'd ask for a lot of money, and I'd stop Mimi from going on.

That was the end of the July 12 entry. Our fingers trembled along the edges of the page, and we hardly breathed.

"Mimi had a whorehouse," Elena whispered. Her eyes were the size of quarters. "That's why she was in prison."

I nodded, while the word *whorehouse* swept through my mind. I knew what it was, although I realized I had never once thought about one. Lizzy had taught me enough about these things for me to understand at least what went on in a whorehouse.

"That's why Lana doesn't want us to know about Mimi," Elena whispered. The wind pressed against the window, sending a cold draft through the cracks, and we dug ourselves deeper under Elena's coat. The mystery of why Mimi had been imprisoned vanished into the chilly night, and it finally made sense to us why Lana had kept Mimi from us all these years. She didn't want us to know about whorehouses. She didn't want us to know a woman who had run one as coldly and dispassionately as Mimi had. It made perfect sense to me why Lana had called her a terrible woman too, and when I remembered how she'd shuddered in the darkness when I'd asked her why, I suddenly understood that as well.

All the vows I made the other night to straighten myself out, to be good, and to leave Lana's journals alone took flight from my mind, and I slowly turned the page. "Let's read one more," I whispered to Elena.

"Okay, but just one." We repositioned ourselves under the warm tent of her coat, and just when Elena bent forward to go on reading, we heard Leo outside in my room.

"Maddie," he called out. "Where are you guys?"

We heard the floorboards creak underneath his heavy footsteps, and we stared at each other, our eyes frozen open. A paralysis overtook Elena immediately, so I grabbed the notebook, slammed it shut, and shoved it underneath my butt.

"If we have to get up," I whispered quickly, "you go first."

Elena nodded and squeezed my hand. Then the door opened and Leo stood at the threshold hunched over and squinting. It took him a few moments to find us back in that red chair.

"What are you guys doing?"

Elena didn't say anything. She didn't have to—she wasn't really speaking to him, so it was up to me.

"We're just sitting here," I said. I shifted my weight and felt the sharp edge of Lana's journal press into my thigh.

"Oh," he said. He didn't know what to think. He just stood there hunched over and stared at us. That's when I noticed the box. The flaps were standing straight up in the air, as if to announce, like waving arms, that we had violated it. It wasn't as bad as if Lana had been standing there, but even so it was bad enough.

"Mind if I come in?" I'm sure he was planning on sitting down somewhere to talk to us about Lana again, but Elena said she was going to bed, and then she heaved up and left me with the notebook stashed under my butt.

"What are you going to do, Maddie?" Leo asked.

"I just want to sit here by myself." What else could I say? I was glad at least that Elena had left her coat with me. I don't know what I would have done had she left me sitting there freezing with the journal under my butt.

She brushed past him, a stiff January breeze, and after he stared at me for a few moments, he slowly closed the door behind him. I waited to hear his heavy footsteps leave my room and then Elena's, before I got up and lowered Lana's journal into the box. As I laid it down I noticed that the journal directly underneath had a small lock on it. I pawed down a few more—they were all locked, all of them except this one. It didn't surprise me that they were all locked. What surprised me was that this one was not. There were at least ten of them, and as I closed the flaps to the box, I kept seeing myself cutting them open with Leo's jackknife.

I hurried back to my room and threw myself under the covers. My hands were stinging cold, and my feet felt like frozen fish. "God, Elena," I whispered. A dozen conflicting emotions convulsed through my body, my insides swarming with fear and excitement, dread and thrill. What had we done? I wondered. I glanced over my shoulder at the small sliver of white moon, and a pang shot through me. We had broken our vow to the moon, I realized, and when it occurred to me that Lana had felt our hands on her journal and had sent Leo into the attic to catch us, my heart banged inside my chest like an old washing machine.

I felt the magnitude of our collective guilt as if it were red and hot and on fire. Then a fever swept through me, a boiling fever of both longing and guilt.

"I'm afraid we've pushed her farther away," I choked out.

"I'm afraid of that too, Maddie." Her voice trembled in the quiet, and it made me worry all over again that I'd sent Lana away in the first place. If that were true, then we had really done it now.

"What if we made her worse?" I whispered. I slid my cold hands underneath my back and lay there frozen.

"I don't know, Maddie."

It really weighed on her, though. She hardly said a word to me or Lizzy the next day, during both our morning walk to school and our afternoon walk home. She still wore Lana's coat and boots and had added her red scarf and black leather gloves, which made me think she must have forgiven Lana for not wanting to talk to us. Lizzy didn't know what to say in our silence and trailed after me as I trailed after Elena. She knew something had happened. She knew Elena and I were concealing something, and she even asked me, but I couldn't tell her about the journals. Anything else, but not the journals.

When we got home Leo wasn't there. Gus was. He couldn't be there so he called Barbara Lamb and asked her to look after us, but instead of coming herself she loaned us Gus. Elena was furious about it and threw a fit in her bedroom. She ripped the covers off her bed and stomped all over them with Lana's boots, and then shoved the mattress halfway off the bedsprings where it teetered like a seesaw.

"I can't believe he didn't come home, Maddie," she yelled. She stormed over to the window and rapped her knuckles so hard against the wavy old glass, I thought it would break.

"He sent Gus," I reminded her. It wasn't as good as being there himself, but it wasn't as bad as eating our bologna sandwiches in the dark.

"He sent Barbara Lamb, and Barbara Lamb sent Gus," she yelled. For some reason, that bothered her more than if Leo had just asked Gus to begin with. I guess she didn't like the idea that we'd been passed down a chain.

"That would kill Lana if she knew he asked Barbara Lamb," she said. "She hates Barbara Lamb." It was true. Lana was none too fond of Barbara Lamb, and the idea that Leo had called her up would have really upset her. Garta would have been a better choice.

Elena leaned her forehead against the cold glass and stared blindly out the window at the fading shadows. "I'm leaving," she announced. "I'm getting the fuck out of here."

She turned and plowed across her room, through the tangle of sheets and blankets and past the teetering mattress, which she gave one last kick. When we asked her where she was going, she said she didn't know. We followed her down the front stairs anyway and out to the porch, and we would have kept going except she wouldn't let us. She said we couldn't come, that she wanted to be alone, so we pressed our faces against the porch windows and watched her disappear down the light-hazy street dressed in Lana's clothes.

Lizzy and I threw on our coats and retreated to the attic, where we sat huddled in the red chair in silence. We could vaguely hear Gus down in the kitchen making our dinner. It was comforting to know that someone was down there keeping the house from emptiness, but nonetheless I sensed a tombish silence. It wore on me, and I felt the strongest urge to tell Lizzy about Effy and Sticks and Mimi, as if that would plug up the quiet.

"Lizzy," I whispered, shrugging under my coat. "I'm going to tell you something I found out about Lana, but you can never tell anyone, especially not Elena."

After she crossed her heart and swore to God she would never tell a soul, I told her that Elena and I had found two pages of Lana's old journal in her papers. I hunched down in the chair and whispered, "I know why Mimi was in prison."

"Why?" she said. Her eyes, so warm and liquid, inspired me.

I shimmied down in the chair until there wasn't more than six inches between our eyes, and said quietly, but very precisely, "Mimi had a whorehouse." I watched with pleasure as the shock registered in her eyes and then radiated out to her face, wrinkling her forehead and settling in her jaw.

"*A whorehouse?*"

I nodded slowly and evenly. "She had Negro whores," I whispered, and then, as best I could, I told her about Effy, Ummy, and Delors, Sticks, Leonard, and Mr. Larkin. When I was sure I had told her everything I stopped speaking, and Lizzy just stared at me, her eyes blinking twice as fast as normal.

"Lana wasn't a whore, was she?" She closed her mouth slowly and swallowed.

"No. Mimi didn't like her to hang around with them. That's why she got so mad when she found her up in Effy's room."

"What did Lana do at Mimi's, then?" she asked me. I hadn't the slightest idea actually, but I knew she had done something there. Why else would Effy have told her she was too good for Mimi's?

Lizzy wanted me to show her the pages, but I told her Leo had caught us last night and had taken them away. She wanted to find them, and if not those pages then some other ones, so I was obliged to let her check Lana's desk. She shook it and pounded it from underneath to see if that would free the drawer. She even stuck the thinnest blade of her jackknife into the keyhole, but I wasn't worried. Elena and I had tried that long ago and had learned that the desk was as impenetrable as Lana. She rummaged through the blank pages on Lana's desk, and only after she checked under Lana's writing chair did she give up.

"Maybe Lana went to buy more drugs from Sticks," Lizzy said while we sat out on the front porch wrapped in our coats. "Maybe Effy didn't send enough money again, and then Sticks came after

Effy and Lana was there. Maybe Sticks beat up Effy and Lana tried to save her, so he beat up Lana too and broke her hip. Maybe the bed broke again too and fell on top of her."

"What about the jazz?" I said. The jazz had to come in somewhere.

"Maybe it was playing on the radio. You said there was a radio in Effy's room. Right?" She was absolutely right. Lana had written that. That was it, then. That is what happened. Sticks had beaten Lana up and broken her hip. It made perfect sense to us, and we agreed that Lana had never told us because she didn't want us to know she had been involved with dangerous drugs.

Lizzy and I were so happy we had finally figured something out about Lana that when Leo came home and made us go out looking for Elena, we floated out into the night. Leo was wretched, though— I think he would have sacrificed a finger to have found her.

"So Gus wasn't good enough?" he kept asking us.

"She wanted you to be there," I told him, which forced him to retrace our steps over to the track again and back up Heart Attack Hill. We didn't find her, and it wasn't until after Lizzy went home and I lay in my bed listening to the faraway sound of Leo doing the wash that I remembered Elena had slept in a barn the last time she had run away. I went down to the cellar and told him, and he slumped against the washing machine, sick at the thought of it.

We asked Garta if we could borrow her car, since Lana had ours, and she was good enough to let us, just as long as she could come along. She brought Lizzy and Jimmy, and on the whole, she behaved fairly well—for Garta, anyway. We all piled into her station wagon and Leo drove around the back roads, stopping at all the barns we could find, looking inside for Elena. He led the way with a flashlight, while Lizzy and I walked on either side of him calling out her name. He said he was afraid if he called her name, she would run deeper into the woods.

We looked inside over twelve barns that night, without finding her. When we got home, Leo finally called the sheriff and told him Elena was missing, and then he sat up at the dining room table half the night waiting for her.

She showed up at eleven o'clock the next morning outside Mrs. Devonshit's classroom. She knocked on the door and asked for me. Given how she looked, so distraught and rumpled in Lana's winter clothes, Mrs. Devonshit couldn't refuse her.

"Where did you go?" I asked her after I stepped out into the deserted hallway.

"Never mind," she said. Her face looked awful; it was tight and pinched, and her pale white forehead was knotted. I looked down at Lana's boots and noticed that they were covered with mud.

"Leo borrowed Garta's car last night, and we drove all over looking in barns for you," I said. She didn't exactly smile, but I saw some of the tension vanish from her brow.

"I want to go up to the Syracuse Hotel to see Lana." She looked over her shoulder to make sure no one was in the hallway. It was empty—there was just a broad beam of sunlight cutting across the floor, which faded almost instantly.

"How will we get there?"

She pulled out a limp ten-dollar bill she had stolen from Leo's wallet and waved it in the air. "We'll take the Greyhound bus."

I wanted to take Lizzy, but Elena said no. She said Lana was in no condition to see people who were not in our family. I told her I thought Lizzy was family, but she reminded me how painful it was for Lana to be seen like that. She grabbed my coat and hat from my locker and shoved them into my hands. "Let's go," she said.

When Mrs. Devonshit wasn't looking I passed in front of the door, and we did that which I thought was impossible—we walked out the front doors and down the sidewalk, unseen and untouched, and headed downtown to the Colgate Pharmacy, where we bought two one-way tickets to Syracuse. I think George, the owner, only sold them to us because Elena looked so much older dressed up in Lana's clothes. He didn't ask us anything. He just took Elena's soggy ten-dollar bill, handed us the tickets, and in less than fifteen minutes we caught the first Greyhound bus to Syracuse.

There were only five other people on board—two gray-haired ladies with fur hats and wicker purses, a heavy-set man wearing a wrinkled navy blue polyester suit, and a young red-haired woman and her red-haired baby—all of whom sat up near the front. We walked to the back of the bus and sat down in the last seat. As soon as the bus left Hamilton Elena shimmied down in our seat and rested her knees against the metal back of the seat ahead of us, pulling Lana's collar up around her ears. She wasn't really talking. Whatever had happened to her last night was sobering enough to silence her. I tried to find out where she had stayed and asked her whether or not she had eaten, but she didn't want to tell me. So I watched the barren trees as we raced past them, noticing with a depressing ache how gray and leaky the skies were. I longed for the summer, for the fragrant green, the embracing air, for Lana's fashion shows and Minnie Harp's tulips, for the sound of children and lawn mowers and television sets spilling out through open windows.

I felt a desperate need to talk, to fill in the stale sound of no one speaking, of the mechanical roar of the bus and the rubbery flop flop of the tires on the cold, contracting concrete. In the silence, I felt my nerves do something that I had never felt them do before—as if some horrible force were let loose upon them, like an impelling wind, they strained, just strained.

"I figured something out about Lana last night," I said loudly. I wanted to drown out the torpored, dreary silence.

The mention of Lana brought her around, not resoundingly, but at least marginally. "What?" she said, glancing over at me. I could only see her eyes and her forehead. The rest of her face was obscured by Lana's hiked-up collar.

"I think Lana must have bought some more drugs from Sticks for Effy, and Effy didn't put enough money in the envelope, just like the last time. So Sticks came after Effy again. He beat her up, and then when Lana tried to save her, he beat her up too and broke her hip." I knew I was talking too loud, but I couldn't help myself—the closed-up silence was sickening. "And the whole time he was beating her up, breaking her hip, the jazz was playing."

Elena stared at me for a few moments. Her eyes went slippery, and I could tell she felt sorry for me. "That's not what happened, Maddie." She hiked the collar up again and shrugged her shoulders underneath Lana's coat.

"How do you know?"

"I just know—that's not what happened. Besides, it was Leo's jazz and it couldn't have been playing on the radio, because it was never published."

The way she said this last—*it couldn't have been playing on the radio, because it was never published*—sounded so informed I knew she knew something more about it.

"What do you think happened, then?" I asked. My voice leapt from me like a radio turned on full blast.

"Shh, Maddie," Elena said, clapping her hand over my mouth. "Jesus, the whole bus is going to hear you."

The man with the polyester suit and the red-haired woman with the baby turned around and stared at me. I slunk down in the seat and rested my knees up against the metal back of the seat ahead of us. "What happened, then?"

"I don't know, but I know it wasn't that." She stared out the window and clammed up after that, and the dreadful silence rolled in again, settling around me like dust.

The bus dropped us off a few blocks from the Syracuse Hotel, and the man with the polyester suit told us how to get there. We bent our heads against the wind and walked straight for two blocks, and then made a left at a busy intersection. Across the street and a few buildings down, the Syracuse Hotel rose up from the dirty concrete looking stately and regal in the poor gray light. Amid the shabby brown buildings and run-down storefronts, it stood like a jewel.

We crossed the street and walked underneath the green awning, where we stopped and shifted our weight from one hip to the other, debating whether or not we should go inside and ask for Lana. Now that we were standing right in front of it there was something intimidating about the Syracuse Hotel. We could see the plush red carpet floors and the soaring ceilings through the revolving glass doors. It didn't look like a place you could just walk into.

"What if she's really bad?" Elena said, staring out at the thick traffic. "If she is, it will be awful to see her, and it will make her worse to see us seeing her so bad."

"But we came all the way up here, Elena," I reminded her. "Let's take her something like a candy bar. We could say we came to bring her a candy bar, and if she's really bad we'll just leave."

Elena liked that idea—it had an escape route in it—so we went inside the lobby of the Syracuse Hotel and stood in front of the newsstand trying to decide whether Lana would prefer a Nestle Crunch or an Almond Joy. "Get the Almond Joy," Elena finally said.

When I reached up to grab the Almond Joy, I noticed a whole neat stack of the *New York Times*. They were piled up on the counter next to the Snickers candy bars, and while Elena paid for the Almond Joy, I laid my hand on top of them just to feel them.

We walked across the lobby to the concierge desk and told the man behind the counter that we were looking for Lana. She was in Room 51B, he said, and then he called her up on a phone and told her that her two daughters were down in the lobby. When he hung up he told us how to get up there. I was relieved that she hadn't asked him to tell us to go away. The thought, awful as it was, had crossed my mind.

All the way up the elevator and down the long, red corridors, the hurricanes blew in my veins, my nerves straining against them. Of all the things they did, this was the worst, worse even than slipping under my kneecaps.

When we got to Room 51B, Harry opened the door. He was so glad to see us that he plowed into both of us and waited while we put our arms around him and kissed his baby-scented head. He pulled us into the room after that. It was bathed in shadows, and there in the darkest pocket lay Lana. She was stretched out on the queen-sized bed, lying perfectly still on top of the white bedspread, her legs uncrossed, her face half obscured by a wet blue washcloth.

"Lana," Harry whispered, tiptoeing across the beige carpet. "Maddie and Elena are here." Elena and I followed him in, walking softly behind him, stopping at the edge of the bed where he stopped.

Lana spoke with a voice neither Elena nor I had ever heard. Her throat sounded raw, and her voice splintered into a raspy whisper. "That's nice, Harry," she said. One of her hands made a slow journey from her side to the washcloth, where she picked up one corner enough so that we could see her right eye.

"How are my girls?" There was nothing left to her voice but a choked whisper. Elena and I looked at one another, and the awful winds picked up inside my veins. She was a lot worse than we had expected, and it was hard to look at her knowing that we might have been responsible for it.

I stepped forward first. "Hi, Lana," I whispered. "We brought you an Almond Joy."

"Thank you, sweetheart." Her hand rose up slowly above her head and pointed shakily at the bedstand next to her. I moved quietly over to it and laid the candy bar next to a glass of water and two aspirin bottles, one of which was empty. She grew up in a whorehouse, I thought. I looked down at her face, at her feverish, cracked lips, and I knew she would never look the same to me again.

"What's wrong, Lana?" Elena whispered. "Are you sick?"

"Yes, I think so." She raised the corner of the washcloth so she could see us.

"What's wrong?" I said. I noticed that there were broken blood vessels in her eye. They looked like little red cracks against the white.

"I don't know," she struggled to say.

We drifted closer to her, and Elena took one of her hands, while I took the other.

"How did you get here?"

"We took the Greyhound bus up," Elena said. "Leo doesn't know."

Lana winced at the mention of his name. "How have you been?" she asked us, her right eye slowly roving our faces.

Elena shifted her weight from one hip to the other, and though I could hardly believe it she whispered, "Leo doesn't come home until late."

"What do you mean?" Lana asked. She started to sit up, but as soon as she moved a low moan fled from the back of her throat, and she fell back on the bed.

"He doesn't come home until after dark," Elena whispered, "and last night he called up Barbara Lamb to come over and make us dinner. She couldn't, but she sent Gus."

"Gus?" Lana said. I watched a wave of something—dread, panic, I didn't know what—sweep through her body and radiate out to her limbs.

"Yes," Elena whispered.

"Oh God," Lana said. She pulled the washcloth down over her hot eye, and I saw her lips twitch. I shot Elena a dirty look and stepped on her toes.

"We miss you, Lana," Elena whispered, and I echoed the same.

"I've missed you too." Harry crawled delicately onto the bed and took up his position next to her. I noticed his coloring books lying there, and his plastic soldiers strewn along Lana's side. He had been playing there for hours, perhaps days.

"You said Leo called Barbara Lamb to come and look after you?" Lana whispered. She reached out and patted Harry's knee, as if to assure herself that he was still there.

"Yes," Elena said.

"And Gus came instead?"

Elena muttered another yes, and Lana's face made a grievous twist under the washcloth. I wondered how Elena could be so cruel as to tell her this.

"Give me that trash can, Maddie," she said in another choked whisper.

I looked down near my feet and discovered a white plastic trash can which was filled partially with vomit. I handed it to her, and after she struggled to sit up, she put it between her legs and heaved three or four times, moaning out the saddest, most pained sounds I had ever heard.

Elena ran downstairs to find a doctor, while I flushed the puke down the toilet. I crept back to her bed and drew small pictures on her forehead with my finger, like she asked me to do, worrying all the while that Elena and I had brought her to this. She grew up in a whorehouse, I kept telling myself. I couldn't look at her anymore without having this thought.

She asked me to get her some aspirin, and when I picked up the bottle, I noticed something which wouldn't leave my mind for the rest of the night. Lana's most recent diary entries, written on Syracuse Hotel stationery, were lying on top of the bedstand, obscured only by a black fountain pen. Having never expected us to come, she hadn't attempted to hide them. I couldn't read them then, but I knew sooner or later I would read them.

Elena came back up about fifteen minutes later with a doctor the hotel had managed to find. He was old and greatly overweight, but he was kind to Lana, careful to whisper and to turn the light on only when it was necessary. He asked her some questions about the headache she described as splitting, and when he shone a small flashlight into her eyes, it hurt her so much she couldn't help but moan.

"You've got a migraine," he told her. "I could give you a couple of pills, but they would put you to sleep. Is there anyone whom I could call to take care of your children?"

"My husband," Lana whispered. "But the girls are fine. They can look after Harry."

The doctor called Leo anyway, but he wasn't home, to which Elena replied, "I told you so." He called Colgate University and left a message. We didn't really need him, though, so it was decided that we would order dinner in our room, and after Harry was packed off to bed Lana could take those pills.

She couldn't eat, but the three of us did, taking turns changing her washcloth while she whispered her thanks and her ever-present apologies. We gave Harry a bath and put him to bed on the small red sofa. After he fell asleep, Elena and I gave Lana two orange pills and watched as she drifted off to a painless oblivion. We sat by her side for an hour or so, drinking her in, grateful to be in her presence, no matter how nominal it was.

"What if we did this to her?" I whispered to Elena. We were sitting up, our backs against the wooden headboard, while Lana lay on her side next to us, the soft blanket pulled up over her shoulder.

"Don't think about it, Maddie. We can't let ourselves think about it." A shudder passed through her and she slid down on her back, closing her eyes in a wince. How could she expect me not to think about it when Lana lay two inches away from us, so sick she had to be drugged?

The telephone rang, but Elena wouldn't let me pick it up. "Let it ring. Let him eat his bologna sandwich in the dark." I worried that all the ringing would wake Lana up, but it didn't.

I waited for Elena to fall asleep before I called Lizzy. I was going to call Leo to put his mind at ease, but I decided not to. I knew he would be pacing around the empty house, sick with worry, but somehow that seemed only right. I stared at the beige walls and the red velvet curtains for a long time, waiting for Elena's breathing to grow long, half listening to the distant sounds of the hotel, to the ding of the elevator, to people walking quietly down the hallway, and to their voices in the nearby rooms. The traffic outside had slowed to the point where I could barely hear it. My eyes drifted over to Lana. It was so hard to imagine her sitting in the room of a whorehouse wrapped in Effy's arms. I tried to envision her buying drugs from Sticks, but I couldn't do that either. The Lana I knew was a very different person.

When I was sure Elena was asleep, I quietly picked up the heavy black phone and dialed Lizzy's number. It didn't even ring once before Lizzy answered it. She'd been waiting all night for me to call.

"What happened?" She sounded a little crazed from waiting so long.

"Lana's got a bad migraine. A really bad one. She puked in a garbage pail."

"Really?" I heard her closet door click shut.

"Yes," I said. "I can't talk long because I might wake them up, but I wanted to tell you that what we thought last night is wrong."

"About Sticks beating up Effy and Lana?" she whispered.

"Yeah." I paused for a moment to make sure neither Elena nor Lana had woken up. "I told Elena that on the bus, and she told me we were wrong, that that isn't what happened. She knows something more than we do, but she won't tell me."

"None of it was right?" she asked. She sounded miserable.

"Not any of it."

I hung up shortly, and Leo called. I picked it up on the first ring and whispered, "Hello." He wanted to know how everyone was. I told him Lana had a migraine and was asleep. He talked about the old times when we'd all been together, when Lana was well and we'd had fun. I don't know why, but his conversation started the hurricane up in my veins. Maybe it was the comparison between our old life and our life now that did it. Or maybe it was the fact that not more than a foot away from me lay Lana, delivered from a hell I didn't understand. Or maybe it was the idea of Leo sitting alone in our house talking to me, not to Lana or Elena, but to me, as if I were somehow their representative.

"I'm coming up to get you all tomorrow morning."

I could just see Elena rolling her eyes and saying, "Yeah sure, Leo." Then I saw Leo walking down those cowpaths with his flashlight, afraid to call out Elena's name, and Lana lying in bed, her face twisting in pain underneath a blue washcloth. I could see Harry sitting quietly by Lana's side, coloring in his coloring books and trying to remember to whisper. Then I saw myself sitting in the midst of them, the only one awake, with hurricanes blowing through my veins.

I did one more thing before I crawled under the covers next to Elena. I folded up the two pages Lana had written on the Syracuse Hotel stationery and slipped them into my coat pocket, down through the rip, into the hem of my coat. Then I lay next to Elena, and while my nerves strained against the hurricanes, I worried that our lives would never be the same again.

10

Leo came to get us the next morning. He took the bus up instead of borrowing Garta's car, since Garta would have wanted to come along. He didn't know what awaited him on the other side of the hotel door, and he didn't like things to fall apart in front of other people, especially someone like Garta.

When he knocked Lana was still asleep. Elena and I were playing whisper hide-and-seek with Harry, waiting for her to wake up. When we heard the knock I told Elena it was him, but she didn't believe me. She thought it was someone from the hotel coming to get our cart of dirty dishes. She was shocked when we opened the door and Leo was standing there. He was freshly shaven, and his dark pants and white shirt were neatly pressed. His face was in pieces, though, just as I knew it would be. He hugged me and Harry, as if he hadn't seen us in a couple of years, and he would have hugged Elena, but she wouldn't let him. She backed away from him, until she was standing on the threshold of the marble bathroom.

He walked in quietly behind Harry. When he saw Lana lying on the left side of the bed in her navy blue dress, he forgot we were even there. He went straight over and knelt down next to her on the beige carpet. He didn't say her name; he just touched the side of her face with his thick fingers, the same way he touched down on the keys when he played something mournfully sweet. He kissed her forehead, then her lips, and he whispered words to her that we couldn't hear. Somehow, the sight of him bent over her stilled my nerves.

Our lives hung suspended in those few moments before Lana opened her eyes. How was she going to react? I wondered. Elena and I pushed closer so we could see her eyes when they opened. After Leo kissed her lips a few more times, they finally fluttered open like eyes do when the morning sunlight falls on them. It took her a few moments to remember where she was and what had happened to her—I saw her memory ripple in stages across her face, until it was clear that she remembered. She turned away from Leo in one slow, lugubrious move—a move which, simple as it was, reached back past Leo to Harry, Elena, and me and slapped us too. It meant things were not normal now, that they weren't going to be for a while, and that possibly they would never be normal again.

"La, don't," Leo begged her.

"You're too late, Leo," she said, her voice still low and washed out. "You were too late then, and you're too late now."

I wondered what she meant by that, but of course there was no way to ask. Leo reached out and touched the white of her neck with his fingertips and whispered, "I'm sorry, La. I didn't know you were so sick."

She glanced over her shoulder at him, silencing him with her frigid stare. He crept onto the bed anyway and laid his hand on her hip, pressing his other hand to her forehead. "I'm going to take you home, La."

She was too drugged to fight him, and besides beyond the drug lay the throb of her migraine, which she said was still there. She lay quietly on the bed with her arm draped over her forehead, while Elena and I helped Leo gather up their things, groping around in the darkness to find everything. We neatly folded their clothes and laid them in the suitcase, putting Harry's plastic soldiers and coloring books on top. When we were done, when we were close to walking out of the room, Lana asked a question that nearly stopped my heart.

"What happened to the papers I put here?" she asked, pointing weakly at the top of the bedside table. No one said anything, least of all me. "Did you take them, Elena?"

"No," Elena said, staring across the darkness.

Elena glanced over at me, and then Lana's eyes shifted from Elena's face to mine. "Maddie?"

"No," I said, trying to say it as innocently as Elena had. It killed me that I had lied to her, while her papers lay burning and concealed in the hem of my coat. I was almost certain she knew I had taken them, and it was only because she was still so drugged that she didn't pursue it. Those pills had fogged her senses and relaxed her terrible grip on privacy.

Leo handed her her dark sunglasses and helped her to her feet. He would have gladly carried her out of there, but she wouldn't let him. Instead, she walked shakily between him and Elena, leaning heavily on their arms, while her dark cane dangled from Leo's wrist.

We went home in silence, Lana languishing up in a front seat, still in the padded clutches of the drug, while Harry spoke every now and then, pointing out the cows that dotted the decaying hillsides. Elena and I kept quiet, exchanging mournful glances. Though neither of us said it, we felt responsible for the state Lana was in, and even if by some fluke we weren't, we had still read her journal. Any way you looked at it we were guilty.

We put her to bed when we got home and gave her two more orange pills. The other two had begun to wear off, and she could sense in the distance that rising, horrible drumbeat of the migraine. Elena and I wanted to look after her and Harry, but Leo wouldn't let us. He stayed with her and sent me and Elena back to school.

All afternoon those pages burned in the hem of my coat. I wanted to read them, but I was afraid to. When Lizzy and I went out on the playground, I thought about digging them up and showing them to her, but when I envisioned Lana lying in her bed, drugged, I couldn't. It was killing me that I had them, but even so I wasn't willing to give them up. I was going bad, I realized. Like a piece of fruit left out too long on the counter, I was slowly but surely rotting. It was something I felt powerless against, as if it had taken over my body and had begun to weave a black web around my heart. It was my nerves, I knew. They were getting worse.

After school Lizzy, Elena, and I sat by Lana's bedside for about an hour and watched her sleep. Leo was in and out of the room, changing her washcloth and dusting the dressers. He had cleaned the house and had gotten down to the bottom of the dirty clothes basket and was now baking a meatloaf for dinner. If it hadn't been for Lana lying drugged in her bed, it might have felt like old times. I even noticed Elena easing up on Leo—seeing him folding the laundry and mashing up hamburger in a bowl unknotted her heart toward him. By the time dinner was over they were speaking whole sentences to one another.

Elena took off after we ate to wherever it was she went these days, and Garta called and said, "SEND LIZZY HOME." I didn't know what Lizzy had done this time, but I knew by the sound of Garta's voice that she was going to get it. I would have gone over to Garta's apartment with her, but Lana woke up and asked for some food. While Leo sat by her bed and watched her eat, I slipped into the bathroom and took up my place behind the grate. She was sitting up, resting her back against the wad of pillows Leo had propped up. The silver tray Mimi had once given her lay across her lap. She was bent over it, slowly spooning up some warm chicken noodle soup Leo had made for her. It was so dark in there I could hardly see them. The drapes were pulled and only a little light from the hallway bled through the crack in the door.

"Are you feeling any better, La?" Leo asked her. His voice was liquid and warm, and he reached up and gently brushed the hair from her damp brow.

"A little." Her voice, though not as deep as it was yesterday, was still no more than a hoarse whisper. "I can feel the headache somewhere behind the drug, but my stomach feels better." She shifted the tray in her lap, and when her navy blue dress fell open a little, I saw the soft, white swell of her breasts.

"La, I'm sorry. I honestly didn't know how sick you were." He pressed forward in his lap and touched her wrist with the very tips of his fingers.

"I told you, Leo. I don't know what else I could have said." She looked at him, and whatever passed between them was enough to push Leo back. He took his hand away and leaned back in the chair.

"Were you sick when you left?"

"No—not physically sick anyway." Her voice rumbled through the air and mingled with the low roar of heat blowing up from the floor registers. She handed him the tray and eased herself down under the covers. "I was only there a day or so before the headache started, though. I guess it had been building up."

"Why did you go?" he asked. "Because of me?" He lowered the tray to the floor and then picked up her left hand, kissing it softly.

"I can't stand the quiet here, Leo," she whispered, staring straight up at the dark ceiling. "I told you. It makes me remember—"

"I know, La," he rushed to say. He cupped the side of her face with his palm.

"I tried to remember it when I was there," she whispered fiercely. "I tried to face it, like you tell me too—" She stopped speaking and closed her eyes to shut out the horror.

"Why don't you see a psychiatrist, La?" Leo said delicately. "We've got the money now. I was talking to Bob, and he said he knows—"

She rolled her head swiftly on the pillow. *"You told Bob?"* There were daggers in her dried-out voice.

"No, no. Of course not," he raced to say. "I just told him you were having troubles. That's all, La, and he said he knows . . ."

She stared him into silence. "I don't want you to ever call Barbara Lamb again for anything. I don't want her loaning us Gus. You know how I feel about that, Leo." This last was spoken like a cold breeze, the tone of her voice like ice. I don't know what it was that reminded her of Gus, but whatever it was, she turned over on her side and pressed her back between them, and said no more. Very shortly, she drifted off into another oblivion.

That night as I lay in bed, I could almost see the hem of my coat glowing. I'd brought it up to my room and had draped it over the end of my bed where I could keep an eye on it. I touched it a few times to make sure Lana's papers were still there.

I glanced through the open doorway at Elena. She was lying on her back, staring up at the ceiling, her hands folded behind her head. She wasn't wearing Lana's white silk robe anymore, I noticed, but rather her own white nightgown. The house didn't feel empty now that Lana was home, but rather it felt stilled and cloaked in silence, as if something huge and blanketlike had been draped over it. Outside the wind had died down to a whisper, and not a single car passed down our street either. It was as if the road had been cordoned off and the traffic shunted to another street so as not to disturb Lana.

"Where'd you go tonight?" I asked Elena.

"Nowhere," she said, keeping her eyes pinned on the ceiling. I knew she was lying. She had gone wherever she had gone the other night when we were looking for her in those barns. She'd found a hiding place somewhere, and she didn't want me to know where it was.

"Now *you're* starting to get like Lana," I said, annoyed by her sudden secrecy. It was bad enough Lana was a whole secret herself, without Elena getting that way too.

She rolled her head on the pillow and looked at me. "You took her papers, didn't you?" she said. Something short and pointed stuck in my heart, and I looked away from her. "Didn't you?" she whispered louder.

I stared at the crisscross patterns of light on my walls and burrowed deeper under my covers. Of course she knew I had taken them. Any fool could have figured that out — there was no one else in the room who could have possibly picked them up, besides Harry, and Elena knew he wouldn't have noticed them. I glanced over at her again and found her staring at me. "I'll tell you if you tell me where you went tonight."

"All right," she said, "but you have to tell me first."

I must have wanted to tell her, because I didn't even argue with her about who should rightfully go first. I just said, "Yes."

"I knew it, Maddie. I knew it." A strange look flooded out her eyes in swift, penetrating beams — one which rooted for the evil in me, one which applauded my stealth.

I looked down at the hem of my coat and could just see the glow of radiation from those papers. "I haven't read them yet," I admitted quietly. "I'm afraid it will make Lana worse."

"I know. That's why I didn't take them. I saw them, too."

"Let's just read these," I said. My voice quivered in the still air, and I felt my heart begin to bang. "And then we won't read anything else."

"Okay," she whispered, and in the next moment she threw the covers off and padded into my room.

As I slipped my hand down into the hem of my coat to retrieve them, I realized it was I more than Elena who was racking up the sins. Not only had I stolen the papers, but I had lied about it. I had told Lizzy about Effy and Sticks, lying to her in the process, and now I was about to read these pages. For Elena, reading them would only constitute a minor sin; for me it was a major sin. Whether it affected Lana or not, it was still a sin. By the time we crept into the attic and huddled together in the red chair, the hurricanes were blowing in my veins again.

November 8, 1967, I read in a shaky whisper. *Dark fingers upon my soul. Can't get them off. Grimy and choking, squeezing my guts. Tried to pry them off. They just slip and dig in deeper. There is no respite from them. None at all. Headache is swelling, growing stronger, a vicious beat in the front of my skull, shattering my thoughts into pieces. It's keeping me from it—if the pain is too much, then I can't think, I can't remember. Everything inside rejects it. My mind won't cast it out. It holds, grips, covers.*

November 9, 1967. The pain in my skull is getting worse. I told Leo, but he didn't hear me. He is so wrapped up in his work, he's forgotten about me—forgotten what happened. He has cast it from his mind. I know he has. I told him this would happen. I foresaw this not long after they took me away.

November 10, 1967. The headache has taken over. Can barely think. My guts are sick. If it weren't for Harry, I would gladly die. Maddie and Elena, too. Shouldn't have listened to Leo—shouldn't have had them. My guilt over them mounts daily. What kind of a mother can I be? I think of Mimi. Surely I am better for my children than she was for me and Teddy. I've kept them innocent. By the time I was their age, I knew everything, had seen everything.

November 11, 1967. Headache so bad now, it's hard to speak. Poor little Harry.

I folded the pages up and shoved them down to the hem of my coat, just in case our trespassing had charged through the walls and hit Lana in the head. We stared at one another, not knowing quite what to say, and then turned our heads and looked longingly at the boxes that stood not more than three feet away. No matter what we learned about Lana, it always led us back to those boxes.

"What's worse," I whispered, "reading these papers or reading her journals from the past?"

"Her journals from the past." She didn't even have to think about it.

"We shouldn't read anymore, should we?" I said, though I desperately wanted to. I knew I wouldn't sleep again, not with Lana's words racing through my mind.

"Not until Lana's a little better."

We left the attic and crawled into our beds. The winds weren't blowing through my veins anymore, but even so I couldn't sleep. Lana's words, *I know he had. I told him this would happen. I foresaw this not long after they took me away*, were going to keep me awake for a long time.

"So where were you tonight?" I asked Elena.

"I went downtown, behind the Colgate Inn where some of the older kids hang out." Her voice sounded pinched and manufactured, and the way she turned away so quickly made me think she was lying.

"What did you do?" I watched her carefully, but she didn't look at me. She didn't even blink.

"Nothing. We just talked."

I didn't believe her. She might have gone out behind the Colgate Inn, but they didn't just talk. They could talk in the park or over at the swan pond. They did something else out there. What, I didn't know, but I knew it was something better than talking.

Lizzy and I gave Lana her breakfast the next morning. She ate a piece of toast and drank a few sips of tea. She was even feeling good enough to let the morning light sift in a little through the parted curtains. The migraine still hadn't retreated, though, and after she ate she had to take a few more orange pills, which hurtled her back into oblivion. We would have sat by her bedside longer, changing her washcloths, had Leo not been there, but he hovered over her like an angel and sent us off to school.

We skipped going up to see Miss Thomas. It was so cold out we doubted she had come out. If she were losing her mind, we agreed, she was losing it inside her house where it was warm. It was still early, so we went down to Minnie Harp's. We hadn't been there since Lana had left, and now that she was back, we were anxious to see what had become of our cross. We drifted down the misty hill and stepped into her stark, barren woods, stopping the moment we spotted it. It seemed a minor miracle that it was still there, jutting out of the cold ground like a knife stuck in an old crusty wound. You could see it from practically everywhere. The leaves had fallen off the trees, and nothing but the tangle of dead weeds obscured it from view. Even Minnie Harp's grass wasn't a screen anymore—it had dried up and collapsed.

We climbed our tree and struggled to find a position in the crotch that was tolerable. It was such close quarters that we finally lined ourselves up, Lizzy taking up the front, while I stood behind her. From there we surveyed Minnie Harp's decaying kingdom. Her flowers had all dropped dead, and in the dull winter light her house looked desolate and stripped, more naked than usual.

We waited there for about ten minutes before the silence started to wear on me. The wind just barely rustled the treetops. I could only hear our breathing and the sound of our coats rubbing up against one another. A few crows drifted overhead like black boomerangs, cawing lowly, but after a while they flew out of view, and it felt so dead inside the woods, it was creepy.

"I've got something to show you," I said. It didn't matter that it was another sin either. I couldn't stand the silence anymore. I reached deep down into the hem of my coat and fished up Lana's papers. "These were lying on the bed table at the hotel. I took them after everyone was asleep." I handed them over her shoulder so she could read them herself. "Lana noticed they were gone, too."

While I watched for Minnie Harp, Lizzy bent her head and read the pages, whispering the very line my mind had caught on last night. " 'I foresaw this not long after they took me away,' " she said. "I wonder who *they* were, and I wonder what they took her away from."

She twisted herself around and was about to launch into her speculations, when we heard Minnie Harp's back door bang shut. It didn't seem possible that she had actually come outside—we hadn't seen her in such a long time—but within moments we watched her round the corner of her house, carrying a dirty white sack in one hand and a black pail in the other. Her cat wasn't leashed to her wrist, so she moved across her decrepit lawn unhampered.

I hit Lizzy with my elbow and she turned around. We held our breath and watched as Minnie stomped toward the woods, coming closer and closer to our cross. She walked quickly with her eyes fixed straight ahead, as if she were late for an appointment. She wore a faded red scarf strapped down to her head, and her rubber brown boots slapped against her thick ankles. After Lizzy stuffed Lana's papers into her pocket, we shifted soundlessly in our perch in the tree, so we could get the best possible view of Minnie Harp's cut-out tongue, in case she dropped her jaw this time.

She stopped abruptly at the foot of the woods, some ten feet away from our cross and stared at it like a cat stares at something it has never seen before. She bent over a little, as if to conceal herself, and scoured the woods with her narrowed, fearful eyes. She glanced nervously over her shoulder to make certain no one was lurking nearby, and when her probing eyes swept past us, we pulled ourselves in. Assured now that she was alone, Minnie hunched over and stalked slowly over to the cross, craning her neck forward, staring at it in absolute bewilderment. She couldn't imagine what it was doing there. Her jaw didn't drop, though—it didn't even shift from side to side. Her mouth never even opened to take a breath. She read the words, HERE LIES 100 DRUNK SOLDIERS, and looked up again, her nervous eyes scanning the woods, her back curved over like a hunchback. She stared at it again, and then she reached out and touched it quickly, the way you'd touch a snake. She backed away from it, as if it were alive, and her head twisted back and forth slowly as she studied it some more. Finally, she strode forward and yanked it out of the ground. Then she fled deeper into the woods toward our tree, the cross pinned against her chest.

She stopped at the fire pit and threw the cross down on the ground. She was breathing wildly, as if she'd just finished a race, and her face twisted pathetically. We had such a perfect view of her, it seemed too good to be true. She knelt down and fumbled to open her dirty white sack. Her hand plunged down inside and pulled out not bottles but long, soiled strips of white cotton. They appeared to have been torn from sheets and were stained yellow and reddish brown. I could see small spots of blood on them, too. They were bandages, I guessed, which she had made herself—bandages for the Nazi. She pulled them out of the bag like confetti and dropped them into the middle of the fire pit. When the sack was empty, she took the black pail and sprinkled the pit with whatever strange liquid it held. I thought it was a religious practice of some sort (I had once seen a priest sprinkle his congregation), but when she struck a kitchen match to it and it went up in flames, I realized it was just lighter fluid.

Lizzy dug her elbow into my side, and I dug mine into hers. It was the fire, no doubt, which heightened the experience, for it was high and huge and maniacal, and it roared in the silence. We could feel the heat seep through our cold shoes, while our hearts pounded in our throats.

Minnie waited until the fire was going strong before she threw the cross on top of it. Through the yellow dance of the flames, I could see Lizzy's perfect bold lettering—HERE LIES 100 DRUNK SOLDIERS. She didn't hum a single note of her opera. Finding the cross on top of her buried bottles had disturbed her, and seeing it now being consumed by the fire was even more sobering. Minnie Harp's father had been a preacher, and I'm sure she didn't take cross burning lightly.

As she made certain that not one bandage escaped the ravaging flames, we shifted our aching weight from one crushed hip to the other as soundlessly as possible. If she had looked up just once, she would have found us—we were no more than three feet from the top of her head.

I didn't know how much longer we could hold our position. Small fires burned in my hips, and the circulation in my feet was starting to cut off. It occurred to me that if we jumped out of the tree, dropping within a few inches of her, we could scare the shit out of her so much she would have to drop her jaw. That way, on our descent, we would get a close-up view of her cut-out tongue.

"Let's jump," I whispered to Lizzy. She nodded and pinched my arm, as if to signal me to drop. I didn't think about it for very long. I just freed my right foot from the tangle of our legs, took a deep breath, and made the plunge. I don't know what possessed me, but a sound came out of my throat which was low and animal-like—it was a brutal growl, something like a prolonged "Auggghhhhhh," which Lizzy reproduced perfectly. The stark terror in Minnie Harp's eyes bore testimony to our savagery. As if we were some horrible beast risen from Hell, she was terrified.

"Nnunggggg, nnungggg," she yelled, her raw voice completely unhinged. She chased us away, striking out violently with her stick, catching Lizzy on the back of the arm, but missing me completely as she tore through the woods on that early November morning. The swiftness and fierceness with which Minnie attacked bottle burying and tulip planting, she now employed as she drove us out of her woods. She was only inches from our heels, barking out her command, her hysterical battle cry. *"Nnunngggggg, nnunggggggggggggggg,"* she cried, with the stick raised above her head like a spear chucker.

I don't know what she would have done to us had she caught us. Lizzy favored the idea that she would have cut us up and fed us to her bandaged Nazi, but I thought she would have just beaten us with her stick. Thankfully, when we crossed her property line into the adjoining field, she stopped immediately. Not so much as one of Minnie Harp's toes left her unkempt yard. We turned around a couple of times on our race out of there to make certain that she hadn't changed her mind, but there she stood, her stick thrust into the air, her mouth opened wide enough for flies to buzz in, while she cried out her painful sorrow. "Nnungggg, Nnunggggg" filled the cold morning air, a lonely wounded cry.

Lizzy and I stumbled up a small knoll and rolled down the other side, laughing like never before. There was sweet pleasure in tormenting Minnie Harp. We couldn't control what Garta or Lana or Leo did, but we had the power to disturb Minnie Harp.

"Did you see it?" Lizzy asked me. She held her sides and tried to catch her breath.

After all this, I realized that I hadn't, not really. The moment I jumped from the tree had been so crowded with impressions, I'd forgotten to look. It had been such a short jump, a few seconds at the very most, and the sound of our barbaric voices had had such a startling power, I didn't remember to look for her cut-out tongue.

"It's cut off halfway," she said. "Part of it's still left." She stuck her tongue out and showed me where Minnie Harp's had been sawed off, but I didn't know whether to believe her or not. Lizzy had the wildest imagination.

11

It took Lana a few more days to shake the headache. She lay in her room with the curtains drawn and a washcloth plastered to her forehead, drifting in and out of consciousness. Elena, Lizzy, and I took turns sitting by her bedside, getting her glasses of water and changing her washcloth, whispering to her when she woke up, eager to hear what she had to say even though her voice still came and went as a hoarse rumble. She didn't say much when she spoke—she thanked us for taking care of her, and she apologized for the state she was in, but thankfully her voice did not permit her to do so too often.

By the weekend she was sitting up in bed. She talked to me and Elena and Lizzy and tried to be cheerful, but I could tell she was forcing it. With Leo she was different. She was quiet and subdued, speaking only when he spoke to her. Something quite huge had come between them, and when I looked in on them in the mornings, I noticed that Lana was never in Leo's arms anymore. He was anchored on one side of the bed, she on the other. Harry, Elena, and I could have fit between them, that's how far apart they were.

By Monday afternoon Lana was up. When we came home from school, she was sitting at the dining room table, waiting for us with some hot cocoa and crumb cakes. She looked pale and lovely in the afternoon light, but even so she wasn't quite herself. She still lingered in the shadows of that monstrous headache, even though she tried not to show it.

Over the next week she didn't get any better or any worse. She walked around the house slowly, quiet as ever, but she was polite and careful not to complain. She didn't speak much to any of us, especially Leo, but she wasn't mean—just distant.

Leo tried to be around more to help her until she felt well enough to take over, but he wasn't really there. His thoughts always drifted up to the theater where Bob Hendrix was waiting for him, and it seemed in an hour's time his eye made ten journeys down to his watch and back. After a while Lana would just say, "Go, Leo," and he would wait maybe ten minutes before he'd leave. I think she preferred to be alone when his thoughts were so obviously elsewhere. She was mad at him anyway—mad that it had taken him so long to realize how sick she'd been, and mad too that he'd told Bob Hendrix something about her.

She was especially angry about being sick. It annoyed her that she wasn't in control, that something vile had come along and temporarily inhabited her. She apologized to Leo one night about it, saying that she knew the last thing he needed was a sick wife. I thought it was an overture of some sort, a peace offering, but Leo heaved up in bed and turned over on his other side, as if she hadn't said anything at all. It seemed his patience could only be stretched over four or five days of the migraine.

She crawled over him and sat down on half of his pillow, waiting for him to open his eyes. "I understand you, Leo," she said delicately, "and I understand what it's like to have work you're passionately devoted to." Her hand rose quietly from her lap, and then very slowly, she pushed her fingers through his hair, like she used to. It looked odd, mechanical somehow, as if over the past few months she'd gotten rusty at it. "You know I understand. I do, but—"

As soon as she pronounced the word *but,* Leo turned over on his other side. She crawled over him again and slipped underneath the covers, until their heads were resting on the same pillow, their eyes no more than ten inches apart.

"I can't do this forever," she whispered. "We're going to have to work something else out."

Leo pinched his eyes shut and turned over again. Lana didn't pursue him this time—she just stared at his back, a few tears rolling down her cheeks. She brushed them away like she couldn't stand them.

Lizzy and I started watching her again to make sure that nothing bad happened to her. We were worried that when the migraine wore off completely, the illness would come back. Thankfully, it didn't. She began disappearing to her writing room, and instead of doubling over in her lap, like she used to, she started writing, which surprised both of us. "Maybe the migraine is good for her," Lizzy whispered to me. "Maybe it numbs the whole illness." Whatever it was, Lana started writing again and, as we soon discovered, cutting out newspaper articles. I found her December 4 newspaper, minus one front-page article, belly up in the bathroom wastebasket. Unfortunately, Lizzy and I hadn't kept up with our copying—not since Lana had come home. We were sure that she wouldn't be reading the *New York Times*, let alone cutting out articles. It was purely by accident that I discovered that one. I just happened to notice it when I was crouched down by the grate watching Lana. I pulled it out and shook it off, and then slipped it down the front of my pants. When I showed it to Lizzy, she said, "Shit, Maddie. Now how are we going to find out?"

I remembered the newspaper stand in the lobby of the Syracuse Hotel, but the problem was getting today's newspaper tomorrow, not to mention taking the bus up there. We decided we'd ask Mrs. Devonshit if she knew where we could find the *New York Times* before we considered anything. "They have it up at the Colgate Library," she said, as if I should have known.

Lizzy and I headed up there after school. We slid the December 4 copy of the *New York Times* from the top rung of a wooden rack and carried it over to a set of green leather chairs. We spread it out on the coffee table and stared down at the article Lana had cut out. It was another article about Negroes. In the middle of the page lay the bold, black headline: DR. KING PLANNING TO DISRUPT CAPITAL IN DRIVE FOR JOBS. We looked up from the newspaper and stared at each other. We couldn't imagine why Lana had cut this article out. We now felt it safe to assume that all the articles Lana cut out of the paper were about Negroes, but even so we couldn't imagine why.

"Maybe it's because of Effy," Lizzy suggested. "Something about Effy."

What, though, we couldn't fathom.

Lana and Leo had a huge fight later that night. While Lizzy and I watched them through the bathroom grate, I couldn't help but worry that discovering Lana's article had brought it on. She was sitting on the bed folding the laundry, the radio playing softly next to her. The drapes were halfway open, and what was left of the daylight spilled in through the windows casting gray shadows. "I think I'm losing them, Leo," we heard her say softly. She bent her head and folded up a pair of Harry's little pants. For a moment it seemed she might cry. "I found half a pack of Winston cigarettes in Elena's coat pocket today." Lizzy and I looked at one another—we didn't know Elena had taken up smoking. "I think we're falling apart, Leo." She laid Harry's pants down and made room for Leo on the bed. When he sat down next to her, she tried to find her way into his arms, but he pushed her away. He took a piece of paper out of his shirt pocket and handed it to her instead.

"This is the name of the psychiatrist, La," he said quietly. "Why don't you call him?"

I could tell from the hot, wounded look on her face that his suggestion hurt her deeply. "I see," she said, backing away from him. "You think this is all my fault. If I'd just go see a psychiatrist everything would be all right."

"I don't know what to do anymore, La." His voice was tense and crowded with emotion, and when he started pulling at his fingers, I knew it wasn't easy for him to say, "Nothing I do or say seems to make any difference anymore." He drew closer to her and brushed her cheek with the backs of his fingers. "It's been almost ten years since—"

"Don't talk to me about that," she said fiercely. She pushed his fingers from her face and stood up. "I knew you would do this, Leo. I predicted it, and you're doing it."

"Doing what, La? *What*, for Christ fucking sakes?" He looked up at her, completely mystified.

"You're pushing me out, Leo. I can feel it—you're closing me out." A deep furrow settled between her eyebrows, and a burning red invaded her cheeks. *"You've forgotten it all."*

"That's what you wanted both of us to do, La," he shouted. "That's what you begged me to do, goddamn it. To forget it, to never talk about it, to never tell our children. *That is what you wanted.*"

She edged away from him in fear and stared at him for a long time, time during which I think she realized the contradiction in her thoughts. Yes, she wanted him to forget it, but she didn't want him to forget it either.

"It's you who won't forget, La," he yelled.

She walked toward him, staring at him as though he were vile, as though he were less than human. "You must have forgotten your part in it," she screamed. Her voice was chilling. "You must have forgotten, Leo."

Leo rose up and grabbed her wrists. "Don't do this, La," he yelled. "DON'T." He slammed her arms down to her sides and held them there, while he bore down on her with his embittered eyes. She struggled to free herself from his grasp, and when she couldn't shake him, she let out the shrillest, most devastating, soul-shattering scream I had ever heard a human being utter. It wracked the air and was so loud and disturbing, the neighbor's dog howled next door.

As if it had sounded an alarm deep within Leo, he let go of her immediately and clutched her to his chest, kissing her face ravishingly. "La," he breathed. "Oh, La. I'm sorry, baby. I'm so sorry." The scream ceased, and for a moment she stood rigid in his arms, perched between one reality and another. Leo sought her lips, and miraculously she began to respond. He moaned and at first Lana reciprocated in a female strain, but, sadly, it deteriorated to a thick sob.

"I'm losing you. I'm losing you all," she cried.

"No, you're not, La," he whispered fiercely. "I'm here. I'm still here."

He picked her up and carried her to the bed, where he held her like a baby, shushing her and stroking her face with the tips of his fingers. She clung to him, her arms folded around his neck, while she sobbed. "You're all right, baby," he whispered over and over again. "You're all right." It was his soothing, practiced litany.

For the first time I looked over at Lizzy. Her black, fearless eyes were filled with tears. Now she knew, I realized. She knew about Lana. She'd finally seen Lana's other side—the dark, troubled side I had never been able to describe. We fell away from the grate and retreated to the bathtub, where we sat down on the cold, porcelain edge and tried to regain ourselves.

"God," Lizzy whispered.

"Now you know what I mean," I said.

For a long while Lana's scream, so utterly naked and terrifying, wracked the silence and echoed through our house. Lizzy and I lay in my room hearing it ricochet off the walls and ceilings, as if it were trying to escape through a door or a window. We were awed by its power.

I thought about everyone — about Lana and Leo and Elena, about Effy, Sticks, and Mimi, about Lizzy and Garta. An image formed in my mind, an image of a human chain of beatings. I saw Sticks beating Effy, and Mimi beating Lana, Garta beating Lizzy, and Don beating Garta, and last of all, Leo seizing Lana's wrists. Then that scream. Was that what this world was made up of? I wondered. Of savage acts against one another? Was that the truth, or what the truth raised?

Where once I had felt separate from it all, barred and distanced, a lonely onlooker eager to join, I now felt like a participant, a player in this game of secrets and lies and violence, wanting only for it to cease.

The next morning I took Lizzy up to see Miss Thomas's birds. I thought it might make us feel better. Lizzy was hoping Miss Thomas would be out on the lawn losing her mind, but it was too cold out now. She was outside, though, spreading straw over her flowerbeds. She had on a pair of black rubber boots that flapped loosely around her ankles and a short red coat that covered all but three inches of her purple crepe dress. Her scarf was a Hawaiian red print with ALOHA written on it in white letters.

When she saw us she said, "Hallelujah! They've come." The air was so cold it came out of her mouth in white, steamy gusts.

She showed us how well Aphrodite was healing in the bird shed, and afterward, she grabbed our hands and towed us across the lawn, her legs working like pistons to gain steam, her arms pumping in counterpoint. "Boy, do I have a feast for your senses," she said, her voice filling the chill December air. "Wait till you see this. You just wait, you looney birds."

Lizzy looked at me and I looked at her, and an unspoken thrill passed between us. We followed her into the house and walked single file behind her, turning down a different hallway than the one which led to the birds. Miss Thomas picked up her momentum, and then her voice came again, fluid and tantalizing and absolutely breathless. "It's the eighth wonder of the world," she said. "Really."

I thought it might be something alive again, like a pit of snakes or a whole bunch of elephants or maybe even a roomful of newborn babies. I didn't know, but I knew it would be good. I trusted Miss Thomas on that count. She stopped at a door and put her back up against it as if to hide what wondrous thing lay beyond. "Now, put your hands over your eyes and don't take them away until I say so." We did what she said. "Okay, are you gooney birds ready?"

"Yes," we both said excitedly, and when Lizzy squeezed my hand I thought my heart might plow straight into my ribs. I heard the door open, and then I felt her hands on my shoulder as she guided us through the door. We shuffled forward blindly, the wooden floor slippery beneath our feet, until she stopped us and commanded us to stand still and quiet without taking our hands away from our eyes.

"Now listen carefully," she said. We heard her move away from us, her feet hitting the floor in a way that sounded backward. Then came the first sound, a click and then mad hysterical laughter. Then the sound of an organ, then another click and more sounds, a whistle, the sound of water, of wind, a harp, and then so many clicks and whirs and songs that I couldn't differentiate the sounds anymore. But above them all came Miss Thomas's voice, imitating them each in turn as she stirred them to life—whatever they might be. It was like nothing I had ever heard before, and it was all I could do to keep my hand covering my eyes.

"When can we look?" Lizzy asked, and I felt a shiver bump through her.

"Okay, you goons," she said. "On the count of three. One . . . two . . . three," she called, and our hands flew from our eyes.

Everything around us was in motion, flying and whirling and turning circles. Everything imaginable and unimaginable was moving and clanging and whirring—it was a circus in miniature, crowded and wedged into every corner of her light-drenched room. There were brown tumbling bears, red monkey grinders, laughing chinamen, and black trains, gadgets of every type imaginable, red-and-blue ferris wheels and white roller coasters, cuckoo clocks all clanging the hour, red-and-black music boxes and singing pink ballerinas and trapeze flyers. It was a spectacle worthy of Miss Thomas and one that could not be taken in in a few moments. It was riveting and electric and so charged, it took your breath away.

Lizzy and I stood spellbound, our hands linked, and when we looked at one another I knew by her expression that her heart was racing just as fast as mine. We were the same, I knew, the exact same. She squeezed my hand as if to communicate that, and then Miss Thomas swooped down on us, took one of our hands each, and pulled us over to the laughing man.

"Do as the chinaman does," she called above the multitude of sounds. Suddenly she started jerking back and forth as he did, imitating his hysterical laughter until finally the sheer force of her zeal compelled first Lizzy and then me into doing the same. The three of us raced from the laughing chinaman to the red monkey grinder, to the pink ballerina, the crying gorilla, the drummer boy, and the screaming banshee, imitating each and every one of them both in action and in sound, whooping and hollering, twisting and writhing about until I was sure the three of us would shortly pass into another life—one of perpetual, life-everlasting sound and motion.

We went through the room like three crazy maniacs, emptying into the air every last bit of raw energy we had. When we reached the end, Miss Thomas threw her baggy arms over her head and shook them like a Kabuki dancer, leading us out into the hallway and then down its long passage, Lizzy and I screaming behind her. We would have followed her anywhere just then—off a cliff if that's where she wanted to take us, that's how much we loved her. She was infectious, utterly captivating, and when she turned the corner and stopped dead, we stopped dead too and stared at her, waiting breathlessly for her next move.

"Shh," she said, putting her crooked finger to her lips. "Shh," she whispered again, as if we might wake someone up.

"What?" I said.

"Shh," she whispered. She bent over, and without so much as a word, she arranged us in a line, my hands on Lizzy's hips and Lizzy's on hers. She turned around then and touched our eyes with her fingertips to close them. Then slowly, as if we were a slow, creeping inchworm, we shuffled forward down a hallway on our way to someplace else.

A wonderful silence breathed all around us, all the more striking since we had just come from that room. The only thing we could really hear was our breath and the soft shuffle of our feet. I couldn't imagine where we were going or what we would see next, but I knew whatever it was would be good. We heard the door open, and when we shuffled in I sensed we had entered a brighter room. I could feel the light on my closed eyelids, and the silence was so padded and immense, it swallowed our sounds. It smelled wonderful in there too, like wet fresh earth.

When she stopped, Lizzy and I stopped. We stood there for a long time with our eyes closed and our hands on each other's hips. Then Miss Thomas started taking in huge breaths of air, Lizzy and I following her, breathing deeply in and out, in and out. She turned around, and very quietly she commanded us to open up our eyes. "But slowly," she said, "ever so slowly."

I opened my eyes ever so slowly to an extraordinary room, not so different from her bird room, except there were no birds but rather flowers—hundreds of beautiful flowers, some great and outlandish and white-petaled, others as tiny as bluebells. The smell was the sweet damp scent of wet earth mingled with the delicate perfume of a thousand blooms. It was like dessert, I thought, and when Miss Thomas resumed taking in deep breaths of this marvelous pickled air, Lizzy and I did the same.

We headed over to the flowers and began inhaling their fragrance deeply, one after another, and something amazing began happening to me. All this deep breathing in and out had made me feel light-headed and more peaceful than I'd felt in a long time. My nerves were so quiet I wondered if they had died. Perhaps I had jumped and whirled around so violently I had broken their necks. I would have to see, but for the moment I was without them. My troubles seemed so dwarfed and faraway, I felt as though I might possibly float out of there on my way to the blue heavens.

12

Lana was never really normal after that penetrating scream, but compared to the woman we had found in the Syracuse Hotel, she was doing well. She lit a few fires in the fireplace: we had beach parties, toasting hotdogs and marshmallows, and we sang songs, though Lana wouldn't sing. She showed us how to make perfect snow angels in the fresh snow, and a few times she even pulled the toboggan up the hill and rode down on the back to steer us through the trees.

Leo was around even less of the time. His musical had gotten bigger by no choice of his own, he told Lana, and since it had there was no way he and Bob would be ready to put it on in December. They pushed it to May (which Lana had predicted), and as to what they did up at the theater night after night, none of us really knew. Elena, Lizzy, and I went up there a few times to see for ourselves, but the curtains were always pulled across the tall windows, and without fail, the door was always locked. Elena began to wonder if maybe Leo was meeting a woman up there, instead of Bob Hendrix, but Lizzy and I highly doubted it.

"He and Lana aren't doing it anymore," Elena argued. It was true, but even so I couldn't imagine Leo going after another woman. I thought he still loved Lana—an idea Elena didn't really share. I some-

times noticed how he admired her when she walked into a room—
the graceful way she moved, in spite of her cane, the way her dark
hair fell across her shoulders.

They didn't say much to each other. I don't think Lana could forget
how he'd given her the name of a psychiatrist Bob Hendrix had
recommended, or *who* it was who was doing all the cooking, the
cleaning, and the looking after. She never mentioned it to him, but
he didn't bring it up either.

She was doing well enough that it began to seem that the damage
we'd done when we snooped through her journals had now either
been stopped or reversed. It was good to know our effect, just in
case we really had one, was not permanent.

My nerves seized on this idea, and one night a few weeks before
Christmas I said to Elena, "Why don't we read some more of the
journal?" I could see her through our open doorway, lying on her
back, reading one of Garta's *True Confessions* magazines with a flashlight. "Just one entry, and then we'll never do it again," I said. "Then
we could swear on the moon afterward."

"When, though?" Elena whispered back. She turned over and
shone the flashlight in my eyes. "Lana's across the hall. She could
probably tell we were reading them. Remember what happened,
Maddie."

When we listened through the darkness, we could hear Lana across
the hall working at her typewriter. It was true, it would be dangerous
to read her journal when she was just across the hall. Even when
she'd been in Syracuse, she'd had the power to sense our trespass
and had sent Leo in to catch us.

"We'll have to wait for her to go away again," Elena said. It was
a terrible thing to hope for, and as soon as Elena said it she took it
back.

"What if she's sleeping?" I said, shielding my eyes against the beam
of her flashlight. "Maybe when she's asleep she can't tell. Remember
when you caught me in there the first time—Lana was asleep then."

"You're right," she said. "But I'll never be able to stay awake until
she falls asleep."

I would stay awake, I told her. She could rest assured of that. It
would be impossible for me to sleep anyway. My nerves would be
up walking around, just waiting for the moment my fingers touched
Lana's journals.

For two hours I lay awake battling off their urges, while Elena slept peacefully in the next room. I heard Leo come home, and after he disappeared into their room, I heard their voices drift across the hall. Lana went back to her typewriter after not too long, and Leo slipped into the bathroom and washed up. He went to bed shortly, and when the slow clack of Lana's typewriter ceased, a stillness descended over our house. I waited for the light in Lana's room to go off, and then gave her fifteen minutes to fall asleep before I crept into Elena's room and picked up her flashlight. "Get up," I whispered, shining it in her face. She bolted up in her bed, and when I reminded her of our appointment with Lana's journal, she shuddered.

We threw on a few sweaters and crept back to the attic, slowly opening the creaky door. When we turned on the light, we saw the boxes standing untouched under the dusty eaves, as if they were waiting for us. We walked over and stood next to them, listening to the night air for any sound of Lana. There was none. It was perfectly still outside too. I looked at Elena, she looked at me, and without a word our hands stealthily undid one flap, then the other. It was our third violation. The first had been mine, the second hers, and now we were about to split one. My hands descended into the box, and slowly, as if it was made of delicate glass, I brought the journal out. I carried it over to the red chair, and after Elena crawled up next to me, I laid it in my lap, and we both stared down at it. It still had the power to shake us.

"Should we start at the beginning?" Elena whispered.

"No," I whispered. I touched the itch at the corner of my eye with an ice-cold finger. "Let's start where we left off last time."

"It was page thirty-two, then." I noticed her breathing had grown a little ragged.

We looked at one another and then down at the journal. "This is our last time," I said.

"I know." She pushed the hair off her face with a jittery hand.

"How much should we read?"

"Just to the next date. And then no more."

I nodded and carefully opened the notebook to page thirty-two, where we'd left off. I laid it across both our laps and waited for Elena to begin reading out loud. Her voice was a shaky whisper, and on the edges of Lana's journal lay our quivery fingers. We somehow knew we were going to discover something this time—something big

and incomprehensible, something which would disturb us for a long
time to come.

July 28 1947.
   After I finished at Mimi's I took a cab over to Sammy's. It was already
late, but Effy had told him I would come over later. I hadn't been there in a
few years, and like Effy said, it had changed a lot. Sammy made it bigger,
and he's got little round marble-topped tables out on the floor now. He's fixed
it up quite a bit, and the bar is beautiful too—dark mahogany and long like
you wouldn't believe. He's got some good singers and dancers, better than
Mimi has anymore. Clara was there and Berty. Louis was playing bass,
Grace was hoofing, and I recognized the guy on sax, but I can't remember
his name. I haven't seen any of them since they left Mimi's club. They're
doing better now working at Sammy's. It isn't weighty like at Mimi's—
wherever Mimi is, there's weight in the air. The place was good and packed,
mostly with whites, but they seemed in a good mood.
   I thought I'd just talk to Sammy and make an appointment with him, but
he wanted me to go up on stage right then. I didn't want to—I was tired and
I didn't have my shoes, but he announced me anyway. After Clara finished
singing "Carelessly," he went up on stage and gave her a break. When she
went backstage, he grabbed the microphone and announced loudly, "Ladies and
gentlemen, we've got Lana Lamar here with us tonight. She's agreed to sing
us a song, so won't you please give her a warm, warm welcome." When the
audience started clapping, he walked over to the side of the stage where I was
standing and pulled me up. "Here she is, folks, the lovely Lana Lamar," he
called out. "The only white lady who can sing the blues." Sammy started
clapping, and when the audience broke out in applause, there wasn't much I
could do but sing for them.
   I hadn't noticed the piano player before. He was white, and when I went
back to talk to him, I couldn't keep myself from staring at his blue eyes.
They were the most striking blue eyes I'd ever seen—cool blue and soft like
a baby's. He asked me what I wanted to sing. I told him "Salty Papa Blues,"
though nobody can sing it better than Dinah. It's not my best song, but the
sight of him threw me off. I should have asked him to play "Let's Call the
Whole Thing Off."
   It was stifling hot in there and smoky as hell, but I had the best time of
my life. We did five more songs, and then I danced barefooted to a song the
piano player had written. It was the fastest stuff I had ever danced to, but it
was wonderful and he was really something. I've never seen anyone play the

piano the way he did tonight. He was all over it—he threw his whole body into it like I've never seen anyone else do. I could have watched him for hours.

I can't describe the feeling I had up there on Sammy's stage without Mimi standing behind the curtain watching me. I felt free and alive again, like there were endless possibilities for a life, like there were whole worlds I hadn't seen yet, like the Fourth of July was in my veins blowing me to Kingdom Come.

We closed the place at 5 A.M., and the piano player walked me home. His name is Leo. It's not short for Leonard or Leon—it's just Leo. There's something there already. I can feel it, as if it is something vital, like a vein or a nerve running between us. His music stirred me, and he said my voice did something to him. "I could write something for you, Lana," he said. My name on his lips was just about the sweetest thing I'd ever heard.

Mimi wasn't home, so I invited him into my room. I opened the slats on the blinds, and the white light spilled across my bed. In the milky haze, we listened to some Billie Holiday records. I couldn't keep my eyes off him. I love the way he looks. He doesn't have that soft, sensitive poet look. He's big and manly, and his arms drive me crazy. They're Popeye arms—the kind of arms you could lose yourself in. He looks like Michelangelo's David.

I kissed him. He didn't kiss me. I don't think he would have, but I couldn't help myself. He said, "You know, you're beautiful, Lana," and my lips were on top of his. He eased me down and crawled on top of me, his hands running over my face like fevers. Our mouths fused, a melting of lips and tongues, and I could barely breathe. My heart loped inside my chest, and I could feel his, as if it were a pulse on my fevered fingertips.

"God, Lana," he said. It was all breath, no voice at all, and my stomach turned over and rose up. He pressed against me, and I pressed back. For a moment we were melded together at the hips, and I realized I had never wanted a man so much. I kept telling myself I couldn't—Jesus, Lana, you just met him. I longed to so much it hurt, so much I had to press my thighs together to still the ache.

I turned us over and crawled on top of him and poured over him. I lost myself in his baby blue eyes. "Leo," I whispered, just to hear his name. The world consisted of the inches between my eyes and his. Billie Holiday was singing, but I didn't even hear her. Sirens could have been screaming down Park Avenue and I wouldn't have heard them either. I couldn't hear anything but the brag of my heart and the rush of his breath. We went under again in a kiss so passionate, so hellbent and so lovely, I almost passed out. I had to roll off him to catch my breath.

"God, Leo," I whispered. I pressed my hand against my heart and felt it

coming loose. "I know," he said. We looked at one another again, our eyes not more than six inches apart. His were blazing, mine were on fire. I never knew such a thing could happen. I'm so used to the filth and disgust of Mimi's backrooms, I didn't think love was possible.

"Where did you come from, Lana?"

I reached over and touched his lips with my fingertips. They were swollen from our kisses—pink and soft and imperfect. One side rose to a higher arch than the other side. It drove me mad, that small imperfection.

We lay on our sides and touched each other's faces. He told me about himself, and I tried to tell him about myself too. My story was too complicated, but I told him what he needed to know—that I loved jazz, and that I'd never felt for anyone like I felt for him.

The sun came up and filtered through the blinds in yellow beams that fell across our legs in wide stripes. Mimi would be home by eight, so I made him go. I can never let her meet him. She'd hack him to pieces in three seconds. "Over my dead body will you marry a musician." If only her body were dead.

Then, in the tiniest letters, she wrote, *I think I love him.*

It was the end of the entry, and Elena stopped reading. Neither of us spoke a word.

"Lana was a jazz singer," Elena finally whispered. Her mouth hung open, and we stared at one another in disbelief.

"And a dancer," I said.

We were utterly shocked. It was difficult to imagine, for as far as we could remember, Lana had never sung so much as a note or danced so much as a step in our lives. I remembered the afternoon when she'd looked through the living room window and had seen Leo playing the jazz like someone possessed, while Elena danced in the middle of the room like a cancan girl. Why had she been upset by this when she herself had once not only danced but sung the jazz as well? It made less sense to me now than it had then.

"Should we stop reading now?" Elena asked.

"I don't know." I was beginning to worry. We'd read a lot—more than we'd ever read before—and I was worried that it might all hit Lana when she woke up. "What if she wakes up and it hits her in the head and she gets a migraine again?" I said.

"Go see if she's still asleep," Elena whispered. "See if she's tossing and turning."

She tucked the journal under her butt, and I went off to the bathroom to see if Lana was sound asleep. She was lying on her side, a foot or so from Leo, and during the time I watched her, she did not toss or turn or sigh or disrupt herself in any way. I took this news back to Elena, hoping that she would make the decision to read on. That way it would be more her sin than mine.

"Should we take the chance she doesn't know because she's sleeping?" she asked me. The wind started up in my veins again. I was beginning to realize that, for whatever reason, Elena wanted me to make these decisions.

"Let's read one more, but a later date," I whispered. I stopped and listened to the quilted silence. There was nothing to hear. No cars passed by outside, and without the slightest trace of wind, the next-door neighbor's dog didn't bark either. "We should only read one more, though. After that, we can't read any more."

Elena nodded, and after she pulled the journal out from underneath her, I carefully opened it to page 34 and thumbed ahead about ten pages. I stopped on *September 20, 1947*, and stared down at Lana's inky thicket of words. *A Sunday*. Elena bent her head and began to read again, her voice tremulous in the airless quiet.

I finished Sammy's at 4 A.M. I don't know how much longer I can keep working both clubs. I've got to quit Mimi's, but for some reason I'm afraid to. I've been working there for twelve years—what did I expect? Sammy's is a better place, but Effy isn't there, nor is Delors or Ummy. Mimi's place, as much as I hate to admit it, is home to me. I grew up in those backrooms, amid the sweat and semen and tears.

Mimi had a convention of salesmen from Chicago, so she didn't come home last night. I brought Leo home with me again, even though I don't like to bring him anywhere near Mimi. He thinks I come from money. Wait'll he finds out what kind of money. He doesn't know yet that Mimi doesn't just run a club. I haven't been able to find the words to tell him.

It was better even than the night before. It started just outside Mimi's darkened apartment. We had our coats off before we'd even opened the door. While I put the key in the lock, he kissed my neck and undid the zipper to my dress, tracing down my back with his maddening tongue. As soon as the door closed behind us, I pulled his shirt off and he slipped me out of my dress.

He undid his pants after that, and I watched them drop to the floor. The sight of him set me on fire all over again. He picked me up in his arms and carried me to my room.

The light filtered through my blinds in white bands of moonlight. They lay across my satin spread like creamy white fingers. He lowered me to the bed and drifted down sweetly on top of me. Our lips met, and our explosion began again. His hands, warm as irons, traveled down my body, and my hands raced across his back.

"La," he breathed. It drives me crazy when he says my name. "La, I love you."

The song he wrote for me floated through my mind. "Being with you is like taking a journey, like disappearing to an enchanted place—a place where blue begins." *This is where blue begins, I thought.*

I pressed against him harder still and let out a small scream. Our lips met again, and he put himself inside me. God, when he goes inside me and stares into my eyes and says, "I love you, La," I could die. There is no better, no greater pleasure in life than this. He moved on top of me, pressing out of me sounds I didn't know I possessed. First a moan, then a scream. The bed is shaking. The world has shrunk to the six or so feet which enclose us. He is all that exists to me. Leo. Oh God, Leo. I cannot get enough of him. I want to devour him, to take him inside me so deep, he is lost to me. I scream again, and his mouth silences me.

"Oh, God, Leo," I say. I take his face into my hands and lose myself in his eyes. "This is too good to be true."

"I know, La."

I tell him I want it harder, and he pounds into me. I want to feel all his passion. I want it let loose upon me. I am enough. I feel my capacity—I am boundless. I breathe him in, drink him up, take him over and over again, until it seems I might pass into another life. We both explode, and for a moment we tremble, on the verge of being one. We breathe the same air, our hearts beat one pulse. I cannot stand it—it is too great a thing to know. I wish to pass on, to meet heaven. I want to scream out my crazy joy. I want him to sink into my body forever. My senses are drenched, and my heart swollen beyond recognition. I cannot speak, for I am paralyzed. But my heart pounds: I love, I love. And we lie on top of one another, like two heated cannons gone off.

Then, shit. We heard the key in the lock. Our clothes were strewn out in the hallway—even our shoes. We both panicked because there was no place to hide him—I have no closet in my room. Only Mimi's room has a closet. Her eyes upon our bedstead would have ruined it for me, so I pulled the sheet around me and raced out to the hallway to pick up our things, but she was already in the door, my dress dangling from her hand. Before I could so much as touch Leo's pants, her foot was on top of them.

"Who's here?" she said fiercely. It was as if ol' Mimi didn't run a bordello, as if she had just come from church and not a whorehouse.

I didn't answer. I ripped Leo's pants from under her polished black toe and fled back to my room and locked the door behind me. "Put them on," I said, throwing him his pants. "She's coming."

I had never really told Leo about Mimi. He had no idea who was going to be pounding on the door. His mother was a normal woman—she baked cookies and cleaned their white house in Lansing.

"Open this door this minute," Mimi *yelled, her fists banging against the door. It wasn't even a normal yell—it was too loud for that. It was the voice a person would use if someone were being murdered.*

"What should I do?" he mouthed, jackknifing into his pants.

"Just sit there," I said, pointing to the chair next to the bed.

I squirmed into one of my dresses and walked toward the door. I had no idea what I might say to her. Hello, Mimi? Why the hell was I nervous? I asked myself. She runs a whorehouse, I reminded myself. Why was it all right for her to raise me in a place where people fucked all the time, and it wasn't all right for me to do it in the privacy of my bedroom?

"LANA, YOU OPEN THIS DOOR RIGHT NOW." Her voice verged on hysteria, so I pulled the door open, and there she stood—big Mimi in her black silk dress, looking as though she'd just come from a Sunday sermon. She took one look at Leo and yelled, "Get out." Her voice commanded him from the chair, to the hallway, and out the door before I could stop her. "Get out," she shouted. "GET THE HELL OUT."

She chased me down the hallway after that, hitting me with her goddamned purse, screaming like an idiot. Bellevue should see her when she's like this. She was on my heels like a Doberman, flushing me out of the hallway and into the living room. I ran into the kitchen, where she ended up pinning me against the cupboards.

"Who is he?" Her face was so close to mine I could see her bleached mustache.

"His name is Leo." My spine crunched against the counter edge, and Mimi stepped on my bare toes.

"Who is he?" she demanded, meaning not what is his name, or is he a good, decent person, but rather what does he do.

"He's a piano player," I announced.

I relished the look on her face. Shock cracked the plaster of her makeup, and her big mouth hung open like a cave.

She grabbed my hair and shoved my head against the cupboard door. "A piano player!" She raised me in a jazz club, and I'm not allowed to love a musician. What the hell am I supposed to do? WHACK—I caught her purse on my shoulder.

"Where's he from?" If the air had been cold, thick clouds of steam would have poured out of her mouth, like a New York sewer.

"Lansing," I said, bracing myself. A musician was bad enough, but a musician from Lansing was worse.

"What the hell is Lansing?" she yelled.

"It's a town in Michigan," I told her, but Mimi has never heard of anything beyond the five boroughs. She doesn't even know where the Pacific Ocean is.

"I've never heard of it so it must not be anything." I caught it on the side of the head for that.

"Whose club?" she wanted to know. She pulled my hair tighter and shoved my head against the cupboard door again.

"Sammy's."

"Sammy's. SAMMY'S. Oh, that's great, that's just great," she screamed. I should have lied. I should have told her a downtown club. She's jealous of Sammy.

She let go of my hair, and I ducked underneath her arm and ran out of the kitchen. Mimi was quick, though. She was behind me in two seconds, her purse snapping at the air.

"I didn't do anything you don't arrange fifty times a day," I yelled. I enjoyed saying that. In fact I relished it. "He's poor too," I screamed. "He lives in a slum with a saxophone player, and they eat Chinese food all the time."

WHACK. I got it on the back of the head this time. Then the living room ended, and I was in another corner.

"You're not going to see him again," she yelled. She pressed her arm across my chest, as if to bar my exit forever, and my back slapped against the cold windowpanes.

"Yes, I am. I love him."

Our eyes snagged and I watched her face twist.

"You don't either." She hoisted her purse above my head, and her eyes filled with poison.

"Yes, I do," I yelled. I left no room for doubt, and she knew it.

She brought the purse down, and for a moment she went silent. I suddenly heard the rush of traffic below us, the shriek of an ambulance and the confusion of horns. Then she looked up at me. "Effy's been arrested," she said. She didn't say it solemnly like anyone else would. She said it to get even with me.

Effy was in the 145th Precinct Prison. I went up there in the afternoon and waited for over two hours in the stifling hot waiting room for them to bring her down. It was jam-packed—there wasn't any place to sit down. The dirty windows were open, but there was no breeze, and the smell of our sweat and malodorous glands was so strong, I had to breathe through my mouth. There was only a handful of whites in there. Most of them were Negroes—mothers, wives, girlfriends, cousins, children. There was one Negro woman who wailed so inconsolably, it became a thread through the thick sound of voices, a mouth for all the grief.

I ended up standing behind a couple of tough-looking white men. One was about twenty-five and had a broken nose and two tattoos on his right arm—a red-and-black serpent and a green iridescent mermaid with breasts the size of balloons. Between the two was the name Veronica written in red, swirling letters. The other guy was older, about thirty or so, and potbellied. His hair was straight black and greasy, and comb marks clawed through it like rows of ditches. He smelled of piss and stale whiskey, and when he turned to the younger man and smiled, I noticed that one of his front teeth was black. I overheard him tell the younger guy something which really struck me, something that I haven't been able to shake from my thoughts ever since.

"If you've got to choose between being a nigger man or a white bitch, which would you rather be?" he whispered behind his hand.

"None of them," the younger guy said, and then he laughed a wheezing, cringing laugh.

"No kidding, but say you got to choose," the older man whispered louder. "Say someone's making you choose. Between a nigger man or a white bitch, which would you pick?"

"A white bitch," the younger guy whispered back. He looked nervously to his friend, to make sure that was the right answer.

The older guy laughed and said, "I picked that too, not that I'd want to be dick meat, but it's better than being a fucking spook." They laughed again, the younger man wheezing so much he broke out in a cough, the other guy falling so far forward, he disrupted a few greasy strands of hair. They fell across his sweaty brow and stuck there like wet, black lines.

When he straightened himself up, he leaned over to the young guy and whispered, "If you've got to choose between being a nigger woman or an ape, which would you choose?" It delighted him to set up this scenario. He grinned and his black tooth popped out on his cracked lower lip.

The younger guy had to think about that. He shoved his hands down into his pockets and looked around the room at some of the Negro women. His squinted eyes skimmed over the poor woman who was bent over in grief, they passed across a thin, wracked woman who was trying to control four small children, and landed on a heavyset Negro woman who had fallen asleep in the heat, her mouth hanging open. "An ape," he finally said.

"You know what I say when Joey ask me that?" the older one whispered.

"What?"

"I ask him what kind of ape."

They both doubled over and laughed hysterically, spit drooling out of the older man's mouth in a long, thin line. The younger one got himself going so much, he broke out in another cough, which brought him to his knees. Most of the Negroes looked at them, wondering what in the hell was so funny, and it crossed my mind to tell them.

I was really struck by this and have been turning it over in my mind ever since. It's sitting in the pit of my stomach like raw dough, and I can't eat. So it's worse to be a Negro than to be a woman, and then again it's worse to be a Negro woman than an ape. Is it really so horrible to white people to be a Negro? Is it really so bad to be a Negro woman that someone would rather be an ape? I cannot imagine this. I cannot fathom what brings people to these thoughts. Has this fucking world lost its mind?

If I had a choice between being a Negro man or a white woman, I'd choose to be a white woman. If I had the choice between being a Negro woman or an ape, I'd be a Negro woman. And what if I had to choose between being a white man or a Negro woman?

I would be a Negro woman.

They finally brought Effy down and took me into the visiting room. There was a huge plate of glass separating the prisoners from the visitors, with telephones to connect them. Eight chairs were on either sides of the glass, and Effy was sitting in one of them waiting for me. Her head was bent, as if her neck were broken, and when she looked up at me, shame flashed across her eyes. It all slipped under my skin again and passed right through me. I take things so badly.

I picked up the telephone with a shaky hand and Effy picked up hers. I asked her what happened. She said she was in Sticks's room when the cops busted in. She looked beaten, and I wanted to put my hand through the glass to touch her face. It used to be so untroubled, so clean, before Mimi took her off the stage and brought her into the house. It almost seemed as if I had never sat in her lap and had never felt her fingers in my hair. Why was she going down the drain now? Why did she choose this moment out of all the moments of her life?

"I'm going to quit Mimi's and move out of her apartment," I said. "When you get out, you live with me."

"Mimi fired me," Effy said. Her voice was flat and straight like a line. The greenish-gray uniform fell off her right shoulder, and I saw how bony it was.

"She's full of shit, Effy," I said loudly. "You know Mimi. She's fired you a hundred times. She'll take you back, but you shouldn't go back. I want you to come and live with me."

"That'd never work." Her face was blank, and small, puffy bags lay beneath her eyes. A purple-and-red scarf strapped her hair down, fuzzy strands of it poking out near her temples. She still looked beautiful, but that noble spirit in her eyes had vanished. Her stare was now vacant.

"Why not?"

"A nigger living on the Upper East Side?" She laughed, and I noticed she was missing a tooth. I knew I would never get that out of my mind, no matter how many nights passed. "What would I do, La? Clean the floors?" she said.

She looked lost and helpless, and it reminded me of the time I was ten years old and she finally took me to meet her grandmother, Saddie, in White Plains. She was always telling me what Saddie said, and Saddie was always saying things like, "Su-gar, come rest your bones, and I tell you something you ain't never heard before." Or she'd say, "Su-gar, shut your big ol' mouth and let me do the talking. I got more to say than ten peoples."

A picture of Saddie grew in my mind. She was this great big, soft tender-hearted Negro woman who could really talk. Even though I'd never met her, Effy and I always talked about her, like she was our favorite person. Whenever something would happen, I'd ask Effy, "What would Saddie say?" Then Effy would step back, splay her legs a little, and snap her hands to her waist. "She'd say: Su-gar, you looking like a long drink of water. Better put your dogs up on this here table, and let me do the talking." It always made me laugh.

Saddie became a permanent fixture in my imagination. She was more real to me than Mimi's Spanish mother, whom I had only met a few times, and somewhere in the summer of my tenth year, I finally got to meet her. I was going to see my hero, the woman who I had loved from afar for most of my life. Effy took me up to White Plains with her on the train, and she filled me up with so many Saddie stories that by the time we got off, I was ready to run into Saddie's great big flabby arms.

Saddie was thin and pointed. She said, "Su-gar," all the time just like Effy said, but she wasn't like I expected. She never asked Effy anything about herself, not even how was she doing. She didn't ask about me either. She hardly noticed I was there. She talked about Effy's sisters and brothers and her cousins, but most of all, she talked about how much she hated white people. "Su-gar, it's the white folks—they take everything, and they don't leave the colored nothing. They can't stand to see a nigger get something. It make what they got look like less when a nigger got it too. Su-gar, let me tell you. . . ."

I was only ten, but I knew she didn't love Effy, not like Effy loved her. And by not loving her back, Saddie made her small. She took away her radiance.

On the way back, Effy slid down in her seat on the train and put her knees up on the seat in front of us. I did the same, and she kept her arm around me the whole way, neither of us saying a word. That was the end of Saddie, though. We never wondered what Saddie would say or do again. It was as if Saddie had died.

I looked through the smudged-up glass at Effy's battered face and her watery eyes. I should have loved her more, I thought. "I won't live on the East Side, then," I said. "I'll live somewhere else. Wherever you want, Effy."

She stared at me for a few moments. "I wouldn't mind living with you, La, but I don't want to live with . . . yours."

With yours. That was the first wall I ever felt slam down between me and Effy.

"You're grown now, La," she said. She glanced over her shoulder as if someone were behind her, but there was no one.

She said those words so coldly it twisted my heart. What did she mean? You're grown up so we don't need to know one another anymore? Or was it, you're grown so let's not pretend—you're white and I'm Negro?

"How would you feel about me living with yours?" I asked. I pressed my forehead against the glass. "We could live in Harlem."

"They wouldn't like it," she said. "You're Mimi's." Her voice trailed off, and she looked away from me, down at her scraped-up knuckles.

My heart started banging inside my chest, and I felt a warm rush of blood flood across my face. "I never thought of myself as Mimi's," I said. My voice was choked, and something lodged in my throat. "I always thought of myself as—as yours." My eyes were stranded on her face, but she didn't look up. She blinked her eyes a lot of times, as if to signal some emotion, but she never looked up. "Why are you doing this to me, Effy?" I cried. I felt the tears sting my eyes. "What did I do?"

She finally looked up at me. "I taught you to sing and dance, La. I don't have anything else to teach you."

Is that how she saw it? She did her job—she taught the white girl to sing and dance like a Negro. I remembered all the times Effy had made me a tent over her bed, and how she and I would lie all day underneath it, singing the gospels. She was a radiant woman then. She was still in her twenties. No one could resist her, not even Mimi, but that was before Mimi brought her into the house. She was still singing then, and I know she never wanted to go upstairs. Before that happened, we'd sing the gospels all afternoon, Effy rocking that tent. I followed every move she made with her head and her arms and legs. We danced on our backs. I copied her then, and I copy her now. We told some tall tales too, but Effy's were always better than mine. "Child," she'd say, "have I ever got one for you." Then she'd laugh, but paper's no good to describe a laugh like hers—it was the laugh of Venus.

I stared through the grimy plate of glass at her. Her face was so utterly blank, it was disturbing. This is not Effy, I told myself. This is someone else. What had Mimi done to her? I wondered violently. For as long as I live I will never forget the day Mimi took her off the stage and dragged her upstairs to one of the backrooms. I was fifteen and Effy was thirty-five. Before they made it up the stairs Effy realized what Mimi was doing, and she dug her heels into the wooden steps and held on to the banister. When I heard her scream I ran out into the hallway, and I'll never forget what I saw. Effy was wearing a red satin costume and a pair of black high heels. She was backed up against the wall, holding onto the banister with both hands, screaming, "No-ooooooooooo," while Mimi yanked her from one step to the next.

"You're going up, Effy," Mimi shrieked. "You're going up or you're going out."

Effy clawed at the wall and her heels scraped loudly against the wooden stairs as Mimi jerked her up, step by step. When they got up to the top, Effy broke down and sagged to her knees, begging Mimi not to do this to her. "Don't, Mimi," she pleaded. "Don't do this to me. Please don't do this to me. I beg you." The sound of her voice was chilling. It was so piteous, I couldn't fathom how Mimi could continue. She did, though—she dragged her down the hall, Effy on her knees, the toes of her shoes rasping against the wooden floors, scratching out her grief. She threw Effy in the room and locked the door behind them. I had to go back on stage, and as I descended the stairs, I heard Effy crying. I don't know how I was able to sing.

Mimi appeared behind the curtain about half an hour later, as if nothing had happened. When I saw her standing there, I knew I would never feel anything for her again. As soon as my numbers were over, I ran up to Effy's room. She was sitting on the window ledge, staring blindly out the window. Her knees were torn up and bloody, and her face was wrenched. I sat down next to her, and she held me in her arms. "Oh, La," she said. "Oh, my La."

A few hours after that, Mimi brought up the first man. He was a middle-aged white man with greasy red hair and a gut so grotesque, the buttons on the front of his shirt gaped open.

How could she ever think I belonged to Mimi? I stared through the window at her beautiful face and pressed my forehead against the filthy glass. "Why did Mimi take you off the stage and put you in the house, Effy?" I asked her again.

She stared at me unblinking. I don't think I will ever know the answer to this.

"You're trying to get rid of me, Effy," I said. A whole stream of tears poured out of my eyes.

"You got better things to do with your life," she said. She pushed her chair back and rose up.

"What are you doing? Effy—" I yelled, but she hung up the telephone. Like an idiot, I slapped the glass with my hand and yelled her name, but she walked away from me, toward the door, where a guard took her by the elbow and steered her out. She glanced back over her shoulder, which told me she didn't want to do this, and a look surfaced in her eyes— a look of such utter black despair I knew it would roll around in my mind forever.

I'm in her room right now, lying on top of her bed, where she has lain on her back so many times, staring up at the ceiling, waiting for one sweaty man or another to blow his wad. Mimi's downstairs. She knows

I'm up here, but she wouldn't dare say anything to me. She knows I've gone under again.

I went inside Effy's closet and pulled the door closed. Her silk robes and all her dresses brushed across my face. I sat down in the darkness and leaned up against the cool wall and breathed her in. That's all I wanted to do—to be surrounded by the smell of her.

Mimi found me in there. She came into the room and found me sitting in Effy's dark closet. She didn't raise her voice, though. She didn't even say, "What the hell is wrong with you?" She just shook her head like I was incurable and sat down on the edge of Effy's bed.

"You wish you were a Negro, don't you?"

I stared at her. *She doesn't know anything.* I pressed my mouth against my drawn-up knees and dug my teeth into my bones.

"She's never coming back, is she?" I said.

Mimi shook her head. "No, not this time," she whispered. I knew she meant it. She crossed one leg over the other, pulled her sea green silk dress over her knees, and poked a finger into her stiff, black hair to scratch her scalp.

The night was starting up. Through the walls I could hear the creak of bedsprings and the low moan of men's voices. Radios played down the hall, and the fans beat out the time.

"Mimi, why did you take Effy off the stage and bring her into the house?"

"Never mind about that," she said. She looked over her shoulder, as if something were outside the window, but there was nothing.

"She's gone now, so why can't you tell me?"

She leaned way over and brushed the hair from my forehead. I could see down the front of her dress—two big, white squishy breasts all strapped down. "Your hair's like a mop again," she said. "I'm going to take you down to Gordy's—"

"Mimi," I interrupted, "tell me why you brought her into the house."

She straightened up and her eyes hardened around the edges. "It's history, Lana. That was over five years ago."

"I know it was, but just tell me," I said. I crept out of the closet a little and fixed my eyes on her face. "What does it matter now? She's gone."

Mimi stared at me for a long time, her eyes inching across my face. "You were a better singer," she finally said. "The people liked you better. I didn't need another singer."

Silence. *The horrible truth screams in it.*

God. I wish I never asked. I wish I didn't know.

I did this to her. I made Effy a whore.

What can a Negro woman be in this world? A maid. A nanny. A whore. And what about a Negro man? A bellhop. A porter. A hustler.

And what about me, singing like a Negro?

There were a few lines that looked as if they'd been scrawled by a child, but that was the end of the entry, so I closed the notebook.

"God," Elena said. She dropped her head backward and stared up at the cold, barren eaves.

I couldn't really speak. There was too much crowding my thoughts—too many new images and too many old impressions of Lana floundering around, uprooted.

"No wonder she never told us," Elena said. "How could she ever have told us this?" She pointed to the notebook, which lay closed in my lap. It felt hot to me, as if I'd just pulled it from a fire. I could almost see the radiation bounding off of it.

"Lana sang like a Negro," she whispered.

"I know." We couldn't imagine, though.

"Effy taught her, and then Mimi made her sing in her club."

Of all that we'd read tonight, this fact most impressed us—that Effy had taught her to sing like a Negro, and that Lana, through no fault of her own, had pushed her off the stage and shoved her into the backrooms of Mimi's whorehouse.

We quietly returned the journal to the box and closed the flaps. We didn't feel ready to leave the attic yet, so we sat down next to the boxes on the cold, wooden planks and thought about it some more.

"We still don't know why she has that cane or why she hates the jazz, though," I whispered. I stuffed my hands up under my sweater and tried to warm them.

"Still, Maddie, we know a lot."

It was certainly true—in just one hour's time we had learned more about Lana than we had in our whole lifetime.

"We don't know what it's going to do to her, though," I said. "She could really be sick tomorrow."

This sent Elena and me into my bedroom, where, before the opened window, we knelt in the cold December air and swore on the full moon that we would never read another word of Lana's journals so long as we lived. Had it been summer we would have walked over to the swan pond with a fistful of quarters and thrown them in, but it was too cold out now. We would do that in the morning.

When I lay down to go to sleep, my mind wouldn't shut off. I couldn't stop the images from racing through my brain. I kept seeing Lana and Leo writhing in bed, and Mimi chasing Lana through the apartment, hitting her with her purse. But most of all I saw Mimi dragging Effy down the hallway on her bloody knees, while Effy screamed, "No-ooooooooo."

13

Elena and I said next to nothing at breakfast the next morning. We didn't know what to say to Lana or Leo, knowing what we now knew about them. Saying "Good morning" even felt strange. We quietly stared at them and felt the confusion of our shifting impressions. In particular we watched Lana to see how she was, to see if there was any change in her since we'd read her journal. She appeared to be normal. I listened to her voice carefully, to make certain it had not gone too high or too low. It was regular—she spoke a normal amount, and her level of cheerfulness was high, considering that Elena and I sat at her breakfast table dumbstruck.

"It could take a few days to hit her," I said when we reached the cold swan pond. "Maybe it takes longer when she's been asleep." I looked up at the sky. It was milky white, with small pockets of gray, and the distant university buildings stood against it on the barren hills, lonely and shivering under their brick skins.

"I doubt it, Maddie," Elena said, but she was very eager to get rid of her eight quarters. We stood on the half-frozen edge of the pond in the hazy morning light, and one by one, we heaved our quarters as far out to the deep center as possible. Elena threw hers first, swearing beforehand that she would never read another word of

Lana's journals so long as she lived. I swore the same, without quite the same passion or conviction, and then, one by one, I threw the last of Leo's quarters into the pond's cold, deep middle.

Lizzy was waiting for us at the corner where the drugstore and the movie theater touched walls, her breath coming out in big cloudy gusts. The traffic was thick on the downtown streets, the school buses plowing through the slushy snow, the cars proceeding slowly behind them. Everything looked dirty—all the shop windows, the cars, even the steamy, inviting windows of the Blue Bird Restaurant. "You better not tell her, Maddie," Elena said. I didn't say I would or I wouldn't; I just nodded my head and fixed my eyes straight ahead on Lizzy. I doubted I could keep it to myself, though.

"Is Lana sick again?" Lizzy asked. She knew something was wrong.

Elena and I looked at one another and then shook our heads. We kept walking, our boots pushing through the heavy wet snow, Lizzy trailing behind us.

"Did Leo do something?" She edged up next to me, her eyes fixed on my face.

"No," I said.

"Then what happened?"

"Nothing," Elena said, but Lizzy knew we were lying. She could tell by the way my eyes angled away that I knew something. I was going to have to tell her the rest—I just didn't know when.

Elena and I watched Lana for a few days to make certain there wasn't a delayed reaction. She seemed perfectly fine, and when a few more days passed without consequence, we felt it safe to assume that the best time to read her journal was when she was asleep at night— not that we were planning to read it again. I was afraid to read anymore. Our minds were swimming in it, struggling to make sense of it, to meld it somehow with our old impressions of Lana. I didn't know who she was anymore. It was so difficult to place her with a woman who hit her with brooms and purses and ran a whorehouse, and it was even harder to imagine her singing like a Negro.

Winter set in not long after. The cold had a way of covering up this last great sin, of sweeping it away or sealing me off from it, because it ceased to sting my conscience. It started to snow a lot, which meant Miss Thomas no longer came outside in the morning to lose her mind on her lawn. Minnie Harp was not to be seen either;

both her burial grounds and her fire pit now lay submerged beneath mounds of snow. It would be spring before we saw her again. We continued with operation newspaper, but my excitement for it had dwindled substantially. We knew what the articles were about, and they never really enlightened us anyway. We kept it up because it was an old habit by now, and with nothing more pressing, it gave us something to do with our cold afternoons.

Lana was doing better. We noticed she was sometimes strained, but she never gave in to it. She kept on top of whatever it was and continued to supply us with new and interesting things to do. She helped us make snow forts outside with snow chairs and tables and snow beds, and when the weather got especially cold we made a snow city.

She hosted scary parties in the cellar, where we all dressed in private and made ourselves look as horrifying as possible. We hid in the shadows, and when Lana said the word, we all came out at once. No matter what any of us did, Lana's costumes were always the best.

She wrote us some short plays, which we put on on a stage she built us in the cellar, complete with a red curtain and two dressing rooms. I couldn't help but notice how attracted she was to that stage. The way she painstakingly built it out of apple boxes, sanding down all the faces until they were smooth and splinterless, made me realize how much she wanted us to have it. She was very particular about the curtain too—any old blanket or piece of fabric wouldn't do. It had to be special, thick red drapery material, for which she paid a lot, certainly more than Leo would have liked. Old chairs from auction houses and church basement sales turned up in the audience, and round mirrors went up on the wall above small tables filled with square pats of makeup. She rehearsed us too, with too much seriousness sometimes, as if we were a real troupe of actors, putting on a real play.

"It's weird, Maddie," Elena kept saying. "It's really weird."

I enjoyed putting on Lana's plays, but I felt a little odd standing on her stage and making up in her dressing rooms, knowing at the root of it all lay her past career as a singer and dancer. A part of her still longed for the stage, I knew, and when she walked around on it, setting it up and blocking our movements, I tried to imagine her fifteen years younger, standing at its edge, belting out songs like a

Negro, while Leo played the piano feverishly off to her side. I never really could, though.

She and Leo didn't talk as much as they used to. Instead, it seemed that silence filled their few waking moments together. Leo was so busy now that a lot of mornings he got up earlier than anyone else and left before we ate our breakfast. When he started missing dinners, it seemed we had lost him for good. Every time his place was empty at the dining table, Elena, Lizzy, and I could just feel their relationship deteriorating.

I think Lana kept herself busy with our plays, with making our costumes and fixing our stage, so she wouldn't have to think about it. She kept busy with Garta too. She visited her in the evenings sometimes, spot-inspection-like, to make sure that Lizzy was being treated right. She kept talking to Garta about her enormous stack of problems too, helping her to fix at least the most fixable. Together, they reorganized her apartment; they wallpapered the living room walls with a rose-colored paper, plugged up the rusty shower stall with spackle, and laid new linoleum down on the kitchen floor. She helped Garta lose a few pounds, and sent away to New York for a special mud mask she hoped would help Garta's war-torn complexion.

Between our plays and Garta, Lana didn't write as often as she used to, nor did she cut out many articles. She hardly ever shook, though, and we only found her in odd places twice that I could remember.

As far as Leo went, I think she started to pretend he didn't exist.

When Lizzy and I watched them through the bathroom grate at night after Leo came home, we noticed that Lana would sometimes walk around in there, as if he weren't really sitting on the bed or in the chair. Occasionally, she'd say something to him about the bills or the taxes, but a lot of times they didn't say anything. After a while, I think Leo started pretending she didn't exist either—sometimes he would just walk into their bedroom late at night, take off his clothes, and crawl under the covers without even walking over to her writing room to say hello.

I didn't know which was worse—the fighting or their awful silence.

"It's all going to break," Elena whispered to me at night. "One of these days, it's all going to just break apart."

It seemed my nerves started getting worse. Either they were growing, or they were having babies, because suddenly they began to weigh more inside my veins. I seriously considered telling Lana about them, and if not Lana, then at least Lizzy. They were almost to the point of taking over my body, I feared, and I worried that slowly but surely they were driving me insane. I couldn't bring myself to this confession, though. I was too embarrassed that I had them, for one thing, and I was afraid if I really told someone the truth, I might be taken away to an insane asylum.

They couldn't stand the peace and quiet of my winter. The silent war between Lana and Leo drove them crazy, as did Lana's journals, which now sat untouched in the attic. They wanted me to read them, especially since Lana had not collapsed after our last trespass. I'd sworn on the moon, though, and every time I suggested it to Elena, she reminded me of that. "We swore on the moon, Maddie," she said, "and we already broke one promise. Besides, we threw close to four dollars into the pond."

It wasn't until Christmas night that I finally broke my vow and read some more. Lizzy had such a lousy Christmas that I had to. Garta had given her only a pair of cheap, black fur-lined boots, while she'd bought Jimmy a whole pile of presents. Then, to make it worse, Don had beat the shit out of Garta for being too sweet to Joe on the phone when he called to say Merry Christmas. Lizzy had tried to save her, but she ended up getting slammed against the refrigerator, her head cracking against the metal handle. I watched it all from the corner, my heart shriveling in my chest.

I took her home with me that night. We walked through the silent streets, our heads bent against the wind, the sky above us a perfect ceiling of stars and moon. We didn't say anything about what had happened. The cold wind seemed to sweep it from our minds, but when we crawled into my bed and turned out the light, it came back to us, as if the dark had ushered it in. I didn't know what to say to her, nor she to me, but it was there, riding between us like an elephant.

I lay awake for a long time, feeling her presence as if it were a dark weight in my bed. She turned over after a while, and when she thought I had drifted off, she pushed her face into the pillow and I heard a muffled sob. I had never once heard her cry. I had seen Garta beat her up. I had heard Garta say the worst things to her, but I had never heard her cry. I pushed my fingers through her hair and felt a hard lump the size of a boulder on the back of her head.

I pressed against her and whispered in her ear, "You'll never believe what Elena told me this morning."

"What?" she sobbed from the depths of my pillow.

"As a Christmas present she told me something about Lana's secret."

Lizzy turned over immediately and stared at me. Hearing about Lana's secret was as good as smelling salts. "What?" she said.

"Wait here." I disappeared into the attic and very carefully opened the flaps to that box and took out Lana's journal. I considered ripping out the pages Elena and I had read so Lizzy wouldn't know there was more, but I decided against it. It was bad enough reading Lana's journal without tearing it apart. I shoved the journal under the red cushion where our copies of the *New York Times* were and went out and got her. We crept quietly down the staircase to the hallway and threw on our coats, and when Lizzy slipped her bare feet into those measly fur-lined boots Garta had squeezed herself to buy, I knew I was doing the right thing.

We climbed the stairs in silence and quietly shuffled into the cold, dusty attic, walking back to the red chair. I picked up the cushion and revealed the journal to her. "It's Lana's," I whispered, while my heart raced like the wind.

"Where did you get it?" She shouldered her brown corduroy coat and crept closer to the chair. Her eyes were the size of quarters, and I noticed how thin her legs looked poking out of those cheap black boots.

"Elena found it in the closet in Lana's room," I lied. "We have to put it back tomorrow." Lizzy crawled into the red chair next to me and stared dumbstruck down at the journal. "Most of it doesn't say anything, but there are a few pages that are good." I turned to page 32, where Elena and I had last started. My fingers trembled along the edges, and I shivered inside my coat. Nonetheless I read it out loud to her in the thinnest whisper. I read her every single page Elena and I had read, relishing every last word of it, looking up every so often to luxuriate in Lizzy's unparalleled joy and astonishment. It was the best Christmas present I could have ever given her.

When I finished the parts Elena and I had read, I stopped. I didn't think we should go any further. I hadn't yet violated my last promise to the moon (I hadn't really read another word of Lana's journal, since I had only read the same words), but Lizzy wanted to keep reading. When she started to turn the page, I stopped her.

"I don't know if we should read anymore," I whispered. "We swore on the moon that we wouldn't read anymore."

"What if we just read one more and then swear on the moon again? This time for good. It's Christmas, Maddie," she said, as if that made all the difference. "The moon won't mind."

The wind knocked against the window and sent in another draft of freezing air. My hands ached so much from the cold that I shoved them underneath my butt. If we read another entry, I thought, it meant one more sin for me. I was losing track of how many I had. I would have preferred not to add another one, but the truth was— I wanted to read it just as much as she did.

I looked over at Lizzy. She was holding her breath, waiting for me to decide. "You can never tell Elena I let you read any of this."

"I promise," she said, crossing her heart.

I opened the journal to an even later date—November 25, 1947— and began reading in the same shaky whisper Elena had read in. The whole time I spoke, my heart knocked against my chest. I was scared of what this might do to Lana and of what it might do to me. I had more sins now than anyone I knew.

Tonight was the worst of nights. I was at Sammy's onstage doing a dance number when I saw Mimi leaning up against the wall by the photographs of Billie Holiday, near the end of the bar, with a drink in her hand. I couldn't imagine what she was doing here. She hates Sammy because he stole all her best singers. I tried to see her face, but it was too dark. She was wearing an old black coat, one I haven't seen her wear since I was in high school. I've got to quit her. I can't keep doing two clubs. It's killing me.

I had to do another set before I could find out why she was here. It was torture, her watching me. I knew she didn't like the new stuff Leo and I were doing. I could feel her nose rising, she's such a fucking snob.

When I finally got to her, she was a little drunk. I knew something bad had happened, because Mimi almost never drinks. The last time she drank was when Teddy left us four years ago.

It was about one in the morning. The place was stiflingly hot and smoky and packed with Negroes, which is why Mimi was standing near the end of the bar—none of them were standing there. I edged up next to her and rested my back against the cool, brass bar.

"What brings you here?" I asked her. The sweat poured down my back in itchy streams, and I wiped my forehead with the back of my hand.

"Your new routine isn't good," Mimi said. She sniffed and rolled her eyes. "Get me another drink, will you." Her hair had fallen—half of it was standing like black straw on her shoulders. Her makeup had worn off, and she looked old, like someone's mother who scrubbed floors all day to put them through college.

I turned around and asked Les for another drink—she was drinking double gins.

"You shouldn't kick your legs so high," she said after I handed it to her. "I could see your underwear. My dancers don't show their underwear."

"I know, Mimi. You only have a whorehouse in the back."

She ignored me and siphoned off half the glass.

"You don't look as good up there as you look at Mimi's," she said. "Sammy's stage is shit." The way she swiveled her head back and forth, scanning the crowd in disdain, really wore on me.

"Why are you here?" I asked her again. It's Mimi's style not to let you know. She likes to drag it out and then kill you with it. When Teddy packed his bags and left, she sat in my room for over an hour before she told me.

"I came to see you." The strap of my black dress had fallen down my shoulder, and she yanked it up. "Cheap dress," she sneered. "Cheap and tacky."

"Why are you here, Mimi?"

She looked around the room again, shooting deadly glances at the people who'd left her for Sammy's. Grace, Louis, and Berty. Her eyes ended up on Leo.

"He looks like a hood," she said. She took another slug of her drink and threw her head back.

"He doesn't love like one."

She hauled off and slapped my face. Sammy saw her and started to come over, but I shook my head. "Mimi," I mouthed, and he nodded. I shouldn't have been embarrassed—everyone knows about her—but I was. My cheeks burned with it.

"Let's go back to your dressing room," she said, draining off the rest of her glass. "I've got something to tell you."

The hallway back to my dressing room was long and dark, and there were a couple of Negro men smoking reefer. They moved out of our way, into the shadows.

"This kind of shit, I don't have," Mimi yelled. "This kind of shit is dangerous."

Since the telephones and bathrooms were along the hallway, there was no way to keep people out of there. It wasn't the best of circumstances, but it *wasn't the worst thing either. She harped on it for ten minutes, as if I took my life into my hands every time I walked down it. Something else was bothering her, something she hadn't said yet.*

When we got back to my dressing room she went through my rack of costumes, pawing through the dresses, checking the seams and sniffing the armpits. "We got better costumes at Mimi's," she said. "He don't clean his. They stink. They're all cheap and they stink."

She pushed the rack away from her, and then sank down in the blue chair near the window, her legs falling so far apart, I could see her girdle pressed around her fat thighs.

"Effy's dead," she said. Her face caved in and her lips started trembling like waves.

"What?" A sheet of something cold and rigid passed through me.

"Effy's dead," she said louder. "Somebody put a bullet in her head." She pulled her dress over her splayed knees and stared at me, her eyes blinking rapidly.

My whole body started to shake, and I dropped to my knees on the gritty concrete.

"She went bad," Mimi whispered. "I don't know why, but she went bad." She wiped her mouth nervously, her fingers racing back and forth across her stale lips as if she wanted to wear them down or silence them forever.

My heart hammered inside my chest like a piston, and all the blackness and disgust, all the horror and cruelty that punctuated Mimi's days and nights, exploded in my mind like a bullet. I fell forward, my hands slapping down on the cold, filthy concrete. It all started with Mimi—every last bit of it. "You put her in the house," I yelled. "You shouldn't have put her in the house, Mimi. You couldn't stand to see her do well. You wanted to knock her down—"

"She didn't have to go into the house," Mimi shrieked. "She could have gone somewhere else." If you could have seen her—her legs spread, her mouth a huge hole in her face, moving at an inhuman velocity, her voice so utterly loud and unstrung, it was raging—you would have understood my hatred.

I stared at her, at her baggy red face, at her straw black hair, and I wanted to wipe her out. I crept forward, crawling across the concrete on my hands and knees, every impulse bent in the direction of ruining her. I was going to hurt her. I was going to bite her ankles or dig my fingernails into her pasty white flesh or squeeze her fat, crepey throat.

"You shouldn't have fired her. She didn't have anyplace to go, Mimi," I cried out. "Where the fuck was she going to go after she's been your whore for twenty years?"

"She was doing drugs, and I couldn't have that." Her eyes swam with black poison.

I kept creeping forward, my eyes fixed on her fat neck. "You should have gotten help for her," I screamed. My throat felt stripped bare. "She was yours to take care of. You made her, Mimi, and you owed her." I screamed this last so loud I almost passed out. I felt my head pulse at my temples, and the blood rushed through my ears so fast, I feared I might faint.

"I didn't see you rushing to help her," Mimi yelled. "You were too busy screwing your hood."

I took one more look at her, and the hate flooded through me with such hot and terrifying intensity, I knew I had to get out of there. I wanted to kill her for all that she had killed inside me and Effy—all of us who'd lived in her sickening wake for the past twenty years. I couldn't trust myself to be in the same room with her any longer. I stumbled to my feet and fled my dressing room, slamming the door behind me. I staggered out to the back alley behind Sammy's and fell down on the wet pavement and wept. I heard sirens screaming on the streets, and rats slashing back and forth in the dark. Above me, black clouds raced across the sky like thieves, and I wondered if they didn't have some evil power.

My mind grew ten mouths that screamed, "Effy's dead," and my heart turned a little blacker, a little more bitter and grew more empty. It wasn't the emptiness that hurt so much—it was the claws that gouged it out. I dug my cold, bare heels into the filthy pavement and threw my back against the brick wall and refused to believe it. I wailed, "No-oooo," into the fucking night and got nothing back. Dead, one Negro whore, I could hear someone say, and I screamed like an idiot.

Mimi's voice sounded out the back door like a fog blast. I sprang to my feet and crashed through the back alley. I coursed aimlessly down a few streets, then a few more, not knowing where I was going, and ended up drinking vodka in a bar called Rames on 85th St, on the tab of a walleyed sixty-year-old loser. I smoked all his cigarettes and swilled down his vodka like it was Kool-Aid, and told him my name was Sophie. I don't remember all I said to him— I only know that I didn't stop drinking until 3 A.M. when he stuffed five dollars into my hand and hailed me a cab.

I couldn't go back to Mimi's apartment. I can never live there again. I went to her club instead, where I lay down on the dark, empty stage and felt my life unfurl. Effy took me out of the house, away from the keyholes upstairs, where I saw enough to reel in my mind for centuries, and she brought me to this stage. She stood behind the red velvet curtain and mouthed the words to *the songs, in case I forgot them, and did the whole dance number in her stocking feet, in case I lost track of the steps. She gave me all she had, and then Mimi punished her for it. How can I ever forget that?*

It was quiet and I heard only my ragged breath and the creak of bedsprings above the black rafters. How many times the sound of my breath has mingled with the creak of bedsprings. It's like a heartbeat to me now. Rasp, rasp, rasp. My life unfolded here, within these tainted walls, where the red curtain cordoned off right and wrong. I have passed back and forth, have gone in and out, have lived on both sides. Amid sordid fucking and screams, among sweating men and foul smells, alongside Negro women and broken dreams, I have grown up. There was one person I loved who made it work, and someone put a bullet in her head.

I went with Delors and Ummy to Effy's mother's apartment for the wake. She was laid out in the living room, but the pine casket was closed, and red ribbons fell where her face should have been. She was shot up pretty badly, someone said.

I had grown up in Mimi's house with twenty Negro women. How was it that I'd never been in one of their apartments? I had visited Saddie's, but that was so long ago I couldn't remember. Effy's mother's apartment was small and cramped, and the walls were falling apart. Small patches of rose-colored wallpaper clung to the plaster where it still existed, and the plaster turned to powder at a touch. Fine particles drifted down from the ceiling like snow and covered the top of Effy's casket.

All the windows faced alleys, and the light was so poor it felt like dusk, though it wasn't much past noon. There was a tiny, scabby kitchen just off the living room, where people heaped their coats on top of a wooden table which stood pressed in the corner. The floor was so worn you could see the floorboards beneath, and the floorboards were so worn you could see the apartment below. If you looked down just right, you could see that fine particles of plaster covered everything down there.

I don't know how many people lived here, but on my way back to the living room I saw a bedroom that had a stack of six mattresses piled neatly in a corner. Clothes—men's, women's, and children's—hung from a strained curtain rod and cut the light. A sour breeze parted a green dress and a black coat and blew over me like cold, putrid breath.

I walked into the living room. There were a lot of children there. They were all dressed in their Sunday best, their hair combed down, their faces shiny clean. I didn't count them, but I would say there were over twenty. Altogether, sixty people flooded Effy's mother's apartment. She borrowed the chairs from

a local church—they were wooden and folding and had the letters HUPC
*stenciled in red on their backs. Almost every inch of the living room was taken
up by them. A plaid green sofa was pushed up against the back wall to
accommodate them, and a small table, wedged in the corner, stood near it,
filled with framed photographs which teetered uneasily beneath a lace curtain
blowing in the cold breeze.*

*Outside of Delors and Ummy, I knew only one other person in the room.
Saddie. She was bent over, almost a hunchback now. She sat near the door
greeting everyone, taking their hands into her white gloved ones, repeating something which I never did catch. She didn't speak to me, nor did she offer her
hands.*

*I was the only white person there, and I was hated. I was alone in that room
like I have never been alone in my life. Delors and Ummy acted as if they didn't
know me. I suppose they had to—everyone else did. It made it more difficult for
me—I didn't have anyplace to put myself, no one to align myself with.*

*I could feel the hostility in the air. I was Mimi's, and there wasn't one
Negro in the room who didn't think it was her fault. They didn't know how
much we had in common.*

*I waited in line to pass by Effy's casket. People pushed ahead of me, as if the
rules for lines did not apply to me. I ended up standing very near to the door,
next to Saddie, waiting for everyone else to go first. She ignored me, staring past
me like I wasn't there, her neck jutting out from her hunched back, stiff with
pride. My presence wore on her, though, and she couldn't keep it up.*

*"Why you come, white girl?" she said loudly. Everyone in the room heard
her. Some of them snickered, though not loudly, and all of them stared at
me. One by one they edged away from me until I stood alone. I looked at
Saddie and remembered how she had treated Effy. It irked me the way she
sat at the door like the Grand Hunchback, presiding, bereft, over her grand-
daughter's passing. She never cared about Effy.*

*"Effy was like my mother," I said. I knew there was no way to communicate
this, that it was ridiculous to even try, but it was out of my mouth before I
could stop it.*

*Saddie sat back in her chair and calmly surveyed her rapt audience, her
proud gray head swiveling back and forth on her stiff neck. She was going to
have me. "We know who your mother be," she roared. "Your mama up here
in Harlem makin' whores of our daughters, that's who your mama be." Her
lips compressed, and her eyes blinked a dozen times in a row, as if she were
fanning her hot thoughts.*

"I know," I said. "She should be arrested."

The room went silent, and no one said anything. Dark, bewildered eyes fell on me, and then on Saddie. She was thinking fast. I could see it racing past her eyes.

"Who you think put those fine clothes on your back? Who you think paid for your speakin' so good? Huh?" She shifted in her seat and folded her arms across her chest, nodding her gray head to Effy's mother and to another woman who stood just beyond the casket. They nodded back, and quite a few of them said, "Yes," and "Uh-huh," but mostly they just stared at me.

"I know," I said. "I feel ashamed about that. That's in the past, though. I pay my own way now, and I don't work for Mimi anymore."

"Yeah, singing like a nigger," Saddie roared. "That how you make your way."

As if it were one mouth, the whole room laughed, and I felt the crush of absolute rejection. I braved a look at the sea of their dark faces, wilting in the mixture of hate and curiosity which flooded out of their black, fathomless eyes. I stared down at my shaky white hands and at the fading bouquet of pink roses I'd brought for Effy. "I can't help the way I sing," I said quietly. "Effy taught me to sing, just like someone in this room taught her."

No one said anything again. They just gaped at me, and I knew it was time for me to leave. I walked rockily up to the casket, completely out of turn, and laid my limp bouquet of pink roses on top of Effy's cheap pine casket.

"White's can't never wait behind niggers," Saddie crowed. "Even at a nigger's layin' out, they got to be first."

I should have realized it would look like this, but I wasn't thinking straight. There are no words to explain how desperately I wanted to get out of there — how desperately they wanted me to leave. I touched one of the pink rosebuds, and without thinking I kissed the top of Effy's casket. As I fled down the hallway on quaking legs, I heard Saddie's voice: "Bubbie, wipe that kiss off. We don't want it dryin'. It dry on there, we got to get it off with a jackhammer."

Everyone laughed again, and I imagined Bubbie wiping it off with a dishrag.

I went to Effy's room and opened the window so the cold air would sweep my thoughts clean. Mimi had stripped it of everything, save the bed and nightstand, but she saved a few things for me — Effy's white silk robe, her radio, the apricot bedspread, and her collection of Billie Holiday records. Saddie took the rest. I put her robe on and lay underneath the spread. When that wasn't good enough, I went into her closet again and pulled the door closed and smelled her. My head grazed the back wall, where her dresses used to hang, and I let the tears roll out of me, while through the wall, I heard my heartbeat—rasp, rasp, rasp.

Somehow, if you parted all the dark waters and plunged down to the bottom of it, through the weeds and scum, Mimi would be there.

I can't get it out of my mind how much those Negroes hated me. They loathed me. I felt it like it was made of daggers. I've never been to one of their gatherings. I've only been in their clubs and have never once felt their hatred. It was very honest, though—only in their surroundings do they dare be honest. In a place like Mimi's, they never could be.

I believe in my heart that I loved Effy more than Saddie ever did. What am I trying to say—that I'm good, I'm above reproach, that they shouldn't have hated me because I actually loved one of them? See how great I am? I loved this Negro woman more than her own grandmother did. You idiot, Lana.

They live here, we live there. We do this for our livings, they do that. How would I feel if I saw white women scrubbing the floors, while Negro women walked past them on their way to walk their poodles in Central Park? What if I were one of those women on the floor? How does it feel, Lana, to be on the floor scrubbing while a Negro woman steps over you on her way out to the opera? It feels wrong, not as it should be.

They had a right to hate me.

One day ago, Effy died, and I died too.

That was the end of the entry so I closed the journal and slipped it under the cushion without saying a word. It wasn't a good entry to read on Christmas, but then no one said it would be.

"I don't think those Negroes should have been so mean to Lana," Lizzy whispered. "Lana never did anything to them. Gus would never have done that."

"She might have," I said. "If she'd been there, she might have. Delors and Ummy did, and they knew Lana better than Gus knows her now."

"I'm a Negro, and I would never do that to Lana."

"You're not a whole Negro," I reminded her. "Garta's your mother and she's not a Negro."

"I know, but if you're half Negro, you're all Negro. Joe told me that. Just a little bit of Negro, he said, and you've got to be a whole one." She pulled her coat around her, and shoved her hands under her armpits. "We have to swear on the moon," she whispered.

I wasn't particularly interested in bending down before the moon a third time, since I highly doubted the moon would believe me. I had already lied twice. I felt very bad about it, terrible in fact, but nonetheless we stood in front of the windows in my room, shivering under our coats, and whispered to the full moon our promise that we would never touch Lana's journal again, so long as we lived.

We crawled into bed after that and watched the lights from the passing cars stalk across the walls.

"It's bigger than I thought," Lizzy whispered. She rolled her head on the pillow, and I stared into her velvety black eyes.

"I know." I squeezed her freezing hand and we huddled closer under the covers.

"I wonder what happened to Lana, though," she said. "We still don't know."

A freezing chill raced through me, and I realized for the first time that I was afraid to really know what had happened to Lana. We didn't bother to speculate either—it seemed those days were over.

I had to wait for Lizzy to fall asleep before I could put the journal back in the box and close the flaps. As if it were an exposed breast or a part of my rear end, I felt naked lying there. I wanted desperately to put it back. When she finally fell asleep, I rushed into the attic and lowered it into the box and closed the flaps. The feeling inside my chest was so disturbing I had no trouble believing I would never do it again. My nerves swarmed in there, overrunning it to such a degree that they were pressed against my lungs, making it difficult for me to breathe.

I went into the bathroom and doused the front of my chest with hot water, wondering all the while why people hated each other so much and why they were always attacking one another. Was that what life was made of? Of one beating after another? Just as I thought that, the light in the bathroom flickered on and off several times, and I heard the sharp cry of a cat outside in the backyard. My heart began to beat really fast, as if it were somehow attached to the flickering light and the screaming cat. The image of Lizzy's frightened face surfaced in my mind, her racing black eyes, and I thought it was me who would save her from a life of beatings. When the light flickered on and off again and the cat cried out, I knew it was true.

It was my first premonition.

14

As the winter wore on through January and February, my nerves got worse. In part, it was because of Lana and Leo. Their relationship didn't get any better. It stayed the same, and after a while it started to feel like it was becoming permanent, as if day by day it were hardening into this awful shape. It drove my nerves wild. There were so many of them now that at times I imagined being run over by a car, the nerves flooding out of me like bees from a hive. They were utterly bored of making snow forts and putting on plays in the cellar. They wanted me to break open Lana's locked journals with Leo's jackknife, and instead of coming out only at night, they started showing up during the day, sometimes after lunch, bugging me about it while I sat in Mrs. Devonshit's classroom.

Since I wouldn't read Lana's journals, they demanded that I do something else, something that was sneaky and thrilling and had the power to absorb them. It was Elena and her mysterious absences they finally settled upon. She kept disappearing after school and sometimes after dinner, and whenever I asked her where she went she said, "Nowhere." I knew that wasn't possible, so Lizzy and I stalked her after school, quietly pursuing her down the cold, snowy streets to find out where she was going.

One day in late February, we found her behind the Colgate Inn with a group of four boys and two girls who were leaning against a couple of cars, talking and smoking cigarettes. That was not her final destination, though. It was only a preliminary one—the real one, her true mission, took her up past Miss Thomas's and through a field where she disappeared into the woods. At first we staked it out behind a small knoll and waited until she crossed the field. When she plunged into the woods, we ran across it, but by the time we got to the woods, she was gone. Then to avoid crossing the field after her and losing her to the woods, we raced up before her and waited in the pines while she crossed the field. We thought we were so smart until we tried to follow her. It was very, very quiet in those winter woods, and there was no cover either. The more she thwarted our attempts, the more I longed to catch her. We tried burrowing into the woods further to pick her up later, but we never chose the right spot, and consequently we never even caught a glimpse of her.

This was supposed to absorb my nerves, but after a while it drove them mad. They started to flock to my stomach in droves, where they floundered around so much I lost my appetite. They took up so much room that sometimes I couldn't even eat a cracker. They kept me awake so long at night that by the next afternoon, I could barely keep my eyes open. When I fell asleep in class three days in a row, Mrs. Blanchard, the school nurse, was summoned to examine me. She checked my eyes and ears with a flashlight, and then searched my head for lice. I was hoping she would find the nerves. That way I would be spared the trouble of having to tell someone, but she didn't.

I finally decided to tell Miss Thomas about them. I remembered her Amazing Life-Saving Potion and thought maybe that might help me. It worried me that she sometimes lost her mind, but I was desperate. I hadn't been up to see her in a month, and when I crawled up the hill just before dark and stepped out of the woods onto her lawn, it gave me an eerie feeling to see her statues half buried in the snow, the thin stalks of her wildflowers poking up through the icy crust. It felt like death or something equally awful, and I worried that Miss Thomas wouldn't be the same, that the tragedy of winter had affected her too. Without the sun and her green flower-stalked yard, perhaps she had lost her mind altogether. I knocked on her door regardless— my nerves were crawling in the back of my throat.

When she opened the door I knew she was all right. She was

wearing a long, gray, pleated skirt and a pair of purple suede shoes. Her white hair was like a soft cotton halo around her head. "I'm thrilled to see you, Maddie," she said. She swung the door wide open with her arm, and even under her blue sweater, I could see her flesh wobble.

She took me into her kitchen, and when I sat down, I wondered how was I going to tell her about my nerves. You didn't just up and tell someone you had nerves. It seemed you should work your way up to it, but without any real warning it came out of my mouth. "I've got nerves," I said. I looked away from her, down at her purple suede shoes, my face burning hot in embarrassment.

"What do you mean, you've got nerves?" When I looked up, there was a smile on her lips, which worried me, but her olive-sized eyes regarded me kindly and encouraged me to go on.

"I've got *nerves*. I've got lots of them. They keep me awake at night, and now they go into my stomach and sit there so I can't eat." The words rushed out of me, the tears concealed but not far behind. They leaked into my voice, which was already too loud, and if I didn't watch myself, they were going to pour out of my eyes.

"Have you told anyone?" she whispered. She folded her gnarled, old hands in her lap and hunched forward the way people do when you're going to divulge a secret.

"Just you." I took a deep breath and tried to relax. I couldn't, though—my heart was beating like a hammer, my nerves swarming in my stomach like fleas.

Miss Thomas's eyes took me in completely. She seemed intensely interested, so captivated that I told her in detail about how my nerves slid down my veins and dented up my muscles. When she asked me what they looked like, I admitted I had never seen them, but I told her I suspected they looked like small black bugs with six booted feet. "How many of them are there, do you think?" she asked, to which I replied, "Thousands.

"Maybe your Amazing Life-Saving Potion could help me," I whispered. I was worried she wouldn't think of it.

"Well, I haven't had too many requests to get rid of nerves, but I think I might know of something."

I followed her down a dark hallway, past the room with all the mechanical toys, great goose bumps welling up on my arms and legs. Where was she taking me this time? I wondered. I imagined a secret room with long shelves filled with jars of magic potions—red potions, green potions, purple potions. She didn't ask me to close my eyes or to be as quiet as I possibly could, like she had the last time. Instead, she opened the door quietly, and I followed her into the darkness.

She walked over to a corner and struck a match, lighting two tall white candles. Slowly, as the flames flickered, I saw a large red box, shaped something like a house without a front. It stood in the far corner, and inside it were odd statues like the ones out on her lawn, only they were much smaller and made of brass. The biggest one was of a woman with eight snakish, dancerly arms.

My first feeling was one of curiosity—my second, fear. I associated these peculiar statues with Miss Thomas losing her mind, and I had the sudden terrifying thought that she was going to go insane right there in front of me in this dark and hidden little room.

We knelt down on a couple of red pillows in front of the little house, and Miss Thomas said, "I'm going to teach you something that will put your nerves to sleep." The candlelight flickered in her glasses, and her eyes danced beneath them.

"Okay," I said, though I couldn't imagine what.

"I want to teach you some Hindu words. They are very old words, very powerful words . . . *ancient.*" The way she said the word *ancient* sent a wind down my back.

I nodded and watched carefully as her eyes fluttered shut and she folded her hands.

"Namo arihantanum. Namo siddhanum. Namo ovajjyanum," she whispered slowly.

I stared at her and felt my heart take off. These were the words, I remembered. When she lost her mind, she used these words. Panic overtook me, and I started to move away from her. I slipped off the red pillow, my knees knocking against the cold wooden floor, and when I glanced around the dark room, looking for the door, I saw Miss Thomas's huge, ghoulish shadow looming on the wall like a monstrous black smudge. I wanted to escape before she really got going, before she turned her face up and started yearning toward the heavens.

"What's wrong?" she said, her eyes blinking open.

I stared at her and started to move backward on my knees. "Is that what you say in the morning on your lawn?" I whispered. The candles flickered as if some invisible presence breathed on them, and

Miss Thomas nodded, her eyes peering at me strangely, as if I were the one who had lost my mind. "What is it?" I said. I held my breath, lest something awful happen, and in the silence, I felt the dark walls close in on me.

"It's Hindu, gooney bird. It's a prayer. What did you think it was?" She laughed and laid one of her soft, gnarled hands on my arm. An immense wave of relief flooded me. Miss Thomas was not losing her mind after all. She was only speaking another language—she was only saying a prayer. The dark smudge on her image dropped away, and all my fears and reservations about this odd woman vanished.

I followed her voice as it rolled, unbreaking, through this thicket of Hindu words until I had the strange sounds and rhythms memorized. *"Namo ovajjyanum,"* we whispered. *"Namo ayaryanum. Namo loey savvuh savanum."* Ten minutes passed, maybe more, and finally she stopped, and silence breathed all around us. When she turned to me and smiled, I noticed there was distance in her eyes, as if she had gone somewhere and had just now come back.

She pulled the statue of the woman with eight arms forward a little. "This is Durga," she said. "I want you to look at her while you speak those Hindu words, and I want you to think of all her hands soothing your nerves, putting them to bed and calming them down with her gentle touch."

"Couldn't her hands just kill them?" I said, staring into her huge, black eyes.

"You don't want to kill your nerves, Maddie. You just want to calm them."

"No, I want to kill them," I insisted. "Can't I get her hands to crush them?"

"They are part of you, gooney bird. You can't kill them. You can learn to tame them, though, so you are their master."

I didn't particularly want to be their master. I preferred them dead, but Miss Thomas insisted that they couldn't be killed—not while I was still alive. They were as much a part of me as my own skin, she said.

I looked longingly at the red-and-yellow powders. It would be a lot easier for me if I could just swallow a potion, rather than involve Durga and all her arms. "You don't have a potion?" I asked.

"This is better than any potion," she said, the candlelight flickering across her face. "Durga has more power than any potion I know of."

I nodded and watched as she pulled herself up and walked over to the closet, where from out of a white box, she pulled a smaller version of Durga. She was metal and stood about eight inches tall. Miss Thomas told me to put her at the end of my bed at night when my nerves got up and to speak those Hindu words while I thought of all her hands putting them to bed. Then she wrapped it up in one of her scarves and slipped her down my sweatshirt.

I hid her in the top drawer of my dresser under my wool socks. When my nerves got up that night, I fished her out, and since there was no place to put her at the end of my bed, I brought her back to bed with me. I made sure Elena was asleep before I stood her on my stomach and stared at her across the hazy darkness. I touched all of her arms with my fingertips, and then very slowly, I whispered those Hindu words. *"Namo arihantanum. Namo siddhanum. Namo ayaryanum. Namo ovajjyanumo."* Over and over again I repeated this mysterious incantation, setting Durga in motion. Nothing happened at first, but after five minutes passed, the words began to transform me. I felt Durga going through my body, her slender arms moving gracefully, her gentle hands putting my nerves in bed eight at a time, shushing them and smoothing their foreheads. Her touch alone made them drowsy, and by the time her warm hand left their foreheads, they were asleep.

After that, I took her to school with me. I slid her down the rip in my coat pocket and carried her around in the hem. I hid her in the back of my desk, and when my nerves started acting up, I slipped her under my blouse and went into the bathroom. With the door safely locked, I perched her on top of the sink and sat down on the toilet and whispered her words, while she lulled my nerves to sleep.

Durga wasn't always perfect. There were times when she didn't work at all. In late March, when I found a letter from Mimi in Lana's mail, she was useless. As soon as I saw the name MIMI LAMAR written in large childlike capitals up at the top of the envelope, my nerves loped through me like gazelles. I tried to see through the envelope, but I couldn't make out any of the words—I could only discern the big bold letters. The page was so pockmarked, though, I could feel Braille-like bumps through the envelope. I quietly slipped it through the rip in my coat pocket and down to the hem where Durga lay.

I was afraid to read it, because I wasn't sure how in the general scheme of sinning it stacked up. What if it was worse than reading Lana's journals, worse than leaking Lana's secrets out in the air? I didn't want to press my luck—I still had a sneaking suspicion that all it would take was something like reading Mimi's letter to push the universe into letting the axe fall on Lana's head.

For two days my nerves marched heavily up and down my legs and arms. It was so monotonous and painful that when Lana took Harry downtown to see the doctor for his earache, I finally borrowed Leo's jackknife and locked myself in the bathroom. I set Durga up on the sink for good luck and then slipped the jackknife under the seal and pried it open. I pulled the letter out and flapped it open, laying it in my lap, where I stared down, amazed, at the childish handwriting. It was the handwriting of a second-grader.

DEAR LANA,

I ONLY JUST DISCOVERED YOU MOVED FROM DETROIT LAST SUMMER. LEO'S FATHER GAVE ME YOUR ADDRESS. BUT HE WOUDNT GIVE ME YOUR PHONE NUMBER SAYING YOU ASKED HIM NOT TO. IMAGINE HOW THIS MAKES ME FEEL, LANA— YOUR OWN MOTHER.

I AM WRITING TO ASK YOU TO PUT THE PAST BEHIND US. I AM ALONE IN THIS WORLD, LANA. I AM GETTING OLD AND DONT KNOW HOW MUCH LONGER I WILL LIVE. I WOUD LIKE TO MAKE AMMENDS WITH YOU AND LEO. I WOUD LIKE TO KNOW MY GRANDCHILLDREN.

I AM SORRY FOR WHAT I DID TO YOU AND LEO AND FOR MANY OF THE THINGS I DID IN THE PAST. YOU SAID YOU DIDNT WANT YOUR CHILLDREN TO KNOW ME, NOT WHILE I HAD AN ESTAB-LISHMENT. I RETIRED FROM THE ESCORT BUSINESS LAST MAY. I WOUD NEVER TELL YOUR CHILLDREN ANYTHING ABOUT ME OR ABOUT YOU, YOU WOUDNT WANT ME TO TELL.

SOMEBODY FROM YOUR OLD LAWYER'S OFFICE CALLED ME LAST MONTH, TRYING TO FIND YOU. I DIDN'T GIVE HIM YOUR ADDRESS. I DIDNT THINK YOUD WANT ME TO. SO I TOLD HIM I'D TELL YOU.

I MISS YOU, LANA. YOU WERE RIGHT ABOUT A LOT OF THINGS. I AM PREPARED TO LET YOU BE. I WOUD LIKE IT VERY MUCH IF YOU AND LEO AND YOUR CHILLDREN WOULD COME TO THE SOUND THIS SUMMER.

MIMI

I heard Elena's footsteps on the stairs, so I quickly slipped the letter back into the envelope and took it downstairs. I mixed it up in the day's mail and laid it on top of the dining room hutch, like I usually did. When Lana brought Harry back from the doctor's, I watched her carefully as she looked through it. She was as stunned as I was to find a letter from Mimi. The shock registered in her eyes first, and then something like an electric bolt passed up her spine — her head jerked backward involuntarily. It was slight, lasting no longer than a moment, but I noticed it. She immediately put it under a bowl of fruit in the kitchen, but it wasn't until later that night when no one was around that she read it.

I watched from the dining room as she took it out of the envelope, and when she turned her back and eased herself down on the kitchen stool, I slipped under the dining room table. I watched the tension creep up her back, where it fanned across her shoulders. Her breathing became gusty within a matter of moments, and I couldn't be sure if it was because Mimi had written, or if it was because somebody from her old lawyer's office had asked to talk to her. When she finished reading it, she jammed it back in the envelope and sat there for a few tense moments, staring out the back door at the dark and distant hills. She took a few deep breaths to steady herself, and then impulsively, she picked up the phone and dialed.

"Mimi," she said. Her voice leapt from her. "I got your letter." Lana shook her hair back and pressed her hand against her forehead, as if talking to Mimi had given her a fever. She cleared her throat a couple of times, and when her lips struggled to form a word, I knew whatever it was she wanted to say was difficult for her. "What did the lawyer want?" she finally asked, her voice lifting an octave. When she squeezed her eyes shut and held her breath, I knew that she feared the answer. As Mimi spoke her body went rigid, and after a few moments, she rose from the stool like a flame. *"Tell him to forget it,"* she yelled. She spoke loudly, too loudly. *"I don't want to talk to anyone."*

Lana went silent and listened to Mimi for a few minutes, her lips compressing shut. She crossed her legs and uncrossed them, and then paced in a small circle, the phone cord tangling around her knees. I saw a red-hot flush race up her throat, spreading across her cheeks like fire, and after her back went rigid again, she slammed her fist down on the counter. "You're doing it again, Mimi," she screamed. "You're telling me what to do again, goddamn it."

There was something about Mimi which had the power to unhinge her, for she hung up the phone in a resounding thwack. One conversation with Mimi, and she was a wreck. Her breathing was like the wind, and her hands trembled like moths. She staggered around the kitchen for a few moments, looking for something. She started to go out the back door, but the blast of chilly air stopped her. She turned around then and moved through the kitchen, bearing down on her cane so hard it squeaked. "She's doing it to you again, Lana. She's doing it to you," I heard her fiercely whisper. She clumsily made herself a cup of tea, and when she finally sat down, it was at the dining room table, her feet coming within two inches of my stealthy knees. I watched her legs knock together, and I listened quietly to the clattery sound of her hand on the teacup. Within a matter of moments my nerves came out in droves.

The front door opened, and it seemed I might be saved, but it was Elena—she crept in quietly and stole up the stairs. I could hear the guilt in her footsteps, and I was hoping Lana's curiosity would be aroused, but she just drank her tea in the darkness and waited for her upset to pass. Leo came home about fifteen minutes later. When he went to turn on the dining room light, Lana stopped him. She said she preferred the darkness, but finding her in the pitch black upset him.

"What happened, La?" he asked, pulling the chair out. Had I not moved back soundlessly, he would have stepped on me.

"Mimi wrote me a letter," she said quietly. "Then I made the mistake of calling her." A huge sigh escaped from her lips, and I heard her elbows drop down on top of the table.

"What did she want?" Leo asked. He sounded nervous.

"For some reason, someone from the lawyer's office wants to talk to me," she said loudly. Her voice snagged on the word *lawyer*, but the rest of the sentence flew from her mouth, as if someone had squeezed it out of her.

"You're not going to talk to them, are you?" He sounded horrified at the thought of it.

"Did I say I was going to talk to them?" She dropped the teacup down on the pale bone china plate, where it rattled delicately.

"No, but—" he struggled to say.

"But *what*, Leo?"

"We put that in the past, Lana."

"It keeps coming back, though, doesn't it?" she said loudly. Her feet moved nervously under the table, and she laughed, though it wasn't really a laugh. It was more a sneer, a cringing sort of sneer I had never heard come out of Lana.

"Only if you let it," he yelled.

"I didn't ask for this letter, Leo. It came out of the blue. What did I have to do with it?"

It was when Lana said, "It came out of the blue," that my heart stopped. I suddenly realized that Elena, Lizzy, and I had caused Mimi to write Lana that letter, especially me. I had tipped the scales, pushed our luck to the edge, and it had come out of the blue now, like an axe, and it was cutting them apart. At the thought of it, my nerves slipped under my kneecaps.

"You're not going to talk to them," Leo yelled. "You're not going to put us through that hell again. We decided a long time ago to put *that* in the past. I won't have it, Lana." His fist lay in his lap like a tight knot.

"You haven't kept up your end of the bargain, Leo," she said bitterly. "We weren't supposed to live in a small town while you worked fifteen hours a day and left me to be . . . *the woman.*"

Lana thrust her chair back and rose up, the delicate teacup rattling on top of the bone china plate.

"So you're going to punish me now?" he yelled to her vanishing back.

She raced out of the room and pounded up the stairs, the sound of her cane a stabbing counterpoint.

"Shit," he said to himself.

He waited for the sound of her door slamming before he got up and shrugged his coat on and left the house. I watched him through the icy porch windows as he headed down the slushy street and crossed over to the snowy lawns of the campus. It seemed he could afford not to get along with Lana now that he had someplace to go.

Once he was out of sight, my nerves charged out from underneath my kneecaps and ran through my thighs, across the ridges of my ribs and over my shoulders. I ran upstairs and pulled Durga out of my drawer and stood her on my stomach, whispering the Hindu words over and over again. Within a matter of minutes, my nerves had stirred up that which in the last month had died down to a tolerable whisper—my tortured curiosity. Why did someone from a lawyer's office want to talk to Lana? I wanted to know. And why did the thought of it make Leo so mad? All that lay dormant through the sluggish winter stirred in me now, like the spring stirred outside, and I thought for sure I was going insane. I said the Hindu words faster and faster and brought Durga up to my chest where I could see her perfectly, but it didn't make a difference. My nerves were too fast— they dodged her every arm.

I couldn't lie still. It became unbearable, and there was nothing I could do but get up and swing my arms around like windmills. I paced back and forth in front of the attic door for over five minutes before I finally opened it and turned the light on. The boxes stood under the dusty eaves, a formidable column, unguarded and intriguing in the weak yellow light. I closed the door behind me and crept quietly across the wide, cold boards until I was standing next to them. I was just going to look at the journals, and maybe thumb through a few pages to see if there was any mention of a lawyer. I felt something wet under my feet, and when I looked down, I saw that the boxes were sitting in a puddle of cold water. The roof was leaking from the thaw, I discovered, and had drenched them, especially the bottom box. I located the drip and watched as it splashed almost soundlessly into the small puddle. I tried to shove the column to a dry spot, but I couldn't budge them. They were heavy beyond belief.

I stumbled out of the attic and went immediately into Elena's room, where I shook her awake. "What, Maddie?" she yelled, lurching up. The light from the hallway cut her face in half, and she squinted her right eye to keep it out. "Something happened in the attic," I whispered. I felt a cold sweat break out on my back, and my whole body convulsed in a shiver. I mouthed the words "the journals," and the sleep fell from her eyes immediately. "What about them?" she asked. I motioned for her to come with me into the attic. She staggered behind me, trying to shake off the sleep, and once inside, I pointed out the leak and watched as her eyes fell from the pitched roof to the floor where the bottom box was slowly but surely disintegrating.

"I tried to push them over," I whispered, "but they won't budge."

"We're going to have to tell Leo, you know," she said. She wrapped her arms around herself and hopped from one foot to the other, to keep them warm.

We stood there for a few moments imagining what would happen were we to tell Leo. It would remind both him and Lana that the boxes were there, which neither of us wanted to do. They might move them out altogether and put them in Lana's closet, where our access to them would be greatly diminished.

"We can't tell him," I said, staring down at the cold, miserable puddle.

"What are we going to do, Maddie? You can't just let it leak like this. The whole house will fall apart." She reached up and plugged the leak with her finger, a small rivulet of icy water running down her arm.

"We could put a pail under it and empty it out," I said.

"For the rest of our lives?" She looked at me, as if I were an idiot.

"No, just for a while—until the summer."

"And who's going to empty the bucket?" she said. "Not me."

"I'll do it."

"You're going to remember every day?"

Elena didn't know me. She didn't know how good I was when it came to carrying out a plan. She had no idea that I went through the wastebaskets every morning looking for Lana's cut-out articles. She didn't know that Lizzy and I copied down the headlines to the *New York Times* every single day. Emptying a bucket of water was nothing.

"I will. Believe me, Elena, I will."

Meanwhile, we tried to shove the boxes out of the puddle. On Elena's command of "Go," we pushed with all we had, and the stack of boxes fell over, hitting the floor with such a resounding crash I was sure Lana would hear and rush in. The top box had opened and the journal we'd read fell out and skidded across the cold attic floor. The sight of it so clearly displaced made my heart race. The last box was ruined—the bottom was a soggy mess and the contents spilled out all over the floor. It wasn't more journals like we expected, but rather dozens of round, silver cans each about an inch or two thick.

"What are they?" I asked as we scrambled down to our knees. Elena opened one of them, and we both stared down at a round circle of something. It looked like something I had seen before, but even so, I couldn't say what it was.

"What is it?" I asked again.

She slipped it from the can and turned it over in her hands. It was about the size of a 45 record, grooved as well, but unlike a record, it was an inch or so thick. When she peeled up a piece of tape on the side of it and began to unravel it, I realized where I had seen it before. In Art's projection room.

"It's film," she said. She held it up to the light, and there between her fingers were the smallest pictures I had ever seen. They were broken by lines and appeared to be all alike. As she continued to unravel it, I counted dozens of pictures, all the same, of a tall, city building with hundreds of windows.

"Why would Lana have film?" I said.

She stared at me for a moment, as if she considered telling me something. "Maybe she was a movie star," she whispered.

Was that the secret Lana had told her during our last days in Detroit? That she had been a movie star? The way Elena had said it sounded like she knew the truth. "Was she, Elena?" I kept my eyes fixed on her face.

"I don't know, Maddie. Why else would she have all this film?" She put the film back into the silver canister and carefully pressed the lid down. If someone had told me Lana had trained lions and flown war planes, I would have believed them. As far as I knew, Lana was capable of anything.

"Is that the secret she told you?" I crept closer to her, laying my icy hand on her arm. "Is it, Elena?"

She shook my hand off her arm and started collecting the other silver cans, stacking them one on top of the other. "I can't tell you, Maddie. You know I can't tell you."

"Why not, Elena?" I said. I felt my desperation pool. "Why not?"

"It does bad things to Lana, for one thing. And besides, Maddie, I don't know. I really don't." She shouldered her white nightgown and went back to stacking those silver cans.

Somehow I believed her.

Together we quietly collected all the silver canisters and stacked them up just beyond the puddle of water. The box itself was ruined, so we folded it up and stuffed it behind the red chair and crept down to the cellar to find another one and a bucket to catch the water. We brought them up to the attic and carefully put the canisters inside the new box, closed the flaps, and stacked the other two boxes on top of it. Then I moved the bucket under the leak, where the drops of water smarted on the rusty, tin bottom.

"The film isn't like the journals," I said. I imagined us unraveling it until it covered the whole floor. "We only swore on the moon about the journals. We never said anything about the film."

"It's really the same, Maddie. Just think about it."

We left the attic and crawled back into our beds, shaking off the cold underneath our covers. As the wind brushed lightly against the windows, I thought about it, and the more I considered it, the more I convinced myself it was different from reading her journals. We'd never said anything to the moon about film.

I realized that Art could show them to us. But even so, it was a risky prospect. It would mean exposing Lana to Art and to anyone else who walked into the movie theater at the time. Reading Lana's journals in the privacy of an attic was one thing—projecting her film onto a public screen was quite another. Who knew what that might do to Lana. And what kind of a sin would it constitute for me? One greater than any I had ever committed, I imagined.

"Elena," I said across the darkness. "Leo and Lana had a big fight tonight, and Leo left."

"About what?" I could tell from the thin sound of her voice that it bothered her.

"She said he wasn't holding up his end of the bargain. She said he's gone all the time and that she has to live in a small town and be the woman."

"I told you it was his fault, Maddie. It's all his fault, and you wait—she's going to blow up even worse one of these days. You watch. It's coming, Maddie—I can feel it."

15

Spring didn't come soon enough. Winter held on one month longer and drove everyone a little crazy. By the end of March, it was still too chilly to stay outside for long; the snow just kept coming and melting and coming again. It was dirty brown from all the melts and freezes and minglings with mud, and none of us were interested in playing in it anymore. Our snow city stood out on our lawn, rounded and shrunken and partially eaten away.

The trees stood as pale specters in the half snowy, half muddy fields. The hills looked more like dingy goose bumps than great lazy elephants, and the sky drew only scorn for prevailing in a despairing slate gray. The wind blew cold chilled air from Iceland, I guessed, and when March ended and it still hadn't stopped snowing, we all lost our patience.

Lana started to go downhill, staying in her room for longer periods of time, staring out at the gloomy skies, occasionally writing on the papers she had spread across her desk. She would have preferred being down in the cellar rehearsing our little plays, but gradually Elena, Lizzy, and I got tired of it, especially Elena since she now spent her free time going to whatever mysterious place it was she went.

It was something Lana had thrown herself into, something she had counted on to absorb her, to fill her cold afternoons. Without it she had only her writing. She still spent some time with Garta in the evenings, but not as often. There wasn't really much left to do on Garta's apartment, and since Garta hadn't done anything horrible to Lizzy lately there wasn't anything much for Lana to fight against.

Lizzy and I noticed that she started having problems breathing again, and her hands shook too. She fought it harder than we had ever seen her fight it before. When her breathing got bad, she'd get up and walk around the room, flapping her arms up and down, taking in deep breaths and blowing them out. And when her hands shook, she'd either sit on them or start beating time on top of her desk, like a bongo player. She talked to herself all the time too. "Come on, Lana," she'd whisper. "Come on . . . *come on.*"

We found her in a few odd places—once she was down in the cellar lying on top of our stage, her arms stretched straight out, like Jesus on the cross. Another time she was sitting in a wicker chair out on our front porch in the freezing cold without her coat and gloves.

She never told Leo about any of it, like she used to. In fact, whenever he was around and she was having a hard time breathing or her hands shook, she tried her best to conceal it from him. She'd put her hands under the table or shove them into her pockets, and when she couldn't breathe very well, she'd start humming or something. Sometimes he would ask her if she were all right, and even when it was obvious that she wasn't, she would say, "Yes, I'm fine."

After the fight they had in the dining room about Mimi and the lawyer, they spoke even less to one another, and when they did speak it was usually with very short sentences. Leo wasn't home much anyway. He stayed away for longer periods, and even though he kept telling her that it would all be over in May, she didn't believe him. She said she had come to see their arrangement as permanent. She never looked for him out the window at night anymore, and once I heard her call herself Lana Lamar.

Elena continued to smoke cigarettes at the back of the Colgate Inn, stealing across the field later to wherever it was she vanished. With the field in a constant state of muddy flux, Lizzy and I never really made any progress. We only succeeded in ruining the black fur-lined boots Garta had given Lizzy for Christmas.

I couldn't always spare the time to follow Elena either. Now that Lana had gone downhill, Lizzy and I watched her a lot through the bathroom grate, and with all the freezing and melting and raining, I had to stay on top of the bucket in the attic. Whenever it rained or there was an especially big thaw, I had to rush home from school to get to it before it overflowed. The leak got worse as the winter wore on, getting so bad that when it rained hard, I had to empty the bucket two or three times a day. Lizzy wondered why I didn't just tell Leo, but that was only because she didn't know Lana's boxes were in there. I told her I was afraid if we told them, they might take the attic away from us, and since she didn't want that to happen, she started helping me empty the bucket. While we hauled it down to the end of the attic and heaved it out the window, I reminded myself that Elena was doing something thrilling in the woods. It was my promise, though, and I had to keep it.

Despite Durga, my nerves didn't improve much. Lana's decline, Leo's absence, Elena's mystery, the bucket, and the film in the bottom box—all converged and made them worse. They could run from my toes to the back of my neck in a matter of moments now. They were in such good shape, they simply raced up like a pack of fine runners. They slept under my kneecaps nearly every night now, making it almost impossible for me to sleep, and they generally got up with me in the morning. I worried that this was all the beginning of the end of my sanity, but Miss Thomas told me they weren't powerful enough for that.

I carried Durga with me wherever I went, concealing her either in the hem of my coat or in an old black purse I borrowed from Lana. No matter where I was, if my nerves bothered me, I excused myself to the nearest bathroom and sat down on the toilet with Durga perched on the sink and whispered the Hindu words. I occasionally visited Miss Thomas to be reinforced by her Durga—a much larger, more durable, shinier version—which I was certain had more powers than my smaller one. I helped her with her birds too, watching Aphrodite's progress with growing interest. I still had hopes for Miss Thomas's Amazing Life-Saving Potion, and after I asked her several times, Miss Thomas finally made me a batch. It was different from the potion she fed Aphrodite; it wasn't a powder mixture, and it didn't need water (which worried me), but Miss Thomas said that a life-saving potion for a bird was much different from a life-saving potion for a human being. Mine was made of oats and wheat flakes, nuts, raisins, and some crushed-up orange and purple granules, which she said were very potent. She put it in a brown paper bag and told me I must shake it thoroughly before I took any. "And only take it when you absolutely need it," she said. "And then only a small handful. It's a very *powerful* potion."

So into the hem of my coat pocket, along with Durga, went this brown paper bag filled with Miss Thomas's powerful life-saving potion. I didn't have to take any until the beginning of April, when a huge rainstorm hit and went on for hours. I could hear the water splashing in the bucket as if there were a faucet in the ceiling instead of a leak, and I had to get out of bed every ten minutes to check on it. My nerves reacted badly to this, and when, during my breaks, Durga could bring me no relief, I fished out the brown bag and administered a very small handful to myself.

I tried it out on Lizzy a few weeks later when Garta beat her up for ruining her cheap black boots. She was shaking and her teeth were chattering when I found her out on the back steps. I wanted to tell Lana, but she begged me not to, so I took her up to my bedroom and made her show me where Garta had hurt her. Two bruises stood out on her upper arm where Garta had pinched her, but the worst was on her back where, just to the right of her spine, near her shoulder blades, was a bluish-purple bruise the size of a fifty-cent piece, which had risen up under her skin like a small mountain.

I pulled out the brown bag filled with Miss Thomas's life-saving potion and offered her a small handful of it.

"What is it?" she asked. "Horse food?"

"Remember Aphrodite? The baby robin? Miss Thomas fed her a life-saving potion and saved her. This is a potion she makes for people. She said to take it when you need to calm down."

"Yeah, but she's crazy," Lizzy said, staring down at the mixture in my hand.

"She's not crazy, Lizzy. She wasn't losing her mind all those times like we thought. She was just praying."

She took the mixture from my hand and put it in her mouth and munched it slowly, staring at me the whole time, lest she die on the spot. We eased ourselves down on my bed after that and waited for it to take effect. In a few minutes, Lizzy stopped shaking, and when her teeth stopped chattering, I told her I thought we should plot our revenge. It was time to get even with Garta, to really get even with her.

We liked the idea of making Garta think she was losing her mind. It was much better than ripping holes in the rear end of her pants. Putting fear in Garta's heart—that was the effect we were after. As our eyes edged along the small, hairline cracks in the ceiling, we came up with it. Letters. We would write threatening letters and mail them to her—letters that would scare the shit out of her.

"We'll write stuff like, 'You better watch out, Garta. We're going to get you,' " Lizzy said. Even in the fading light, I saw her eyes flash.

"Or even worse stuff," I whispered. "Like, 'You better watch out, Garta. We're going to *kill* you.' "

Lizzy rolled her head on the pillow, and her eyes swelled deeply from the inside. "Yeah, then we could tell her how we're going to kill her."

While the shadows on my walls went from gray to black, we imagined a hundred different ways we would tell Garta we were going to kill her. Lizzy liked the idea of putting poison in her morning coffee, but I thought it would be better to skin her alive and then cook her on long sticks and feed her to the dogs. If we were going to do something like that, Lizzy preferred that we hit her over the head with a brick, saw her up into little pieces, and then feed her to the dogs. We considered torturing her first, like hanging her from a window with a rope for a few hours and then dropping her on the concrete. Or putting a noose around her neck and making her wait for days all tied up before we pushed the chair away. The possibilities were endless.

We decided we'd use the typewriter in the nurse's office at school — Mrs. Blanchard's old, unwieldy Remington. It was hardly ever used, and we doubted Garta would ever be smart enough to figure it out. We would wear gloves, Lizzy decided, so none of our fingerprints would be on the paper, the stamps, the envelopes, or Mrs. Blanchard's old typewriter. I was glad she had thought of that, because I wouldn't have. For the paper, we decided to use brown paper bags. We would cut out a small square and type something on it. It was a good idea, because neither Lizzy nor I carried a lunch, and it was something everyone had plenty of. For the envelopes, we settled on the small, plain, white kind, which we bought the next day in the grocery store for fifty-nine cents. We also got some plain stamps at the post office—a dozen of them for starters.

When I asked Mrs. Blanchard if I could use her typewriter, she didn't look too happy about it, but she rolled the old Remington out from behind her desk anyway. I noticed she kept staring at my black gloves. Nonetheless, I turned my back on her and put the brown paper down into the roller, plunking out the words with my index fingers. GARTA, I typed. YOU'D BETTER WATCH YOUR STEP, BECAUSE I'M WATCHING YOU.

Lizzy and I had decided to make our first note the least threatening, realizing that if we said we were going to kill her right away, there would be no place to go. We had thought about how to sign it too, but we hadn't come up with anything good. Lizzy had wanted to sign it THE WATCHER, but I didn't think that was quite right. I thought about it again, and after a few moments it came to me.

I poised my index finger again and typed, THE EYES OF GOD.

I thanked Mrs. Blanchard and headed down to the bathroom, where Lizzy was waiting for me in one of the gray stalls. With our gloved hands we folded the brown paper note and stuck it in the envelope.

"We can't lick it with our tongues," she said. "They might be able to trace it back to our spit."

I had never heard of spit prints or tongue prints, but I didn't want to take any chances, so we dunked some toilet paper into the toilet and wet the flap and the stamp.

"The Eyes of God," Lizzy whispered. "That's good, Maddie. I like it."

I put the envelope down into the hem of my coat, next to Durga, where it stayed until after dinner. Once it was dark, Lizzy and I met down at the post office. When no one was looking she opened the mailbox with her gloved hand, and I dropped the letter down the chute. It was probably the cleanest letter ever mailed.

When Lizzy found it in Garta's mail two days later, she had to have some more life-saving potion.

She stayed for dinner, and just after Lana cleared away the dishes, Garta banged on the front door. I watched Lizzy freeze as soon as she heard Garta's voice. I squeezed her thigh under the table. "Don't look guilty," I whispered. "Just act like nothing happened."

Garta plowed into the dining room and slapped the letter down on the table for Lana to read. "The Eyes of God," she sniffed. "Who in the hell would write this?" She was wearing an oversized green nylon parka, and her face was red from the cold April wind. She yanked Leo's chair out and slumped down, pulling out a mushed-up pack of Benson and Hedges from the back pocket of her tight blue jeans.

Lana sat down at the table and took our small brown paper square out of the envelope and read it. "I don't know," she said, looking up. "Who do you think?"

"I haven't got the slightest idea, unless it's that asshole Jimmy Ringer, up at the dining hall. He hates me because I made head cook over him." She shook a bent cigarette from her pack, straightened it out, and lit it with her rhinestone lighter. She plucked the note out of Lana's hands after that and read it again. " 'You'd better watch your step, because I'm watching you,' " she said mockingly. "What in the hell does that mean? 'The Eyes of God'?"

I braved a look at Lizzy. She sat quietly, perfectly poised. Hearing Garta blame it on Jimmy Ringer had eased her nerves.

As Lana and Garta went through all the people it could have been, Lana trying to calm Garta down, Lizzy and I squeezed hands under the table. It was all perfect, and the sweetest part was that we could do it again.

A few days later we sent another one. With my back to Mrs. Blanchard, I plunked out the words with both of my gloved index fingers. ONE WRONG MOVE, AND YOU'RE IN *BIG* TROUBLE. I underlined the word BIG, and signed it, THE EYES OF GOD.

"Did you have to underline the word BIG?" Lizzy said when I showed it to her in the bathroom. It made her nervous to push the threat an extra yard. "It's bad enough we said she was going to be in big trouble."

We tried to erase the line, but it wouldn't erase, so we mailed it as it was, late that evening, and waited two days for it to appear in Garta's mail. When we found it after school, on top, Lizzy had to have some more life-saving potion. She was afraid this time Garta would figure it out.

"She won't," I promised her, as we trudged through the slushy streets. "She's going to think of all the people she hates, and she's going to blame it on them."

Lizzy stayed at my house for dinner, just in case. She didn't want to be alone with Garta in their apartment when Garta discovered the note. It wasn't until after Lana did the dishes and put them away in the cupboards that Garta finally turned up at the door.

"I got another one," we heard her tell Lana. She followed Lana down the hallway and came into the dining room, where she slammed the envelope down on the table. "Read this one."

While Lana took the note out and read it, Garta sat down in Leo's chair again and lit another cigarette. She was wearing her green nylon coat over her white dining hall uniform, her hair still pinned underneath a black hairnet. I couldn't be absolutely certain, but I thought I detected a slight trembling in her hands. She was upset — there was no doubt about that.

She must have felt our eyes, because she looked over at me and then at Lizzy. "WHAT ARE YOU STARING AT?" she yelled.

"Nothing," Lizzy said. I pinched her under the table to remind her to act like nothing had happened.

"What does it mean — one wrong move?" Garta yelled. She jabbed her cigarette into her pinched mouth and took a deep drag. "How in the hell am I supposed to know what a wrong move is? And what is *big* trouble?" she wanted to know, spitting out the blue-gray smoke.

Lana did her best to calm Garta's rattled nerves. She smoothed Garta's arm with the palm of her hand. "It's just someone very childish who wants to scare you," she said. She tried to convince Garta to just ignore the threats and go on with her life as though nothing were different, but Garta thought she should do just the opposite. She talked wildly of arming herself, of sleeping with a gun under her pillow, of carrying a switchblade with her whenever she went out, until Lana finally shushed her. When she got up and made some tea, Lizzy and I ran outside and up the hill, into Miss Thomas's woods, where we exploded in laughter.

"WHAT DOES IT MEAN, ONE WRONG MOVE?" Lizzy roared, imitating Garta's gruff voice. She was holding her sides, writhing back and forth on the ground, the pine needles sticking in her hair.

"HOW IN THE HELL AM I SUPPOSED TO KNOW WHAT A WRONG MOVE IS?" I went on, rolling onto my back, laughing past the tall pine trees, up to the reddening sky.

I could almost feel Lizzy healing — it helped her to know she had some power over Garta, that Garta was not almighty, that a little note could bring Garta down. Laugh, I thought, as I watched her double over in a spasm. Laugh your head off.

A week or so later spring finally took hold. Green grass appeared everywhere, and soft, baby-green halos outlined all the bushes and trees. The air smelled of fresh earth and red hyacinths, and beautiful yellow forsythia bloomed along the sidewalks. The dingy gray skies were gradually replaced by gentler ones, which swirled with purple and white. Lizzy's favorite field on top of the hill was covered in a soft, healthy green, and we started hiking up there after Elena vanished into the woods. We walked over to the waterfalls quite a few times too and perched ourselves on the cliff, watching the cold, spring water plunge into the engorged stream.

Art gave us a bunch of free movie passes, and by the end of April, Elena, Lizzy, and I had used them up. Every time he started the projector and light hit the screen, Elena and I looked at each other. Neither one of us could forget the silver cans of film in the bottom of Lana's boxes.

Lizzy and I returned to the attic, where we emptied the bucket and pursued operation newspaper with a vengeance. In the month of April alone, Lana cut out at least six more articles about Negroes. Martin Luther King, Jr., had been assassinated, and for days there were articles about him, all of which Lana cut out. It inspired us to copy whole paragraphs from the front-page articles about Negroes. We just opened up the window, the sweet-smelling breeze wafting in, and while Lizzy read, I scrawled.

We ended up reading great portions of the front page, learning about a lot of things besides Negroes, like the Vietnam War and all the rioting on college campuses. We read an article about a man named Simon Wiesenthal too, a famous Nazi hunter who'd been tracking down Nazis ever since World War II had ended.

"What if one of the Nazis he's trying to catch is Minnie Harp's Nazi?" I said, stretching my bare legs out on the dirty attic floor.

"Yeah, what if?" Lizzy said. Her eyes widened, and her lips parted in a smile.

The thought of it was riveting. "I bet Simon Wiesenthal would pay a lot of money for a Nazi. He'd probably pay one thousand dollars for him."

"More," Lizzy said. "Way more."

We didn't get down to Minnie Harp's right away, partly because of the spring rains, but mostly because of Lana. Something unusual began to happen to her, and we didn't know what it was. We spent a lot of time watching her from the bathroom grate, trying to figure it out. It seemed she wasn't the least bit shaky anymore; she hardly ever doubled over in her lap, nor did her voice ever get too high. She never wrote either. She spent her afternoons rifling through her closets, heaping her old clothes in piles and sealing up large stacks of her papers in big boxes. When Elena asked her what she was doing, she said, "I'm spring cleaning," but Elena highly doubted that. We saw her pack a whole suitcase with old clothes, and when she pushed it underneath her bed instead of putting it back in the closet, we all began to worry.

Elena thought Lana was getting ready to leave us, but after we discovered her out in the backyard late one night, burning her papers, she said it was much worse than that. "She's going to kill herself, Maddie. People always burn their letters and papers before they kill themselves." We pushed the attic window open and quietly watched as she stirred her roaring fire, feeding it papers from her boxes. She had on a navy blue skirt and a black sweater which hung down past her waist; her hair was tied up in a haphazard knot at the back of her head, long strands of it flying loose in the spring breeze. She never looked up, not even once—she just stared into the fire as if she were mesmerized by it.

We knelt down on the dirty wooden floor and watched her burn every last paper. "What if we did it to her?" I whispered to Elena.

"I don't know, Maddie." She stared at me across the darkness, a huge crease cutting across her forehead. "We can't watch those films, you know," she said. I swear she looked haunted.

I told Lizzy everything the next morning. We decided that we'd have to watch her even closer, so instead of hanging around Shorty's or going up to Lizzy's favorite field, we came straight home from school and kept our eyes on Lana. She just continued cleaning out closets and packing things up, never once getting shaky or doubling over in her lap. She didn't look like a person who was getting ready to kill herself, but, then, what did we know about that?

When another letter from Mimi came in the mail, I wasn't sure what I should do with it. I slid it down to the hem of my coat and carried it around for three days. I told myself to put it back, that it could really hurt Lana, but my resolve had grown shabbier by the day. Knowing that didn't help me either—it only made it easier for me to lock myself in the bathroom when Lana was outside with Harry and slip Leo's jackknife under the seal. I set Durga on top of the toilet to ward off any evil spirits, and pulled the letter out, laying it in my lap.

LANA,

I AM SORRY ABOUT OUR PHONE CONVERSATION. I DIDNT MEAN TOO TELL YOU WHAT YOU SHOUD DO, EVEN THOUG I THINK YOU SHOUD TALK TO THE LAWYER'S OFFICE. I AM NOT SAYING TO REOPEN OLD WOUNDS, I AM NOT SAYING TO BRING UP OLD BUSINESS. DON'T EVEN TALK ABOUT THE PAST. TALK ABOUT THE PRESENT. TAKE UP WHERE YOU LEFT OFF IS WHAT I MEAN.

ITS NOT TOO LATE. SOME PEOPLE STILL REMEMBER YOU.

WHAT ARE YOU DOING IN A SMALL TOWN CALLED HAMIL-TON? I COUDNOT FIND IT ON THE MAP. YOU BELONG HEAR IN NEW YORK. I KNOW THAT MUCH. ME AND YOU LANA, WE ARE INDEPENDENT CITY WOMEN. YOU NEED EXPOSURE, NOT ISOLA-TION. YOU FIGHT ME BECAUSE YOUR SCARED. BUT YOU CANT RUN SCARED FOREVER.

PLEASE THINK ABOUT WHAT I SAY.

MAYBE YOU DONT FEEL READY TO BRING LEO AND YOUR CHILLDREN HEAR. MAYBE YOU WOUD RATHER COME ALONE. I WILL BE IN NEW YORK TIL JUNE 1. AFTER THAT, I WILL BE AT THE SOUND. KEPT YOUR ROOM IN BOTH PLACES. KEPT TEDDY'S ON THE SOUND. MIMI.

I put the letter back in the envelope, taped it shut, and slipped it into the day's mail before Lana came inside with Harry. I crept through the kitchen and watched her from the back porch as she pushed him on the swing. I wondered what she was scared of. And what about what Mimi had written? "It's not too late. Some people still remember you." Maybe she really was a movie star. When I remembered the film up in the attic, my nerves raced from my thighs to my shoulders, but I couldn't look at the film—not after I had just read Mimi's letter.

As I watched her give Harry a few underdunks on the swing, I had to admit that she looked lovely and very much alive. Her long hair flowed down her back, blowing in the spring breeze, her gray dress riding up and down her graceful legs as she pushed him. I wondered if she really did long for New York. Is that where she wished she was when she stared out at the hills? It seemed I would never know the answers to these questions.

When she found the letter in the mail, she put it under the fruit bowl again. I had to wait over four hours, hanging around the dining room and the bathroom, depending on where she was, until finally sometime after ten o'clock, she sat down on the kitchen stool and read it.

She read it twice, and then ripped it up into tiny pieces and dumped them in the garbage pail. Her breathing didn't become rackety, nor did her hands tremble in the least. She didn't pace the kitchen in confusion either, looking for something that wasn't there. She made herself a cup of tea and sat down on the stool and sipped it. The only thing she did was push the pieces of Mimi's ripped-up letter deeper into the garbage—such was her instinct for secrecy.

When Leo came home and found her in the kitchen, I half expected her to tell him Mimi had written her another letter. She didn't, though—she didn't even mention it to him. They went up to bed, and I hung around the grate for a while to see if she was going to tell him in the privacy of their room, but she didn't. In fact, they hardly spoke to one another.

I knew then that something had changed inside of Lana. I didn't know how or why or even what, but I knew she had changed.

When she told us the next installment of the bear and sparrow story, there was no doubt in my mind. One night late in April when Leo didn't come home, Harry suggested we tell some tall tales. We were all sitting in the backyard in the wicker chairs, drinking root beer floats, admiring the cool blue sky. Lana wasn't particularly interested in telling tall tales, but since Harry wanted to so much she finally agreed. He led off with one about a boy who couldn't control his appetite and ate up whole cities, and Elena told one about a teenage girl who quit school and lived in a barn. Mine was about a girl who mysteriously died at the age of eleven, and when they opened her up to find out what had killed her, they found thousands of black bugs inside her veins.

It was Lana's turn after that, which Harry loudly announced. "The bear and sparrow," he squealed. "The sparrow was under the snow."

She tried to get out of telling us the story. She said it would be better to save it for another time when she felt up to it, but we insisted, Harry the loudest. "All right, all right," she finally said. "But remember, you asked for it." She stretched her legs out in front of her, and while the sun set, she gave us what would be the last installment, although we didn't realize it at the time.

The sparrow lay under the snow, while above her in the tree, the man sparrow waited for her. It snowed heavily all night without stopping, and the longer the man sparrow waited, the angrier he got that the sparrow hadn't come back with his food. He yelled out the door a few times, telling her to hurry up, that he was hungry, but there was no answer. The sparrow could hear him faintly, and though she tried to call back, her voice was too weak and muffled by the snow.

When it got very dark, the man sparrow finally realized something must have happened to her and went out to look for her. He worried that he'd pushed her so hard she had collapsed, which would make things bad for him. Who would bring him his food now? He vowed when he found her, he would treat her better so she would hold up for the rest of the winter.

He didn't find her that night, nor did he find her over the course of the next few days. The sparrow just lay under the mounting snow, struggling to stay alive. She heard the man sparrow call for her, and she called back, but he never heard her. He even walked over her a few times without knowing it.

A few days later, she heard the man sparrow talking to another bird, a lady bird. The sparrow couldn't tell what kind of a bird she was—she just knew she wasn't a sparrow. The lady bird was lost, she told the man sparrow. She had gotten separated from her flock and had flown the wrong way. She asked him for directions, but he told her she didn't need to worry about flying south. "Stay with me," he said. "I have a nice warm nest. You don't need to fly south this winter. I know how to find food. We'll find it together." The lady bird was so cold and tired and hungry, she accepted his offer. The sparrow heard all of this and was deeply hurt. The man sparrow had forgotten all about her.

During the next week the sparrow lay under the huge mound of snow and listened to the man sparrow and the lady bird as they laughed and talked and searched for food. She was deeply wounded by this.

Days passed and the sparrow began to lose hope. The man sparrow would never find her now. He wasn't even looking anymore. He didn't love her. He loved the lady bird. When another week passed, and she started to hear the lady bird searching for their food alone, while the man sparrow stayed warm in his nest, she knew it wasn't true. Slowly but surely she began to understand what had happened. The man sparrow was no good, she realized. He lured females into his nest and then tricked them into searching for his food. He didn't love anyone, nor did he have a shred of decency. She longed for the bear, for his kindness and love, but he was deep in hibernation and wouldn't awake until the spring.

The sparrow prayed that the snow would melt, keeping herself alive on a blaze of hope. She had to set things straight with the man sparrow. She couldn't die before she spoke the truth about him. She had to expose him, to tell him who and what he was, and she had to warn the lady bird about him. It was this desire that kept her alive, and finally, after days and days, the huge mound of snow on top of her began to melt. Each day it melted more and more, until her beak poked through the icy crust, then her feet, and when finally she could flap her wings, she was free.

She shook herself off, and the first thing she did was dig herself some roots. She needed her strength before she confronted the man sparrow. She dug up as many roots as she could find and gorged herself until she could not eat another bite. She slept peacefully that night in a discarded nest she found in a neighboring tree, and when she awoke in the morning, with the sunlight in her eyes, she felt strong and sure. She ate some more roots, and after she flew around for a while, to get her blood flowing, she flew up to the man sparrow's nest. She burst in and found him eating breakfast with the lady bird. She edged inside their nest, close to the table, and stood there tall and proud. "You just used me to get your food," she cried. "You didn't love me. You only looked for me because you didn't want to search for your own food, because you're lazy and selfish, and you think you're better than I am." She told the lady bird that this would happen to her as well. "He has no heart," she said passionately. "He can only use others and discard them when they are not needed anymore. He has no conscience either." The man sparrow rose up from the table and grabbed his shovel. "Get out of here," he yelled, wielding the shovel, but the sparrow wouldn't move.

"Come with me, lady bird," she implored. "We don't need him. We can survive without him. He's nothing but a liar and a con artist."

"I SAID, GET OUT OF HERE," the man sparrow roared.

When the sparrow stood her ground and told him she would tell everyone in the forest about him, he couldn't stand for her to say another word. He raised his shovel and hit her over the head again and again until she fell to the floor, dead.

Dead, Lana said. Dead.

She stopped speaking. We were all so stunned that none of us said anything. The sounds from the neighborhood came swimming back to us, and suddenly we heard a chorus of bullfrogs swell in the distance. It was Harry who first spoke. He slipped out of his chair and walked quietly over to Lana. "Did the bear make her better?" he asked her, his little eyes moist with confusion. It was as if his baby voice brought her around, for after he'd asked his question, she stared at me and Elena helplessly.

"Did the bear make her better?" Harry insisted.

"Of course he did, Harry," Lana said, running her fingers through his hair. "He found her in the spring and took her back to his cave and made her all better." She looked at me and Elena boldly. "The end."

And it was the end, for we never again heard another installment of the bear and sparrow story.

Lana rose from her chair and collected all our glasses, placing them on top of the silver tray Mimi had once given her. "Come on, you guys," she said, as though nothing had happened. She glanced over at me and Elena and motioned us with her head. We were still too stunned to move. Instead, we sat in our wicker chairs and watched her carry the tray across our back lawn, chatting idly with Harry as he ran by her side, as if she hadn't just left the sparrow on the floor, dead.

"You're right, Maddie," Elena whispered from her bed that night. "She has changed." She rolled over on her side and hiked herself up on her elbow, the light from the hallway illuminating half of her face. "I think it's because she feels separate from Leo now. We're not much of a family anymore." Her pale forehead knotted, and the corners of her mouth turned down.

"Elena, I have to tell you something." I rolled over on my side and stared at her.

"What?"

"I have to tell you in your bed."

She shoved over and threw the blankets back so I could crawl in next to her. I hadn't been in her bed in such a long time that there was a certain comfort in lying next to her now, in straightening out by her side. I sank deeper under her covers and listened to the sound of the rain on the rooftop. It was a sound I used to enjoy, but now because of the leak in the attic, it caused me anxiety. It was coming down harder now, and I knew that before too long I would have to get up and check the bucket. I figured I had about a half an hour.

"Mimi sent Lana two letters," I whispered.

"*She did?*" I felt her eyes on me immediately.

"I found them in the mail on the floor before Lana did," I said. While Elena drifted closer to me, I told her about the lawyer's office wanting to talk to Lana, and about how Mimi said people still remembered her. As I spoke I watched her face carefully. Her eyes wandered across the ceiling and down the half-lit wall out in the hallway, her thoughts churning underneath. When I finished, she turned her head on the pillow, and our eyes met and locked for a few moments.

"You really want to know what happened to her, don't you, Maddie?"

I nodded and tried to get out from underneath her heavy gaze.

"You've really changed, Maddie," she whispered. She stared at me for a few moments longer. It was as if she had never really seen me before, as if she'd never before considered me a force to reckon with.

"So have you," I said. A car drove by outside, the beams of light drifting across the wall, passing over us as if it were some kind of ethereal wand, dusting us with something unseen.

"We've all changed," she said. "None of us are the same as we were last year in Detroit. Leo's different, and so are you, and Lana is changing. Something is going to happen to us, you know," she said. "*Something bad.*"

My nerves rose up beneath my skin and fled to the four corners of my body.

"Let's promise each other something," she whispered. "No matter what happens let's not break apart." Her voice sounded small and shy in the watery air.

"Okay," I said. It was such a puny word to express how deeply I felt about it. I wanted to take her hand, but it didn't feel comfortable to do that anymore, as if we had grown too old or too awkward for it. I didn't leave her bed, though—we lay side by side, our shoulders touching, while we listened to the punishing rain.

"Elena," I said, after a long time passed. "Do you think Leo was the man sparrow who beat Lana up?"

"He could be."

"But I always thought Leo was the bear," I said.

"Maybe he was the man sparrow," she whispered. "Maybe that's what's wrong with them."

"You think Leo beat her up?" A shock registered in my mind like an electric bolt, and I honestly couldn't imagine it.

"I don't know, Maddie. I really don't."

She pressed her temples between her hands, as if to still the pulse of her thoughts. "It's all mixed up, Maddie." She turned over after that and fell asleep, but I never really slept that night. I dozed off and on, waking up a couple of times in a cold sweat, the strangest images fleeting through my twisted dreams — Leo with wings and a beak pecking Lana's eyes out; Leo trapping Lana under a huge black shovel; and Leo taking Aphrodite out of her cage in Miss Thomas's bird room and pulling her wings off.

The next morning, I dragged Lizzy down to Minnie Harp's. The tall, dead grass in her yard lay now in a brown, soggy ruin. Her barren house was completely in view, a little more battered and raw-looking after the winter. Some of the shutters hung now from one nail, and a few of the eaves had broken away and fallen down the side of the house where they rested like big, gangly crutches. From the edge of the woods we could see her tulips breaking through the ground, but as far as we could tell, Minnie hadn't come out yet.

We poked around in the awakening woods looking for signs of a fresh burial, and not finding any, we wandered over to the fire pit to see if Minnie had burned anything else. We stirred the dark matted ash with a stick, turning it over to see what lay beneath, and found bits and pieces of the bandages which hadn't burned completely. I overturned a clump of wet leaves and laid bare something that looked like a whole bandage. I pushed the leaves off it and bent over and picked it up. After I shook it free of ash and leaves, I held it up between my fingers.

"Look," I said to Lizzy. It was the burned collar of a man's shirt.

"The Nazi," Lizzy whispered. We looked from it, to the house, and then back at each other. "It's from his shirt," she said.

Somehow holding his shirt collar between my fingers made him more real than seeing the bottles he presumably drank from.

"Maybe he's still alive," I said. A heavy-handed chill crept up my spine, and we stood frozen, our eyes fixed straight ahead on Minnie Harp's arthritic house.

"What if he's one of the Nazis Simon Wiesenthal is looking for?" she said.

I stared at the dirty, wet shirt collar between my fingers, and a field of gooseflesh rose up on my arms and raced up the back of my neck. "We should find out if he's still alive," I said.

"How? The newspaper is all over her windows."

I thought there had to be at least one place where there was a tear or crack in Minnie Harp's newspaper. It was so old there had to be, but the only way we could find out was to check all of her windows. The idea of getting that close to her house gave us both the creeps, but it seemed there was no other way to find out if the Nazi was still alive.

We crept nervously out of her woods and stole quietly from tree to tree, finally hiding behind the great elm which anchored her side lawn. The sound of her opera flooded out from the back of her house, a high, breathy aria which Minnie often hummed herself. I pointed to the bay windows that jutted out from the side of her house and suggested we look in those first. The idea scared the hell out of me, though. It was one thing to jump out of a tree in the safety of Minnie Harp's woods—it was another to actually lay a hand on her rotting house. Somewhere in the distance I heard the sharp, ominous bark of a dog, as if it were warning us away from touching her house. When I glanced up at the sky and saw a fat, dark-edged cloud, I knew we shouldn't do it.

Lizzy wasn't as worried about touching Minnie Harp's house as I was, but even so I couldn't get hold of myself. It was just like Lana's journals—once I'd started something I couldn't stop myself. It was my nerves, I knew. Slowly but surely they were eating away at my moral fiber.

I followed Lizzy out from behind the tree. We crept stealthily across her lawn to the bay windows, where we quietly searched the yellowed newspaper for any cracks or tears. Some of them dated as far back as 1948, but nonetheless there were no cracks.

We heard something then which we would never forget. From deep inside the tomb of Minnie Harp's house came the unmistakable sound of a tumultuous, gunky cough that belonged no more to Minnie Harp than it did to me or Lizzy. It was distinguished first by its sickening gooeyness, next by its maleness. We had never heard Minnie Harp cough, but we'd heard her hum, and this was not the cough of an opera singer. It was the cough of a Nazi.

Lizzy drifted over to me and we stood together, our ears pressed to the window, listening spellbound as he hacked out whatever grotesque sickness gripped him. Until this very moment, I had never quite believed that Minnie Harp was harboring a Nazi. It was when we found the shirt collar that it finally seemed possible there had at least *been* a Nazi—whether or not he was alive was another question. But now as I listened to the sound of his lung-eating cough, I was convinced he was still alive and living in Minnie Harp's house.

From that moment on, we scoured every page of Lana's *New York Times* in search of further news of Simon Wiesenthal and the missing Nazis. We crept across Minnie Harp's lawn every chance we got and went from one window to the next, searching the newspapers for any tears which would afford us our first glimpse of her Nazi.

We checked all the windows on the left side of Minnie's house and were about to brave the front, when Lana needed to be watched again. Near the end of April, Lizzy and I came home from school and found her in the kitchen throwing a fit. We stepped onto the back porch just in time to see her heave the metal cover of a pan across the room. The plastic cup and bowl Harry had used for lunch followed, the remaining bit of milk and chicken soup slopping all over the kitchen floor. She grabbed a sponge from the sink and sank to her knees, angrily crawling on all fours while she swiped up the mess. She muttered to herself, words we couldn't make out, and when she left the kitchen, I dug down in the garbage and found it—there was another letter from Mimi, ripped into tiny pieces. They lay between some rotting banana peels and moldy mashed potatoes.

I watched her at the dinner table and noticed that she hardly touched her food. Her voice wasn't shaky, though—it bristled with anger.

"What's wrong with you?" Elena asked her after she yelled at Harry for dropping a macaroni noodle on the floor.

"Is your father here?" she yelled. "Do you see your father at this dinner table?" Her face was deeply red, her eyes burning like lasers.

Elena shot me a look, as if to say, I told you so, but I knew the truth. She was mad at Leo, yes, but Mimi's letter had set her off. She didn't disappear to her writing room, like I suspected she might.

Instead, she did the wash. I watched her from the cellar steps as she heaved our clothes into the machine, threw some powder in, and slapped it on. Then she scrubbed the kitchen floor on her hands and knees, slamming the brush down so hard I thought it might break. She took out the vacuum cleaner after that and threw it around the living room rug.

Just before the sun went down, she pulled Harry outside and watched him from the porch steps as he played in his sandbox. I quietly sat down next to her, and for no reason at all she turned to me and said, "For your sake, I wish you'd been born a boy, Maddie. They don't have babies, so they own the world." She looked back at Harry as he dumped a bucketful of sand on the grass. "Do that again, Harry, and you'll never play in that sandbox again." These were the words of Garta, I thought, not Lana.

I watched her through the bathroom grate after she put Harry to bed. She went into her writing room and began typing with a brutal vengeance—the same way she had washed the clothes and scrubbed the kitchen floor. When Leo came home she didn't stop. In fact, she assaulted it more, her fingers raining down on those keys faster and harder, as if she were punishing it. Leo said hello to her, and she muttered something, and then fifteen minutes passed before she came into their bedroom. She walked hurriedly across the floor, disappearing into the closet, where I heard her rummaging through one of those boxes she had sealed up. When she emerged with a sheath of papers and crossed over to her dresser, Leo made the mistake of speaking to her.

"Sorry I missed dinner," he said quietly. He was sitting on the edge of their bed, rolling up his white shirtsleeves.

"You might have called," she yelled, her voice already bitter.

"I told Therese to call, but I guess she forgot." He tried to smile (as if that would have helped), but his lips didn't make it very far.

"What does it take, Leo, to pick up—"

"There's no phone in the theater, La." He shoved both of his rolled shirtsleeves up past his elbows, as if he were going to fight her.

"That's no excuse, Leo," she shouted. "Not when your wife and children are waiting for you."

She stared at him violently. He stared back, not knowing what to say, and then it came—her terrible, fiery anger. Her arm sliced across the dresser, knocking over all her bottles of perfume and colognes and jars of creams. The sound of it was startling—it mangled the soft, evening air.

Instead of yelling back, Leo sat there in silence, staring blindly down at his worn black shoes.

"Just sit there," she yelled, stamping her foot. "That really helps." Rage fled from her eyes and hit Leo with laser precision.

"What do you want me to say?"

"I want you to say you're sorry," she yelled. "I want you to tell your children you are sorry you don't even have time to eat a meal with them anymore."

"I'll tell them in the morning," he muttered. He hung his head and sighed deeply, his posture sliding down on his breath.

"I want you to tell them tonight. Right now, Leo. I want you to tell your two girls you're sorry, so they don't have to fall asleep another night wondering if their father gives a shit about them anymore." Her face was red and chapped, and her eyes flashed like beacons, signaling doom.

"I said I'll tell them tomorrow," he yelled back.

Lana yanked open the top drawer of her dresser. "You're killing me."

"And what am I supposed to do, Lana?" he screamed. "Teach piano lessons in the fucking living room to little girls for the rest of my life? That's what you want, isn't it? You want me to give up my life, because . . . *because you think I took yours away*. You think it was my fault. I know you do, but if *you hadn't been so goddamned impatient . . . it . . . never . . . would . . . have . . . happened*."

Lana stopped breathing. You could suddenly feel the air in the room as if it wore boots.

"You bastard, Leo," she hissed, her voice sliding down to the lowest octave. She wheeled around and ripped the drawer out of its socket, and despite its weight, she heaved it across the room, where it landed some ten inches from Leo's feet. Her slips and nightdresses flew out of it and landed, one after another, like reckless parachutes all over the room.

"You couldn't stand it when I was in the limelight, could you?" she yelled. Her eyes narrowed, and she stalked slowly toward him. "You couldn't take that, could you? So you bring me to this little town and tell me to forget the past."

His back went absolutely rigid, and his fists clenched in bitter knots. "You're the one who won't tell your children about—"

"Don't you *dare* say it, Leo," she yelled. She flew at him. "You say it, and I'll leave you. Do you hear me?" She shook her fist near his face, and for a moment I thought she was going to slam it into the side of his head. I know she wanted to.

As if something inside her clicked off or shut down, she backed away from him, her eyes registering shock. "Look what you've done to me," she said in horror. She hit herself hard on the chest with her fist, as if to point herself out. The thud, the sound her flesh made, fist against chest, made my stomach roll. "Look what you've reduced me to."

"You did it to yourself," he said.

Lana heaved her cane against the wall. "I'll undo it, then," she yelled fiercely. "I'll call up the lawyer." She raced over to the dresser, her feet colliding with all the fallen jars and bottles upended on the floor.

Like a terrifying giant, Leo rose up and pursued her across the room, his face breaking into those ragged red pieces.

She turned on him, spitting out her words. "You have your goddamned life, so why shouldn't I have mine? I'll call the lawyer—*I'll call them all.*"

Leo wanted to silence her—his hands rose to her mouth and fell and then rose again. For some reason, he couldn't, and instead he seized her wrists and slammed them down. She struggled to free herself, and when he clamped down even harder, her mouth opened and that same terrible shrill scream pierced the still night and froze my heart. It rose from her like a siren from her soul, and as if it touched a spot of reason deep inside of Leo, he stopped. He dropped her hands immediately, and her scream ceased as quickly as it had come.

It had summoned both Harry and Elena, whom I could see standing in the doorway, clutching one another.

"I'm sorry, La." His eyes melted, and his voice came as a crushed whisper. "I didn't mean that."

Lana stared back at him unblinking. She went absolutely rigid as she teetered between two edges. I was afraid she would collapse on the floor and weep, that Leo would sink to his knees and cradle her in his arms like a baby. I know she fought off this temptation—I saw it pass over her brow and lodge in her jaw. It was what she usually did; it was where these awful fights generally led. But not this time. She pulled her hand back and slapped him hard across his face. "I'll never forget what you said, you bastard."

I thought for certain that Lana was about to exit our lives again. It seemed she would walk out the door and climb into the car and speed away. Perhaps it was Harry and Elena's presence in the doorway that stopped her, for she turned around and vanished into her writing room, slamming the door behind her.

Leo glanced over his shoulder at Elena and Harry, not so much as moving. "Take Harry back to bed, Elena," he said loudly. His shoulders fell forward, and he turned away from them. When Elena and Harry headed shakily down the stairs, he stepped up to her door and banged softly with his knuckles. "La," he said quietly. "I'm sorry. I don't know why I said that. I didn't mean it." His voice was thin and washed-out, strangled sounding.

There was no answer, just the scratchy silence. I wondered what there was in Leo's words—*"If you hadn't been so goddamned impatient, it never would have happened"*—which had the power to transform Lana. Why had they brought out in Lana such a ragged loss of control? I didn't know, but I knew it wasn't simple. I knew it was a dark and seething mess.

My head felt like it was going to split open, so I lay down on the cold tiles and pressed my hands against my temples, where the beat was fiercest. What if it was Leo who had beat her up so long ago? That awful scream when he held her wrists down, I thought—it was as if he had done it many times before.

I sat up and looked through the grate to see what had become of them. Leo wasn't in their room anymore, and the door to Lana's room was still closed. I didn't hear the sound of voices, so I guessed Leo had gone back to the college.

When I crept through Elena's room, I noticed that she was either asleep or feigning sleep. I didn't say anything to her. My nerves were in such a sad state of confusion, I just headed straight to my dresser and fished Durga up from underneath my wool socks. I carried her back to my bed, and after I climbed in I started to put her on my stomach.

"What's that you've got?" I heard Leo say.

I looked around my darkened room and was shocked to find him sitting in the corner. It scared the hell out of me, for one thing, and for another, he had seen Durga. When he moved slowly from the chair to my bed, I pushed her deep under my covers and pressed my leg on top of her.

"Maddie," he said, sitting down next to me. "I wanted to tell you I'm sorry I haven't made it home for dinner lately." I didn't know what to say. I just stared up at him and watched his face twist. "I couldn't keep on teaching piano lessons," he whispered. "I just couldn't do it anymore—not because of Lana, but because I couldn't do it anymore. You understand?" he asked me.

I nodded, and he touched my face with the tips of his fingers, the same way he used to touch Lana. He said good night to me, and I heard him walk down the stairs and head out the front door. I took Durga out from underneath the covers and was about to stand her on my stomach when I heard Elena whisper, "This is what I told you was going to happen, Maddie. It's never going to be the same between them either. Not now." She turned her face toward me, and in the hazy light she look haunted.

I pushed Durga back under the covers and gripped her tightly.

"Who would you want to go with?" she asked. "Lana or Leo?"

I thought of Leo holding Lana's wrists down, and of the horrible look on Lana's face when Leo had said—*"If you hadn't been so goddamned impatient, it never would have happened."*

"I'd pick Lana," she said. She pulled her covers close to her and brushed her long hair out of her eyes. "Who would you pick?"

I stared at the comforting shadows on my wall, my eyes drifting slowly across the pattern of the windows, to the patterns of the barely moving tree branches. I didn't know who I would pick. It was too awful a thought, and I couldn't think anyway—I still had a splitting headache. It kept me awake and restless, and when Elena finally fell asleep, I took Durga into the attic and stood her on top of Lana's boxes. Then, as if it would help, as if it would still the throb in my head, I pushed my hand through the flaps of the bottom box and touched her silver canisters of film.

16

Leo was gone the next morning when I got up, but Lana was down-stairs in the kitchen making us breakfast. She wouldn't look at us right away, but even so she wasn't shaky. Whatever change had overtaken her seemed permanent—she held her head high, her neck jutting out of her blue linen dress, as if streams of stubborn pride ran beneath her skin.

"I don't want you two to get the idea that the trouble between me and Leo has anything to do with you," she said. Her back was to us, her arms working briskly at her side as she turned the eggs over in the frying pan. "It has nothing to do with you. I'm sorry you had to hear it."

We didn't say anything. We just ate her eggs in silence, and when we were done, we left out the back door, hoping she would be there when we got home from school.

I never heard one word Mrs. Devonshit uttered that whole day. My mind was seized with fear, and my nerves ached inside my veins. I knew something profound had taken place inside of Lana, and it terrified me. I worried about what it might make her do, because I knew she was preparing herself to do something. I could feel it as if it wore boots and walked all over me.

It ate Elena up so much that she disappeared from school during recess. When the principal asked me where she had gone, I told him I didn't know, but it worried me. I sat in a puddle of sunlight all afternoon and drew small circles in the palm of my hand with a blue pen. Then when the sun went behind the clouds, I locked myself in the bathroom and lay down on the cool tiles and shut my eyes.

By the time we left school, it was raining so hard Lizzy and I had to race home to empty the bucket. I was afraid to walk into the house for fear that Lana was long gone, but she was down in the cellar playing hide-and-seek with Harry. Lizzy and I sat on the top step for a while and listened to her pretending she didn't know where he was. She sounded perfectly all right, so we left her, and while Lizzy ran up to the attic and emptied the bucket, I hung around the front door waiting for the mailman to bring the *New York Times*. Garta called not long afterward and told me to send Lizzy home. "She's got to watch Jimmy," she said. "My sister got sick and I got to get back to work. SEND HER HOME NOW."

Leo called right after that and asked to talk to Lana. I yelled down the cellar stairs, and she came up to the top step and leaned against our hanging winter coats and sweatshirts. "Ask him what he wants."

"She wants to know what you want," I said to Leo.

"Put her on the phone, Maddie." He whispered, "Jesus," under his breath, and I heard him drop something heavy on his desk.

"He wants to talk to you," I told Lana, holding the phone out to her.

She squeezed her eyes shut, as if to summon her patience. "Ask him what he wants."

I asked him what he wanted and he told me to put Lana on. It went on like this until finally Lana took the phone. "Go down and find Harry," she said. "He's hiding under the stairs."

I went downstairs and pretended I didn't know where he was, shuffling past him while he held his breath, letting him relish his secrecy. When I walked to the back of the cellar, I was shocked to discover that Lana had dismantled our stage. The apple boxes were neatly stacked against the wall, all the props we'd collected were packed away, and the red velvet curtain was folded up and now lay wrapped in plastic. The dressing rooms no longer existed, and most of the chairs were stacked in the corner. Why had she done this? I wondered. It seemed to say something, to indicate her deeper state of mind. She's pushing us away, I thought. Or else, she's leaving. Why else would she pack up our stage? It disturbed me to know that it was gone—while I hid among the apple boxes and chairs, playing hide-and-seek, I mourned its loss.

When Lana finally came downstairs, I took up my post on the front steps and waited for the mailman to bring the *New York Times* and, hopefully, another letter from Mimi. The phone rang again, and terror seized my heart. It was Garta, I knew. I had forgotten to tell Lizzy to go home. I picked up the phone, and before I even finished saying hello, Garta was screaming.

"WHERE THE HELL IS LIZZY?"

"I forgot—"

"SEND HER HOME RIGHT NOW."

As Lizzy and I raced down the rain-slicked streets, the world went by in a blur, all the colors smearing together as if they'd been dumped into a huge tank of water. I could hear my gusty breath as if it were at my ear, and a desperation rose up from somewhere deep inside of me.

"I'm sorry, Lizzy," I croaked loudly. "I'll tell her it was my fault." I put my hand on her arm as if that would bring her back to me.

"She won't believe you," she said coldly. She ran ahead of me, her head bent against the rain.

When we reached the landing at the top of the stairs, Garta grabbed Lizzy by the shoulders and whisked her into the apartment. I followed on their heels, but I wasn't quick enough. The door slammed shut in my face, and the next thing I heard was the shattering crack of the lock. I pounded on the door with two knotted fists, yelling Garta's name, but my voice, no matter how loud and unstrung, was lost under Garta's rage.

"I COULD LOSE MY JOB BECAUSE OF YOU, SHIT-HEAD," she screamed from inside. I heard a dull sickening thud, which told me she had slammed her fist into Lizzy's head. Then the clattery sound of Lizzy falling to the floor, her legs and arms scratching out her agony on the linoleum floor. Somewhere in the midst of it all came Lizzy's small, remarkable voice. "Mom," she breathed, "Maddie forgot to tell me."

"Garta," I yelled, pounding the door. *"She's telling the truth."*

Something crashed against the wall, and then I heard the sound of Garta's stampeding feet, punctuated by the heartbreaking plaint of Lizzy's voice.

I pounded the door more intensely. "Please, Garta," I cried, tasting the saltiness of my tears. *"Pleas-sssssssssssssse."*

Art stepped out of the projection room into the dim, gray hallway.

"Garta's beating Lizzy again," I cried. He jabbed his cigarette into his mouth and started down the hallway immediately. When he stepped up to the door, he laid his fist into it. "Garta," he hollered, "you'd better leave her alone if you know what's good for you."

A few moments later Garta opened the door and shoved past me and Art.

"MIND YOUR OWN BUSINESS, ART," she said. "GO BACK IN YOUR ROOM AND BEAT OFF, WHY DON'T YOU?" She stormed down the stairs after that, the curse words flying from her mouth like spears.

Art and I pushed the door open and found Lizzy sitting in the corner of the kitchen, tomato soup dripping from her hair and running down her face. The bowl lay turned over near her feet, the soup smeared on the linoleum by Garta's huge feet. Jimmy was hiding underneath the table, silent tears plowing down his face, his knuckles turning white as he clung to the metal leg.

The first thing I did the next morning was visit Mrs. Blanchard's office. Lizzy and I had decided we would write, ANOTHER WRONG MOVE AND YOUR LIFE IS ON THE LINE, but under the circumstances I felt the need to make our note stronger. I poised my two index fingers and pecked out this message: ANOTHER WRONG MOVE AND YOU'RE DEAD. I signed it, THE ANGRY EYES OF GOD.

"Did you have to write *dead*?" Lizzy asked me in the bathroom, our small brown note shaking silently between her gloved fingers. The word *dead* terrified her. "I thought we were going to write, 'your life is on the line.'"

"It's the last time I can use Mrs. Blanchard's typewriter. She knows I'm doing something wrong, and she won't let me use it again. Besides, Lizzy, she knows about me typing on brown paper. If Garta ever asked her—"

It was so unbearable a thought that Lizzy clapped her hands over her ears.

"She won't ask, though," I said loudly, pulling her hands down.

"And besides, if she did, she would tell Garta it was me. She's never seen you down there with me. She doesn't even know you're in on this."

The realization that none of it could be traced back to her fortified her and gave her the courage to mail this difficult message to Garta.

When Garta turned up at our dining room table two days later, she was sobbing. She yanked out our small brown note and thrust it over to Lana, snuffling loudly into the sleeve of her green nylon jacket.

"It's the worst one. It couldn't get much worse." She turned her head and glared first at Lizzy, then at me, the hate flooding from her eyes. Lizzy's shaky hand sought mine under the table, and together we trembled, our knees knocking lightly against one another.

"I know what the wrong move is now," she sobbed. She shot Lizzy and me another bitter look, and the small hope that she didn't know it was us vanished.

"What is the wrong move?" Lana asked.

Lizzy squeezed my hand so hard, the bones in my fingers cracked.

"It has to do with Lizzy and me fighting," she said, glaring openly at Lizzy, shooting me another brutal look. I heard Lizzy's breathing — it came and went as if an elephant sat on her chest.

"How do you know?" Lana asked her. Her eyes went swiftly from Garta to Lizzy and then back again.

"Because this came just after Lizzy and me had another fight," Garta sobbed. She wiped her nose with the back of her hand, and grabbed her pack of Benson and Hedges from her coat pocket.

"What was the fight about?" Lana wanted to know.

"I called Maddie up to tell her to send Lizzy home, because my sister got sick," Garta cried. "I had to go back to work, and Lizzy didn't come home for about an hour, and I caught it back at work." She plucked one of her cigarettes out of her pack with the stubby ends of her fingers and jabbed it into her mouth.

I was too worried about the ultimate outcome of this conversation to protest Garta's blatant lie, but then Lana turned to Lizzy and asked, "Is that true?"

Lizzy didn't nod or shake her head; she didn't offer so much as a word. Her breath stopped, and she stared at Garta.

"Maddie?" Lana said. I looked at Garta and then down at my untouched peach cobbler. I looked up again at Garta's teary face.

"No, it's not," I said. My voice was loud and quaking. "She called, and I forgot to tell Lizzy, because Leo called right after that, and you sent me downstairs to play with Harry."

Lana looked at Garta, and Garta looked at me. Had Lana not been there, she would have split my head open.

"Never mind," Garta said, spewing out a mouthful of smoke. "It don't matter about that."

She picked up our note and read it out loud. " 'Another wrong move and you're dead. The angry eyes of God.' " When new tears coursed down Garta's face, Lana rose up from the table and got her some tissue.

"I know who it is," Garta cried, blowing her red nose into the pink Kleenex.

"Who?" Lana asked.

Garta glanced over at us again, giving me an especially vile look. I swore after this whole thing was over I would straighten myself out.

"Who?" Lana said again.

"It's Art up in the movie theater," Garta cried. "That old man who runs the projector. He listens to everything that goes on up there, that nosy little fucker. He's always got his nose stuck in someone's business. He thinks I don't know where he gets that Eyes of God shit. Just because he sits up there in that room day and night, watching all those films and all the people who sit in there, don't mean he's got the Eyes of God."

Garta was crying quite openly now, a shock in itself, but I was too busy congratulating myself to marvel over it. She was convinced it was Art. How perfect, I thought. Out of everyone Garta knew, it was Art who best knew the systematic cruelty she carried out against Lizzy.

I braved a look at Lizzy. She was as unburdened as I had ever seen her—her eyes blazed and her hands, now silenced, lay quietly on top of the table. I nudged her with my elbow, she nudged me back, and while Garta cursed Art to hell, we slowly dipped our spoons into the peach cobbler.

"I'm going to have him arrested," Garta yelled. "I'm going to take these to the police and have him arrested. You can't go around threatening people like this."

I don't know why, but I wasn't worried about the police discovering it was me and Lizzy and not Art. Somehow I sensed, so long as another note was not written, nothing would be done about it.

Lizzy and I retreated to the attic. We didn't laugh this time, not really, for it suddenly seemed too real, too serious to laugh about anymore. The reason we had written the notes still existed—Garta could beat her up again. We could only hope that with the Eyes of God permanently installed in the projection room, she would think twice about it.

Lizzy and I agreed that we'd gotten our revenge for the time being, and during recess the next day, we took the envelopes, stamps, and brown paper bags out of our lockers. After school we smuggled them out of the building in the hem of my coat and dropped them into Minnie's fire pit and threw a lighted kitchen match on top of them.

As they blackened in the flames, we heard the faint sound of opera coming from Minnie Harp's house. It wafted back to us on the sweet-smelling breeze and reminded us that we hadn't yet searched her front or right-side windows for any cracks or tears in the newspaper. Once our papers were reduced to ashes, we stomped on them and then ran from tree to tree, across Minnie's budding green lawn, con-cealing ourselves behind the big elm tree which stood in her front yard. We had a perfect view of the front of her house. On the left side was a three-sided bay window, on the right was the screen porch, and in the middle lay her front porch. The porch steps were still there, though they didn't look too sturdy, and there was a large wooden door, naked of any varnish, which stood between two long, thin-shuttered windows.

"Let's open the shutters," I whispered, though the prospect of ven-turing onto her porch gave me the creeps.

"The porch looks rotten," Lizzy said. It did look rotten, but the whole house looked rotten, I reminded her. "It's still standing," I pointed out.

She finally nodded, and when Minnie's opera rose to a particularly poignant swell, Lizzy and I ran from behind the tree to the left side of her porch. We crept onto it slowly and carefully, the boards be-neath our feet groaning miserably. Thankfully, the lefthand shutter was very near the edge of the porch, so we didn't have far to go. I expected it would be nailed shut, but it swung open when I pulled it and revealed to us our first miracle—a newspaperless window. The glass was filthy, but nonetheless we caught our first glimpse of the inside of Minnie Harp's house. The stairway lay in a state of ruin; the wooden banister had fallen over and now hung so precariously over the dim hallway that it seemed a good crack of thunder could wrest it free. The stairs had huge holes in them where boards had either disintegrated to dust or had been accidentally stepped through, and the walls were nothing more than yellowed, flaking plaster.

The door at the far end of the hallway gaped open and Minnie Harp appeared like a ghost. My heart shot up to my throat where it beat like a sledgehammer, and immediately we turned and fled her porch, forgetting the edge, opting instead to race madly down the steps. I went first, Lizzy following desperately behind me, her right foot stabbing through the bottom step, stopping her completely. "Maddie," she yelled. I ran back to her and pulled her foot out, leaving her new shoe lodged somewhere in the sawdust and decayed boards. She ran ahead of me, and before I followed her, I looked up to see what had become of Minnie Harp. She stood at the filthy window, unmoving, her gaze fixed directly on me. If she had screamed out her mournful "Nnunggg," or rapped an angry fist against the glass, or pursued us down the sidewalk, brutalizing the spring air with her war cry, I would have felt all was right. But instead she stood there, stilled and silenced, and gave me not a mournful cry, but her defeated, helpless stare. Her look pierced my callousness, and for the first time since I had laid eyes on Minnie Harp, I pitied her.

The smile fell from my lips like unnecessary weight, and I turned around and followed Lizzy across the front lawn, into the woods, and out to the field. We raced up the knoll and tumbled down the other side, lying still in the baby grass, trying to catch our breath.

"I lost my shoe," Lizzy gasped. "It was my new shoe. My mom's going to get me for that." She pulled up her pant leg and we surveyed the long cut around her ankle. It was bleeding quite a bit, and around it had formed a deep, blue bruise which had welled up like an anthill. "She won't care about the cut," Lizzy said, "but she'll care about that shoe."

We thought of returning to Minnie Harp's porch to extract it, but neither of us had the stomach for it, especially me. It had only been a brief impression—locking eyes with Minnie Harp—lasting only a moment, but even so I couldn't get it out of my mind. As if our deed had more evil significance, the memory of it left a dark blot on my conscience.

We fixed up Lizzy's ankle with some alcohol and Band-Aids and found a pair of Elena's old shoes for her to wear until we could gather our courage to go back down to Minnie Harp's again. Garta would notice, we knew, and we could only hope that the Eyes of God would prevent her from beating Lizzy again.

While I waited for Lizzy's call that night, I heard Lana and Leo fighting in their room. I couldn't make out their words, but their sharp and raised tone of voice told me that they were arguing bitterly. I didn't get up to listen at the grate, because my responsibility for their troubles weighed on me too much already. I was sure I had helped bring them to this awful place, and with each raised, sharp piece of their voice, I felt our old life crumbling.

I had affected Minnie Harp too, I realized. I couldn't get her face out of my mind, and though I asked Durga to erase it with her hands, it lingered in my conscience, disturbing me. Although we hadn't seen the Nazi, I was sure he was in there. The look on her face, pitiful as it was, told me it was true. Her eyes, so devastating, had begged me not to come any further, not to break down that precious wall that kept us apart.

I had affected Lana and Leo, I thought, and now they were affecting me. I had affected Minnie Harp, and she, in turn, had affected me. Lizzy and Art and I had affected Garta. I imagined this huge web, an enormous long, webbed chain of people affecting one another. It seemed you couldn't do something and have it go unnoticed. It had to end up affecting someone, somewhere, always. Here I was living in a small town, and I had affected Mimi, who had in turn affected Lana, who now affected Leo, and as a result affected me, Elena, and Harry. If Garta were to beat Lizzy, it would affect Lizzy and me, and also Art, who didn't even know he was part of Garta's web. I imagined millions of webs, connecting all the people in the world, and was stunned by the thought that something I did might one day affect someone in India, where Durga had come from.

I heard the phone ring. I ran downstairs and answered it.

"Maddie," Lizzy whispered. "She didn't get me." She sighed, and I heard her press against something that squeaked in the closet.

"That's amazing," I said. The strident sound of Lana's voice floated down to me through the floor registers, and I plugged my right ear up with my fingertip so I couldn't hear her.

"She said we'd just get another pair of shoes," Lizzy whispered. "I told her one of the boys took it and threw it in the creek."

"And she just said she'd get you some new ones?" I sat down on the kitchen stool and let my eyes drift out the back door where they came to rest on the lazy, black hills. They were like my lucky charms, those hills.

"Yes," Lizzy whispered.

It was the Eyes of God, we realized, perched high up in the projector room, watching all.

17

The enormous weight of Garta's problems helped relieve Lana of her own. Despite her troubles with Leo, she marshaled her forces once again and waged another campaign against Garta's cruelty to Lizzy. The special mud masks went back on Garta's face to restrain the boils that slowly but surely had crawled underneath her complexion. Lana's diet was again imposed, and Lizzy found Lana's lists taped to Garta's bedroom mirror. We took this as a hopeful sign—the last time Lana had made lists for Garta they ended up in the garbage. With Lana on Garta's back again, and with the Eyes of God permanently installed in the projector room, Lizzy felt safe for the first time.

We didn't go down to Minnie Harp's again for a while. Garta made good on her promise to buy Lizzy a new pair of shoes, so we didn't have to worry about the one lodged in Minnie's porch step. Lizzy thought we should at least go down to check the last of her windows for any cracks in the newspaper, but I didn't want to. The image of Minnie Harp's face came back to haunt me every now and then, making the prospect of viewing her Nazi less appealing.

Soon we were all distracted from our lives by Leo's musical production. It was starting up in a week, and since he had persuaded Lana to do the costuming, our house had been turned upside down. The dining room was wholly usurped by Lana and her volunteer crew of three college girls. Two sewing machines were set up on the table, and costumes hung everywhere—on the backs of chairs, from the edge of the hutch, and from all but one doorway surrounding the dining room. They altered and redid dozens of costumes, Lana and the older volunteer, Maria, manning the sewing machines, while the others fixed hemlines and sewed buttons and sequins on everything. Leo's cast of twenty came by appointment to be fitted, and it sometimes got so crowded, they had to wait on our front stairs.

I didn't understand how Lana could devote herself so completely to Leo's project when she and Leo weren't getting along. She threw herself into it with great energy and kept it up even when they weren't speaking to one another. It must have been her attraction to the stage and to all its attending parts that gave her the enthusiasm, because I know it wasn't Leo.

I looked forward to Leo's production, or rather to its end, for it seemed only after it was over could we return to a normal life. I had great hopes that we would come back together again, that perhaps we might even take a vacation or go and visit Leo's family in Lansing, but Elena didn't think so.

"It's too far gone between them," she said from her bed one night.

"But Lana's fixing all the costumes for him."

"She's only doing it because she promised him a long time ago. And she only acts nice about it because those three girls are always here, and all those actors keep coming over. She's just putting on a show. Believe me, things aren't any different between them, Maddie. If anything, things are only worse."

For two more weeks we ate in the kitchen, either on the floor or up on the counters, while Lana and her crew labored in the dining room, eating their meals between the sewing machines and all the costumes.

Finally May 15 came, and on a beautiful Sunday evening, Elena, Lizzy, Garta, Lana, and I and the two boys climbed Heart Attack Hill, dressed in our best clothes. Lana wore a beautiful long black velvet gown with a red waist, and Elena had on a navy blue dress. Lizzy and I wore the dresses Lana had made for us—mine was pale gray linen, and Lizzy's was a rich, deep purple. We took our seats in the front row of the theater and watched it fill up quickly. I turned around and spotted Barbara Lamb, and way in the back I saw Gus sitting alone. Quite a few of our classmates were there, including Louis, who sat quietly between his overweight mother and his red-haired sister. He was only three rows in back of me, so I tried not to stare at him, but I couldn't help myself. Miss Thomas sat across the aisle and six rows back, and when she saw me, she threw her arm up in the air and began waving it furiously as if she were signaling a ship. Even Mrs. Devonshit had come—she sat some ten rows behind us next to her startlingly thin husband.

I looked down at the program we'd been given and was surprised to learn that Leo's production had a title. *One Man's Life*, it was called, and beneath the title lay a quote from a man named Emmet Goodall: "The best musical ever bred in a university. Broadway bound."

A small band was seated in wooden chairs on the floor beneath the stage. The musicians were tuning up, while Leo milled about them, saying a few words and patting them on the back. He was dressed in a black suit with coattails, which he had bought especially for the occasion. He looked elegant in it, and for a while I couldn't take my eyes off him. Bob Hendrix poked his head through the curtain a few times, and finally motioned for Leo to come backstage. As he walked up the stairs and hastened across the stage, I noticed Lana's eyes nervously follow him.

Moments later the lights were dimmed and a hush fell over the audience. Leo reappeared from behind the curtain and walked down the steps, his coattails flapping behind him. I watched carefully as he picked up his little white stick and raised his arms high above him, the tails of his coat rising with a flourish. I remembered the last time he had raised his hands high above the piano, and I feared that when his arms came down, we would hear the same sound as we had heard then—the jazz. Elena pinched my thigh, and we both looked at Lana. If she was worried about it, she didn't show it.

Leo's arms came down, and suddenly the air in the theater was filled with the sounds of "Meiling," the only piece from his musical he had ever played for us. The curtains parted, the stage lights came up slowly, and we saw an old man in a dark green trenchcoat leaning against a black lamppost, smoke swirling around his feet. A great moon hung in the background, and a row of houses stood behind him, with white picket fences that gleamed in the bluish light.

He began to sing a song about the past, about the glory of his life, while he began to dance a mournful dance. His movements were stiff, he stumbled and lost his balance, he missed the beat often, and he fell down twice. It was all calculated and done so well, it was mesmerizing.

As the lights began to dim, the old man stumbled to the side of the stage, where he leaned against another black lamppost. Leo's music picked up speed, and a spotlight came up on center stage, revealing a younger man dressed in tight black pants and a dark flowing coat. He proceeded to dance the old man's dance with youthful vigor. The jumps the old man had fumbled the young man did now with power and beauty. The turns which had caused the old man to fall down were now executed so perfectly it took your breath away.

As the music slowed down, so too did the dancer, until he began to move as if in a dream. The old man drifted out of the shadows and joined him, the two of them dancing side by side, the same slow dreamy steps, until they both stopped and melted to the floor. With the last note of "Meiling," the stage went black and the audience clapped.

I looked at Lana. The tension had gone out of her face, and she looked relaxed, relieved even.

There was a moment of silence before Leo raised his arms again. When he brought them down, the lights came up on stage, and the old man was leaning against the side lamppost in a yellow spotlight, while the younger man stood center stage in a strong white light. As he began to sing the story of his youth, various young men and young women appeared in other dimmer spotlights around the stage, dancing slowly under a diaphanous net, as if wrapped in a dream. They were his sisters and brothers, and the woman he finally married.

I heard bits of the jazz creep into Leo's music, strains of it here and there. It wasn't that noticeable—it went by very fast, but even so I noticed it and so did Elena. We both braved a look at Lana. If she detected it, she didn't react; she sat still, her eyes taken away by the dancers, as if she had fallen completely under their spell.

The three sisters drifted out of their circles of light and pulled their brother center stage, where they took turns singing their separate songs, gliding and twirling around him. The music was full of life and fun, and as far as I could tell, there wasn't a note of jazz in it. When two of his brothers leapt from their circles and chased their sisters away, the music, playful and feminine, took on a darker, more masculine tone, picking up speed and passion. It wasn't until they began to tap dance in unison, that I heard the jazz steal into the music. It held strong for about fifteen measures and then disappeared. It broke out again when the dance reached a pitch, but it quickly receded.

The woman he was to marry unwrapped herself from the netting and strode forward, the brothers drifting backward to their dim spotlights. She was barefoot and her brown hair flowed down over her shoulders. Her movements were bold and earthy, and she swung her arms and her hips provocatively, while she sang, *Look at me. Notice me. Here I am, look at me, look at me.* The young man, completely spellbound, stopped and watched her in awe.

When the music began to race I heard the jazz. It was stronger and more obvious than the other times, but even so it wasn't constant. It came and went in short spurts, and I wondered if Leo even realized it was there.

"He's going to do it, Maddie," Elena whispered to me.

We both looked at Lana. Her back had gone a little rigid. She was staring straight ahead, her eyes filled more with wonder than with anger, but even so, she shot Leo a dirty look. I knew he was going to hear about it.

The young man began to respond to the woman, and as their song and dance began to merge, the jazz crept in bit by bit, until it began to take over. As they danced together now, taking the stage with great leaps, the music picked up. It was no longer a classical sound riding over the jazz—it was the jazz. It wasn't the song Leo had played for us in the theater, nor was it the one he had played for Elena and Harry in the living room, but it was the jazz, and it invaded me in the same crazy way.

I glanced at Leo. He looked the same as he'd looked when he had played the jazz on the piano, only there was no piano now, only the air. His body, so big and awkward without the music, was his again. He moved as if possessed, his body rocking in time, his arms soaring up and down in the air like some great big elegant bird.

Elena squeezed my hand and whispered, "This is it, Maddie," while Lizzy spoke into my other ear. "Is this the jazz?"

We all looked at Lana. She had ceased looking at the stage. Her right hand shielded her face like a visor, as if there were a blinding sun overhead. Her eyes were clenched shut, and her thumb and middle finger worked her temples as if that awful migraine had begun to bloom inside her skull.

Those scorching questions returned to me—what had happened that the sound of this jazz now inspired in her such dread? What was it, goddamn it? Everyone else in the theater loved the music. The air was charged with it—people were tapping their feet, nodding their heads in time. Even Garta was moving to it.

When the two dancers began to slow down, the music changed again. They put their arms around one another and danced slowly, gazing into one another's eyes. The lights dimmed on center stage, and a spotlight came up on the side of the stage where the old man was leaning against the lamppost. As he watched the young man and woman dance sweetly in the red-hazy light, he began to sing a slow, sentimental song. Lana took her hand away from her face and opened her eyes again. There was no more anger flooding out of them; she didn't even look at Leo. She watched the lovers drift through the swirling smoke, while tears welled in her eyes.

The worst was over, I thought. I didn't know what would happen between them now, but I wondered why Leo had done it, why he had let the jazz reign when he knew Lana would one day sit in the theater with her children and hear it. She had slaved away on his costumes, while all the time he knew he was going to play the jazz. I was beginning to wonder if Elena was right—if everything were all his fault.

As the lovers stood center stage, stilled and wrapped in one another's arms, the lights dimmed and finally faded to black. The old man's voice carried for one or two seconds longer, and when it ceased there was a moment of ethereal silence before the audience erupted in applause. Neither Elena nor Lana clapped, nor did Lizzy and I. Garta and Harry did, but they had no idea what had just happened between Lana and Leo.

When the dancers disappeared, the great moon rose, the light flooding it, until it hung in the blackness, like a beacon.

"He's going to do it," Elena whispered.

When the lights came up on the stage again, the young man was standing in the center surrounded by eight women. It was the same pose Elena and I had seen when we opened the theater door the morning after Lana had gone to Syracuse. They stood very still while the lights rose and the old man took up his post on the side of the stage. Leo's arms ascended again, and when they came down, the jazz flooded the theater. It didn't ease its way into the auditorium — it exploded. Had it had arms it would have raised the roof. As the dancers broke out in a flurry of fast footwork and a wild display of circling arms, I realized in horror that this was the song Leo had played in our living room. It wasn't just any song — it was Lana's song, the song he'd written for her, the song which to Lana was the worst possible song he could play in front of her children, in front of anyone, ever. But there it was — Lana's song tearing through the auditorium, ripping up the air, while the audience went wild. They loved every last nerve-ticking beat of it.

My heart started pounding like a sledgehammer, and when I spun around in my seat and saw the horror etched in Elena's face, I knew it was true. Lana grabbed her cane and rose up. She clutched Harry's hand and shoved past Garta and Jimmy on her way out to the side aisle. She didn't say a word — she didn't even look at us. She moved rapidly, pulling Harry along, her cane knocking against the chairs and stabbing the floor. Her flight was reckless and unsteady, and we watched in horror as her dark receding form moved up the aisle and out the door. Elena shot up and shoved past all of us and ran up the aisle. I stood up then and so did Lizzy, but Garta pulled her back down. "Sit down," she whispered loudly, while I pushed past her and raced after Elena.

I turned around once before I rushed out the door and saw that Leo was sitting at the piano. It was he who played this song — with his own two hands, he played this song which he had promised Lana he would never play in front of her children, in front of anyone. His head moved in circles, his legs pumping up and down, his hands racing along the keyboard, as if he alone were made to play this song. For the first time in my life I hated him.

I turned around and raced out of the theater. Elena was already halfway down Heart Attack Hill, running at breakneck speed. I couldn't see Lana or Harry, but I started running anyway, my feet aching in the tight black patent leather shoes Lana had made me wear. When I reached the bottom there was still no sign of Lana and Harry. I kept running, and when I finally made it to our street, I could see the light blazing in our kitchen window.

I staggered up the porch steps, gasping for breath. Right away I noticed that it was dead quiet — I could only hear my own harried breath. I walked down the dimly lit hallway, my heart beating like the wings of a bird, and came into the dark dining room where I found Elena sitting silently at the table, amid the sewing machines and scraps of cloth.

"She's not here," she said. She slumped forward, her elbows knocking against the table. A piece of light fell through the window and lay across her face like a white strip.

"Did you check the garage?" I asked gingerly, laying my sweaty fingers on the back of Leo's chair.

She hadn't, so we hurried outside and found the car sitting in the garage. It hadn't moved since Lana last drove down to the store to buy some thread. We sank down to the back steps in silence and surveyed the ghostly lawn and the lazy hills in the distance.

"She left us again," Elena said quietly. She picked up a twig and gouged out small trenches in the dirt with it. Then she stabbed it into the ground a few times, as if to punish it, and heaved it out into the darkness where it fell in a soft scratch on top of the picnic table. "Leo's no good," she said, scraping her heels across the trenches. "I don't know what happened to him, but he's just no good."

"He was playing the piano when I left," I said.

"He was?"

I nodded and swallowed past the lump that had formed in my throat. "Just like he played it in the living room."

"Fuck you, Leo," she said bitterly. Then, she yelled it louder. "FUCK YOU, LEO." Her voice echoed in the clear, spring air, and she grabbed one of Lana's garden rocks and threw it at the garage where it hit in a loud thunk against the side. The neighbor's dog, always vigilant, snarled next-door in the darkness.

We sat out on the steps, suspended in time, half waiting for someone to come and claim us. I could only imagine how Leo would discover that his entire family had left the theater long before the final act. I wondered how this would look to the Hamilton public — the composer's family racing away, deserting his first musical production.

When the chill spring air seeped through our linen dresses, we retreated to the dining room where we had lived and breathed these last few weeks. It felt like a huge party had ended and everyone had gone home and left us to clean up the mess. We slumped down gloomily in our chairs and glanced around at the damage.

"It was all for nothing," Elena said, heaving a cupful of red sequins across the table. They hit against the hutch and fell to the floor like sparkling rain. She threw her feet up on the table, between the two sewing machines, and pushed her chair back onto two legs. "It's probably ending right now," she said solemnly.

"They're probably behind the curtains celebrating," I said, imagining the whole cast throwing their arms around each other.

"I hate to say it, Maddie, but it was pretty good. Even though he played the song, I thought it was pretty damn good."

"It was," I said. "Even Garta liked it."

A few more minutes passed, and Elena checked her watch. "They're probably out front by now, and Leo's probably looking for us." It made her smile, knowing he wouldn't find us there.

Elena turned off the kitchen light and lit a candle. "I want him to come home to a dark house." The candle threw a ghoulish light on the room, casting hideous shadows on the wall in the shape of monstrous sewing machines.

When we heard the front door open, Elena blew out the candle, and we held our breath. In the next moment, Leo's darkened silhouette appeared in the doorway against the backdrop of the streetlight outside. I don't think he saw us right away, but he sensed we were in there; I'm sure he heard my breathing—it was loud and pneumatic. He came in and sat down at the table, cattycorner from me and Elena, and no one said anything for a number of long, painful moments. I shifted my weight twice, and Elena swallowed hard a few times, while Leo folded his hands on top of the table and stared at us across the darkness.

"Where is she?" he finally asked. His voice was flat, almost a whisper.

The silence continued to mount, until I found it intolerable. "We don't know," I said. "When we got outside she was already gone, but the car's still here."

"She's got Harry, then?" He unfolded his hands and slid them off the table.

I nodded, and the wind fluttered through the trees, the leaves rustling in soft applause, blowing Lana and Harry further and further away, I thought. When I shifted in my seat, Leo's knees began to pump up and down under the table. "I want you two to come up to the theater with me." His voice sounded thin and washed-out, as if he had just come from a shouting match. "They're having some wine and cheese, and someone from my family—"

"You can forget it," Elena said, breaking her silence. Her voice came as a stab, and she shoved her chair back as if she were going to get up and run out of there.

"I need you to come," he said with great difficulty. It sounded like something large was wedged inside his mouth, and he had to talk around it.

"You should have thought about that before, Leo," Elena said. She pushed her chair back further and rose up. "I wouldn't go to a dog-fight with you."

"Don't say things like that," Leo yelled. The strength of his voice was startling in the dark silence.

"Fuck you," Elena whispered lowly. She twisted her neck off to the right, as if she were calculating her escape.

"Listen here, young lady. You don't understand. You have no idea what goes on between me and your mother. Do you hear me? *You do not know what you're talking about!*" His voice was stretched-out and hoarse, and it hung in the air like a blast.

"*Then why in the hell don't you tell us?*" Elena yelled back. She gripped the back of the chair so hard, I heard the tense, uneasy sound her fingers made as they rubbed hard against the wood.

"It's her story, goddamn it," Leo cried, jabbing his fingers through his hair. "I want to tell you, but if I told you she would never forgive me."

"She's never going to forgive you now," Elena spat back.

The truth hung heavy in the air, and no one said anything for quite a while. Somewhere down the street a woman called her cat to come home. "Tabbatha," she sang out her back door. "Here, Tab-ba-tha." It stunned me to know that just a few doors down, a woman could sing out a back door calling for her cat. It seemed our pain stretched at least down a whole block.

Leo returned his hands to the top of the table where he folded them quietly. "Will you two please come up to the theater with me," he said patiently, softly even. "They're all waiting for me up there."

"I'm not going," Elena yelled. She picked up Lana's pincushion and threw it against the wall, where it fell to the floor on top of the red sequins in a soft, metallic plink, plink.

"Please, Elena," he begged her. "It's important to me. It will only take a half-hour, and then afterward we'll get in the car and look all over for Lana just like we looked for you."

I think it was Leo's reference to our search through those barns which melted Elena's heart, because she reluctantly agreed to accompany him up to the theater for a half an hour. "But only a half-hour, and I don't plan on saying anything either."

Leo didn't care if she spoke or not. He just wanted us by his side for show. None of us even said anything as we crossed over the campus and crawled up Heart Attack Hill. We walked slowly, our heads bent, while Leo's coattails rose and fell in the spring breeze.

"I've told them that Lana had a stomach flu and that you took her home," he said when we reached the theater. His hand was on the doorknob, and we could hear the swell of voices inside.

"So we're supposed to lie for you?" Elena said.

"Yes, if you would, please," he said. "I'd appreciate it."

We followed him in and stayed by his side while he shook people's hands and sopped up their compliments. He never forgot to introduce us as his girls, pushing us out in front of him, his big hands sliding down our dark hair and resting on our shoulders. I couldn't help but think how much better he looked in his coattails, shaking people's hands, telling them thank you, than he did escorting those young girls to and from the piano bench in our old living room.

It took us an hour to get out of there, which Elena graciously allowed him, the party continuing on after we left, with Bob Hendrix taking up the limelight. It bothered Leo to leave as early as we did, but he knew he had to take his children and make a gallant effort at finding his wife and son.

We made sure she wasn't home first before we piled into the car and drove up and down the deserted streets looking for her. We stopped at every diner and restaurant in town, Elena and I waiting in the car while Leo went in to look. We didn't find her in any of them, so we drove outside of Hamilton and looked in all the seedy bars and restaurants along Highway 12. I sat in the backseat alone, the silence settling around me like walls. I couldn't speak, not even when Elena leaned over the seat and whispered things back to me. My tongue felt like someone had shot it full of Novocain, and my nerves spread through me, racing to the remote corners of my body, as if a bomb had gone off somewhere near my heart.

"She's long gone," Elena said after a while. We were so far out of town there wasn't another car in sight. Only the streetlights kept us company and the perfect sky, which was stretched out above us like a sequined ceiling.

"Where could she go without a car?" Leo said. He rolled his window down halfway, as if there weren't enough air, and it whistled in, blowing over me like warm breath. It seemed to speak to me, to say, "She's not out here. She's gone away."

When it was past one o'clock in the morning, Leo finally turned around and headed home. Lana hadn't come back while we were gone, or if she had she'd left again, because the house was empty and pitch-dark. While Leo called Garta to see if Lana had shown up there, Elena and I sat in the dining room next to the sewing machines, dreading the morning light. As long as it was still dark it felt as if there were a place to hide, as if there were still some hope of figuring things out. Leo called Gus next, and when he found out Lana wasn't there either, he called the sheriff, as he had when Elena had run away. I wondered what the sheriff thought of Leo when he heard his wife and son had left him too.

He made us go to bed after that. He said good night to Elena, and then he walked quietly into my room, a dark, giant silhouette wearing coattails. He sat down on the edge of my bed and just stared down at me, the pattern of light from the window falling softly across his face.

"What?" I said, though my voice wasn't much. It came out of me like a thick fog.

"I'm sorry about what happened tonight, Maddie. I shouldn't have used that song."

I stared up into his troubled blue eyes and watched them mist over. "Why did you, then?"

"I don't know, Maddie," he said softly. "I wanted to use it. It's the best song I've ever written, and I thought it worked really well. Without it, I don't think the show would have been as good."

"But you knew she was coming," I said. "She sewed all the costumes."

He hung his head and laid his hand on top of my covers, its sweaty warmth radiating through me. "I know, Maddie," he whispered. "I didn't do it to hurt Lana. I know it's hard to understand, but I had to do it."

I understood what he meant, because I had felt compelled to read

Lana's journal even though I knew it was wrong. But even so, I never would have stood on a stage and read it out loud to an audience. I knew what Leo had done was not exactly this; it was his song after all, one he'd created, and it was only natural that he would want to play it, but to wound Lana like that seemed unforgivable.

None of us slept that night. It seemed we all lurked in the darkness, weighted down by the same poisonous dread. I finally crawled into bed with Elena, and after a long stretch of silence, she whispered, "This is it, Maddie. This is how it's going to be from now on." I pinched my eyes shut, and in the mottled darkness behind them, I felt the red-hot beat of another headache. A hammer marked the passing moments on the underside of my forehead. Maybe Elena and I would go to Lansing and stay with Leo's father, I thought, or maybe we'd just stay here with Leo. The bang of the hammer drove it from my thoughts, and I lay there still, feeling the tide of my life drifting further and further out to sea.

At about six o'clock in the morning, we heard Lana come in. The morning light was already pouring in through Elena's windows, falling across her floor in thick, yellow beams. We sat up in bed and listened carefully as she opened the front door and walked quietly down the hallway. She must have been carrying Harry because we didn't hear his footsteps. She took him back to his room, and when we heard the shrill whistle of her teapot, we knew she'd made herself a cup of tea—a hopeful sign.

"Maybe she decided to forgive him," I whispered to Elena.

"I doubt it." She flopped down on her back, and I watched her pale forehead knot in the morning light.

I eased myself down next to her where we lay stiffly, listening for the sound of Lana. She must have sat down at the dining room table to drink her tea, because we couldn't hear her anymore. When my head began to throb in the silence, I got up and walked over to the door to see what had become of Leo.

"He's sitting up on the edge of the bed," I whispered. His face was sunk deep into the palms of his hands, and a shaft of morning light fell across him in one long, unbroken beam.

"He must know she's here," Elena said, "but he's too chicken to go down there."

I hardly blamed him. I wouldn't have wanted to face Lana if I had played her song in front of a whole audience. I crawled back into bed with Elena, where we listened quietly for their sounds, wondering where they would finally collide. In the bedroom? In the dining room? On the stairs?

After what felt like an interminable stretch of time, Lana finally climbed the stairs. Her steps were slower and heavier than usual. She'd hurt her hip climbing Heart Attack Hill, I knew, but I imagined she was also exhausted. Elena and I got up and crept behind the door, where we watched her through the crack. I was surprised to see she was still dressed up. I knew, of course, that she hadn't changed her clothes since last night, but even so it was odd to see her climb the steps so early in the morning dressed in a black velvet gown. When she reached the top step, she stopped and put her hand over her heart. We could see them both, though as yet they could not see each other. Leo was waiting out these last few moments seated on the edge of the bed, his face yet plunged into the depths of his palms.

Lana finally walked the last ten feet to her room and paused in the doorway just long enough for Leo to look up. Then she stepped inside and slammed the door so hard, the whole house shuddered.

Elena followed behind me as I crept across the hallway and into the bathroom. When I lowered myself behind the grate and motioned for her to do the same, she was amazed. She didn't even know it was there. Lana was sitting in a chair just out of our view. We could see her knees and her feet, but we couldn't see her face. Leo was still sitting on the edge of the bed, pulling nervously at a black thread which hung from the cuff of his jacket.

"Where did you go?" he asked her.

"Does it matter?" Her voice, instead of being high and thin, was low and hoarse.

"We looked all over for you. We drove everywhere we could think of—all over the town, all over the campus. We even went about ten miles out of town and looked in all those bars." He spoke rapidly, supplying her with this information as if it would somehow lessen his crime.

"It doesn't matter, Leo," she said. "You could have sacrificed your arm and it wouldn't matter." Her voice was so calm and controlled, it was chilling.

He stared at her, his blue eyes bloodshot and aching. "I'm sorry,

La," he said softly. "I should have told you." He looked lost and lonely, sitting in that flood of sunlight.

"Sorry isn't good enough, Leo. It won't work this time."

He looked up at her, and I could almost see his patience evaporating. "What else can I say?" he said loudly. "I played *The Song*. What can I tell you? The theater is still standing, for Christ's sakes, and you're not dead either. What the hell else is there to say, but I'm sorry I played the fucking song?"

"Nothing," she shot back. "There's nothing left to say, Leo, because *you said it all.*"

She rose up and stalked across the room, sitting down on the chair across from him. She leaned over in her lap and spoke so softly it was eerie. "I've done a lot of thinking in the last eight hours, Leo, and I think I finally understand what's going on." There was something frightening about the softness of her voice. It lay stretched and taut over a steely anger, and I saw it work its way under Leo's skin. "It galls me to think that only a few weeks ago you ordered me not to talk to the lawyer. You said we had made a bargain a long time ago, and you didn't want me to bring up the past, while you were up at that theater rehearsing your show girls with *that* song, Leo—the song *we* made a bargain about—the song *we* agreed you would *never* play in front of me or my children. We agreed to put that in the past, as well as the lawyer. And *we* don't need to ask ourselves why either, because *we* know why, Leo. *We know why.* I don't need to tell you what that did to me to hear that song last night, either. You know only too well."

"It's my music, goddamn it," he yelled back, "and I haven't played a note of it for nine years, Lana. *Nine fucking years.* We should be over this—we should be way the hell past this. Nine years is a goddamned long time. It's just a song, goddamn it, a string of notes. It's not a fucking sledgehammer, Lana. It's not poison. It's my music, goddamn it, and I am entitled to use it."

"I know it's your music. I understand that, and I hope you'll understand when I tell you it's my life." Her voice rose now, the thin coat of softness torn open by her anger.

"What the hell does that mean?"

"It means this," she said, leaning closer to him. "Our bargain no longer exists. You have broken it completely. I am no longer writing.

I am no longer doing anything, but living in this small shit town, raising three children. I never see you anymore, and now I discover that in your absence, you have completely violated your promise to me. You knew what it would do to us, and so now I can only conclude that you want this to be over with."

Something invisible shot up his spine and jerked his head back. "That's not true, La," he yelled defensively. "I just want to put the past behind us. You're not the only one who's had to live with it, goddamn it. I've had to live with it every day of my life. I can't talk about it, yet I am bound to remember it. I can't tell our children about it, I can't play my music, and I'm not even allowed to have a job because of it. I'm sick of *it*, Lana, and all I ever wanted to do was to put it the fuck behind us." The anger was so thick in his eyes, he could not even blink.

"You want to put behind what suits you, Leo," she screamed. "You won't let me do what *I* want to do either. I am not supposed to talk to anyone—I am not even supposed to consider it. I am supposed to write a book I never really wanted to write. You don't care about me. You've got me just where you want me—*as the woman*—as a completely subservient, domesticated woman with no life of her own, who cooks and cleans and does the goddamned wash."

He stared at her wildly. "You think it was my fault, don't you, Lana? You do, you think it was all my fault, and you want to punish me for it for the rest of my life. You want me to clean and cook and teach those fucking piano lessons—YOU WANT ME TO BE THE WOMAN, GODDAMN IT," he screamed.

Lana stared back at him, not blinking, not breathing.

"Goddamn it, La, admit it," he yelled. "Admit you blame me. Admit you think everything was my fault."

She glared at him for a moment, measuring him with her narrowed, bitter eyes. She spoke then, spitting her words out like venom. *"If your ego hadn't been so big, it never would have happened."* Her voice was loud and bitter cold, like a chilling wind, and when she rose up and walked briskly to the door, slamming it behind her, we knew these were her final words.

Leo's mouth dropped open, as if she had just slapped him hard across the face. All these years that truth had festered in her heart, and now the poison of her accusation spilled into the room, filling every corner with a thick, deadly air. She blamed him. Lana blamed him for everything.

I staggered over to the bathtub and rested against the cold porcelain until I felt I could stand up. Elena made it over to the window before she collapsed on the sill.

Her jittery eyes roved the bathroom wall, her thoughts reeling underneath. "It was all his fault," she whispered.

"What if he *was* the man sparrow," I said. That malignant beat resumed in the front of my skull, hammering out the seconds, like a ticking clock.

"She's changed," Elena whispered. "Did you hear her voice?" She shifted her racing eyes from the wall to me.

I nodded. It was a chilling voice, cocksure and dispassionate—a voice that was ripping us apart. "Do you think she's going to take the car and leave?" I whispered.

"I don't know."

Terror seized us, and we loped down the stairs to find out where she'd gone. Instead of backing down the driveway, she was in the kitchen making pancakes in her black velvet gown.

"Good morning," she said, flipping one of them over. "I'm sorry I left you in the theater last night." She turned around and looked at us. Her eyes were on fire. "You were all right, I hope," she said.

We both nodded.

We watched her quietly as she moved the sewing machines and put them where Leo always sat, and, as if he didn't exist anymore, she set the table for herself, me, Elena, and Harry. When we sat down to eat, we heard him come down the stairs and leave out the front door. That's when the tears came to her eyes. When the door banged closed, they rolled down her face silently, and she neither moved away from us nor sought to hide them. She just let them spill down her cheeks and drop on her pancakes while she continued to eat them without a sound.

For the next three days I sat in Mrs. Devonshit's class without even realizing I was there. When she called on me, I never even had any idea what her question had been. I just said, "I don't know," and shrugged my shoulders.

My nerves felt fat and lazy as they crept through my veins—they were in a stupor, but even so their presence was torture. I excused myself quite a few times and took Durga into the bathroom where I stood her on the sink and whispered those Hindu words.

It was almost impossible to sleep at night. There was so much static in our house, you could hear it crackling. Lana slept on the sofa or else in Harry's room, and we never knew if Leo were going to come home or not. He stayed in his office a few nights, and when he did come home, he slept in his clothes under a small beige afghan. They didn't speak to each other—they wouldn't even stand in the same room together. I don't know where Leo ate his meals, but I know he didn't eat them at home. He continued with his musical, and though Lana told us we could go up and watch it, we never did.

In four days, everything broke apart again. When school let out, Elena went as usual to the back of the Colgate Inn, where I'm sure she smoked more than her share of cigarettes. It looked like it might rain, so Lizzy and I headed home to hang around the bucket in the attic. When we walked into the house, I knew right away that something was wrong. It was too quiet, and the air felt loaded down.

"She's gone," I said to Lizzy, as panic rose inside me. We walked slowly down the hallway and stepped into the dining room. I noticed that the sewing machines had been put away and the breakfast dishes were washed and heaped in the dishrack.

"Maddie," I heard Lana say. I turned my head and saw that she and Harry were sitting quietly on the sofa. "Where's Elena?" she asked.

"She's with her friends," I said. "What are you doing?" There was something wrong with the way Lana just sat there, while Harry colored next to her.

"Go and find her and bring her back here," she said. "I want to talk to you both. I have something to tell you."

Lizzy and I ran down to the Colgate Inn as fast as we could, only to discover that Elena had already left. We turned around and raced up to the field, forgoing all stealth, plunging across it, our elbows pumping at our sides. The sky was a brilliant blue and the field so lush and green, I almost couldn't imagine a bad ending to this day. The rapid pulse of my heart told me otherwise—it's over, it's over, it seemed to beat.

The muddy ground inside the woods provided us with Elena's fresh trail. From the distance between her footprints, we could tell she had run at top speed through the pines. We weren't really thinking about where she went or what she did. It never even crossed our minds that we might stumble upon her secret. All we wanted was to find her and bring her back to Lana.

Suddenly her tracks stopped, and Lizzy and I looked up. An old black, junked car stood amid the pine trees. It was a Chevy, all rusted and banged up, and not only were its front doors missing, but the windshield was so finely cracked you couldn't even see through it. We crept up to it, not knowing whether Elena was inside or not. Very cautiously, we walked along the side and looked in the front seat. It was all torn-up—yellow stuffing oozed out of the stiff black cracks, and half a steering wheel lay on the floor near the rusted gas pedal, the other half lodged in the dashboard where a radio had once been. We inched along the side, our fingers snagging on the cracked, rusted paint, as we tried to get a good look inside the back window. It was so filthy we finally had to press our faces up against the glass. We squinted and peered in for a closer look, and there, stretched out on the backseat, was Elena, sprawled on top of a boy. Their mouths were welded together, their hips grinding into one another, and their breathing so out of control that even now, as Lizzy and I stood pressed against the car, they didn't hear us.

"Elena," I said, rapping on the window.

She heaved up and twisted around, her face registering utter shock. "Maddie," she yelled. The boy lurched up too, his eyes wide, his jaw hanging slack. While he struggled to button his shirt, the life drained out of me. It was Louis. Louis Bartalucci. I backed away from the car, my feet sticking in the mud. "Lana wants you to come home," I said too loudly. I didn't wait there another moment. I turned around and tore through the woods. I heard their voices as if in a dream, my heart pounding so wildly, it filled my ears. It didn't matter that I did not know Louis, that I had lost track of him; it didn't matter either that he hardly knew me at all. What mattered was that Elena had taken him away from me.

She caught up to me when I was halfway through the field, Lizzy following closely behind her. "What the hell's wrong with you?" she yelled. She pulled my sweater, but instead of stopping, I let it slip off my arms and fall to the muddy field. "Jesus, Maddie," she screamed. "What the hell's wrong?"

I don't know what it was about the combination of Elena and the boys I liked, but whenever they got mixed up together, I couldn't speak. It triggered something deep down inside, something dark and primal, which lay beyond common jealousy.

We raced down the hill in silence, and as soon as we saw our house, my thoughts lurched back to Lana. My nerves stirred in the pit of my stomach when I remembered how she was going to tell us something. We crossed over our back lawn and walked slowly up the porch steps, disappearing into the kitchen where the soft breeze disturbed the curtains. Lana was in the dining room, arranging the chairs. She had set the table as she always did for a tea party — Mimi's cups and saucers were out and filled with hot cocoa and marshmallows, and a plate of chocolate chip cookies sat in the middle. We took our seats without saying a word, each of us painfully aware of the sudden formality, of the great difference between this tea party and all the others.

Lana sat down and passed us the cookies. She was wearing an off-white blouse with a beaded collar, and a long, tan straight skirt. Her dark hair was swept back into a makeshift French bun which she had hastily jabbed bobby pins into, uncaptured wisps of it falling down around her shoulders. Her face was pale, and thin blue veins stood out in relief at her temples.

"I wanted to talk to you," she said solemnly. I noticed a trace of lipstick on her mouth.

We nodded, but only scarcely.

She stared down at the table, at her fingers as they edged across the bumpy top of a cookie. When she looked up, I noticed the blue veins at her temples. "Leo and I have reached a point where we can't agree on how to live anymore. I'm sorry you have to see this. I never meant it to be this way." She pushed her plate away and rested her hands on top of the table. "You will grow up and become women one day. I don't like to have to tell you this, but it isn't going to be easy for you. Women aren't taken as seriously as men, and what women do with their lives is generally thought of as less important than what men do with theirs."

A sweet breeze blew through the dining room, billowing the curtains into a balloonish swell. It stirred a lock of her hair, which fell across her face, and she brushed it back lightly. It seemed her expression changed with the breeze; it darkened and her brow furrowed, as if a cloud had passed over her, and we knew the worst was yet to come.

"I used to lead a life much different from the one I lead now," she said. "My life isn't what it should be. I am capable of much more." She broke off here and took a slug of tea as if it were as fortifying as whiskey, her eyes resting on the spoon for a moment, where a distorted image of her appeared. She looked up then. "It's very hard for me to tell you this, but I need to straighten my life out now, and it means I'm going to have to leave for a while."

The words *leave for a while* washed up in my mind like a wave. "Where are you going?" I said, my voice far too loud in the still air.

"I'm going to New York."

"Can we go with you?" Elena asked. I could tell from the prickly sound of her voice that a panic had begun to rise inside her.

Lana waved her hand in the air as if to clear away our voices. "I can't take you out of school when you only have a month left."

"We don't care," I rushed to say.

"Yeah, who cares?" Elena said.

Lizzy just stared at us with her mouth open, her big black eyes moving from my face, to Elena's, across the table to Lana's.

"We can't do that," Lana insisted. "You have to finish school first." She tried to sound logical and calm, as if what she were proposing were some sort of short vacation, but underneath the tension rose in her voice like heat.

Elena slammed her back against the chair. "I'm not staying here," she yelled, her knees rasping against the underside of the table.

"Once you're out of school you can come to New York and visit me," Lana said loudly.

I noted the word *visit* instead of *live*, and my nerves charged through me like bulls.

"Does Leo know you're leaving?" Elena yelled.

"I told him this afternoon," Lana said. She shook her head back in defiance.

"And he's not going to stop you?"

"I've made up my mind, Elena. What can he do?" she said. "I'm a grown woman."

Tears fell soundlessly from Elena's eyes. "Why do you have to go now?" she asked. "Why can't you wait until we're out of school?"

"I'm sorry, sweetheart," Lana said softly, "but things have reached a point where I can't wait any longer." She reached across the table and stroked Elena's hand with her fingers, promising her that we could come and stay with her in New York as soon as school was out, reminding us that it was only a month. She told us she had arranged for Gus to stay with us until Leo's musical was over, and after that, she said, Leo would be free to take care of us right. "Like he used to," she said.

The breeze blew through the room, so stiffly this time that it knocked over the vase of red tulips Lana had set on the windowsill. The sound of it seemed to wake her up, to remind her of what lay ahead. She had to leave in a few minutes to catch the 4:10 bus to New York, she said, and she wanted us to walk downtown with her and Harry. It didn't quite seem possible that we were going to lose her in a matter of minutes. I had imagined she would leave later that night or tomorrow even, not in a few minutes. She is leaving us, I told myself, but it couldn't quite get a footing in my mind. When I saw her packed suitcases in Harry's room, it began to make sense, but still I continued to move and speak as if in a dream.

We walked her downtown to the drugstore where the bus was stopped outside. She carried one suitcase, while Elena, Lizzy, and I took turns carrying the other one. The brilliant blue sky above us was a lie, and the warm sun a sham. The traffic went by in a blur, and the people seemed to float just beyond my fingertips, as if they had no relation whatsoever to me. But even so, it angered me that they just kept walking, that the cars kept driving, as if nothing had happened. Lana is going away. Don't you see? My mother is leaving. They kept going though, just like Lana's sea—"It just keeps going, back and forth, back and forth," she'd said to me once, "and it doesn't care who's been born or who's died or who's dying."

I followed behind her, watching her cane stab the ground and move forward. How did it happen that on a sunny day in May, Elena and I were escorting her to a bus that would take her away from us? In some distant pocket of my mind, a thought surfaced like a dead fish and floated there. Everything that had ever happened to us, it said, had all the time been leading us to this very moment, as if the whole of our lives had only been a prelude to this final scene.

When we reached the drugstore, Lana went inside and bought her tickets, while Elena, Lizzy, and I waited out on the sidewalk with her suitcases. I stared across the street at the bank clock that revolved around and around. It was 4:00.

Lana came outside with her tickets, and after she handed them to the bus driver, he threw her suitcases into the luggage compartment and then slammed the door, the loud thwack sounding final. He headed up the steps and swung into his seat, where he waited for Lana to say good-bye to us. She dropped to her knees on the warm sidewalk and flung her arms around Elena, then Lizzy, then me, until the four of us ended up thrown together in a huge knot. She kissed our cheeks and promised us over and over again that she was not leaving us. "Just one month, just one month," she cried, as if it were a prayer. When the bus driver honked his horn, Lana finally pulled away from us and stood up. She swept Harry into her arms and took one last longing look at us before she quickly climbed the stairs and reappeared in the side window. She and Harry waved to us, Harry comically pressing his nose and lips against the glass, while Lana's arm drifted out the window. They kept waving as the bus pulled away and probably continued to wave long after the bus left us on the curb mournfully alone.

My own tears didn't come until late that night after Gus put us to bed. Elena asked me to sleep next to her, but I couldn't. I still felt betrayed by her, and even though I longed for the comfort of her company, a black stubbornness persisted in my heart.

Leo hadn't come home from his musical, and Lana hadn't called yet either. I thought she would, and when there was no call, a bitterness began to descend. She wasn't even going to call us, I thought. It seemed the least she could do. My nerves were dulled and didn't do much more than stagger around, but even so I couldn't sleep. Was Lana going to stay with Mimi? And if not at Mimi's, then where? Why hadn't she just made Leo leave? I thought. Maybe she just wanted to go to New York by herself. Maybe she just wanted to get away from all of us.

When Leo came home late, he stopped at Elena's bed. He whispered something to her, but she didn't answer. He pulled the covers over her shoulders and kissed her ear, whispering something else I didn't hear. When he came into my room, I pretended I was asleep. I didn't know what to think of Leo now that Lana was gone, but after he kissed my ear and left, I wiped it off with the edge of my blanket.

The tears flowed from my eyes like warm blood let from a wound. I didn't want anyone to hear me, so I crept into the attic and sat down next to Lana's boxes, snuffling into the sleeve of my nightgown. I stood Durga next to me, as if she could possibly do something to mitigate my sorrow. I thought of Lana's journal, but I decided I wouldn't read it tonight, that under the circumstances I couldn't. I would just look at it in the box and maybe count how many locked diaries lay beneath it. I moved Durga to a higher spot, as if she could ward off evil spirits, and slipped my fingers under the flaps. I pulled them open and looked down inside. The box was completely empty; there wasn't so much as a shred of paper in it. Lana had taken them all with her, I realized. She had packed them away in the suitcase we had struggled to carry. The film, I thought, panic striking my heart. I quickly pushed the top boxes over and thrust my hand into the bottom box. When my fingers collided with the cold, silver canisters, relief swept me. She hadn't taken them. I tore open the flaps and stared down at them, and as the wind stirred the metal chimes next door, I wondered how long it would be before the Eyes of God touched them.

18

Over the next week, Lana called a few times, but not enough for my liking. I wanted her to call every day, but she said it was too expensive. She didn't have a phone anyway, so whenever she wanted to call us, she had to walk down five flights of stairs and use a phone booth two blocks away, which meant we could never call her. She said she wasn't living with Mimi, although she admitted she'd seen her once. She was living in a small apartment in Greenwich Village. It only had one room, she told us, with a tiny kitchen and a small bathroom with no bathtub—just a shower. It didn't have any furniture either, except for a mattress which the landlord had been good enough to lend her, and a broken-down chair she had found out on the street. We couldn't imagine why she wanted to live there, but she said she was fine. It was Harry who was having a hard time adjusting to the city with all of the street noise, but she thought he would get used to it.

When we asked her what she was doing, she said, "I'm straightening out my life." And whenever Elena asked, "Do you have a job?" she would say, "No, not yet, but I'm working on it."

She never sounded very good. Her voice was sometimes too high and thin, and other days it was low and shaky. A week after she left, she was cut down by another migraine headache and could hardly speak at all. It took no leap of imagination to envision her lying on a mattress in a dark, empty apartment, while Harry colored quietly by her side.

"Do you miss Leo?" I asked her once, to which she replied, "Sometimes."

She declined to talk to him, though, so Elena and I were obliged to tell him what she'd said. He was around a lot more since his musical had finished, but he wasn't always good company—at least not at first. His face was carved up a lot of the time, and he sometimes spoke very little. He didn't mention Lana much, but he often said things like, "We're still a family," and "We're going to be just fine," and he took us out for ice cream and drove us anywhere we wanted to go. He was good about including Lizzy too. That was the one thing Lana had asked him to do, and he never once forgot it.

He didn't keep the house up very well, but we didn't tell Lana. He never left us alone at night, though—not even once. He sat at our piano instead and composed songs—some of which Lana wouldn't have approved of. He never played her song again, at least not around Lizzy and me, but when Elena wasn't around, he did play the jazz. She hardly spent any time with us as it was, traipsing up to that old black car where she and Louis clutched one another in the cruddy backseat. I still found it hard to talk to her, and whenever she was gone and I thought of the two of them, it stuck in my heart.

If it hadn't been for Lizzy, I would have sunk into a depression. We spent every moment we could together, trying to keep up at least a semblance of our past life. We hiked up to Lizzy's favorite field a lot and lay on our backs with our hands thrown behind our heads, while we gazed up at the blue sky and looked forward to the day we would take the Greyhound bus to New York.

We spent a lot of time going through the *New York Times* in search of Nazi articles, and we continued to empty the bucket whenever it rained, which thankfully was less often. We checked more of Minnie Harp's windows even though it wasn't so easy—now that it was warm, Minnie came out to take care of her tulips and to bury the bottles which had accumulated over the winter. We watched her from our treetop perch, hoping that she'd do something new, discovering instead that her range was rather small—she tended tulips, buried bottles, and burned bandages. We'd pretty much exhausted her outdoor endeavors. It was what lay within her house that we began to set our sights upon—namely, the Nazi.

Neither Lizzy nor I felt ready to force our way inside her house, though we realized it would eventually come to this. We had very little hope that the rest of her windows had any cracks or tears in the newspaper. We figured that a woman as obsessed with secrecy as Minnie Harp would invest a lot of time in the repair and upkeep of this most important armor. Besides, say we found one crack—what were the odds that the Nazi would be sitting in plain view?

When Leo went out and bought us our first television, we were spared the terror of putting together any real plans against Minnie Harp. It was another defiant thing he did against Lana since she'd left—buying this television—but one we all appreciated. It kept Elena home at first, and for a while anyway, it drew what was left of my family back together.

If nothing else, we were all there when Lana called. She never sounded very good, though. Her voice wasn't always high, but there was a consistent tiredness to it, as if she never slept at night anymore. We worried about her, particularly Leo, but out of all of us he was the most powerless to help her.

"Why don't you go down there and get her?" Elena asked him one night.

"She doesn't want to be with me," he said. "The last thing she wants is for me to force her to come back."

That made sense to us, considering Lana felt like he'd forced her to live in a small town to begin with, but it did little to soothe us. It seemed there was nothing we could really do but wait for Lana to do what she had to do. It drove my nerves wild and pushed Elena deeper into the backseat of that junked car and caused Leo to sit in our darkened living room some nights drinking Jack Daniels whiskey—something that was as new to our diminishing household as the television set. Sometimes when I couldn't sleep, I would go downstairs and sit with him in the black silence. We rarely spoke (we knew what troubled us), but one night near the end of May, he said something to me which I never could shake from my thoughts. He said, "I'm afraid she might kill herself."

That thought had never crossed my mind, and I was sorry Leo had put it there. It was an extra burden I could have done without, for it now gave me something very tangible to worry about. Instead of imagining Lana floating around in the darkness, I worried that she might take too many migraine pills or hang herself from the window of her fifth-floor apartment. "Or what if she slits her wrists?" Elena would say from her bed. "Or sticks her head in a gas oven?" It was the worst sort of talk to have at night, but it seized our imaginations, and when days would go by without a phone call from her, we could think of little else.

It wasn't long after that Lizzy and I started making plans to break into Minnie Harp's house. The idea of uncovering her Nazi and handing him over to Simon Wiesenthal began to take on an irresistible appeal.

Lizzy wanted to capture him, but I didn't think it was such a good idea.

"How are we going to capture him?" I asked her up in the attic.

"We'll tie him up," she said. She was draped over the arms of the red chair, her hands pressed behind her head, her eyes roving the blackened ceiling.

"What about Minnie? She's not going to stand there while we tie him up. She might have a lot of things wrong with her, but she wouldn't just stand there while we tied him up." I lay down on the cool floor and rested my feet on the windowsill, where if I looked just right I could see Elena out in the backyard chucking stones at a lilac bush.

"We'll knock her out with our flashlights," Lizzy said. The thought of it didn't even make her flinch.

However much it appealed to me to knock Minnie out rather than to face her in the dark, I knew we couldn't do this. "We could get in trouble for knocking her out," I told her. I asked her what we were supposed to do with the Nazi once we tied him up and knocked Minnie out, and she said we'd just drag him outside and call the police. I told her that we could get in a lot of trouble for that. "You can't just knock out old women and tie up men."

What I proposed was this: we'd steal inside Minnie's house at night when we knew she was asleep. We'd use Lana's old camera with the flash and take a couple of shots of the Nazi, and then we'd get the pictures developed and mail them to Simon Wiesenthal, telling him where the Nazi was *only* after he sent us the money. Lizzy worried it would take too long since Simon Wiesenthal lived in Austria, but I maintained that if we did it really soon, it wouldn't take us more

than a month. "We could be done with it by the time school's over,"
I said. It wasn't as instant as Lizzy liked, but she finally came to see
it my way.

Over the course of the next week, we cased Minnie Harp's
house, trying to figure out the best way to get inside. There were
two entrances, both on the right side of her house—the side door
Minnie herself came and went through, and the hatch doors to the
cellar, through which Minnie had emerged the first time I saw her.
I was in favor of using the entrance Minnie used herself—the idea
of going down into her cellar gave me the worst kind of creeps,
but we tested her door one afternoon and found it locked. We
discovered the cellar door was half unhinged and would require
only a minimal push to open. If we wanted to get inside, we realized, we'd have to go down through those hatch doors and into
her cellar.

We decided it was better for Lizzy to hold the flashlights while I
took the pictures. Between the two of us, Lizzy had more of a ten-
dency to freeze up. "You've got better nerves," she said, which under
the weight of my nerve problem was laughable.

We dusted off Lana's camera, and to make sure it worked we
bought some film and took some pictures of Minnie's house from the
woods. I stole the money from Leo's wallet to pay for the film and
the developing, and then I stole a little more to buy some flashbulbs.
All in all I took ten dollars. It was another sin, but I figured when
Simon Wiesenthal paid us I could put the money back.

A full moon appeared in the sky the night we decided to break
into Minnie Harp's creepy house. We hadn't planned it this way, but
when I noticed it beaming luminously in the dark sky, I hoped it was
a good omen. I couldn't be sure, though, for the full moon was the
time to make promises and not necessarily the time to ask for good
luck. Nonetheless, I did.

At one o'clock in the morning Lana's small alarm clock went off
underneath my pillow. The sound of it in my ear was shattering. I
shut it off and woke Lizzy up, and we scrambled nervously out of
bed, quickly pulling off our nightgowns, dressing in the clothes we'd
handpicked for this night—black pants, black sweatshirts, and black
shoes.

"Are you sure you want to do this?" I whispered to Lizzy, pulling
the sweatshirt over my head.

"Are you?" she said. Her hands froze on her zipper, and we stared across the darkness at one another. I think we were both separately hoping that the other would back out, but neither of us said anything. It seemed we were in too deep now.

"Come on," Lizzy finally said.

We grabbed our flashlights from underneath the bed, and I slung the camera around my neck. I never knew how many creaks and groans were lying in wait in the floors and stairs of my house until Lizzy and I tried to walk over them silently. It was a small wonder that we didn't wake up Leo or Elena.

We headed out the back door and ran down the hill, the crickets and frogs swelling the air in what sounded to me like a chilling chorus. We crept into the woods where the trees stood like tall dark fathers, blowing slightly in the wind, warning us with their shaking branches not to go any further. The twigs bent and snapped under our feet, rending holes in the silent night, sounding more like breaking bones than sticks.

We left the woods behind and crept across Minnie Harp's dark lawn, our feet snarling in the tangled weave of her dead grass. The shutters banged against her house, sounding out their protest, and the rotted gutters moved back and forth across the house like shaking heads, scratching out their no's. We stalked quietly past the front porch, grateful at least that we didn't have to pass through the hall-way—through the opened shutter, we could see the ghostly outline of the dark banister hanging against the flaking plaster walls.

When we came to the hatch doors on the right side of her house, we stopped. The combined sound of our heavy breathing seemed too loud for safety—we doubled over and tried to still ourselves. My heart pounded like a jackhammer in my throat, but nonetheless I bent down and grasped the metal handle on my side of the hatch door. Lizzy took hold of the other, and very slowly, we pulled them up and laid them gently on the ground. With the exception of one good squeak, they were fairly quiet. The cement stairs, sticking with old wet leaves, yawned before us. I went first, holding my flashlight out in front of me as if it were a sword, and Lizzy followed closely behind me, her breath at my ear. We came face to face with the door at the bottom of the steps, and after standing there for a long time shud-dering, we leaned against it and pushed. It gave way almost immedi-ately, although not without complaint. It rasped on the old hinges, and when we pushed it open, it cracked and moaned and let out one long, wavering shriek. We could only pray Minnie and her Nazi hadn't heard it.

The cellar was a horror. Our flashlights illuminated it bit by bit — the walls were as bumpy and rounded as an ill-lit cave, and the ceiling was made up of greasy black crossbeams and old rusty pipes, many of which hung in questionable suspension above our heads. There were stacks of newspapers everywhere, making our passage more difficult; they stood in piles, some taller than me, but most of them had fallen over, like huge rows of dominoes. Old coats and clothes hung from the beams, some of which we had to move through, and dozens of pieces of broken furniture — chairs, tables, bedframes, bureaus — were heaped in various poses of disrepair, sticking together in an unnatural conglomeration, as if Minnie Harp and her Nazi had stood at the top of the stairs and thrown them down year after year. Old sinks and washing machines stood in one corner, and rusted motors and greasy metal parts crowded a dusty wooden table, over which countless black ants flowed.

There was a putrid stench which hung in the air like thick, gagging smoke. It smelled of mustiness, of closed-in dust-pickled air, of rotting cloth and paper, of waterlogged wood and mildewed cement, but most of all it smelled of rotting food, as if in those old sinks lay bits and pieces of decomposing meat and bones.

We turned the corner and discovered the cellar steps. A closed door stood at the top, gouged with rows and rows of squiggly lines as if Minnie Harp and her Nazi had trapped something with claws down there. I didn't know if my heart was strong enough to continue. It loped and bolted and thundered so violently in my chest that I worried it might plow through my ribs and drop to the floor.

I don't know what compelled us to walk up those stairs. They were a nightmare. They were noisy and groaning, and I feared they couldn't take our weight, that our feet would crash through them, plunging us into a darkness I dared not think about. We carefully passed over the broken steps and tried to step in unison to cut down the noise, but even so the stairs cracked and moaned, shattering the tombish silence. The closer we got to the top, the stronger the smell of rotting meat became, until finally I quit breathing through my nose and breathed through my mouth where I swore I could taste it. Lizzy pushed her nose into the dark sleeve of her sweatshirt.

When we finally reached the landing, it was so small and rotted away that Lizzy and I had to stand one behind the other. The old coats pressed against us on either side too, stinking and heavy with dust. I illuminated the worn doorknob with my flashlight and lifted my hand twice and then dropped it.

"Do it, Maddie," Lizzy whispered in my ear.

I raised my hand slowly and touched the doorknob again. I took in a quiet gulp of air and turned it. It clicked open almost soundlessly, and immediately we were assaulted by the most vile smell. It emanated from this room or a room nearby, a putrid, gagging stench, which smelled like rotting flesh. As I slowly pushed the door open, it whined in an unbroken, stinging peal, which seemed to go on forever—during which time I felt my heart in serious jeopardy. It bucked against my rib cage furiously, threatening to tear loose. I stopped, and it was so quiet it seemed we could hear the ants marching across the floor.

The door opened into a room so black, so absolutely lightless, it was terrifying. We shone our flashlights to the right, illuminating a small space, a closet perhaps, which was crammed with more newspapers and broken furniture. Against the back wall stood a rickety table, covered with a staggering variety of jars of creams and make-ups, of cans of hairspray and bottles of fingernail polish and perfumes. We lingered over them for a moment, stunned not only by their sheer volume, but by their presence in Minnie Harp's house.

There still wasn't a sound, so we moved into the room a few inches and threw our light to the left. We illuminated a few small tables littered with lamps and books and ashtrays, spilling over with unfiltered cigarette butts. My light passed over Minnie Harp's old phonograph and her collection of battered opera records, and my heart picked up speed. Lizzy clung to my side, squeezing my arm, her breath like a tornado at my ear. Was this her room? I worried. Were we going to collide with Minnie Harp in this bitter darkness? We kept moving, our flashlights passing over a dark blue easy chair and a long thin table, on top of which stood a bottle of Seagram's Seven and a bundle of dirty bandages of the exact sort Minnie burned in her fire pit. Next to the bottle was an old doll who stood armless, her hair a matted black mess, her dress pink and stained.

We heard our first sound—the wavering creak of bedsprings. It was earsplitting in the stultifying silence. We moved forward and suddenly a bed appeared in our light—*the bed*. My heart almost shut down, and I could hardly breathe anymore. It was the mattress Minnie had dragged out of the cellar; it was thin and black-striped, and a yellowed sheet lay tangled at its bottom. The bedsprings continued to screech in a series of creaks, and when my light fell on two bandaged feet, I stopped breathing. They were wrapped up like a mummy, stained with pus and blood, and they were moving slowly and jerkily off the mattress and down to the floor. I followed them with my light, and when I saw the hairy, white legs, I knew they belonged no more to Minnie Harp than they did to me. They were the Nazi's. My heart skipped a few perilous beats and then stopped; my lungs all but shut down.

He was wearing a dark robe which fell open, the light illuminating his gray boxer shorts and his thin, withered legs. As he tried to stand up, his hand clutched at the table where the bottle of Seagram's Seven and the armless doll stood. He was palsied, we could see, and the table shook violently beneath his hands. The bottle and the doll crashed to the floor, the glass breaking in what seemed the loudest sound I had ever heard. My shaking light crept up his withered body, past his grayed, sunken chest, and finally fell on his face. He was utterly terrifying. He was hideous, grotesque—his face a mask of horror. He stared wildly out of one milky, clouded eye—his other eye was covered with a bandage stained with yellow ooze. His lips were gray and so horribly cracked they looked shredded. His hair was stringy white and shoulder-length, his beard nearly a foot long. He moaned as if the light wounded him, his breathing filled with so many rattles and gasps, I thought his lungs leaked. He began to cough, a horrible gooey cough which was so full of disease, Lizzy and I backed off. He staggered forward, his shaking arm outstretched, his mouth hanging open, revealing a few blackened teeth amid gums so puss-filled, they looked like cottage cheese.

Lizzy grabbed my flashlight and I pulled the camera up and slammed it against my eye. I pushed the button, and the flash exploded in the darkness like lightning. As if the light had darker powers, the Nazi collapsed to the floor, the clattery sound of his old body heartbreaking in that awful blackness. Lizzy followed him with her light, and there he lay on the floor amid the shards of broken glass, groping piteously for someone, for something. I poised the camera again, and just as I was about to push the button, Minnie appeared out of the blackness like a bat and flew at us, her arms held high above her. The sound which fled from her mouth was primordial, inhuman. It was not the sound of "Nnunnngggg," but rather a low and terrifying growl, more of an "Arrrrruuggggghhhh" than anything, which quickly escalated to a shrill scream.

All thoughts left us, and we turned around and crashed down the stairs, tearing through the cellar, knocking over her stacks of newspapers, her inhuman growl propelling us forward. We flew up the concrete steps and into the night, racing across Minnie Harp's dark tangled lawn and through her woods, stopping only when we reached the field. We collapsed in the wet grass and held our sides, coughing out the putrid stench from our noses and mouths, gulping in the fresh, cool air.

"Oh my God," Lizzy gasped. "Oh my God, oh my God."

We lay on our backs in the dewy grass and stared up at the unmarred sky, letting the quiet wash over us.

"Oh my God," Lizzy said again. "Oh my God."

I couldn't speak. I was silenced by the memory of the Nazi's horrible face and by Minnie Harp's terrible scream, neither of which retreated from my conscious mind as we staggered up the hill and stole into my unbreathing house. I lay frozen in my bed for hours, staring up at the ceiling, my nerves barely breathing, while Lizzy slept restlessly by my side. When I finally fell asleep, sometime after four o'clock, the Nazi's grotesque face and Minnie's awful scream plunged into my dreams.

When I awoke in a pool of light the next morning, I knew I would never be the same again. I had seen something which was not meant for my eyes, something which I couldn't even begin to fathom. When Lizzy woke up, we looked at each other and squeezed our eyes shut. I think we both wished it had never happened.

"Oh my God," Lizzy whispered, digging herself deeper under the covers.

"She would have killed us," I said. I turned over and pushed my face into the pillow.

"Did you get the picture, though?" she asked. Neither of us had wanted to think about it last night.

"I think so," I said, though I couldn't be sure.

We took the film down to the drugstore after school and ordered two copies of it from George. The rest of the afternoon we spent up in the attic going through some library books, looking at the photographs of the missing Nazis, trying to figure out if any of them looked like Minnie Harp's. Looking at them somehow helped us feel better about what we had done, but even so it was hard to tell which one was Minnie Harp's; he was older by some twenty years now, and so hairy and withered, it was impossible to match his face.

When the photographs were returned five days later, we had a nearly perfect picture of him. His good eye was wide open, his mouth also as he hacked up his disease, and his arm was rigid and outstretched. I couldn't look at it very long, though—it was too horrible, so I thrust it underneath the red cushion in the attic.

We found Simon Wiesenthal's address in one of the books. In case anyone had any information on the whereabouts of any of the missing Nazis they were to reply to Dokumentation Szenprum, Salztorgasse 6–IV–5 1010, Austria. I had to steal the money from Leo's wallet to pay for the stamps and for the envelope we needed to mail the photograph, but I was fairly confident that I would soon be able to put it back. We wrote a small letter and paper-clipped it to the photograph, which we dropped into the envelope. *We discovered a Nazi living in the Madison County part of New York State*, it read. *This is his photograph. Please let us know if he is one of the ones you are looking for.* We gave him my address and signed it L and M. We didn't mention the money—we thought we should wait to hear from him first. If he wrote back and said he was interested, we would tell him to send us five thousand dollars, and then and only then would we provide him with the address.

While we waited to hear from Simon Wiesenthal, Lana seemed to get better. In fact, after a while she started to sound too good. It seemed she was doing too well without us. She didn't miss us enough anymore, and she seemed happier than she'd been in a long time, which pained us all, particularly Leo. Elena even began to lose track of why she hated Leo so much and began to wonder about Lana.

"Maybe he drove her away," Elena said to me one night out on the back porch. "But he's not keeping her away." She kicked a few of Lana's garden rocks out of the flowerbeds with her bare toes and sent them sailing across the back lawn. "She's never coming back," she said. Her words seemed to hang in the warm air like rain clouds, and when the porch light flickered on and off, I worried that it was a premonition.

Elena got up and wandered over to the old picnic table, where she stretched herself out on top of it. "She'll never take us back either," she said bitterly. "She'll make us stay with Leo."

I moved quietly across the lawn toward her, until my knees knocked against the picnic table. "How do you know?" I asked her. I reached out and touched her bare shoulder with my fingertips.

"You think she wants us around?" she said. She yanked a stick out from underneath her back and started breaking it into tiny pieces, heaving them one by one against the wicker chairs. "That would mean we would find out about her. You think she wants us to find out about her, Maddie?" She turned and looked at me, and I saw her eyes in the porch light. An icy wave swept up my spine—they looked exactly like Lana's.

When it seemed it was true, when it seemed Lana was never coming back, Elena and I made a deal to tell each other our Lana secrets. I couldn't really remember the first secrets Lana had given me, it had been so long ago, but I remembered the one about how men would never mean that much to me.

"I only remember the last one she told me, and it's not really about her," I told her.

"I'll trade you that one for the one I have."

I nodded, and she asked that we go into the attic. I don't know why—Lana certainly wasn't within earshot and Leo had begun playing something mournful on the piano downstairs. I followed her in nonetheless, and we settled down on the floor next to the boxes. "You tell me first, Maddie, because yours isn't about Lana."

As I sat there in the quiet of the attic, I realized how little Lana's personal secrets meant to us anymore. It didn't really pain me to part with them, as it would have a year ago. In fact, I didn't even whisper it into Elena's ear. I just said it straight out into the air, where it would presumably float and drift for centuries. "She said men would never be the most important thing to me," I said. I didn't tell her the rest—the part about how I would do something great with my life.

"She said that?" Her forehead knotted in confusion, as if it weren't a proper Lana secret, and I nodded. "That's a stupid secret," she said.

"She told it to me when Andrew carved your name up in the tree, instead of mine."

"I'm sorry about that, Maddie."

It was ridiculous, but I felt tears welling up behind my eyes. "I liked Louis, too," I whispered. I never meant to say it. It just slipped out. In fact, I didn't even know it was in my mind.

"Is that why you won't talk to me, Maddie?"

That awful paralysis came over me again, and I was powerless to speak. I could only hang my head and fight back the tears.

"I didn't know you liked him, Maddie. If I had known, I wouldn't have liked him."

I didn't believe her, but I liked her for trying to make it up to me. The tears fell from my eyes anyway and spilled soundlessly down my cheeks. I pushed my face into my lap and pressed my eyes into my kneecaps.

Elena's hand came out of nowhere and touched down lightly on my shoulder. "I'll tell you two of Lana's secrets," she said. "Okay?"

When I heard the words *two of Lana's secrets,* my small sorrow melted away, and I raised my head. She cleared her throat, and just like me she spoke her words directly into the air, where with their weight and power I knew they would drift for centuries. "She's got a steel plate in her hip that the doctors put there to save it," she whispered. "It was more than broken, Maddie. It was shattered into a whole bunch of pieces, and some of them are still floating around in her hip. That's why it hurts her so bad sometimes," she said, squeezing my hand. "That's why she could never dance again."

I shuddered to imagine what sort of violence had caused that, and without any warning a picture exploded into my mind, a brutal picture of Leo beating Lana's hip with the blunt end of a shovel.

"You still want me to tell you the other one?" she asked.

"Yes," I answered.

"I don't know what happened to her," she said, "but I know it happened on May tenth, nineteen fifty-nine, in New York City." She paused for a moment. "We moved to Detroit four months later."

Goose bumps welled up under every inch of my skin, and I raised my head higher and looked at her. "That's when she and Leo promised they would put everything in the past," I said.

She nodded. "I think that's when they made their bargain."

It was all starting to make sense. All the secret bits and pieces of Lana's life were finally starting to come together. I was beginning to understand that Lana's history was not boundaryless and floating, but rather was precise and fixed, never to be altered. It had happened on May 10, 1959, in New York City, and four months later we had moved to Detroit.

I wanted to catch Elena when she was hot, so I reached down inside the box and took out two silver canisters of film. I handed one of them to her, and we slipped the film out and turned it over and over in our hands.

"I wonder what's on it," I said. I looked up at her face and watched her eyes widen.

"I don't know," she whispered.

As we ran our fingers across the tiny grooves, our eyes edging around and around the film, Leo attacked the piano keys downstairs, sending up something dark and racing, which mingled with my heart-beat, merged with it even. When the moment was right, I suggested that we take a few of them up to Art's projection room tomorrow and watch them on the screen. I whispered it slowly and quietly, but nonetheless I saw the guilt steal over Elena like a rain cloud.

She looked up at me, the shock registering in her eyes like tiny ripples, and I knew the small spell she was under had shattered. "We shouldn't have told her secrets," she said. There was panic in her voice, and she stared down at the film. "We told her secrets, and now we're touching her film," she said. She dropped it into the open silver canister as if it were contaminated and slammed the cover on.

"Jesus, Elena," I said, "it's not like Lana's sick. She's in New York, and she's really happy. Remember?" At the thought of Lana living happily without us, something cold and angry took possession of me, and I pulled up the tape on the side of the film and unfurled some of it, throwing it across Elena's lap. She recoiled, as if I had thrown a snake on her, and moved away, knocking into the bucket, where the water sloshed back and forth in the bottom.

"I know, Maddie," she whispered loudly, "but that's not a good enough reason to watch her film." She watched in horror as I unraveled more of it, her anxiety increasing with each unfurling.

"Why not?" I asked her, watching the dark ribbons of film falling in my lap.

"We can't, Maddie. Not right now." She reached over and stopped my hand from unraveling any more. "If Lana does something worse to us, then we can, but not yet." Leo's piano music ceased, and suddenly I could hear the crickets' constant summer song. I finally stopped and looked into Elena's eyes—they were filled with so much fear, I couldn't help but think she knew what was on the film already.

"Do you know what's on it, Elena?"

She stared at me for a long time, the thoughts running back and forth across her eyes. "No," she finally whispered, "but I'm afraid it's something awful." A shudder passed through her, plowing straight up her back, and an image flashed through my mind—that of Lana looming over Mr. Larkin in Mimi's whorehouse, whipping his bare butt. I looked down at the ribbons of film in my lap and felt my stomach floating sour. I rolled it up and dropped it softly into the silver canister, pressing the lid back on. Elena moved next to me, stretching her legs out on the dirty floor, and while we sat there in the quiet, lulled by the warm sound of the crickets, I knew it was only a matter of time before we watched Lana's film. I only needed to wait.

That horrible photograph of Minnie Harp's Nazi came back to us two weeks after we mailed it to Simon Wiesenthal, marked INSUFFICIENT ADDRESS. Thankfully, Lizzy and I found it before Leo did. We took it up to the attic and immediately stashed it under the red cushion, along with the other copy, where together they burned fiercely. All the while it had floated around Austria, it had been on my mind, and now that it had been returned to us, I felt terribly disturbed. The idea that he was down there in Minnie Harp's house, rotting and stinking, kept me awake at night, and no matter what I did, I couldn't shake him from my thoughts; his arresting, repellent image haunted me.

What were we supposed to do with the Nazi now? Certainly he could not continue to live in secrecy with Minnie Harp. Not now, not after we had discovered him. I wanted to tell someone about him. I felt the desperate need to let someone know he existed—an adult—someone like Leo or Gus or even Mrs. Devonshit.

"We've got to tell someone," I said to Lizzy out in my backyard.

She slumped down in one of the wicker chairs and started digging her heels into the sun-warmed grass. "Who, though?" she asked.

"Leo." As far as I could tell, he knew more about Nazis than either Gus or Mrs. Devonshit.

"Yeah, but we'll get it for going down there," she said. "And if my mom ever finds out, she'll—"

"He's a Nazi, though," I interrupted. "Who's going to get mad at us for catching a Nazi?" She thought about that for a moment, her eyes climbing from the peak of the roof to the clean blue sky overhead. It bothered her to have the Nazi on her hands too, I could tell by the way her forehead pinched together between her eyes.

"Okay," she finally said.

We waited until Elena left the dinner table and disappeared out the back door before we told Leo. He didn't quite know what to say when we put the photograph in his hands.

"Who is he?" he asked as he laid it down on the table.

"He's Minnie Harp's Nazi," I said.

Leo didn't really know who Minnie Harp was, although he admitted he'd heard of her. Lizzy eased herself down in Lana's chair while I stood next to him, and very calmly we tried to fill him in on the details. As best we could we described the horrible, decrepit condition of her house, and then very slowly, as dusk settled outside the dining room windows, we worked our way around to telling him how we happened to have a photograph of the Nazi.

"Simon Wiesenthal is looking for Nazis," I said. "So we took a picture of Minnie's Nazi to send to him."

Leo didn't say anything. His jaw fell open a little, and he just stared at us as if he'd never seen us before.

"We went inside her house a few weeks ago and took his picture," I said. I stepped away from him a little and gripped the back of his chair with my sweaty hand.

"You went inside Minnie Harp's house?" he asked. He was horrified. He turned his head and stared at me hard, his eyes barely blinking. I realized right then that I should have lied and told him we'd taken the Nazi's picture out on Minnie's lawn.

"The door was open," I lied. "We just stepped in and took his picture. We weren't in there for more than a minute. Right, Lizzy?"

Lizzy nodded. "He was all stinking and his feet were bandaged up like a mummy's," she said. She reached out and touched the edge of the photograph with her jittery fingertips, her eyes moving nervously between me and Leo.

"He couldn't hardly walk either," I went on. "He fell down right after we took his picture."

We were both so desperate for Leo to know that we took turns telling him about the Nazi, the words gushing out of us so quickly he was rendered speechless. We told him about the Nazi's face, how his eyes looked, and how his mouth was all filled with puss, and we tried our best to impart to him the exact stench of Minnie's house and the harrowing pitch of her tongueless growl.

However uneasy Leo was about it all, he was riveted by our details. He even asked us to tell him a few of the parts a second time, just so they could sink in. When we finished, he sat at the dining room table in the fading light, dumbstruck, and stared out the window as the last of the shadows crept across our lawn. When the room was almost black, he pushed his chair back and walked into the kitchen, where he called up the sheriff and told him he ought to go down to Minnie Harp's and take a look. "There seems to be a sick old man living in her house," he said. The sheriff must have asked him how he knew, because Leo said, "My daughter saw him down there." I wondered what the sheriff thought of Leo's family now. His thirteen-year-old daughter had run away, his wife and son had too, and now his youngest daughter had discovered a sick old Nazi living in Minnie Harp's house.

The next morning Lizzy and I headed down the dewy hill and crept silently through Minnie's woods and across her lawn, where we lowered ourself in the tall grass and waited for the sheriff to drive up. Cicadas droned in the nearby bushes, piercing into our anxious thoughts, and huge wadded clouds drifted lazily through the sea of blue sky above us, filling us with worry.

Somewhere after the town chimes rang eight times, a police car pulled into Minnie's overgrown driveway. The sheriff didn't come himself, but had sent Deputy Kezzner to take a look. He was a younger man, somewhere in his thirties and already thick around the waist. He wore a brushcut and shoes so shiny black they glinted in the sun when he swung them out of his car. We drifted over to the driveway and stood knee-deep in weeds, watching him. He knocked timidly on her side door, uncertain as to what he might find inside. Just moments later Minnie opened the door a small crack and peered out with one crackling black eye. He spoke a few words to her and then pulled his badge out of his coat pocket and flashed it. It hardly seemed possible, but Minnie opened the door and let him in.

"He's probably gagging right now," Lizzy said. I didn't doubt he was, but I could only guess what was happening inside. In the back of my mind I imagined that the sheriff or Leo would contact Simon Wiesenthal or someone like him. The Nazi would be taken away to a prison, I supposed, and as to how we were going to make any money, I couldn't say. I only hoped that someone would see to it that we were rewarded. In any case, I felt a deep sense of pride steal over me. Lizzy and I had done something extraordinary, I couldn't help but think—at the age of eleven, we had caught a Nazi.

When the door finally opened, the deputy emerged from the darkness of Minnie Harp's tomb alone. The first thing he did was blow his nose into a white handkerchief, which he couldn't get out of his pocket fast enough. Either he was blowing the stench from his nose or he was crying. He was shaken up, that was for sure. He walked right past us and stumbled into his car. Before we could even ask him what had happened, he backed recklessly out of Minnie Harp's weed-strewn driveway.

We were shocked. He hadn't said a word to us. It was as if we weren't even there. "Why didn't he say anything?" I asked Lizzy. We watched as he swung the car out onto the street and lurched forward, speeding away.

"He's in shock."

We stared at the back end of his vanishing car. When it was completely out of sight, we sank down into the weeds and, after deciding we'd skip school, we quietly watched Minnie Harp's side door for an hour, to see if she would come out. Lizzy was worried that she might try to sneak the Nazi out, but I knew he was too sick to go anywhere. We waited and waited, hidden in the wet weeds, and as the morning sun rose higher in the sky, a sick feeling descended into the pit of my stomach.

"What if he wasn't a Nazi?" I said. I brushed the weeds away from my face and stared at Lizzy.

"We'll have to run away," she answered in all sincerity. Her dark eyes flashed fear, and my head started to throb.

"Where could we go?" My head was really aching now, and my stomach felt pumped full of air.

"Canada maybe." She threw her arm over her eyes, as if a radiant sun were beating down on her, and tapped her foot nervously in the grass.

The sheriff called Leo after dinner, and Lizzy and I hung close to his elbows, desperate to know what had happened, even as we were desperate not to know. Leo said almost nothing, a few "ah-huhs" and "I sees," but nothing of any great import. His face only grew more disjointed, grave red lines deepening in his forehead. When he hung up the phone, he walked into the dining room and sat down at the table, staring out the window at the fading light.

"Sit down," he said sternly, turning to us. His eyes were crawling with anger, and as I staggered over to the table, I became aware of a growing, numbing fear. It started in my mind and spread to the region of my chest, radiating out to my legs and arms, which began to shake almost violently. I glanced at Lizzy and noticed that her eyes had frozen over and that her legs had gone rubbery. We sat down and fixed our quavering gaze, not on Leo, but on the lacy tablecloth Mimi had once given Lana.

"That man is no Nazi," Leo told us. He thumped his knuckles against the table until we looked up. "He is Minnie Harp's boyfriend." He stopped speaking, and while his blue eyes searched our faces, my heart fell to my stomach, where it beat like a gasping fish. I looked away from Leo, down at my fingers as they traced a shaky outline on the tablecloth. "He suffers from diabetes and had a stroke," he said louder, "and for years she tried to care for him by herself. She was too afraid to take him to the hospital, because she didn't want to lose him. They're going to have to take him away from her now, and he'll never be able to come back."

Leo didn't say any more for a while. In the silence I heard the town chimes tolling the hour—seven bongs seemed to go on forever—while a few flies buzzed maniacally in the windowpanes, setting my nerves on edge.

"You girls broke into her house," he finally said. "The sheriff found the cellar door pushed in." This is what angered him the most—the fact that I had broken into Minnie's house and had lied about it.

We had broken into an old woman's house and had ripped open her pitiful secret. Lizzy grabbed my hand under the table, and while Leo told us what a horrible thing we'd done, my nerves began leaping from my brain, falling down to my shoulders, where they raced down my spine and paralyzed me. Of all the sins I had committed this seemed the worst, and when I considered what the universe might do to get me back, I nearly fainted.

As if it might help, as if it could possibly sway the universe away from me, I apologized loudly to Leo, my quaking voice lacerating the night air. He listened for a while, but when it became unbearable, he put his hand over my mouth and silenced me. He accepted my apology, he said, but nonetheless I was grounded until school was out and Lizzy couldn't come over until then either. He sent her home, and I spent the next hour pleading with him not to tell Garta. When the night had fallen completely outside the dining room windows, he finally agreed, and when he said he wouldn't tell Elena or Lana either, I threw my arms around his neck and hugged him.

During school the next day, I stared out the window in a daze. When it finally ended, I walked Lizzy to the movie theater and then crept up to Minnie's house alone. I stood on her lawn not too far from where Lizzy and I had stood the day before and stared at her house, as if through my eyes, I could communicate my apology. An ambulance pulled into the driveway not too long afterward, and I watched in grief as two men climbed out and took a stretcher into Minnie's house. Within five minutes, the door opened, and they carried the man out. He was still wearing the dark maroon robe he had worn that night, and a gooey bandage was yet taped against his festering eye. A white blanket was tucked neatly around him, and his arms were strapped down, as if he were capable of violence. While his head writhed back and forth slowly on the small pillow, the breeze stirred a lock of his hair, blowing it straight up in the air, where it swayed for a moment before it fell across his face like a gash. He looked anemically white and more sickly in the stark afternoon light, and now that I knew he wasn't a Nazi, I felt pity for him deeper than any I had ever known. Because of me these men were taking him away, I thought. Just as they hoisted him up to the back of the ambulance, my eyes chanced to fall on Minnie Harp. She stood at the door, staring after the man, her mouth open, her jaw slack, in the very position Lizzy and I had waited so long to see. All thoughts of her cut-out tongue vanished when I saw her face, so unmasked and piteous. A strange, sad horror flooded from her eyes, as her lips struggled to form her silent, dammed protest.

I went without dinner that night. I felt physically sick, as if my nerves were wracked with fever. I had taken the man away from her, I realized. It sickened me to think of it, but I couldn't keep myself from it—the thoughts just kept turning over and over in my mind like a wheel. I brought out Durga and stood her on my stomach, although I don't know what I expected her to do. My nerves weren't racing around—they were pouring through my veins like fiery molasses, making my skin boiling hot. I stared at her arms nonetheless, imagining what I might possibly ask of them. They could cool my skin, I thought, or unclog my veins, but what I really wanted them to do was more than I could ask. I wanted them to give back Minnie Harp's man.

Is this what happened when you uncovered the truth, when you unveiled secrets? Something about this whole thing seemed to warn me away from Lana's secret, to caution me against pursuing it any further. What would I find? I wondered. Another tragedy? Would there be no Nazi, only a sick old man?

19

My last two weeks at school were quiet ones. Leo didn't relent, nor did he reduce my punishment until the very end. He made me stay inside at night, and he wouldn't let Lizzy so much as step foot on our lawn. He let us talk on the phone, but even so I couldn't wait for my sentence to be over and for school to end. I wanted to be sitting on the bus with Elena, staring out the window, waiting for New York City to come into view.

I didn't have too many hopes about going, though, because Lana had all but stopped calling us at night. She called, at the most, once a week, and her calls were always so short it almost wasn't worth it. When Elena and I reminded her that we were all coming as soon as school was out, she would say, "Yes, of course," but there was something tepid and unsubstantial about the way she said it.

"She better not call and tell us not to come," Elena would say across the darkness at night. "Because if she does, that's it."

In any case, Elena and I packed our clothes two days early in the brown suitcases we hadn't used since we'd moved last summer; and though Garta hadn't yet said Lizzy could come, Lizzy secretly packed one of Gus's old suitcases. We put everything we needed into them, and every time we wanted to brush our teeth or comb our hair, we

had to open them up. It seemed they were our insurance against
Lana's changing her mind.

Leo knocked off the last few days of my sentence and let Lizzy
come over again. We went straight up to the attic, where we stared
out the window, not saying much, instead just listening to the sound
of whirring fans and television sets and children playing outside. We
were both a little worried that Garta might not let her come. We
feared that in Lana's absence, her power over Garta had diminished,
and it scared me now to imagine what might happen to Lizzy were
I to go away too. I doubted the Eyes of God could last much longer—
surely his power was wearing off. Lizzy couldn't sleep at night thinking about it.

"What about Lizzy?" I asked Lana the night before we were to
leave. "Garta still hasn't said she can come. Are you going to call
her?" I squeezed my eyes shut and pressed my back against the
counter, as if that would make her say yes.

"I'll see, Maddie." She sighed deeply, and when she spoke again
it was to say, "Put Leo on."

I held the phone out to Leo, and while he stood alone in the kitchen
talking to Lana, Lizzy, Elena, and I waited nervously in the dining
room. It was pitch-dark outside already, and the black skies were so
leaky, a fine mist swirled in the air. It was chilly too, and after a stiff
breeze blew in through the window, Elena got up and slammed it
shut.

"Is Lana going to call my mom?" Lizzy whispered. I nodded and
she half-relaxed.

"She's telling him we can't come," Elena whispered. She rapped
her knuckles nervously against the glass and stared out at our dark
somber lawn. "She's going to make him tell us, too." She turned
around and leaned her back against the cold, wet windows.

When Leo hung up and turned around, we knew it was true. His
face hung loose and muscleless, and his shoulders fell forward.

"She said we couldn't come, didn't she?" Elena said. She tensed
up, and I sensed that whatever lay coiled inside of her was going to
go off any minute.

"She needs another week," Leo said softly. He looked diminished
standing in that doorway in the faded light. "She said she's very busy
this next week. She needs a little time to get a couple of mattresses
for you to sleep on."

"Who cares about stupid mattresses?" Elena yelled. She knocked Leo's chair over and swept the fruit basket off the dining room table, the apples and oranges dropping to the floor like bombs.

"She's only talking about one more week, Elena," he said louder.

"Yeah, and in one more week, she'll say she needs another week. I know she will," she cried, "because she doesn't want us anymore."

Leo tried to tell her it wasn't true, but there wasn't much backbone to his words. I don't think he was too sure she wanted us either. He tried to appease us by taking us out for ice cream, but a chocolate/vanilla swirl didn't have the power to reach down and touch the spot Lana had hurt again.

"She'll never ask for us, Maddie," Elena said from her bed that night. She was lying on her back, knocking her knee against the wall in quick, stabbing rhythms. It sounded like the beating heart of a hollow, winded giant. "She's got a new life," she said bitterly. "She's got the life she really wanted. She was probably waiting all these years for Leo to fuck up royally so she could have an excuse to leave."

"That's not true," I said, remembering all the times Lizzy and I had watched her suffering silently through the bathroom grate. "It just happened that way. She didn't plan it."

"I didn't say she planned it." She hiked herself up on her elbows. "I said she was waiting all these years for Leo to fuck up. There's a difference, you know."

Despite what I knew about Lana, it was hard not to listen to Elena. Her words took on a certain persuasive power, and under the weight of Lana's latest rejection, I couldn't ignore her. We knew she'd left because Leo had broken their bargain and played the jazz, but it was becoming more difficult to keep track of.

I heard Elena's knee slam hard against the wall. "That's it," she said. She threw off her covers and shot up from the bed, a white flame in the dark. She rushed into my room and went straight to the attic door. "That's it, Maddie," she yelled. "That's all I can say. I've waited long enough."

"What's wrong?" I said, though I knew what was wrong. She pulled the door open, and when she didn't so much as pause to embolden herself against the ghosts, I knew her anger had taken full possession of her. Finally, I thought, as I followed her into the attic. Finally. I leaned against the eave and watched with a certain amount of satisfaction as she tore open the box of film. She shoved her hands down inside and came up with five silver canisters.

"What are you going to do?" I asked her. I feared that in her anger she might heave them out the window like boomerangs.

"I'm going to watch them. What in the hell do you think I'm going to do? You're going to ask Art to show them to us." She threw her hair over her shoulders and thrust her hands into the box, bringing up five more canisters.

"Lizzy's going to have to see them, then," I said, edging up next to her, "because Art's her friend."

She loaded me up with five canisters. "I don't give a shit if Garta, Gus, and the whole town sees them, Maddie. If she's going to leave us here, I'm going to see what the hell's on them." She took out more canisters and stuffed them under her white nightgown. "Put them up your nightgown, Maddie," she said. "We're taking them outside."

While Leo played the piano in the living room, we ran down the stairs and walked quietly out the front door. We raced around to the back and quickly unloaded the canisters underneath the porch, stacking them in piles of three. I looked up at the sky—it was pitch-black, without the slightest trace of the moon or stars. "What if it rains?" I said. Elena glanced up at the blank, leaky skies and then scrambled up the stairs where she opened the back door soundlessly. She reached inside and grabbed Lana's green raincoat from the hook, and very carefully, we wrapped the canisters up in it.

"What if it does something really bad to Lana?" I asked her when we got back upstairs.

"It serves her right," Elena said.

I didn't feel quite so harsh about it, but I was in favor of knocking Lana down a little bit. I was all for sending a small force out into the universe to sober her up, but I didn't want anything really bad to happen to her. I worried about that too, because fifteen cans of film was a lot of film. It was worse than reading a few of her journal entries, far worse, but even so I had no intention of stopping it. I wanted to see those films more than I'd ever wanted to see anything, and actually it was working out quite nicely. Lana needed a little bringing down, and since it was Elena who had instigated the whole thing, it wasn't so much my sin as it was hers. I didn't need another whole sin—not after Minnie Harp.

⸙   ⸙   ⸙

We wolfed down our breakfast the next morning, and after Leo left I called Lizzy to come over and help us carry the film to school. I told her to meet us in the backyard. I said it was urgent, but I didn't tell her why. I just said we needed her.

We waited out on the porch for her—we weren't sitting there for more than five minutes before she came racing around the corner of the house. She was so completely winded that all she could say was, "What happened?" before she bent over to catch her breath. We pulled Lana's green raincoat out from underneath the porch, and when we threw it open for Lizzy to see, she didn't know what to think.

"They're film," Elena said. "Lana's film, and we want you to ask Art to show them to us." I noticed her anger had not been diminished by a night of sleep.

"Where did you get them?" Lizzy wanted to know. She knelt down in the dewy grass and popped one of them open, running her finger across the grooves, her eyes growing huge.

"We found them in a box," I told her.

We picked up five of them each and hauled them out of the backyard. When we got to the school, we each slipped them into the dark bottoms of our lockers, and then we waited—for hours.

I never heard a word Mrs. Devonshit said. I didn't even pay much attention when my classmates asked me what I was going to do with my summer. I told them I didn't know, and while they told me their plans, my thoughts went and rested in the bottom of my locker with the film.

The afternoon was torture. It was hot, for one thing, and for another, Mrs. Devonshit actually spent an hour telling us about bauxite and aluminum, like we really cared. It was the longest afternoon of my life; it seemed the big hand on the clock had a weight strapped to it. It crept so slowly up past the seven and the eight, it took ten minutes to reach the nine, another fifteen to reach the ten, and a half an hour went by before it landed on the twelve.

When I heard the bell I was the first one out of my seat. Lizzy, Elena, and I met out in the hallway and grabbed the film canisters from the depths of our lockers, and then raced through the muggy streets up to the movie theater. We climbed the stairs to the second floor as fast as we could, and then rushed down the dim, dreary corridor to the projector room.

The Eyes of God was sitting inside smoking a filterless Camel cigarette, sipping a cup of coffee from his gray Thermos. It was so warm up there, the sweat fell from his short, silver brushcut and streamed down the sides of his face. He walked over to us and stared down at the fifteen canisters of film in our sweaty hands. "That's a lot of film you got there." He took my top can and popped it open, pulling out the thick reel of film inside. "What's on it?" he asked, turning it over in his hands.

"We don't know," I said. "We found them in our basement."

The Eyes of God didn't care what it was or where we'd found it. He just told us to go sit downstairs in the theater while he set things up. "It'll just take me a few minutes."

We loped down the back stairs and filed down the empty aisle, sitting down in the middle seats, five rows from the front. It was humid in there, and our bare legs stuck to the red velvet chairs, but even so I started to shake. Now that we were really going to see the film I was afraid of what it might contain. I was scared that it might make Lana look worse than she already did.

"What if it's awful?" I whispered to Elena.

"Then we'll know the truth," she said. She slid further down in her seat, and I noticed she couldn't keep her eyes still. They roamed all over the theater—across the ceiling, down the walls, and past the thick red curtains that hung on either side of the screen. "The truth is always the best, Maddie."

Lizzy and I looked at one another. We didn't necessarily think so, not after what had happened with Minnie Harp, and suddenly I was terrified of what the truth might do to us. It could fling us apart even more, I worried, or it could gouge out a chasm so huge between us, it could never be bridged. No, the truth wasn't always the best. There were times when it was the worst thing in the world.

Just when I felt the strongest urge to rush out of the theater into the warm embrace of the afternoon, the lights died and the Eyes of God spoke. "Okay," he said. "Let's see what we've got." I turned around and saw him standing next to the projector, his left hand sitting on top of it as if it were his best friend.

The whir of the projector cut the silence and the light hit the screen. The sound of jazz came up, distant at first, slowly filling the theater with its rich, snappy sound. Elena took my hand and squeezed it, and Lizzy dug her elbow into my side. That sound, no matter how bright it was, filled us with dread. Another image faded up, and we were suddenly looking at the outside of Sammy's Club. It had red doors and a red awning, with the words SAMMY'S CLUB painted on the awning like a signature in bold black. On the left side, just beyond the red doors, was a glassed-in marquee that had a poster inside it. FEATURING LANA LAMAR, it read, and underneath it was a glossy picture of Lana dressed in a sleeveless red sequin dress, standing with her red high-heeled shoes boldly apart. Her painted red mouth was wide open behind a big round microphone she held in her left hand, and her right hand was stretched to the heavens. Her hair was short and cropped in a way I could only vaguely remember, and her eyes sparkled with points of light, as if someone had painted them with stardust. Around her image were small circles featuring the musicians, Leo being in the largest one, and the only white man. He was seated at the piano, his hands a blur on the keyboard.

Suddenly, Lana was standing in a spotlight at the center of a large wooden stage. The band was spread out behind her, Leo sitting at the piano to her left in his own white spotlight. She was dressed in a black sequin dress and dark high-heeled shoes, her mouth painted a lurid red. While she sang boldly into a round microphone—*"He don't treat me right, not even at night when I fall to the floor on my knees"*—Leo rocked back and forth like he always did when he played the jazz. Lana was the one who caught your eye. She was arresting with her luminous skin and her breasts heaving provocatively from the top of her black dress. Her voice was even more stunning, though. Without a doubt, it was the belted-out singing voice of a Negro woman— rich and flexible, wailing and soaring into the upper ranges. It sounded so strange, so foreign, so utterly mismatched—that sassy, acrobatic voice coming out of Lana. It was as if a Negro woman stood behind the curtains while Lana mouthed the words.

She danced in a way I could never have fathomed—her hips and shoulders moving in shimmies and waves, her feet tap dancing on the wooden stage. She grabbed the microphone from the stand and then dropped to her knees, her head falling backward, her white throat vibrating with the song. On her knees, with one arm outstretched to the audience, she belted out the words, *"And he ain't gonna see my face no more, no more, no more, no more, no more."* As her voice hung on the last *more* in a high, prolonged note, her sound and image vanished.

Suddenly, white dots danced across the screen, and Lizzy, Elena, and I turned around and looked anxiously up at the Eyes of God in the projection room. "There's more," he said. "That was just the first reel." We looked at one another. It was hard to have known our mother all these years as Lana, the writer, and to see her come to life on screen now as part sex goddess, part Negro singer, part siren. "Jesus," Elena whispered. Lizzy pushed her hair off her damp face and exhaled loudly. I didn't say anything, but I felt my eyes bulging.

A young man appeared on the screen next. He was tall and thin and dark-haired and wore a navy blue suit with a white shirt and a skinny red tie. He stood in a dimly lit hallway, holding a microphone, while black men and white men stood together in the shadows, dressed in dark suits, smoking cigarettes and talking lowly.

"We're backstage at Sammy's Club in Harlem," he said. He turned and started walking down the hallway, the camera following bumpily after him. "We're on our way back to the dressing room, to talk to Lana Lamar."

The screen went black for a moment and then Lana appeared, not as the singer, but as the Lana we had always known. She was sitting in her dressing room, in a dark blue chair, her back to a mirror, which was outlined by a dozen white light bulbs. She wore a white blouse and a pair of black slacks, and behind her in the mirror, people kept coming and going out a door. The man sat across from her on top of a stool, and after a moment he thrust the microphone underneath her chin.

"It's been said that you got your start in a whorehouse." Lizzy, Elena, and I were shocked, but not as shocked as we were when Lana told him it was true. "Yes," she said, "my mother ran a bordello in Harlem for years, until she was arrested." We looked at each other, our mouths hanging open like caves.

"There are rumors that one of your parents is Negro," he said. "I've heard it both ways—that your mother was Negro and your father white, or your father was Negro and your mother white. Which is true?"

"Both my parents were white," Lana said, "though I never knew my father." She smiled faintly. "I was raised by a Negro woman named Effy." She looked down, first at her lap, then down at the floor. Fifteen years had passed since Mimi had put Effy in the house, and ten years since Effy had been shot, and it still bothered her. You could see the sadness settle on her shoulders like a weight.

The man leaned forward and pressed the microphone a little closer to Lana's mouth. "You've been referred to as the Dragon Lady," he said. "How does that make you feel?"

She looked up and smiled at him, and behind her back in the mirror I saw Leo walk in. He said something to an older woman ironing, and she pointed to Lana. As Leo walked toward her, the screen went black again, a few of those white dots flashing across it.

"There's still more," Art called down to us.

What came next I would never forget—raw film takes, unedited, as Art told us, of a Lana we had never seen or heard or even imagined.

She appeared on the screen sitting on a wooden stool at the edge of Sammy's stage, holding a microphone. She sat in a pool of stark white light dressed in a pair of black pants and a white blouse, the sleeves of which were rolled up past her elbows. Her face was damp, her eyes blazing like I'd never seen before. She was speaking to a noisy crowd, which was pressed into every corner of Sammy's small club—people were crammed in the doorways, others stood on top of the chairs, some even stood on the tabletops. There were over a hundred people wedged into that space, white and Negro. As if the crowd were one huge body, it seemed to vibrate. Some of them were rooting for her, while others shouted at her. You could almost feel it ticking, seething in parts, knotting up here and there in anger, as if it were poising itself for some sort of eerie attack.

"Slavery is still alive in America," she called out. "We may have abolished it one hundred years ago, but it has never really vanished. We play it out every day, every hour, every moment of our lives—this game of inferiority, superiority—both whites and Negroes. We must stop. It has gone on long enough."

There were pockets of applause, amid protest which sprang like wells from other parts of the crowd. Lana stood up and walked to the edge of the stage, where she waited a moment for them to settle down.

"It's all in our heads, folks," she cried out. "White people aren't superior, and Negroes aren't inferior. There's not an ounce of it in our genes."

Parts of the crowd writhed like some living beast and horrible words, thick and garbled, fled from its mouth: *Go preach to the niggers. Go home, you stupid bitch. Who asked you anyway?* Lana stood at the very edge of the stage, her eyes scanning the crowd, as if to measure it, to check its volatility. She stood tall and strong and took it in, as if it were her job to ferret out the disease, to take it on her shoulders, later to haul it off some place where it would no longer hurt anyone.

It went on like this for a long time—the camera restlessly shifting back and forth like an oscillating fan, passing over Lana as she spoke fervently, her eyes deep and hot and ignited, and then back to the reddened faces of the crowd, some of their mouths moving with the velocity of fear, hatred even, others crying out their agreement, their hands a blur in applause. Her voice was lost and then heard again, like a lone and poignant song, amid a backlash of fury and hollered-out praise. Large photographs appeared and disappeared on easels which stood behind her—photographs of opened human chests, one white, one Negro, with the lungs removed to reveal the hearts—hearts that were exactly the same size, the same color. Then somewhere a chilling voice rose above them all. "Get this bitch off the fucking stage," it said. "Get her off the stage." Suddenly the camera was violently disrupted, the picture veering up to the black rafters and careening across the ceiling as if it were strapped to a dysfunctional plane. It slid down the wall, and for a moment it held on a middle-aged man as he pounded the edge of the stage violently with his fists. Just moments later the crowd parted and two large men surged forward and dragged him away. His voice came again as a stabbing refrain. "Get that bitch off the fucking stage."

When the camera was righted again, Lana said, "There's no such thing as inherent inferiority based on skin color—the white man made it up," and the camera began its restless movement back and forth, as if it were recording a game. It seemed it was a sport, some odd form of entertainment, as if these people had come to gape at her, to hear her say things no one else would say.

A white flash raced across the screen, as if to wipe it clean, and then a crowd of Negroes appeared. They were standing bunched together, crowded around the stage, while Lana paced near its edge. Her black suit was rumpled, her white blouse damp with perspiration. "On behalf of the white race," she called out, "I apologize to each and every one of you for what's been done to you."

There was applause, but in small pockets here and there, a fury began to rise like a geyser. Some shouted as if from one booming mouth, "It's too late now. *We don't want your mother-fucking apology.*" Others simply clapped. Then they argued amongst themselves about it, chaos descending within moments. They were torn in half—some were excited, others outraged—the fury rising like a tidal wave in parts of the crowd. Those men moved in immediately, pushing everyone back, fueling the rage even more. The camera shimmied forward to the front line, where the action was thickest. It coursed over the floor, across worn and dusty shoes, and once again careened across the ceiling, passing by the white lights, lighting up the screen with bright, blinding shards of light. Lana was nowhere to be seen, but suddenly we heard her voice. It rose over the crowd like a high-throated aria, a voice of reason in the madness. "Please, you're making it worse," she cried. "Just leave them alone. Please, just leave them alone."

The screen went white again for a moment, and then another crowd appeared and it continued. It kept going—a whirling, dizzying sequence of film clips of Lana speaking, of the crowds reacting, until it began to seem like it really was a game—a game where Lana's job was to say provocative things and theirs was to respond, while she took it all in and the camera kept up its relentless movement, back and forth, recording it all. "Take your boots off the Negro's back, or he'll do it for you," she would say, and then a whole, mixed tide of approval and rebellion would roll in.

There were Lana's fathomless eyes and then a dark sea of moving mouths—over and over, back and forth. One crowd after another. Negro and white. Elation and rage—some shouting, "Amen," others cursing her to hell. Moments of silence, Lana speaking passionately of whites, of Negroes—moments of heightened raw emotion, the crowd moving in waves, those two huge men darting here and there, pushing the crowds back, keeping control. And Lana's eyes, always her eyes—windows into an inflamed soul. It kept going and going, back and forth, over and over, this fierce, hectic partnered dance, until I could hardly breathe anymore.

When the screen finally went white and we heard the film flipping as it went around and around up in the projection room, I felt a whorling in the pit of my stomach and a dull ache behind my forehead. The images continued on in my mind as if they were somehow tattooed to the underside of my eyelids. Somewhere in the midst of it all I felt a prickly uneasiness; I sensed that she was a curiosity to them—this white woman who sang like a Negro and said strange things no one had ever heard a woman utter. It seemed it was all a sideshow, a public exhibition where she was the main attraction—a curiosity, a freak, and to some nothing more.

We all turned around and looked up at the Eyes of God. He was standing next to the projector, his eyes yet riveted to the white screen. When he noticed we were looking at him, it seemed he woke up. He turned to the projector where the end of the film was whipping around and shut it off.

"That was four rolls, guys. I can't show you any more this afternoon," he called down to us. "Maybe tomorrow we can see some more."

He pulled the house lights up, and Lizzy, Elena, and I finally looked at each other in the brightness. "Oh my God," Lizzy said. Elena said, "I know." For my part, I couldn't really speak. We wiped the sweat off our foreheads with the backs of our hands and pulled our sticky shorts off our wet legs. There was a dizziness in us all, as if someone had knocked us over the head with a bat. We stumbled up the aisle and crept silently up the back stairs to the projection room, where Art was rewinding our film on those gray arms.

The Eyes of God glanced over his shoulder at us. "Who was that?" he asked.

"She's our mother," Elena said. I thought I detected a note of pride in her voice, but I couldn't be sure.

As the sweat slid down his face, the Eyes of God reddened. "She had a lot of guts."

Elena, Lizzy, and I looked at each other and shuddered. There was something spooky about it all, something nervous and unforgettable.

He kept the film for us and promised to show us some more tomorrow. We thanked him and drifted down the stairs and out into the late afternoon. We didn't walk more than a block before the skies cracked open and it began to pour. Lightning spread across the sky, and then a clap of thunder broke the silence.

"It would have to come now," Elena said, as we started to run down the street.

We all looked at one another, and a fever swept through us. It was Lana, we feared. She'd felt those four rolls of film as if they had flickered across her face. Elena pulled ahead of Lizzy and me and sprinted down the street. We ran faster too, as if with a little more speed we could run right out of our guilty skins. The rain pelted down on us, like tiny fists of punishment, filling our hearts with dread. What had we done now?

We followed Elena into the house and up the front stairs. We disappeared into the attic and closed the door behind us, dropping to the dirty floorboards where we tried to catch our breath. It was suffocating in there, so Elena threw open the window. Just after she dropped backward in the red chair, lightning slashed across the sky and pierced the distant hills.

The rain fell through the ceiling and stung the bucket, plunking out an anguished tune that matched the haggard beat of my heart. Lizzy stretched out between the boxes and a rusted bedframe, and I sat huddled beneath the eaves, the rough splintered wood poking the back of my skull.

"I bet Lana got that way because of Effy," Lizzy whispered. Even though it was sweltering in that attic, her teeth chattered.

Elena shot me a dirty glance, which faded almost in an instant. What did it matter now if Lizzy knew about Effy?

We lay there in the silence for a few moments, Lizzy finally breaking it again. "That's why Gus thought she knew Lana," she whispered. "She must have heard about her."

I thought back to the day of Barbara Lamb's welcoming party when Lana had stepped into Barbara's hot washroom where Lizzy sat with Gus. After Lana had extended her hand, Gus had said, "Do I know you?" as if she had recognized Lana from somewhere.

The three of us looked at one another, and though none of us said anything, we knew for certain that Lana's involvement with Garta had very little to do with Garta and everything to do with Lizzy.

"We still don't know what happened to Lana, though," I said. My voice was half the size it usually was. It sounded raspy and low as if someone had shredded up my vocal cords.

The thought of what had happened to Lana edged down our spines like hacksaws, and no one said another word about it. We didn't want to know, not now anyway, not today. Instead, we listened to the rain as it pelted the roof and splashed haphazardly into the bucket, half watching the clouds as they raced across the sky like dark bandits.

When Leo came home, we sat at the dining room table and ate his macaroni and cheese without saying anything. He thought we were mad at Lana because she hadn't let us come, so he left our silence alone. We kept looking at him, though. We couldn't help ourselves. Where was he when Lana stood on that stage? we wondered. And what did he think about it all? I could only guess that he'd hated it.

He kept looking up when he felt our eyes on him. "What?" he finally said. We all looked down at our cold macaroni and cheese and prodded it with our forks. "It's not my fault," he said. "It was Lana's decision." He meant about not letting us come to New York, but even so it seemed he spoke of those films.

"Why did Lana do that, Elena?" I asked her when we went back to the attic. I whispered it, but even so it sounded too loud. It seemed we couldn't speak about it quietly enough.

"I don't know, Maddie," she said softly. She tossed her damp hair over her shoulders and dug her chin into her drawn-up knees. "It's weird though, really weird."

"I could never picture her doing that," I said. It was true—I could not imagine the Lana I knew now speaking feverishly in front of half-hostile audiences.

"She's not the same person anymore, Maddie," Elena whispered. "She was still young when all that happened."

I moved closer to her, my hands edging across the gritty floor. "Do you think she was crazy?" I whispered faintly. I couldn't get rid of that idea. I kept seeing her standing there apologizing to those Negroes for the whole white race.

"No, she wasn't crazy, Maddie." Her eyes were still pinned in the distance, and her voice sounded dreamy, as if her thoughts had gone and rested with Lana's films. "She was passionate, and everything she said was true. And Art was right—she had a lot of guts." She lay back on the floor and slipped her hands behind her head. "She's not a regular kind of mother, Maddie."

Thunder rumbled in the early evening, and a small flash of lightning flickered across the dull gray sky. Elena stretched her legs out in front of her and rested her feet on the small window ledge. Her black shorts were wrinkled and damp from the rain, I noticed, and now dust from the attic floor covered them.

"What happened to her, though?" I whispered. "She's not like that at all anymore." I remembered how her hands used to shake and how her breathing could deteriorate to gasps when she was just sitting there.

"I don't know, Maddie, but something did," she whispered. Her voice trembled, and she closed her eyes for a moment.

"Something with her hip," I said. A shiver passed through me when I remembered how it had been shattered into pieces. That brutal picture exploded again in my mind—that picture of Leo beating Lana's hip with the blunt end of a shovel.

Elena pressed her dusty finger to my lips. "Don't talk about it anymore, Maddie," she whispered.

"You really don't know?" I asked.

She shook her head, and I believed her. What did she have to lose now—we'd already watched four rolls of Lana's films, we'd broken all our vows to the moon, and I knew we would never make another one. I knew too that we would never again throw quarters into the swan pond, promising anything. It felt as if I had crossed over a line I would never cross again. It was as if a scissors had come along and cut my life right here, at this odd, uneasy juncture, and from this point forward everything would be different.

I turned and looked at Elena. Her fingers were filthy, her damp black hair was coated with dust from the floor, and a big smudge of dirt lay across her cheek like a stripe of black war paint. I looked at my hands and down at my pants and realized I was filthy too, but I didn't care. Somehow it felt right that, while it rained outside and washed everything off, we lay in the attic covered with dirt.

We slept together that night in Elena's bed. We didn't wash up or change our clothes either. We just crawled under the sheets and lay in the darkness feeling gritty, uprooted and lost.

"We'll find out what happened to her, Maddie," Elena whispered. Her eyes roved the ugly pink wallpaper, stopping on the part which had dried out and fallen over backward.

"I know," I said. "But what if it breaks us all up?" Pieces of fear coursed through my veins, like bits of poison, and stirred my hive of nerves. I crept closer to Elena, to her warmth, and stared at the dark smudges on her face. They looked like spots of sadness that had leaked through her thoughts.

"We could live with Grampie in Lansing," she whispered. "Or maybe we'll stay here with Leo. It's not really that bad here. But whatever, you and me will stay together, okay?"

"Okay," I said.

She reached down and squeezed my hand like she used to before we ever moved to these hills where everything had unfurled and broken apart, scattering into the loose, unmarred air. We fell asleep holding hands, while the mournful notes of Leo's piano drifted up to us, and the rain outside slowed down to a misty drizzle and then ceased altogether.

20

Over the next two days, the Eyes of God showed us the rest of Lana's film. We watched Lana sing and dance across the wide screen in glittering costumes with flowers in her hair, while Leo played the piano feverishly off to her side. She was interviewed in her dressing room, on the streets, in small drab offices, and on and off Sammy's stage. She always wore the same black suit and white blouse, and sometimes a thin black tie. Every time she spoke, she said something different, her speeches continually evolving. It seemed she was searching for the right words that would unlock people's minds, always changing them, always trying new ones. She must have believed if she just kept trying, she would one day stumble upon the words that would work. It was never easy for her, not even for a moment. There was always some kind of disturbance, some kind of tawdry violence or another.

She called a few nights later and talked to Leo. Elena and I were over at the swan pond with Lizzy, lying in the grass, staring up at the clear, bright sky. There was something about reading Lana's journal and seeing her films that finally bound us together again. It was as if we had formed an alliance in her name. We would find and keep her secrets—just the three of us—and no matter what, we would figure out what had happened to her. It became our unspoken pact, and as we drifted through the days, we could think of little else.

"Lana wants you guys to come the day after tomorrow," Leo told us when we got home. He was sitting at the dining room table in the fading light, staring past the fluttering curtains out at our backyard where the wicker chair Lana had always sat in stood white and lonely against the hills.

"Lizzy, too?" I asked.

"Garta says it's okay," he said.

We all looked at each other and shivered. We were going, then, I thought. We were finally going.

Elena walked soundlessly over to his chair, laying her fingers on the back of it. "How long can we stay?"

"She didn't say, Elena," he said quietly. "She said you'd just play it by ear."

Lizzy asked him if he were coming, and when he said he wasn't invited, I felt something stick in my heart. He walked into the dark living room after that and turned the television on. The light flickered across his face, and when he took a slug of whiskey from the bottle next to his chair, I thought I heard a sob catch in the back of his throat. He shifted in his seat, as if to move out from underneath our stare, and when he looked up at us, I felt the crush of his sadness.

That night Lizzy, Elena, and I repacked our suitcases, and then spent the next morning perched high on top of Heart Attack Hill. Though she hated to admit it, Elena had grown fond of the green hills. She wanted to look at them one last time, in case we never came back. In the afternoon, Lizzy pulled us up to her favorite field where we could see forever, and afterward we walked up to the fort behind the gas station, where Elena lit up a cigarette and gave Lizzy and me our first puffs. She thought we were old enough now—not in years really, but she recognized that seeing Lana's films had aged us. We walked across the street after that and crept up the stairs to the projector room, where we said good-bye to the Eyes of God.

"We're going to New York tomorrow," Elena told him. "Lana asked for us."

"You're coming back, aren't you?" When we told him we might not, he looked almost as sad as Leo had. He extended his hand with the crooked finger, and after Elena and I shook it, Lizzy threw her arms around his neck. "I'll stay here for a while," she whispered.

When the Eyes of God squeezed his eyes shut, I knew he would miss her more than he could say.

Elena and I left them alone and stepped out to the street. The sky overhead was a blanket of dull leaden gray, out of which leaked a fine misty rain. Elena said she had to say good-bye to Louis and headed up to the woods to their abandoned car, where I imagined their embrace would be more impassioned than usual. I didn't know what to do with myself, so I put on Lana's green raincoat and went up to say good-bye to Miss Thomas. I helped her feed the birds, and when I told her Lana had finally asked us to come, she said, "Hallelujah." At my request she made me an extra large batch of life-saving potion, which she put in a big brown paper bag. "Only take it when you absolutely have to," she said very gravely. "I made it very strong this time." Then, for good luck, we sat in front of the real Durga and spoke the Hindu words, while the rain streamed down the windows and dripped from the eaves.

When I woke up the next morning, Durga lay between me and Elena, four of her arms pressed under Elena's hand. I pulled her out gently and shoved her underneath my bed, just in case Elena woke up. As I lay in the weak morning light, staring out the window at the cloudy blue sky, I knew our lives were going to change again. We are leaving today, I told myself. I may never sleep another night in this bed, I thought; I may never look upon these mercurial skies again. These green hills, which I had come to love, may only become a memory, and my own father, the man who had raised me, may never live with me again.

Elena woke up shortly. She must have had the same thoughts, because when we washed up in the bathroom together, she didn't say anything. We ate a quiet breakfast with Leo too, none of us saying much.

Around twelve o'clock he drove us down to the drugstore with our suitcases. The bus hadn't come yet, but Lizzy and Garta and Jimmy were already inside buying Lizzy's bus ticket. When Leo went inside to buy ours, Elena and I stood outside on the hot sidewalk, while I secretly said my silent good-byes to Shorty's gas station, to the movie theater, and to the Blue Bird Restaurant across the street. I didn't know if I'd ever see them again.

The bus pulled up in front of us shortly, and after the driver threw our three suitcases into the luggage compartment, Leo's hands fell gently to our shoulders.

"Well," he said, "I guess this is good-bye." A knot formed in his throat, and he struggled to swallow. "Tell Lana I said hello, and call me tonight when you get there, okay?"

Elena nodded, and Leo put his arms around her. "We'll see you again, Leo," I heard her whisper.

"I hope so," he whispered back.

When he gathered me up in his arms, I wanted to stay there, to loll in them for a long time. I threw my arms around his neck. "Leo," I breathed.

"Don't take things too hard, Maddie," he whispered in my ear. "Try not to worry so much. You're only eleven years old. And take care of Lizzy."

I nodded and watched as he embraced Lizzy. "Take care of Maddie," he whispered to her.

Garta hugged the three of us too, if you could call it that. She opened and closed her arms so quickly it felt obligatory, completely mechanical, and so far from heartfelt that we laughed about it later.

We climbed on the bus and fell into two of the empty side seats, pressing our faces against the windows as we waved to Leo, Garta, and Jimmy. "GIVE MY REGARDS TO BROADWAY," Garta yelled.

"Like they really want your regards," Elena whispered. When the bus finally pulled away from the curb and drifted out of town, we watched them grow smaller and smaller. They looked like a family, I couldn't help but think, and when I realized we had left Leo with Garta, I felt a little sick.

"Wouldn't that be weird if my mom left Don and married Leo?" Lizzy said. Her face was still pressed against the window.

"It would never happen," Elena said, shooting Lizzy a horrified look. We pictured it for a moment, and then we all burst out laughing.

"GET OVER HERE, LEO," Lizzy mimicked, "AND PLAY SOMETHING SWEET ON THE GODDAMN PIANO."

We doubled over in the seats laughing so hard everyone in the bus turned around and stared at us.

When we got out of town, we moved to the back, where a middle-aged woman with dyed black hair chain-smoked Chesterfield cigarettes. We hunched down in our seats, and Elena lit up one of her Winstons, which we passed back and forth until we smoked it down to the filter. As the hills slid past our eyes, we wondered what we would find in New York. What would Lana be like? Would she still be happy? We were hoping we'd at least meet Mimi. It seemed she might be our only hope of ever finding out what had happened to Lana. We were counting on her big mouth to open and tell it all.

I fell asleep on Elena's shoulder after we left Binghamton, and when I woke up it was almost dark. I found myself stretched out on the backseat alone, with Elena's sweater balled up under my head. My heart started pounding immediately. I bolted up and discovered Elena and Lizzy sitting in the seat ahead of me, smoking another cigarette.

"Where are we?" I asked, rubbing the sleep from my eyes.

"Ten miles from New York City," Elena said.

This shook me up. I hadn't had time to prepare myself. I pressed my cheek against the cold glass and stared ahead at the white glow in the sky. At least I'd woken up now, I told myself. I could have woken up in the Port Authority Bus Station. I could have missed riding up on the city and driving over the George Washington Bridge. But even so, I was unnerved.

I watched out the window as we raced past the trees, keeping my eyes on the white glow which hovered above Manhattan like a halo. I couldn't see anything yet, but I could feel it out there, as if it had a heartbeat. Elena and Lizzy started watching out the window too, their eyes fixed above on the starless sky, as they waited to see the tops of the skyscrapers. After a few more minutes of watching the trees speed past, suddenly on our left, Manhattan swam into view. We could see part of the George Washington Bridge as it reached across the river and touched down on the other side. The bus made a few turns, and then we were driving across the upper deck of it. The foreboding feeling I had had was replaced by one of awe. I had never seen anything so vital as Manhattan in all my life. It loomed in the distance like a giant with a million lighted eyes. Energy seemed to radiate from it as if it had fingers which reached out and pulled us in.

Elena, Lizzy, and I pressed our faces against the glass again and held our breath as the bus crossed the bridge and plunged into Manhattan. Elena lit another cigarette, and as we passed it back and forth, our eyes were stolen away by every passing building, by every light, by every person we chanced to see. It seemed this city had a thousand mouths and a million heartbeats, which all pulsed and breathed and spoke at once. Lana lived here, I thought, and in the midst of this great seething place we would find her again.

The bus turned and sped down Ninth Avenue, finally turning left on 42nd Street, where the traffic was thicker than any I'd ever seen before. Yellow taxicabs darted everywhere; the air was filled with the impatient sound of horns, of people hurrying through the summer streets like they were all late for something. The bus finally pulled into the underground station, and before Elena butted the cigarette out in the steel ashtray, she gave us each one more drag.

"She better be here," she said. We looked at one another and shivered.

"She will be," I said.

We stood up and shifted our wrinkled pants around, smoothing them over with our hands, tucking our white blouses in. Elena quickly raked her fingers through her hair, while Lizzy pulled her ponytail tighter. I took off my red sweater and tied it around my waist. Already it was hot, and I felt a few drops of sweat roll down my back.

As soon as we stepped off the bus, we merged with a huge tide of people who were flooding in and out of the gates like ants. We picked up our suitcases and then hurriedly joined the stream flowing into gate number six. It didn't take us long to find Lana. She and Harry were standing near the front of the crowd which had knotted up near the door. If Harry hadn't been with her, though, I doubt I would have recognized her right away. She had cut her hair off—it was short, just below her chin, and was parted on the side. It wasn't exactly the same way she had worn it in the films, but it was close enough that it made me shudder. She was wearing a pair of navy blue pin-striped pants and a white blouse with rolled-up sleeves. Only in those films had we ever seen her wear pants. At the thought of it a chill ran through me.

Elena, Lizzy, and I stopped about six feet away from her. As the people pressed around us we looked across the heated air at her, and she stared back at us. It was only for a few moments, but we all hesitated. We didn't know who she was anymore. She looked different than we had ever seen her, and we knew she'd changed. She didn't know what to make of us either—it seemed as if in our absence

we'd become figments of her imagination, and suddenly we had materialized before her eyes. She looked radiant, though. Her cheeks were
flushed, and her eyes shone as if two warm candles burned behind
them. It seemed in her absence she might have healed.

"How are you guys?" she finally said. She didn't move forward,
nor did she open her arms. She just stood there with Harry clinging
to her right leg.

"We're good," Elena said, but her voice cracked and she banged
her suitcase against her knees. "You cut your hair." I could tell by
the thin sound of her voice that it bothered her.

"Yes," she said, reaching up and touching it. "I got tired of it long.
Do you like it?"

We all nodded, though we weren't sure how we felt. It looked
good, but what did it mean?

"Come here, you guys," she finally said, opening her arms up to
us.

Elena dropped her suitcase and rushed forward first, then me and
Lizzy, and we flung ourselves into her arms. She smelled wonderful,
of gardenias, as if a flower were pinned near her heart, and her arms
felt strong and sure.

"Maddie and Elena and Lizzy," she whispered, as if she were just
naming us. She kissed the tops of our heads and breathed us in. "I've
missed you."

We took the escalator up to the main floor, which was so gorged
with people it was hard to walk. Lana paved our way to the street,
where we climbed into a yellow taxi—the first cab Elena, Lizzy, and
I had ever ridden in.

Lana said, "The corner of Bleecker and Eleventh streets," and the
cab lurched forward and sped down Ninth Avenue, the summer
streets coming in through the opened windows, the lights and smells
and sounds spilling all over us. While my ears filled up, and my eyes
took it all in, it ravished me. It was almost like Miss Thomas's room
with all those moving objects that sang and danced and whirred, her
room of perpetual sound and motion, but it was much better, much
grander. "Isn't it grand?" I wanted to say. *"Isn't it just grand?"*

"You grew up here?" Lizzy asked Lana, and when Lana nodded,
we couldn't imagine. No wonder she hated our silent, deserted streets.
No wonder those hills didn't move her. She'd been born in this. Mimi
was right, I guessed—Lana belonged here. I could sense it as if it

were embedded in her straight back, in the way her eyes swept fondly
across the streets, as if they were hers.

Lana lived on Eleventh Street, five flights up, in a redbrick building. We stumbled up the stairs, lugging three suitcases, Harry leading
the way. On our way up the third flight, we met a pair of old sisters
who lived on the fourth floor. One of them bent down and kissed
Harry's cheek, the other touched Lana's arm. "These are my three
daughters," Lana told them. "Lizzy, Elena, and Maddie." We all said
hello to them, and afterward I glanced over at Lizzy. Her big black
eyes swelled from the inside like they used to before Garta had beaten
her up so much.

When we finally reached the top, Harry proudly jabbed his key in
the lock and opened the door, his little hand reaching inside to flip
on the light. He pushed it open and held it there until we were all
inside. It didn't take us long to look at it—it was one big room, with
a small bathroom and a kitchen that stood behind folding doors that
were pushed back. Four large windows faced the street, and the white
rice paper curtains Lana had hung over them were half raised and
fluttered in the breeze. The walls were white and barren, with the
exception of a few photographs. They were tacked up on the wall
above the pillows on Lana and Harry's mattress.

Besides the mattress she and Harry used, there were two others,
which lay on the wooden floor—one double for me and Lizzy, and a
single one for Elena. They were all made up with white sheets and
blankets. A potted gardenia sat in the window blooming, its thick
sweet smell filling the room, and next to the closet door stood a blue
wooden chair with a half-broken back. Her journals must be in the
closet, I thought, because they weren't in this room. Besides the mattresses and the chair, there was nothing else in there.

Elena, Lizzy, and I lay down on our mattresses and looked around
us. The white rice paper curtains wagged back and forth slowly in
the hot summer breeze. With the white walls, the white sheets, and
the scent of gardenias wafting through the air, I felt as if I were lying
in the warm petals of a great flower. I couldn't be sure, but it felt as
though I might like it here.

When Lana took Harry into the bathroom, I darted quietly across
the room and opened the closet door. I wanted to see where she had
put her journals. I looked up and noticed that the top shelf was
crammed with Lana's underwear and stockings and all of Harry's

clothes. Her dresses hung on a pole, pressed tightly together, a few of her nightgowns looped over them. I knelt down on the floor to get a look in the back, and before my knees even touched down, I felt Elena and Lizzy behind me.

"What are you doing?" Elena whispered.

"I'm looking for the journals." After I said it I remembered that Lizzy didn't know there were more of them, but it hardly mattered now.

"Shove over," Elena said. I moved over, and both of them dropped down to their hands and knees. We all bent our heads down and looked past Lana's shoes to the very back of the closet. I was the first one to see the silver canisters of film—they were wedged in the very back, behind her suitcase.

"The film," I whispered. A wave of fear surged through me at the thought that Lana had gone back to giving those speeches.

"How many?" Elena asked.

I scrambled inside and pushed the suitcase back far enough to count them. "There are six of them."

"Oh God," Elena whispered. "She's doing it again."

It sunk all our hearts.

We heard the door to the bathroom open, and we quickly closed the closet and scattered. Lizzy ran back to our mattress, while Elena and I flung ourselves on Lana's. We didn't do it quick enough, though, because Lana opened the door and saw us in mid-flight.

"What's going on, you guys?" We stared at her, but none of us said anything. She walked across the room and stopped in front of Elena. "What are you doing, Elena?"

"Nothing," Elena said. She rolled her eyes and sighed.

Lana looked around the room to see if anything were out of place, and her eyes fell next on Lizzy, then on me. "What's going on, Maddie?"

I looked at Elena. She was staring down at her brown sandals, flipping the silver buckle back and forth.

"Maddie," she said. "Tell me what's going on." Her eyes pierced me.

I looked at the closet door and noticed that Lana's white bra was hanging from the doorknob. "Elena was trying on your bra," I said.

Elena's eyes shot up to mine, and Lana looked from me to her, and then behind her at the bra hanging on the doorknob.

"Is that true?" she asked Elena.

Elena nodded dutifully, but then she made the mistake of looking up at me—we burst out laughing, and just moments later Lizzy broke up too.

"I know you're up to something, you guys," she said. "Just so you know I'm not stupid." She wasn't really mad—just a little put off, but she didn't let it bother her. She started tucking in Harry's shirt, and we tried to stop laughing, but it kept coming out of us in fits and starts. It seemed to purge our souls of the worry those cans of film had ushered in.

"We're meeting Mimi tonight," Lana said when she finished combing Harry's hair. "She's going to take us out to dinner."

At the word *Mimi,* something electric shot through me. Elena, Lizzy, and I looked at one another, and a wordless thrill passed between us. We were finally going to meet Mimi, and though none of us could say it, we all shared the same hope—that Mimi would somehow open her big mouth and tell us everything.

Before we met her we called Leo from a corner phone booth. Elena, Lizzy, Harry, and I piled inside, all sweaty, our legs and arms sticking together, while Lana leaned against the glass and waited for us. Elena talked to him first, and then I got on and gave him my scattered impressions of New York City in one long breath. He said he was glad I liked it as well as I did. He thought out of everybody, I'd like it the least, but I don't think he was really happy about it. He was counting on me not to like it, to be on his side about those green hills. He told me to put Lizzy on after that because Garta and Jimmy were over there watching a John Wayne movie with him, waiting to talk to her.

Elena and I didn't even have to try to hear what Garta had to say. We could have been standing out on the curb and we would have heard her.

"YOU ALL RIGHT?" she yelled.

"Yeah," Lizzy answered.

"YOU DIDN'T SPEND ALL YOUR MONEY YET, DID YOU?"

"No."

"WELL, DON'T, 'CAUSE I AIN'T SENDING YOU ANY MORE."

Lizzy pressed her eyes shut in a wince, and a moment of silence passed between them. "Mom," she whispered shakily, "if Lana stays here and so do Maddie and Elena, I want to stay here too." I could tell by the look on her face that it took all her courage to utter those words.

"WHO SAID LANA WANTS YOU?" Garta yelled back.

Lizzy licked her lips nervously and before she spoke again, she cupped her hand over the phone and pressed herself against the glass. "She said I was her daughter," she whispered.

"YEAH, WELL, YOU AIN'T, SO GET THAT OUT OF YOUR PEA BRAIN."

Lizzy took a deep breath anyway and spoke the most difficult words she'd ever spoken. "I want to stay with Lana." She pressed her eyes shut after that, and her breathing grew so rackety, I could only imagine how hard her heart was banging inside her chest.

Garta took a loud deep breath and exhaled. "LEO WANTS TO TALK TO LANA, SO PUT HER ON, SHITHEAD."

Lizzy and I hovered around the booth trying to listen to what Lana said, but for the sound of the traffic, we couldn't hear a word. After a few minutes we retreated to a closed-up storefront and leaned our backs against the metal window grates and waited for her, the anxiety filling up in us like smoke. Lizzy's eyes drifted down the light-hazy block and came to rest on the distant waters of the Hudson River, where a few ships slipped past in silence. Her lips moved soundlessly, and when she tilted her head back and gazed up at the foggy sky, I knew that under her breath she had just spoken a prayer. She moved her lips close to my ear and I felt her warm breath. "Are you kind of scared?" she asked. I nodded, and when I turned and glanced at her I saw the fear rise in her eyes like a tide. I understood in some hazy, distant way that this trip meant something deeper and more significant to her than it did to me. Mine had been a race forward into Lana's arms. Hers had been that too, but it was also a desperate flight from Garta. For that reason, Lana's shaky life scared her more than it scared me, and it scared me plenty.

"You won't leave me, will you, Maddie?" she whispered in my ear. Her voice was so tiny, yet it came directly from her heart like a small, sweet wind.

"No, Lizzy," I said.

We met Mimi after that by a little market with flowers, not more than a few blocks away from the phone booth. A yellow cab pulled up to the corner, and the back window rolled down. "Lana," she yelled, sticking her head out the window, "let's take this cab uptown." She had an accent, though I didn't know what kind. "Pile in, kids," she yelled to us. She was wearing a peach crepe suit, which buttoned all the way to her neck, and her hair was exactly as Lana had described it in her journal—dyed black and so starched and stiff, a tornado could not have moved it. Her face was so old and wrinkled, it looked like she was a hundred years old. She tried to cover it up with light brown cream and a whole layer of beige powder, but it showed through anyway. Her eyelids were streaked with two different shades of blue eye shadow that went all the way up to her black, penciled-in eyebrows, and she wore lipstick the color of frosted bubble gum.

Lana hurried us over to the cab and opened the door. "Be nice now," she whispered, digging her thumbs into our backs. Mimi shoved over, and Lizzy, Elena, and I crawled in, Lizzy ending up sitting next to Mimi. Lana climbed in the front seat with Harry, and as soon as she pulled the door closed, Mimi said loudly, "Sixtieth and Park," and the cab lurched away from the curb. There was a considerable amount of traffic out on the streets, and the air was choked with fumes. The sky was almost completely dark too, as if all the exhaust had drifted up and dirtied it.

Mimi reached across Lizzy and patted Elena's leg, her beige nylons scratching noisily against one another. "You must be Elena," she said loudly. She talked almost as loudly as Garta. "She looks more like you than Leo," she called up to Lana. "Thank God." She grabbed the back of the front seat and pulled herself forward. "Harry's the one that looks like Leo, but we love him anyway."

"Mimi," Lana said coldly. It sounded like a warning.

Mimi leaned back in the seat and turned to me. "You must be Maddie," she said, patting my knee. "She looks more like you than any of them," she yelled up to Lana. She acted as if we either couldn't hear or couldn't talk, as if we were just photographs or something.

Lana turned her head and glanced back at Lizzy. "Mimi, this is Lizzy," she said.

Mimi finally acknowledged Lizzy's presence. "Hello, Miss Lizzy," she said. She smiled and revealed a set of white dentures. "You must be Maddie's little friend." Lizzy shrank from her and pressed closer to Elena.

"How do you girls like Lana's haircut?" Mimi said. Both Elena and I started to open our mouths, but she cut us off. "I think it's a shame, beautiful, long curls, and she cuts them off. Pretty soon it's going to turn gray, and then you'll be sorry."

An uncomfortable silence settled inside the cab, and Mimi turned her head and stared out the open window at the clogged traffic. She touched her finger to her chin, and I noticed the huge diamond ring she wore. It was the size of an M&M and gleamed like a star. She made her money on Negro whores, I thought, on girls like Lizzy.

Elena pinched my thigh, and when I looked at her she shifted her eyes to the left, to point out Mimi, and then rolled them up to the ceiling, where she fluttered her eyelashes. Lizzy leaned across Elena and whispered, "Elena was trying on your bra," and we all started laughing again.

Mimi turned and looked at us. "What are they laughing about?" she asked Lana.

"I don't know," Lana said. "They've got their secrets." She glanced over her shoulder at Mimi and rolled her eyes.

Mimi said, "I wonder where they got that from," and we started laughing even harder.

Somehow that put Mimi on our side, because after that she started talking to us instead of talking to us through Lana. We shared the same frustration — Lana's secrecy.

We took the cab up to Park Avenue and went inside a posh restaurant called Antoinette's. All the tables were covered with thick, white linen tablecloths, and each had a small vase of red roses on top. The floor was black marble, and pink stone columns rose out of it like slender trees. We'd never heard of anything on the menu, so Lana ordered for us.

A thin, dark-haired waiter brought us each a bowl of cold, horrible soup, and while we ate it Mimi started to pick on Lana's dress. "It's a rag," she whispered. "Where did you get it? Macy's basement?"

"Hardy, har, har, Mimi," Lana said. She closed her eyes to summon her patience and wiped her damp brow with a napkin.

"Why don't I take you all over to Bloomingdale's and buy you a couple of dresses. The girls look like they could use some too," she said. "Elena," she whispered, "don't put your elbows on the table. Not in here."

Elena's elbows dropped to her side, and while I slipped mine off the table I reminded myself that this woman had once run a whorehouse and couldn't write any better than a second grader.

"We don't need any new dresses," Lana said. "And besides, Mimi, you don't have the money."

"I've got a pension," Mimi said defensively.

"They don't have pensions in your line of work," Lana insisted.

"What was your line of work, Mimi?" Elena asked. Lizzy and I kicked her under the table.

A flush stole up Lana's face when Mimi answered, "I was in hair and makeup."

The dinner was slowly but surely deteriorating. When Lana got up to use the bathroom, Elena at least tried to make it worthwhile. She leaned across the table and asked Mimi, "What happened to Lana?"

Mimi turned around and glanced over her shoulder to make sure Lana wasn't on her way back. She turned back to us, and just as her eyes shimmered and her lips formed around a word, I saw Lana come out of the bathroom.

"Lana's coming," I whispered.

Mimi slid her hands off the table and leaned back in her chair, and we all went silent. When Lana sat down she knew something had happened. We were too quiet, and no matter how hard we tried not to, we all looked guilty, especially Mimi.

"What's going on, you guys?" she asked us again. When no one said anything, she immediately turned to Elena. "What are you doing, Elena?" she said.

"Nothing," Elena said.

Lana's eyes swept past me and Lizzy and landed on Mimi. "What are you doing, Mimi?" she said.

Mimi looked up at her, completely undaunted, and locked eyes with her. "Sit down, Lana," she said. "Take a load off your feet, will you. I'm not doing anything. We were just talking about Leo. The girls were just wondering what's going to happen. They're not stupid. They can see your apartment isn't big enough for them to live there permanently."

Lana believed her and sank down to her chair. The subject of Leo depressed her, though. "I know," she said wearily. "It's too small in there, but I don't know what we're going to do. I have to talk to Leo about it, but—" Panic spread across her face, and she stopped speaking for a moment. She brushed her fingers nervously across her forehead, her eyes narrowing on Mimi's face. "I don't want to talk about this now, Mimi." Her voice was hard and tense. "The girls haven't even been here six hours yet. Can't we just relax for one night without bringing it all up?"

Mimi nodded and patted Lana's hand, and the tension lifted from our table like a morning fog.

When we left the restaurant, the sky overhead was dark and teeming with swift black clouds, but Mimi still insisted that we go to Central Park. We took a cab over there, and while Mimi and Lana edged along the wide sidewalks, talking softly, Elena, Lizzy, Harry, and I ran ahead of them. We didn't know what they were talking about, but judging from Lana's torn-up expression, we guessed Mimi had brought up the subject of Leo again.

It started to get under my skin, this business about Lana and Leo and what they were going to do with us, and when I looked from Lana's dark expression up to the sooty black clouds, I felt my thin armor of peace melt away. As if someone threw a switch, my nerves came awake immediately—it was such a sudden shock that I dropped to my knees in the grass. In their mad panic, my nerves raced into my heart and lungs and all but stopped my breathing. It felt like the moment when Lizzy and I had opened Minnie Harp's door to utter blackness, except there was nothing terrifying like that. I was kneeling on velvety green grass, with huge old trees soaring above me.

"What's wrong, Maddie?" Lana asked me, helping me to my feet. "What happened?"

"Nothing," I said, though she knew from my eyes that I was lying. They were huge and bulging, I felt, and I couldn't keep them still. I slipped away from her, running ahead, and caught up to Lizzy, where I jogged lightly by her side, breathing like an asthmatic. I longed for Durga, and when I remembered she was underneath my bed, my nerves surged forward inside, spreading through me, as if I had sprung a thousand leaks. What was I going to do about them? I wondered. The life-saving potion was no good without Durga, and I didn't have anything else. Fear spilled into my heart, and when I glanced up at the blackening sky, my head began to throb.

"So what do you want to do, Maddie?" Elena whispered. She

looked over her shoulder to make sure Lana couldn't hear us. "Do you want to stay here, or do you want to go back to Leo?"

Her question rattled me even more. I glanced nervously around me, at the crowded benches and sidewalks, and my nerves swept through me again, like an invasion. The traffic boiled out in the street, filling the air with the sound of chaos, and when I stared up at the menacing sky, I felt a knot as big as a fist lodge in my heart.

"I don't know."

"I think I want to stay here," Elena whispered. "If she'll really let us. I think it's better here. We belong here, not in those hills."

I longed for those peaceful, green hills. "Maybe they'll get back together," I said. That was the only solution I could bear to think about.

"I doubt it," she said.

We left the park not too long afterward. Mimi invited us up to her apartment, but Lana declined, so we took a cab down to Greenwich Village.

On our ride home, Elena whispered, "I bet you anything she's going to send us back. She's going to tell us her apartment's too small, and she's going to send us back."

This drove me over the edge. Not only could I not breathe right anymore, but now I couldn't see very well either. The world looked blurry to me, and when I climbed the five flights of stairs up to Lana's apartment, I felt as if I were on shaky, trembling ground. The walls seemed to breathe, to pulse in and out of focus, and with each rocky step I felt myself coming more and more unglued.

When we got upstairs, Elena, Lizzy, and I lay side by side on our mattresses, our hands behind our heads, eyeballing the ceiling above us, half listening to Harry's sweet, untroubled voice as he sang, "The itsy bitsy spider climbed up the waterspout," from the bathroom where Lana was giving him a bath. After a while, Lizzy whispered, "Elena was trying on your bra," and she and Elena cracked up laughing again, but my nerves had taken control of me so completely, I couldn't even smile.

"What's wrong?" Lizzy said, because I usually laughed the loudest.

"Yeah, what's wrong?" Elena said. She pulled her sandal off her right foot and threw it at me. It landed on my stomach, but I could only stare at it.

I wanted desperately to flee, but there was no place to go. I longed for the attic, for the sanctuary of that red overstuffed chair where I could open the window and rest my eyes on the still, enduring hills. I yearned for the sound of Leo's piano drifting up to me from the living room, for the sound of Lana's typewriter punctuating the lazy, night air. I wanted the sweet breeze to linger over me, for the leaves to rustle in the highest branches in soft, muted applause. I ached to hear the sound of children playing frozen tag in the neighbor's backyard, of canned laughter spilling out of opened windows. I wanted to hear the stray bark of somebody's dog, the name of someone being called in after dark.

The sounds outside of Lana's window weren't singular enough. They were an indistinguishable din, stung every now and then by the desperate whine of an ambulance siren.

"Lana," Elena yelled, "Maddie's gone weird again."

"No, I didn't," I said. "I've got a headache." It was true—on top of everything else my head was pounding.

When Lana finally shut off the lights and crawled into bed, my nerves came out like a pack of wolves. Lizzy and Elena fell asleep almost instantly, and while I waited for Lana's breathing to grow long, I listened to the soft rustle of the rice paper curtains as they moved lazily in the breeze. My eyes roamed the unfamiliar walls, lingering on the new patterns of light, drifting over to the closet door again and again where those silver cans of film had now gained a force of their own. As if they were radioactive, I could feel them inside the closet, breathing and emitting light.

I reached for the life-saving potion and piled three handfuls onto my stomach. I had no appetite whatsoever, so it was painful to keep swallowing mouthful after mouthful of the stuff. My nerves were crawling around in my stomach, setting small fires, the flames of which were high enough to scorch my heart.

When I finished eating it, my head throbbed more, and I felt so sick to my stomach that I worried I might puke. It hadn't done anything to calm my nerves down either. They were now so completely out of control, I doubted even Durga could have done anything.

A streak of lightning lit up the room in a pale, ghostly white, and a crack of thunder splintered the silence. It had been building up to this all evening, I remembered, but when I heard the mad rush of rain, panic seized me again. The bucket, I remembered. I had forgotten to tell Leo about the bucket in the attic. It could be raining up in the hills now too, I realized, and if it were coming down as hard as it was here, there was no hope for the kitchen ceiling. It would burst, and Leo would kill me.

A sick wave of nausea swept through me, and I raced across the room. I pushed open the bathroom door and dropped to my knees in front of the toilet, just moments before my stomach made a tumultuous heave. The rain pounded down on the rooftop above me, and I retched again and then once more before I collapsed on the cold, dark tiles. Tears fell from my eyes and wounded cries escaped from deep inside me. I felt all torn up, and my mind reeled in confusion, those steams and vapors racing in the blackness. The bucket was overflowing and Lana was speaking on stages behind our backs, and still we didn't know what had happened to her.

I pressed my eyes into my kneecaps and plugged my mouth up with the hem of my nightgown, but it didn't help. Something larger than myself had wrested control of me, and I was powerless against my grief. My eyes burned with tears, and my sobs grew so loud, I turned on the faucets full blast to drown myself out. I fixed my eyes straight ahead on the cold, steel pipe underneath the sink and cried out those Hindu words. *"Namo arihantanum,"* I sobbed. *"Namo siddhanum. Namo ovajjyanum."*

I can't be sure how long Lana stood in the doorway watching me— long enough for the shock to have registered on her face. "Maddie," she gasped. She reached over and slammed the faucets off and then dropped down to her knees. "What are you saying?" she said. "What are those . . . *words?"* The sound of them had terrified her, just as they had terrified me when Miss Thomas had first spoken them.

I looked up into her blazing eyes, and I told her. "My nerves," I sobbed. "My nerves are so bad." I had to tell her. I had to tell someone. They had finally driven me to the brink.

"What nerves, sweetheart?" Her hands raced over my face, her eyes swallowing me up.

"They're bad because I left Durga home," I cried. I tried to still myself, but I couldn't. The sobs kept coming out of me, as if I'd pulled the plug to some fathomless well.

Lana slammed the toilet cover down and thrust her hands under my armpits and hauled me up. She dropped to her knees beneath me, her eyes roving my face like hot searchlights. She was utterly mystified. She had no idea what was going on, and I think for a few awful moments, she thought I had lost my mind.

"Maddie, what are you talking about?" she yelled. "What's Durga and what are those words?"

"Miss Thomas gave me Durga for my nerves," I wailed, "but I left her under my bed, and now my nerves are everywhere." I could feel them bolting through me like wild horses.

"She taught you those words?" Lana said. Her thumbs were on my cheeks, furiously brushing away the flood of my fears.

"They're Hindu," I cried, "but they don't help if I don't have Durga and her arms."

"Her arms?" she said. She couldn't imagine.

"She's got eight," I sobbed. I remembered the attic then and the imminent explosion in the kitchen, and a new wave of anxiety overcame me. "The bucket," I cried.

"What bucket?" she asked, creeping even closer to me.

"There's a big leak in the attic," I wailed, "and Leo doesn't know about it." I pushed my arms into my stomach and pressed forward. When I looked up at her, I realized she was completely lost. She had no idea who I was anymore, nor could she imagine all I had done. Her secrets swept through my mind like a hurricane—Mimi, her whorehouse, Effy, the films—and I lost my reason.

"Why do you have those films?" I cried.

"What films?" she said. Her thumbs worked overtime on my cheeks, wiping away my tears.

"The ones in the back of your closet," I said, pressing my arms against my crawling stomach.

"Mimi kept them for me from a long, long time ago," she said. A cloud passed over her expression.

"You don't go on that stage anymore?"

A stark look of horror washed over her face. "What stage, Maddie?" The sound of her voice, hard and tense, came as a shock, and the chilling look on her face cut through my misery and brought me around. The sobs caught in the back of my throat, and I went silent. Our eyes locked, and as shudders coursed through me, I wished to God I had never said that. It had escaped into the rain-soaked air, never to be retrieved, and I knew somehow things would never be the same. My stomach heaved again, and I leaned over and puked in the small sink.

Lana stood up and banged the bathroom door open. Elena and Lizzy were standing outside, huddled in the darkness. I pressed forward in my lap and watched them, my heart beating like the wings of a moth.

"What did you do, Elena?" Lana yelled.

"Nothing," Elena said defensively. She backed away from Lana, Lizzy following after her, and even in the hazy darkness, I saw her face turn a miserable white.

Lana pursued her across the room, her white nightgown sweeping after her. "Goddamn it, Elena. You did something and I want to know what it was."

Elena knocked into the mattress and sat down, Lizzy drifting down to her side. I saw the rain pour down outside the opened windows, the rice paper curtains flapping in the wind.

"How does Maddie know about those films?" Lana yelled. A streak of lightning lit up her enraged face in an eerie flash of white.

"They're in your closet," Elena yelled. Her fingers pulled at each other in her lap, and her legs pumped madly.

"How does Maddie know about stages, Elena?" Lana insisted. A hoarse rasp sounded in her voice, and when she took another step forward, I thought she was going to slap Elena's face.

"I don't know," Elena cried. She dug her bare heels into the floor and heaved one of Lizzy's shoes across the room. It hit on the edge of the bathroom doorway, just inches from my face.

Lana reached down and grabbed Elena's chin and yanked it up. "How does she know, Elena?" Her teeth were clenched, her voice was fierce, and as if her anger had fingers I felt it claw the air.

She dug her thumb into Elena's chin, and I heard Elena's small quavering voice. "We saw your films." Her eyes were huge and filled with fear.

"What else?" Lana demanded to know.

Elena's eyes shifted and sank into me like fishhooks. I felt my guilt as if it had tentacles which reached up and choked my throat. These were not Elena's sins alone—they were mine as well. In fact most of them were mine. I lurched up and stumbled across the room and sank down on the edge of the mattress next to Elena. I felt her stiffen, and when she moved away from me, my stomach heaved again.

"We read one of your journals," I said. My voice was high and washed-out and choked with post-sob shudders.

Lana teetered back and forth, as if she might faint, and stared first at me, then at Elena. "What did you read?" She looked shocked and hurt, betrayed even.

"About Mimi and her whorehouse and Effy," I said quietly, though I don't know how I could have spoken the words. My throat pinched off, and I felt my heart flap inside my chest like it was coming undone.

Something went through Lana then—a wave of shock, a dark invisible knife, I don't know what, but she straightened up and staggered across the dark room to her mattress where Harry was still sleeping. She bent over and turned on the lamp, and I noticed how much her hands shook. We all watched as she stumbled over to her closet and took out a pair of dark pants and a white blouse. She slung them over her arm and then disappeared into the bathroom.

Elena turned to me and gave me the vilest look. "You've got a big fucking mouth, Maddie," she said.

I glanced over at Lizzy. She turned away from me and stared down at her bare feet.

"I didn't tell her we saw the film," I whispered. It was a pathetic thing to utter, but I didn't know what else to say.

"We heard you, Maddie," Elena whispered fiercely. "You asked her if she went on the stage anymore." She bore down on me with her eyes, and I turned away from her.

I felt forsaken, and when the wind blew against my back, I shivered violently. She didn't understand what had happened to me, I thought. Neither did Lizzy. They had no idea about nerves or what they drove you to do. "I was going nuts," I whispered, as if that might help me.

"You are nuts, Maddie," Elena said in disgust. "You're just like Lana. Little Lana," she said. "Little puke-puke Lana."

She stood up and walked over to her mattress, where she threw herself down and pulled the sheet over her head. Lizzy crept back to bed too, and I sat frozen on the edge of the mattress, shaking. I heard the rain outside again, and I remembered the bucket. "The kitchen ceiling probably burst," I whispered, but neither Lizzy nor Elena was speaking to me.

Lana opened the bathroom door and stepped out into the room. She had changed into her pants and blouse, and after she threw her nightgown inside her closet, she slammed her feet into a pair of shoes and grabbed her black umbrella.

"I'm going for a walk," she said. Her voice was stern and filled with angry backbone. She yanked the door open, then closed it loudly behind her and vanished down the stairs. I heard her climb down two flights, and then a minute or so later, I heard the front door bang shut.

I crawled over the mattress and watched out the window as her umbrella passed below. She crossed the street quickly and hurried down the next block, slipping into the phone booth on the corner. I saw her struggling to close the umbrella, and when she finally picked up the telephone, she didn't turn her back like I thought she would. She faced her apartment, and I could almost feel her eyes moving between those top four windows.

"She went into the phone booth," I said. "I bet she's calling Leo."

A moment passed in silence, and then Lizzy scrambled up to the window next to me.

"Where?" she said.

I pointed to the phone booth on the corner, and Lizzy squinted past the sheets of rain to see it.

"She's probably telling him she's sending us home," Lizzy said.

That roused Elena. She threw her sheet off and clambered up to the window, kneeling next to me. Her eyes combed the streets below, and when she found Lana standing in the phone booth, anguish fell across her face like a shadow.

"She'll probably put us back on the bus tomorrow," she said. She pushed her long black hair off her shoulders and leaned out the window, the rain falling on her face. "I don't care, Maddie," she said. "It's better she knows. We can't go through the rest of our lives pretending we don't know anything about her. So who cares?" she yelled out into the night.

"Yeah," Lizzy yelled back, "who cares?"

We all did, but it was easier this way, to merge in defiance. It helped bring us together during a time when it felt like we might fall apart.

"So we'll live in the hills," Elena yelled out the window. *"So what."*

"Yeah, so what?" Lizzy yelled, leaning out the window.

"Who gives a shit?" I yelled too, though there wasn't much left to my voice.

Elena lit up one of her Winston cigarettes, and as we passed it back and forth, blowing the smoke out the window, we watched Lana standing in the phone booth two blocks away. She talked for over a half hour, and when she finally hung up, she didn't walk home like we thought she would—she crossed the street and kept walking. She came home about fifteen minutes later. We heard the angry beat of her footsteps on the stairs and the stabbing clomp of her cane. She was leaning on it hard again, as if all our trespassing had sunk into her hip. When she opened the door, she was out of breath and soaking wet.

"So you've started smoking, Elena," she said, while she slipped her wet shoes off. "That's great, just great." She shot Elena a dirty look and then surged forward to the kitchen. Elena didn't say anything. She just sat on her mattress and stared at her. We all did. Her anger hadn't dwindled much, but it wasn't a shaky anger—it was bold and strong and had a thick spine.

She quickly dried her hair with a towel and slapped the teapot over the fire. Then she stepped behind the closet door and took off her wet clothes. When she reappeared, she was wearing a pair of gray pants and another white blouse. She moved into the kitchen and noisily took down a few cups from the cabinet and set them on the small counter, her hands moving quickly, haphazardly almost.

When the teapot started to whistle, she yanked it off the fire and poured the hot water into our three cups, splashing it all over the place. She pulled out a small tray, banging it against the cupboard door, and slammed it down on the counter, where she recklessly placed those three cups of hot tea. She carried it across the room to the mattress, where she set it down. We watched her hands, but they didn't shake—they didn't even tremble. Her face was white as milk, though, and when her weight fell on her bad hip, she winced. She pushed Harry over, making room for herself, and dropped down to the mattress, stretching her legs out in front of her.

"Come over here," she said in a loud, flat voice. We just stared at her. "Come on," she said again. "Come and drink your tea."

It was hard to read her face just then. It seemed to flicker on and off, to flash conflicting emotions. I saw weariness and misery pass over her, and then warmth seemed to radiate from her. The furrow which lay between her eyebrows deepened, but then she smiled weakly at us, and we didn't know what to think. I felt something churning inside her, though, as if beneath the layer of her skin ran a swift and turbulent river.

"Come on," she ordered us.

I finally got up and moved quietly across the room and sank down at the foot of the mattress. Lizzy followed and sat down next to me, and while we all watched Elena, she made her way over to us almost soundlessly. Lana drew her legs up and rotated them to the side, wedging a pillow behind her head. She pushed her wet hair from her forehead and took a long, thoughtful sip of tea. A few moments passed in utter silence, and when she rested the cup on her hip, she finally spoke. "I think you guys are too young for me to tell you what happened to me, but Leo said he thought I should tell you. And it seems now that I have no other choice." A vague smile appeared on her lips, but it vanished almost immediately. "I hoped I could tell you when you were much older, but—" Her voice trailed off. She took a quick sip of tea, and when she put it down, lightning tore up the sky again, and a clap of thunder split open the silence. "Elena," she said, "give me one of your cigarettes."

Elena got up and walked over to her mattress where she pulled a pack of cigarettes out of her suitcase. She handed them over to Lana, and after Lana shook one out, Elena lighted it for her. She took a few long drags and watched the gray-blue smoke fan out into the air. "I guess you know I was a singer and a dancer at a club called Sammy's," she said. Her foot tapped against the mattress like a nervous beat.

We all nodded.

"And you know Leo worked there too."

We nodded again, and for a few moments she stared down at her teacup, her eyes hardening around the edges. When she looked up, her eyes were so depthless and pained I had to look away for a few moments. "I'll tell you what happened to me," she said sternly, "but I'm only going to tell it once. And after I do, I don't want to ever speak of it again. Do you hear me?"

We nodded again, and after she searched our faces, she hurled her gaze out the window, where the rain continued to fall and the wind tugged on those fragile, rice paper curtains. Her foot tapped against the mattress, as if it alone drove her forward, and when her fingers gripped Elena's cigarette I knew she didn't want to tell us this. A minute or more passed, the time clawing through us—we hung there, barely breathing, just waiting for her. When she finally looked up at us, her eyes were so large and distant, I knew she had somehow transported herself back in time. She opened her mouth then, and though it hardly seemed possible, she told us everything.

It was May 10, 1959, she said quietly. She was in her dressing room at Sammy's, a small room with dirty white walls and gray concrete floors. A dressing table stood up against one wall, a rack of her costumes up against another, and a good-sized window at the far end of the room opened to a back alley. She hung her black suit in the clothes rack, placing it between her costumes so Leo wouldn't notice it. She was going to speak after the show tonight, and she didn't want Leo to know until it was absolutely necessary.

She sat down in the blue chair in front of her dressing table and lit one of Irene's Pall Mall cigarettes. She was Lana's hairdresser, and she was such a chain-smoker she left a pack of cigarettes in every dressing room. Irene poked her head inside the door. "You got a half hour, baby," she said. A yellow pencil was pushed behind her dark ear, her curly black hair pressed under a red turban.

"Okay," Lana said, glancing down at her watch.

"They're lined up around the block tonight, sugar. White and Negro. More than last night even," Irene gushed. "You're gonna have to sing 'em sweet tonight, child."

They've come to see the white lady sing like a Negro, Lana thought. She knew she wasn't a great singer, not nearly as good as some of the Negro women who used to sing at the Apollo, but the people wanted to see what she looked like. They wanted to see what went on after the show, when she spoke and riled up the crowds. She never deluded herself about that. Maybe it was a lucky thing, she thought. Things were different than they used to be. There were hardly any jazz clubs anymore. Mimi's had gone under almost ten years ago, and Sammy's only hung around because he had her on the weekends. Everything was changing. The air was charged with something new, something she wasn't sure about.

She threw her cigarette out the window and sat down at her dressing table and lit another one. She could hear the crowd outside. The sound of them was building, and she wondered who'd be out there tonight. Last night a white man turned up at a center table, and two songs into the first set, he yelled, "Leave the business of niggers with the niggers." Spears, the bouncer, hauled him out, but still.

She wasn't sure why, but white men couldn't bear the idea of a

woman trying to lead men. Somehow, it was the same thing as Negroes telling them what to do.

She slipped her foot into a black stocking and rolled it up her leg.
Why did she keep doing it, she wondered? She smiled when she
remembered the time someone had asked her why she felt so much
for the Negroes, and she'd told them, "In a former life, I was a slave."
He'd laughed, but she often thought it was true. The feeling was so
strong in her, she imagined it had to be something like that.

Leo walked in and sat down in the small chair across from her.
He was dressed in his white shirt and black vest. His legs were
already filling with energy, starting to work. "Jesus, it's really crowding up out there, La," he said. He shook one of Irene's cigarettes out
of the pack and lit it with a gold lighter he fished out of his pocket.
His eyes fell on Lana's black suit hanging on the costume rack. She
hadn't hidden it well enough—the sleeve was sticking out. His back
stiffened.

"You're planning on going out there tonight," he said, lifting the
pants up.

"I was thinking about it," she said. She put her foot into the other
stocking and rolled it up her leg.

He stood up and raked his fingers through his curly brown hair.
"Jesus, La," he said, "I can't believe this." He started to pace in
front of the costume rack, his blue eyes filling with poison. "This is
getting out of hand," he yelled.

Lana stood up and brushed past him stiffly and grabbed a purple
costume dress with black sequins off the rack behind him. "You're
making a lot of money here, Leo," she said sternly. "If I didn't go
out there and speak, we might be out of jobs."

"Do you think I give a shit about that?" he yelled.

She glanced up at him and raised her eyebrows in a look that said,
"Yes." He would never understand, she realized. Never. I shouldn't
have married him, she thought. I shouldn't have married. A woman
like me should never have gotten married.

She walked over to the door and opened it a crack. "Irene," she
yelled. "I'm ready for you."

Leo walked up behind her, pushed the door closed and leaned his
arm against it, hemming her in. "It's got to stop somewhere, Lana,"
he said. The cigarette was still clenched between his teeth, and his
right eye was closed against the smoke.

"Why?" she said.

He pulled the cigarette out of his mouth. "Because this is not the kind of thing you should be doing," he yelled loudly. "That's why."

He pointed his cigarette at her, and she slipped it out from between his fingers and pushed it into her mouth. She ducked under his arm. "Why," she shouted, "because I'm a woman?"

"Yes, precisely," he yelled, following on her heels. "Because you're a woman, a beautiful fucking woman, Lana. Do you think those men in the audience are listening to you. I'll tell you what they're doing. They're thinking how great it would be if they could lay you down on that stage—that's what they're thinking, La. Believe me. It's dirty work you're doing."

"I wear a suit," she said. They locked eyes for a moment, and no matter how she hated to admit it, she knew somehow it was true— that the men didn't always listen to her, that they had other thoughts.

Leo pushed a space clear on her table and wedged himself in next to her. "This is serious business now," he said. "You can't even walk down the hallway here, because of what you do. I have to lead you back and forth every night because it's not safe anymore for you to walk down a fucking hallway. This is not life, Lana. This is not the life I wanted us to live. Why in the hell do you keep doing it? It's not like anyone is asking you to do it. There's no one out on the street chanting your name. Not one fucking person would lose any sleep if you quit."

She stared at him, her eyes narrowing, her mouth tightening. "Because I feel for it, goddamn it," she yelled. She hit herself hard in the chest with her fist, and Leo moved away from her in disgust.

Irene poked her head in the door. "You ready, baby?"

Lana nodded and Leo stormed out, slamming the door behind him. "I'm not waiting for you," he yelled back to her.

"As if he ever does," Lana whispered.

"He worries about you," Irene said.

"He worries about more than that, Reeny. He worries that I'm bigger than him."

Their eyes met in the mirror and something wordless passed between them. Irene nodded, and they heard a few of the musicians in the next room tuning their horns and laughing. The sounds in the front kept building too, like a boiling pot. "It's gonna smoke out there tonight, baby. You're gonna have to dance them up a tornado."

Lana smiled and slipped three gold bracelets onto each wrist.

When she was dressed, Irene walked her down the hallway where she stood backstage behind the curtain. She pulled it back a little to see what the crowd looked like. They were mostly white, she noticed, which disappointed her. She preferred the Negro crowds. They were looser and things seemed to flow better in their midst. Most of the musicians were on stage, tuning up and putting that first drink in them, including Leo. He was already sitting behind the piano, his sleeves rolled up, a drink in his hand, while he talked with Louie the drummer, and Bertie the sax player. He was laughing, and it irked Lana. The way he slapped his hand down on top of the piano when he thought something was funny really wore on her. She wondered what he was going to do tonight to get even with her, because for all his goodness, he had a bad habit of getting even.

Lana spotted Sammy bustling around, shaking people's hands, giving away drinks, steering people here and there by their elbows. She searched the crowd for Spears. He was standing over in the corner, near the door, talking to a young white woman wearing an off-the-shoulder black dress. He's too impressed with white women, she thought again. She'd have to talk to him about that later.

The lights in the house came down a little, and the stage lights came up. The musicians settled themselves, and Sammy bounded onto the stage, straightening his thin black tie. He looked old now, like a man from another, more gentle time. He grabbed hold of the microphone stand and pulled it toward him, the round base rocking back and forth between his feet. "Welcome to Sammy's," he called out. "We've got a hot night for you up here in Harlem. The Black Notes are here with us . . ."

Lana wondered how much longer they could keep this club going, how much longer they could all drift along on the past. She straightened her back and flapped her arms up and down to get her breathing going. She waited for Sammy's old, tired lines—"and our own Lana Lamar, the only white lady who can sing the blues"—before she parted the curtains and strode onto the stage. As soon as the audience saw her, they erupted in applause. Sammy retreated off the stage, and Lana strutted up to the microphone, taking it off the stand.

"How are you all tonight?" she said loudly. As the audience clapped and whistled, she felt the skin around her mouth stretch taut in the smile Effy had taught her to use. "Thank you for coming all the way up here to Harlem to see us." She turned and nodded to the musicians, careful to avoid eye contact with Leo. "We got some wonderful songs for you tonight, folks," she called out. "We're gonna start off tonight with an old favorite of mine, a George Gershwin song—'Let's Call the Whole Thing Off.' "

The audience applauded again, and while she put the microphone back on the stand, the musicians readied themselves. The lights in the house dimmed, and the spotlight on Lana brightened.

"A one and a two and a—" Leo said.

"You say eether and I say eyether," Lana sang. *"You say neether, and I say nyther. Eether, eyether, neether, nyther—Let's call the whole thing off! You like potato, and I like potahto. You like tomato and I like tomahto. Potato, potahto, tomato, tomahto, . . ."*

Leo was rushing her. She glanced over her shoulder at him and gave him a look with her eyes, keeping her smile intact. He ignored her, so she turned back to the audience and scanned the people in front of her, looking for any unsafe, immovable faces. There was one man who caught her eye. He was sitting alone at one of the front tables, watching her with impassive eyes. He was a tall thin man, somewhere in his early sixties, who had a skinny gray mustache and pencil-thin lips. What was striking about him was the way he just sat there and watched her. He didn't move to the music at all. It was as if he didn't even hear it. He just sat there, and once, ever so faintly, he smiled at her with one side of his mouth. Lana looked away from him after that.

"But oh, if we call the whole thing off," she sang, *"then we must part. And oh, if we ever part, then that might break my heart. So if you like pajamas and I like pajahmas, I wear pajamas, give up pajahmas. For we know, we need each other, so we better call the calling off . . ."*

Leo was dragging it now, so she was obliged to turn around and shoot him another look. He smiled back at her knowingly and winked. The bastard, she thought.

He messed with the next two songs too—"A Sailboat in the Moonlight" and "How Could You?" but when he rolled into the fourth one, "Rockin' My Baby Home," the song he'd written for Elena, he didn't screw around anymore. He played it straight, lighting into the piano, rocking back and forth like he was made to do, while Lana danced. The audience went wild. This is what they came for—to watch her shake and gyrate like a bombshell, to hear her torchy voice ignite the house.

Her eyes caught Leo's, but it was still no good. The high feelings didn't ride between them tonight—only a scratchy silence. She was ready to give it up, but he wasn't. He was giving it to the piano though. His fingers pounded the keys like ten thick mallets.

After they finished the first set, Leo went up to the bar and ordered himself two shots of whiskey, so Spears had to escort Lana down the long dark hallway. He wasn't too happy about it either. He was finally making some headway with the woman wearing the off-the-shoulder black dress, he said. But they didn't want her to walk down the hallway alone, especially not when there had been an incident last night. If only the phones and the bathrooms were someplace else, she thought.

Spears steered her down the hall and checked her dressing room before he headed back. "Nobody in here, Lana, but Irene," he said. When he left, he locked the door behind him. Irene was sitting near the window, smoking a cigarette, her feet propped up on the window-sill. "You guys are cooking tonight," she said.

Lana sat down in front of her dressing table and mopped her sweaty face with the white cotton towel Irene had laid out for her. Leo usually came down, and while Irene fixed Lana's hair they talked about how the first set had gone and went over the songs they were going to do in the second set. He didn't come down, though, nor did he send Spears to get her. Irene had to walk her up front.

Leo was a little drunk when they started the second set. Lana noticed he had brought back another glass of whiskey, which sat on top of the piano. After the show, she decided, she'd tell him to grow up.

They started off with "I Love You, Yes I Do" and "I'm Getting Old Before My Time," like they usually did. Then Leo took it offtrack again and played a couple of Jelly Roll Morton songs. Lana shot him a few dirty looks, but he didn't pay any attention to her. He went ahead and played two of his own songs after that, two high-steppers in a row. He didn't even give her a chance to catch her breath. Then he ended the set with the hardest-driving piece he'd written. It was his favorite, a song he'd written for her shortly after they'd met. "Where Blue Begins," it was called, and it went through more piano riffs than any other song around. Not only was it long—it was fast and unrelenting and by far the most difficult dance number for Lana. It was their last song for the night, so she indulged him and the crowd and gave it all she had, ending it on her knees with her left hand stretched to the rafters. The lights went to black, and the audience broke out in whistles and applause, which was deafening in such tight close quarters. Lana took her bows, and after she clapped for the musicians, she went backstage and waited for someone to walk her down to the dressing room.

She rested up against the wall and caught her breath. The audience was still clapping, and when she heard the band again, she decided she wasn't going back out there. He can forget it, she thought. She pulled the curtain back and glanced out at the stage. Sammy had pulled the lights back up, and the spotlight was on Leo as he moved on the piano like a man possessed. His hair was soaked and sweat streamed down the sides of his face. Let him have his moment in the sun, Lana thought. Our days at this are numbered. She leaned up against the wall and waited for him, but when he finished that song he lit into another. When a third followed, Lana got tired of waiting. She opened the curtains and looked around for Sammy or Spears, but she couldn't see them. The place was jam-packed and dark, and the air was thick with smoke. She noticed the man with the half-smile, though. He was still there, his impassive eyes fixed on Leo.

She stepped out into the hallway and noticed that it was clear, except for one white man using the telephone. He was young, in his twenties, and was pleading with his girlfriend or wife not to be mad at him for not calling until now. He wasn't anyone to worry about, Lana thought. She thought twice about venturing down the hall nonetheless, because there was a slight bend in it, about midway down, and from where she stood you couldn't exactly see who, if anyone, was standing there. She looked down at her watch—Irene had already left.

"Hey," she called out to the young man, "is there anybody down there besides you?"

The young man turned around and looked and then shook his head. "There was someone by the back door a few minutes ago, but they're gone. Why, you looking for someone?"

"No," Lana said.

When she heard Leo light into his fourth song, she started walking down the hallway. Almost immediately her heart began to beat faster, and she told herself to stop being ridiculous. But then again, she remembered the reason why she'd stopped walking down the corridor by herself. There had been too many incidents. She tried not to think about that. She crept along slowly and kept one hand on the wall. Her eyes stretched wide open, and with each step her heart pounded a little faster. Maybe Leo is right, she thought. This is no way to live. You can't even walk down a hallway without fear. She took a deep breath and swallowed. You've faced worse things than a long dark hallway, she told herself, but even so there was something terrifying about it. When she passed the young man and could see that no one lurked in the shadows of that small bend, she eased up. And when she saw that the back door was closed, she got hold of herself. It wasn't bolted, she noticed, but it was closed. There was still a ways to go, she reminded herself—some eight doors down, and she hadn't made it yet. She held her breath and passed the first three; but before she went on, she slipped her shoes off. Nothing like the sound of heels scraping on the concrete to let someone know a woman was coming.

She passed by the fourth door, then the fifth, her heart thudding inside her chest. This is a hell of a way to live, she thought. When she passed the sixth door and then the seventh, the idea left her thoughts. After she sailed into her dressing room and locked the door behind her, she completely forgot about it.

She checked behind her costume rack to make sure no one was in the room before she unzipped her purple dress and let it drop to the floor. She pulled out her black suit and draped it over the back of the chair. She'd go out as soon as the band stopped playing.

She noticed Irene's Pall Mall cigarettes were still on her dressing table. She took one and lit it before she sank down into her dark blue chair. When she started to rub her knee, she heard the band stop playing. She listened to the faraway sound of applause, and when another song didn't follow right away, she guessed they'd finally quit. She wasn't looking forward to the moment Leo walked through the door. He would be drunk, and she would have to hear it all over again.

She turned the chair around and started taking her hair down, pulling the three irises out first. She could save them if she put them in water, she thought. She could wear them again on Tuesday. She heard the band members out in the hallway, and she braced herself for Leo's drunken arrogance. One of them must have needed air because she heard the back door open and then close. She laid the irises down next to the ashtray where her cigarette sat burning, and when she looked up in the mirror, she saw the door break open behind her. She heard it too—a clean crack. Immediately fear pumped through her heart, and she grabbed the purple dress off the floor and clutched it against her. She expected to see Leo, but instead four or five Negro men rushed in. At first she thought it was Spears and some of his friends, that he'd come to check on her. She even spoke his name. "Spears," she said, but Spears wasn't there. They rushed at her so quickly, so furiously, she didn't know exactly how many there were. She had two seconds, no more, to stand up and scream. She made it to her feet, but just as she was about to cry out a hand lunged out from behind her and clamped down on her mouth, pushing her down and yanking her head back brutally. She twisted to see who it was, but he held her so tightly, she couldn't see him. As they swarmed around her she kicked at them violently, swinging her arms as they latched onto her, slugging the one who was barking out the orders—the talker. "Get her arms," he whispered savagely, and suddenly her arms were thrown behind her back, where she felt them tearing loose from her shoulders. He had no front teeth—his mouth was like a roaring black hole, and one of his eyes was yellow with pus. Fear, like poison, fled through her body—her eyes bolted open, her heart banged maniacally, and she couldn't breathe fast enough through her nose. She was suffocating. What's happening, what's happening? Goddamn it, stop it, she screamed, but it came out as a high-pitched sound and nothing more.

A tall, thin Negro with cuts all over his face was standing by the door, looking out, whispering feverishly every few seconds, "Come on, man. *Come on*," while the talker barked out another command, "Take her legs," he yelled, shoving another one forward. "Get her legs." Another Negro man appeared from behind and grabbed Lana's kicking legs and clamped them under his arms. His hands were shaking uncontrollably and she noticed the black fear in his eyes. He was no more than nineteen or twenty years old. He had one dead eye, and his head was shaved bald. Did she know him, did she know him? she wondered violently. Fear was so thick it blotted out her thoughts.

They quickly lifted her off the chair, into the air, and the one who did all the talking kicked it out of the way. Lana screamed shrilly, wildly behind the man's hand, but it was nothing—a muted note. What she heard was Leo's piano playing her song, "Where Blue Begins," the piano sliding up and down in a chilling, unforgettable chorus. She kicked her legs furiously, her upper torso heaving back and forth, as if she could wriggle free of their gripping hands. The one who held her arms back yanked them so hard, so violently she felt her right shoulder break. His dark face contorted evilly, the scar across his cheek twisting, while the pain ripped through her like shrapnel. They moved her wildly across the room, the black ceiling racing by in a rocky, hellish blur, the talker screaming, "Hurry the fuck up," while the tall, thin one at the door kept yelling, "Come on, come on, man. *Jesus, come on.*" Lana's eyes bulged in horror, her heart beating recklessly, perilously, like it might tear through her chest. This can't be happening, her mind screamed. Words, words, flying through her thoughts. This can't be, this can't be. It can't be. Stop. Stop. Stop. Goddamn it STOP, while Leo's piano pounded in the background, like an evil, vile, revolting beat which drove this shattering thing forward.

The one who held her legs lost a grip on them for a moment, and Lana kicked him brutally, her heels slamming into his sides. "Come on, man, help me," he yelled to the talker.

"Just break her legs, boy," the talker screamed. Sweat was beading up on his forehead, sliding down his black face. "Mr. Williams say to break her legs."

"How?" the one who held her legs yelled. He was so nervous, his head started twitching off to the right, his legs buckling underneath him.

"Pull them the F apart," the talker yelled. He reached over and slapped the scared one's face.

"We should do her first," the one who held her mouth raced to say. She still couldn't see him, but his hand was digging so deeply into her jaw that she could feel the bones in his fingers. The one who held her arms said, "Yeah, don't want to do no one with broken legs." The talker laughed, so did the one who held her mouth. Wild, sick, cringing laughter.

Lana's heart started working like a red-hot piston, slamming up and down, up and down, a horrible, deathly black passing in front of her eyes. Her mind was screaming, help me, help me—words, all kinds of words—stop, help, why, God, Leo. She could hardly breathe anymore, and her shoulders were screaming in pain. They raced past the window and then threw her down on the floor, her head cracking down on the concrete, where she writhed and squirmed like a fish thrown on dry ground. She screamed too, stripping her throat bare, but the one who held her mouth never let go. The sound went nowhere but back into her body, where it ricocheted past her heart, through her soul.

Lana stopped speaking. For a few long moments she sat paralyzed, her mouth frozen open, her eyes moving back and forth in small tremors, as if something horrible were unreeling in her mind. We just sat there and watched the horror race past her eyes.

"Go first, boy," the talker said to the one who held her legs, but he didn't want to.

"You go," he yelled back. His lips trembled and sweat dripped off his forehead, falling onto Lana's black shredded-up stockings.

The talker hauled off and slapped his face. "Go now, man," he yelled. "You fuck, go now."

He rushed around and grabbed hold of Lana's legs, yanking them apart, clamping her right leg under his knee, holding the other one down with his hands. The scared one stepped back and unzipped his pants with violently quaking hands, while the one who clamped her mouth reached down and ripped her underwear off—the sound of it cut through their voices like an earsplitting shriek. "Hurry the fuck up. Hurry the fuck up," the guard kept yelling in maddening counterpoint to Leo's eerie, ticking piano, while the one who held her arms down pulled them up so high in back of her, something snapped in her left shoulder. The pain was deafening, and a horrible moan flooded out of her throat.

"Shut up," the one who held her mouth said, and he kicked her skull with the toe of his shoe, until the network of black pipes overhead went completely out of focus.

"Don't kick her, man," the scared one yelled. The talker impatiently motioned him with a quick jerk of his head. "Come on," he yelled, while the guard stamped his foot and screamed, "Fucking get going asshole." The scared one dropped down on the floor between her legs and thrust himself into her, pumping five or six times, careful not to lay down on top of her, while the talker pushed her legs further and further apart. The scared one kept his eyes

closed and held himself up on his arms, pushing his head back as far as he could. The one who held her mouth started goading him on. "Fuck her man, fuck her," he chanted wildly. "Just fuck her, boy. Pound her man, pound that cunt. Pound that cunt." It helped the scared one to keep going—his face alternately twisted between pain and pleasure, his neck writhing back and forth on his shoulders. Lana's mind went wild. Oh my God, oh my God, No, no, no-ooooooooooooo, she screamed. Her spine crunched against the concrete floor everytime he slammed into her. Her legs were screaming in pain, her shoulders too. It was so grotesque, so unspeakably sordid, so vile and inhuman, so filthy and bestial, and finally so completely incomprehensible, she felt her sanity bend and then snap. "Slam that pussy, boy," the talker cried. "Slam it hard. Give it to her, boy. Fuck that white pussy. Fuck that cunt." Lana saw him over the scared one's shoulder. He loomed there like a piece of horror— a cold, rotten piece of horror. His mouth was like a black hole, and his eye oozed with yellow pus. She couldn't breathe anymore. She was suffocating, her lungs inflated with fire inside her wrecked chest. She tried to move, to writhe, to fight, to claw, to dig, to murder, but three of them were holding her down. They all went silent—the only sound was Lana's strangled, muted screams, sounding thin, concealed behind thick winds, and the sound of Leo's piano playing Lana's song—a vicious, insidious tick, tick, tick. Her jaw and her shoulders burned, the tendons in her crotch pulling away thread by thread. Her mind was screaming with words, words, futile words, her throat now burned and torn to shreds. The pain was unbearable, and black kept racing past her eyes like streams of death.

Lana managed to free one of her hands and clawed at the scared one's face, cutting him just under his dead eye, her arm rigid, her fingers like spastic hooks. The one who held her mouth kicked her skull again, the scared one yelling, "Don't kick her. I said, don't kick her, man." He jumped up, and after he shoved himself back into his pants the one who clamped her mouth shut switched places with him, the guard yelling, "Hurry the fuck up. Hurry the fuck up." In the time it took for them to make the change off, one long shriek fled from Lana's scorched throat, but for the sounds of Leo's hellbent piano, it went unheard.

She would never forget the next one. He was white. He had a scar over his nose and greasy blond hair that hung down over eyes so bestial, they were searing. He tore his pants down, as if he couldn't get them off fast enough, and he scrambled down on the concrete floor between her legs, the talker yanking them apart again. While he stabbed into her, he laid on top of her, his face not more than three inches from her own, his breath the smell of *stale rum. "I'll fuck you," he whispered fiercely, gritting his teeth, spit flying from his mouth. "I'll fuck you, I'll fuck you, I'll fuck you," he said in time to his pounding beat. He ripped her bra off and fondled her breasts, biting them until they bled, while he slammed into her over and over again, with grunted savage thrusts. "That's right, man," the talker cried. "Fuck that pussy good. Fuck that pussy good." Lana's sanity bent again—it reached down and touched a spot she had never known, words racing through her mind like a hurricane. The pain between her legs was excruciating, her back crunched against the hard floor, her skull felt split in two. And those words, stop, help, God, Leo kept going and going and going. She saw the scar across his nose, his fierce crazed eyes, the maniacal smile which twisted his lips, and she wanted to kill him, to tear his body to shreds, to run it over with a car until it was bloody pulp. His breath exploded as he climaxed in terrible, cruel bliss, falling limp on top of her for a moment, while the guard yelled, "Okay, get the fuck up, man. Hurry up." He rose on his knees and pushed himself back into his pants and then took his right fist and slammed it into the side of her face, near her jaw. Then his left fist smashed into her temple.*

She blacked out, how long she'll never know, and when she came to she discovered they had stuffed her underwear into her mouth and tied her hands behind her back with her bra. The talker was on top of her, slamming into her, his face screwed up in twisted, disgusting pleasure. He wasn't really slamming into her, though. He was pretending—she felt his limpness on the inside of her crushed thigh, but just barely. A vile, disturbing hatred fled through her again, and she wanted to castrate him, to sever his head with an axe, to dash his ugly, demonic brains against a brick wall and then crush them under her heels. The talker finished his charade, stuffing his limpness into his dirty gray pants, and they rolled her over, the white one kicking her in the spine, someone else slamming their knee into her skull. The bitter dark erased them and she passed out again—the last sound she heard was Leo's amazing piano riff from "Where Blue Begins." It played on and on and on like a verse from the devil's tongue, coming from deep down in some black and gritty hell. "Being with you is like taking a journey, like disappearing to an enchanted place—a place where blue begins." *This is where blue begins, she had thought.*

Lana closed her eyes tightly and swallowed. When she opened them, she spoke again. Four men raped her, she told us quietly—three Negroes and one white man. They ripped her clothes off and held her down, and then they took turns raping her. They said horrible things to her, words she could never speak out loud, and all the while the song Leo had written for her played on. Before they were even finished, she blacked out. They kicked her skull and spine with the toes of their boots and she had passed out.

When she came to, the man who had held her arms back was kneeling between her legs zipping up his pants. There was blood on his hands, and when he noticed it he started madly wiping it off on the filthy floor. Beyond the underwear stuffed in her mouth, she could taste her own blood. When she closed her eyes, she heard the talker say, "We got to break her legs." She opened her eyes again, but she could hardly make out their faces anymore. The pain threw a dark screen up between them. The horror too. Her mind had passed through a few warps and had plunged down into utter blackness.

"How?" the scared one said. Somehow he was holding her legs down again.

"Pull them apart," the talker screamed.

The scared one kept shaking his head. He couldn't do it.

The door opened, and Lana looked over long enough to see an older white man step into the doorway. It was the one she'd seen sitting at that front-row table. She recognized his thin lips, his skinny gray mustache. He said something about her getting her niggers, but she couldn't be sure. She was a long way from reality. Then he smiled that half-smile, his lips like a red slot, his teeth like white tombstones.

The white man with the scar across his nose pushed the scared one out of the way and grabbed her right leg. The talker grabbed the other one, and they pulled her apart like a wishbone. Someone kicked her right hip in a series of brutal thrusts to make it break easier, and then she blacked out completely.

Lana stopped speaking and closed her eyes as if she had blacked out all over again. I couldn't take my eyes off of her. Neither could Lizzy nor Elena. We sat there at the end of her mattress nearly paralyzed, just staring at her drained, white face. Tears welled briefly in her eyes and fell silently down her cheeks, but she brushed them away with the back of her hand, as if she didn't want them.

No one said anything for a long time, although the sky outside the open windows rumbled lowly like a groaning stomach. The rain had slowed to a hissing drizzle, and the lightning came now only in white flashes. We didn't know what to say to Lana—at least I didn't. I had been pushed to a place where words didn't mean anything. We all had, I think. It was the most horrible thing I had ever heard of in my life, and I knew somehow too that it was even more terrible than that. It wound through my guts like poison and hacked open a hole inside my brain, where knowledge of such things could suddenly exist.

We hung in the silence, Lana sitting perfectly still, her eyes yet closed, her forehead pinched together, as if she were going through the painful process of stuffing the horror of those memories back down into a box deep in her subconscious, sealing it up again with the strings and glues of the mind.

She sat alone against the wall, as if her experience had cordoned her off forever from those who hadn't known such cold terror. Almost instinctually, we moved closer to her. I crawled up next to her hip, but was careful not to touch it—a black fog seemed to radiate from it, so I put my hand on her thigh instead. Lizzy sat behind me and touched her foot, and Elena picked up her hand. It looked strange, but it felt like the right thing to do.

She finally opened her eyes. They landed on each of us in turn and finally came to rest on her hands.

"What happened after that?" Elena whispered. It pained her to ask, and it felt like a cruel thing to do, but even so had Elena not asked I would have.

Lana brushed the last of her tears away and lit another one of Elena's cigarettes. She took a deep drag, as if there were sustenance there, and then told us she'd woken up in a hospital room, a private room Mimi had gotten her in Beth Israel Hospital. She was in a body cast that encased both of her legs and went up to her ribs. Both of her shoulders were broken, her skull was fractured in three places, her jaw too, and most of the tendons and ligaments between her legs were in tatters.

I wracked my mind for any memory of Lana lying in a hospital bed wrapped in white gauzes and casts, but there was nothing, not even a glimmer of recognition. "I don't remember that," I said softly. My voice came as a shock to me—it sounded as if it had ascended from a grave.

"You never saw me," she said. She took another stabbing drag off her cigarette. "The babysitter took care of you, and then Leo took you to stay with Grampie for a while."

I couldn't remember that either, although Elena said she could. She mentioned some highlights of that particularly long visit, like the night Grampie took us on the ferris wheel ride and the time he put

Elena and me in an old buggy and ran us up and down the street. I remembered this, but somehow I couldn't remember that Lana wasn't with us.

She was in the hospital for over four months, she said, where two operations were performed on her hip and a few on her inner thighs. Mimi paid for the best surgeons money could buy, and that was the reason she could walk as well as she could. She took another drag off her cigarette and then touched the ash to the side of the ashtray, where it fell off and rolled to the bottom. "I knew I would never dance again," she said. "At first I hoped I would be able to, but that was out of the question. I never really sang after that either. I tried, but I couldn't. I could never stand the sound of that music again."

Leo didn't want her to perform in public anymore anyway, she told us. He never wanted her to stand on another stage again. He wanted to take her away from New York, away from the racial tension which ate her up, and away from Mimi, who had great, crazy hopes of Lana becoming some sort of national public figure—someone like Betsy Ross or Florence Nightingale, or even Amelia Earhart. It didn't matter what Lana was fighting for or about—Mimi was attracted to any kind of flame, like a rabid moth.

On Lana's first walk outside the hospital, Leo begged her to leave New York. They were creeping along the sweltering August sidewalks, Lana taking baby steps, while Leo held her elbow. She wore a white hospital gown and a pair of pink slippers Mimi had bought her. Her hair had grown back some, but it was still boyishly short. The trees were standing still, it was so hot, but nonetheless Lana was grateful to be outside of the hospital. It had been almost three months since she'd walked anywhere besides down her corridor. She could hear the traffic in the distance, but it seemed from another world, a world she had never meant to leave so far behind. Most of the people who edged past her were from the hospital. They all wore white, and they looked safe, benign even.

"I want to take you out of New York, La," Leo said softly. He put his arm around her and gripped her elbow with his other hand, as if to absorb the shock.

"And what will I do?" Lana asked. She pushed her fingers through her short cropped hair, her thumb snagging on the crusty edges of a long scar.

"Whatever you want, La," he said. "You'll do whatever you want."

"I could never be a housewife. I have to have some sort of work, Leo. I've worked since I was seven years old." She couldn't imagine being anything, though. It was hard enough just to walk down this sidewalk, without thinking about work.

"You can't go up on stages anymore, La. Not in this city. There are too many crazy people. You could have been killed."

Even though it was an especially hot August day, a series of shivers passed through her like a storm. The bad feelings started to surface like sharks, and she clutched Leo's arm. "It's coming over me again," she whispered. Fear of the fear swept through her, and Leo eased her down on a nearby bench. She pressed her hand against her thudding heart and took deep gulps of the humid air. Her heart beat like this so often, she was amazed it hadn't quit.

She watched a couple of young nurses walk by, free and unfettered, swinging their purses in the late afternoon heat, talking back and forth. "I'm not the same person anymore," she whispered bitterly. "I'm not the same, Leo." Every day she said this. It had become like a cruel password, a prayer almost.

Leo pulled her into his arms and held her tightly for a long time, while she tried to imagine herself stepping onto a stage in front of an audience. The thought of it was too overwhelming. In fact, she almost couldn't believe she'd ever done it to begin with.

"I'm not the same," she cried. "I'm not the same person." Fear was so thick in her heart, it felt like tar.

"Shhh, La," Leo said. "I'm here, baby. I'm here. You're all right. You're all right, La."

She looked up at the trees, and when the leaves rustled lightly it scared her. Everything scared her—any loud or sharp noises, sudden movements. Anything that darted or jerked in any way frightened her. Birds, cars, people moving too quickly. The sound of her own beating heart sometimes terrified her too. Panic took possession of her—it came and inhabited her like the devil, sometimes for hours at a stretch, sometimes for days. It came out of nowhere, it seemed, and sometimes it would just vanish into thin air. That was the thing about it—she had no control over it whatsoever, and she had come to fear it more than she had feared anything. Fear. She feared fear.

The thought of leaving New York frightened her. The thought of staying did too, but even so she couldn't imagine just leaving. It was the only place she'd ever lived. It was hers and everything in it and about it was hers, but Leo didn't think she was safe.

"You could be walking down the street, La, and some lunatic will remember he heard you speak and start calling you a nigger lover, and that's it." He looked away from her, over to the parking lot, where the sun glinted off a hundred scorched car rooftops.

When he said, "that's it," those dark, churning thoughts turned over in her mind and released bits of fear, like poison. There used to be horror in imagining what someone might do to you, but now that it had been done, *horror* wasn't even the word anymore. *Terror* was more like it. Freezing cold terror.

"What will I do though, Leo? I can't just sit someplace all day. I still feel those things, Leo. I still feel the exact same way about it as I always did . . . *before.*"

Leo turned to her, his mouth falling open. They had never spoken about that part of it, about how she felt about it now. Somehow Leo had just assumed that the whole thing had turned her mind away from the Negroes, that it had turned her heart against them. It had had that effect on him.

"How could you, La?" he asked her.

A whole group of nurses walked past them—the day shift was over and a sour breeze seemed to follow them from the hospital. They heard the whine of an ambulance pulling up in the back, and just moments later Lana's hands started shaking. She had no control over that either. Whenever the panic stole inside of her it made her shake, whether she wanted to or not. "I don't want to have to keep telling you this, Leo—there were two white men involved too. What the white one did was the—" She couldn't finish her sentence. Her voice left her, as it did during the worst moments.

Leo stroked the back of her hand. "La," he said quietly. "There were no white men there, baby."

She jerked her hand away from him and laid it in the white cotton lap of her hospital gown. "Leo," she said sternly, "I may not be the same person as I was then, but I know who I saw. I was in the room, goddamn it. I saw both those white men with my own eyes."

She stared at him, bewildered, while he looked at her with slippery eyes that told her he felt sorry for her.

"La," he said, reaching for her hand again, "your mind wanted to see those white men, because you couldn't stand the idea that Negroes would have done such a thing to you. You imagined them, La. You imagined them, baby."

She drew away quickly, turning her back on him. How many times she had been told she had imagined those white men. The police had told her, the lawyers, then the doctors, and now Leo was convinced of it too. They made her worry that on top of everything else, she was losing her mind. Yet she remembered them distinctly. How could she ever forget the white one's assault. It was burned into her psyche forever. Mimi was the only one who believed her, but every time she said that to Leo, he always yelled, "Mimi would eat your shit if you put it on a plate and gave it to her—she's nuts, Lana. The woman ran a whorehouse for twenty years."

"I saw them, Leo." Her jaw was clenched and her fists lay coiled in her lap. "I saw the pink scar across the white man's nose. His white flesh came as close to my eyes as anything ever has. Goddamn it, I saw them. *How many times do I have to tell you?*"

She hit the back of the bench with her fist, and Leo moved closer to her. He laid his warm hand on her shoulder. "They never found any white men, La," he whispered gently. "They only found three of the four Negroes. You weren't in any state to know exactly what you saw, La. Even those three Negroes said there were no white men."

She turned around and locked eyes with him. "I know what I saw, Leo. That older man who sat in the front row—he hired them. Goddamn it, I'm telling you he hired them to do it. And they covered it up because he's white."

He stared at her again, his eyes melting in pity. "La, I know you think you saw them, but you didn't. You imagined them. It's perfectly understandable."

She couldn't speak of it anymore. Her hands were jumping, they shook so hard. She got up and started hobbling forward, as if she could run from it. Leo scrambled after her, taking her elbow, steadying her. "Okay, okay, La," he whispered. "Maybe I'm wrong. Maybe there was a cover-up."

She looked at him long enough to know that he didn't mean what he said. "Don't patronize me, Leo. I may not be myself, but I'm not a fucking child."

They walked along in silence after that, the sidewalk beneath their feet baking in the hot August sun.

That night in her hospital room, she and Leo struck their bargain. While the fan whirred endlessly on top of the nightstand and the sweat soaked through their clothes, he tried to convince her that they had to leave New York.

"What will I do, Leo? I don't want to take some awful job, and I can't just live in some small town and sit home and cook. I can't be the woman, Leo. You know that, so don't ask me to be. I'd go crazy." It shook her up to use the word *crazy*—she felt that close to it. "That was my work," she said quietly. "It's not something I can just forget about."

Leo had already thought about that. He'd thought about it all. "Write it down, La, in books for people to read. You can reach a lot more people that way."

Lana sat there for a few moments thinking about it. While her eyes wandered across all the paintings and photographs Mimi had hung on her walls, Leo told her that she never had to sit home and cook, that she could write, for the rest of her life if that's what she wanted. "I'll help you raise our children," he said softly. He asked for one thing from her, just one thing—he wanted another child, a son.

She agreed to that, although she knew it wouldn't be for a while. The thought of making love was still remote to her, thousands of miles away. It would take a long time for those bitter, repulsive feelings to fade. She agreed to it, though, to start trying in a year, if he would agree to two other things. She asked him to never play the jazz around her or her children, especially his song, "Where Blue Begins," because she couldn't bear to hear so much as a note from any of it.

"Of course," Leo whispered. "I would never, La. Never." He even shuddered in the heat to imagine it.

Lana worried that he wouldn't be able to keep his vow. "I know human nature, Leo. It never works to suppress anything, especially passions. Never. I'm afraid it will come back to us."

He pressed his finger to her lips to silence her. "It won't, baby," he whispered. "How could I ever play that music after—"

He pulled her into a warm embrace that lasted for a long time and said the same words over again. They came straight from his heart, she knew, but even so she didn't believe him entirely. She had a feeling that somewhere, sometime it would come out again, but she couldn't think about it anymore. It rocked the small place she'd found to stand on, so she let it go.

"I don't want Maddie and Elena to know either," Lana whispered.

"Not for a long time, Leo. Not until it leaves me. I mean that, Leo. I mean it more than I can tell you."

"Okay, La," he breathed. "We won't tell them until you're ready. We'll start over. We'll put it all in the past. We'll get out of here and start a new life. We'll leave Mimi and Sammy, all of them, and we'll change our lives," he said. He touched her face with the tips of his warm fingers. "I love you, La, more than anything."

Her hands started shaking, so Leo put them between his and held them for a long time, rubbing them, as if that would drive the demons out.

Lana stopped speaking and looked up at us. She closed her mouth and swallowed, and when she pressed her fingers against her lips, I knew she wasn't going to say anymore. "That was our bargain," she said. "It was a long time ago."

We all stared at her again, unable to find the words to speak. It was hard to understand that while all this went on, I had been alive and blissfully ignorant. It was all out now—thrown into the air where it could float and drift without consequence. It had come from Lana herself, and no words she uttered about her past had the power to do anything more than heal her.

"What's going to happen now?" Elena whispered.

She looked at the three of us. "I don't know," she said. "I really don't know." She glanced at the little clock on the floor next to her mattress. It was quarter to four in the morning. "We're not going to figure it out tonight," she said.

"What have you been doing now?" I asked her.

She looked at me and patted my arm. "I'll tell you tomorrow, sweetheart," she said. "Not tonight. I've talked enough. Tomorrow I'll tell you." Somehow I believed she would.

She put the ashtray on the floor and got up long enough to pull the blankets back. "Get in, you guys." We didn't want to part with her any more than she wanted to part with us, so we crawled underneath the covers, pushing Harry over as far to the wall as he could go. Lana lay down between me and Lizzy, and Elena lay next to me. I noticed she didn't change into her nightgown. I almost said something about it until I remembered how just a week ago Elena and I had fallen asleep in our dirty clothes. Sometimes you couldn't keep yourself from doing something like that.

Lana turned off the light, and for a good twenty minutes we lay there on our backs in the silence. The sky still rumbled outside, but only faintly, and every now and then a white flash appeared, but rarely. The storm had left a cool breeze, which pushed and tugged at the rice paper curtains. It was a soothing sound, one I found refuge in.

I don't know how they did, but Elena and Lizzy fell asleep. I couldn't, though. My mind kept me awake shifting and sorting and fitting together all the pieces which had been floating in my thoughts for almost my whole life. I remembered the night when Leo had grabbed Lana's wrists and that stark, shrill scream had come up from deep inside her like a siren. I realized why now: she couldn't bear to be bound in any way, held against her will like that—not after what had happened. I understood too why that scream had sounded such a deep alarm in Leo that he let go immediately, both of her wrists and his anger. The scream was a powerful reminder of what had happened to them so long ago.

I thought about the words Leo had said to Lana one night: "If you hadn't been so goddamned impatient, it never would have happened." They finally made sense to me. He wanted to blame her because he couldn't bear the idea that she blamed him, or worse yet, that he blamed himself. And what about Lana's words? When he'd said, "Admit it, La. Admit you blame me," she had turned to him and said, "If your ego hadn't been so big, it never would have happened."

All these years they'd been tossing the blame back and forth like a hand grenade, waiting to see whose hands it would finally blow up in. It seemed the blame rested on more shoulders than just theirs. Didn't it? It wasn't a matter of Lana's impatience or Leo's ego, was it? Wasn't it bigger than that? Hadn't it happened because Lana had opened her mouth and told the truth? She was the sparrow, I realized. She'd been beaten just like the sparrow had been for speaking the truth.

It was only a vague, formless thought, all of this. It was more of a feeling than a thought really, and one I couldn't hold onto for very long. It was too difficult and so amorphous and hazy I had to let it go.

There was something else that plagued my mind—the idea that Leo had played that song in front of Lana and her children, in front of an entire audience. I could not understand how he could have played that song now that I knew why she couldn't bear to hear it. How he even considered playing one single note of it was beyond me.

I had an idea that she would never be able to forgive him. It was more than him just playing a song she didn't like. It was much more than that, I understood, but even so I couldn't begin to calculate just how much that was.

At the thought of what might happen to Lana and Leo, to all of us, my nerves reared up. Quite a few of them raced up to my neck where they swarmed like ants, but most of them headed underneath my kneecaps. What I wouldn't have given for Durga just then. I couldn't lie there still, not when they were under my kneecaps. I wanted to get up and pace, but there was no place to do it other than in this room. It wasn't a private enough place to get rid of nerves, so I started jiggling my legs under the covers.

"What's wrong, Maddie?" Lana whispered to me. Her sleep must have been very thin, because I wasn't jiggling my legs very hard.

"It's my nerves," I said. "They're under my kneecaps."

She thought about that for a moment, deciding, I guess, that the subject of my nerves was too big a thing to talk about at five o'clock in the morning. "Put your legs over my stomach, and I'll rub your knees," she whispered.

I doubted it would do much good, but I draped my legs over her anyway, my feet ending up on Lizzy's stomach, my head nestled under Elena's arm. Lana started rubbing my kneecaps, pressing her fingers into them. "Whenever I can't sleep, I lie in bed and take my mind off myself," she whispered. "I think to myself how big this world is, how it's filled with more people than I can imagine. I say— right now, right this instant, somewhere a baby was born. Its mother just heard its first cry. And I see them in some room. I'm in that room with them for that moment, and then I think, right this second another one was born somewhere else. In South America or China. And right now, this very instant, a boy kissed a girl for the first time, somewhere, some place in the world, and right now their hearts are beating like crazy. They could be in Russia or France. I go inside their rooms, or I stand out on their streets, and I watch them. One moment someone is being born, and then, right now, somewhere, someone died, and someone's crying."

"And right now, someone just fell down," I whispered, "like maybe in India, or in Lansing. And now they just got up."

"Somewhere, someone did," she whispered.

21

I fell asleep sometime after five-thirty with my legs draped over Lana. Harry woke us less than four hours later. Lana got up and took him into the bathroom, where she cleaned him up, while Elena, Lizzy, and I stayed in bed, under the covers. As soon as the sleep fell away, the images Lana had pressed into our minds resurfaced, and we glanced at one another helplessly. Somehow it had been better before we really knew—the truth was so utterly black and ugly it squatted in our hearts like an elephant.

"Can you believe Leo played that song?" Elena whispered. She pulled the sheet up under her chin and squinted her eye against a thin shaft of sunlight.

"No," I whispered. Lizzy shivered next to me.

"Maddie, remember when Leo came to get Lana at the Syracuse Hotel and Lana said, 'You were too late then, and you're too late now'?"

A chill crept through me when I considered what Leo had been too late for.

I was grateful, at least, that the sun was out and the sky was a soft blue. A few puffy clouds lingered, but they'd lost their dark power. It was already warm too—I could feel the heat rising as if the sidewalks were baking underneath my back.

Lana brought Harry out of the bathroom, and we quietly watched as she moved around the apartment, our eyes shifting in unison. She was looking around for Harry's gray T-shirt, pawing through their piles of clothes, as if it were just another morning. It felt odd to us. How could she walk around the apartment looking for something so small and insignificant as a gray T-shirt after what had happened to her? To us, it seemed it had only happened last night.

When she finished dressing him, she went down to the phone booth. From the fifth-floor window, we watched her make a couple of phone calls. When she came back ten minutes later, she told us we were going to spend a few days with Mimi on Long Island Sound. We were all relieved to be let out of the city. The prospect of sitting all day in Lana's stuffy little apartment in the sweltering heat didn't appeal to any of us.

Mimi picked us up outside Lana's apartment in a navy blue Cadillac just after ten o'clock. She was wearing a white sundress and a pair of beige sandals, which made her look more like a regular person, but even so her dyed black hair was still poofed up and as stiff as straw. She wore so much blue eye shadow, I wondered how she could keep her eyes open.

She had no idea what had happened last night, and for a while she tried to make conversation with me, Lizzy, and Elena, but none of us could really talk. We were all sunk deep in our thoughts, struggling to bring some order to our shifting impressions. We kept watching Lana to make sure she was all right. It seemed all she'd told us last night would be floating on top of her thoughts, like oil, intruding every few moments, but she seemed free of it, as if she had succeeded in pressing it deep down into that box at the bottom of her mind.

When our silence in the backseat got to be too much, Mimi started to tell us a story. She prefaced it with the words, "When I was in the hair and nail business," but Lana stopped her before she got too far along.

"They know you ran a bordello, Mimi."

"Oh," was all Mimi said. We saw her eyes shift in the rearview mirror, from the sweltering pavement to our faces in the backseat.

"They know everything," Lana said. "I told them last night."

Mimi just nodded and snapped her mouth shut. Her mind must have spun back to those days as well, for she didn't say anything more. She just gripped the leather steering wheel, fixed her eyes straight ahead on the steaming hot pavement, and drove us out to Long Island Sound.

I don't think Elena or I had ever realized how much money Mimi had made in the whore business until we saw her house. It was a beautiful rambling clapboard house, two stories high, which sat back a perfect distance from the beach. It was far enough away so that you didn't feel you were on top of it, yet it was close enough that someone could step out the front door and call you if you were sitting down near the water. It had a small cupola on the top, which sat between two gables, and a beautiful screen porch which faced the ocean. On either end of it were old weathered porch swings, creaking lightly in the sea breeze.

Mimi had decorated the inside lavishly with fine oriental rugs and beautiful mahogany furniture which sat amid white upholstered divans and chairs. There were huge bay windows on three sides, all of which faced the ocean. It was really elegant, but even so I couldn't quite forget where the money had come from. Effy had paid for some of these things, I thought. She had spanked Mr. Larkin's pink ass so Mimi could sit on a white sofa and gaze out the windows at the ocean.

The walls in her dining room were covered with photographs of Lana and Teddy, but mainly Lana. It seemed she had one for every age of Lana's life. Lana swimming in the ocean, Lana swinging on the porch, Lana in her bed, Lana singing and dancing on Mimi's stage, sometimes alone, sometimes with Effy.

We climbed the stairs to the second floor, where Mimi had kept Lana's and Teddy's rooms exactly as they had been. They were like shrines now, testaments to another, lost time.

Lana ducked into Mimi's office on the second floor—a room that looked very similar to the office in Mimi's whorehouse, which Lana had once described in her journal. Thick, velvety curtains hung from the windows facing the sound, and an oversized mahogany desk stood in the middle of the room. It looked like the desk of a giant.

When Lana got on the phone and started dialing, Mimi closed the door behind her and led us downstairs to her living room, where through the bay windows we could see the ocean unfurling. We sat down on her white sofa and stared at all the photographs on the wall, our eyes lingering over the ones of Effy and Lana. You could see their link, as if a fine web had grown between them.

Mimi came out of the kitchen carrying a silver tray with four glasses of lemonade, which she set down on top of a long, wooden coffee table. We each took one and then shifted in our seats, staring out the window at the ocean. The pain of Lana's story had settled on our tongues, silencing us.

An old man and a stark boy, no more than eight years old, passed along the shoreline. The boy was skinny, cadaverously so, his knees and elbows like knots in his stringy limbs. His head was completely bald, and his chest was so sunken, his ribs stood out like thick fingers. He half staggered, half ran ahead of the old man, plunging in and out of the water clumsily, his arms flapping up and down awkwardly like a big, drunk bird. The ocean intoxicated him, and the more I watched him, the more I realized how sick he was. I noticed the old man then, how he stopped and watched the boy, as if the union of this skinny boy and the sea were somehow magical, as if it were something to witness. He reminded me of the Eyes of God.

"That's Howard and his grandfather," Mimi said, grateful for a topic of conversation. "He's only got two more days before he goes back to the hospital. He's dying of leukemia. He's a nice little boy, but his mother," she said, rolling her eyes. "Saracyn-*tia*. Don't make the mistake of calling her Saracyn-*thia* either, or she'll paint your butt blue."

I glanced out at the ocean, at the bald-headed little boy, and suddenly he looked more tragic, but Mimi was so funny, I didn't think about it for very long. "The grandmother's a real winner too. She's always calling me Mimikins, like we're best friends. Her name is Hora—Horror, is what I call her. She complains so much about the bursitis in her arms and the arthritis in her legs, I wish she'd just cut them off and get it over with. She's got a wart on the side of her cheek too that's so big it's got a lawn growing on top of it, and whenever I say, 'Hora, why don't you get that taken off,' she says, 'It's the only beauty mark I've got left.' A beauty mark for Attila the Hun, I tell her, but you can't tell Hora anything."

Lana finally came downstairs. It was so warm and humid that Mimi suggested we put on our bathing suits and go down to the beach for the afternoon. None of us had a bathing suit, but Mimi had kept a lot of Lana's old ones. She had wrapped them in plastic bags and had laid them away in the attic years ago, as if she had known all along that this day would come. She even had a pair of Teddy's old trunks, which were a little big for Harry, but he wore them nonetheless with the waist folded over a few times. She gave Lana the last bathing suit Lana had ever worn on the sound—a black two-piece with thin shoulder straps and a short ruffled bottom.

We looked forward to being in the midst of sand and water, sun and sky. It was so faraway from the concrete dressing room with the black ceiling where Lana had known the worst moments of her life. It seemed our minds were held hostage in that room, our hearts too, and the sand and water, the sun and sky offered us a way out. We raced across it and ran down to the wet, foaming shoreline where we cooled our scorched feet. The waves were enthralling—they weren't too big to be terrifying, nor were they too small to be a disappointment. They seemed just the right size for us, and for two hours Elena, Lizzy, and I lost ourselves in them, riding them one after another, over and over again, forgetting everything. The way they churned and foamed and swept forward and backward helped to purge us all of our heartache.

We ate a picnic lunch on a blue-green blanket Mimi brought down for us. While the waves crashed on the beach and the white foam popped on the sand, we bit into her fancy ham and cheese sandwiches and munched on the thick Bavarian pretzels she kept dropping on our plates. The way the gulls glided, their wings beating like some sort of silken refrain, and the blue sky stretched out above us, seemed perfect until I remembered again about Lana.

My eyes fell on her right hip, where just beneath the black bottoms of her bathing suit, that long empurpled scar lay like dark hemp on her pale skin. I watched as she scooted over on the blanket to pull up Harry's soggy red trunks. Elena and Lizzy noticed too. It was as if the loud, crunching sound of our pretzels had brought the memory back to us. I tried not to think about how it had happened, but my imagination seized on it. It was the worst kind of imagining too, worse even than visualizing Leo beating her hip with the end of a shovel, because I knew it was true, that it had happened, that one night, almost ten years ago, four black men and a white man had come into her dressing room and shattered her hip and her life into pieces.

I wanted to see Lana's scar, to finally touch it. I knew we had promised her we wouldn't ask about it again, but it didn't seem like asking to see the scar was like asking about it. It was a scar after all, something you didn't have to ask about—you could see it and touch it without saying a word. When Mimi walked up to the house to get us popsicles, I asked Lana if we could see her scar. Her back went a little rigid, her forehead knotted, and for a moment it seemed as if she'd forgotten what she'd told us last night. She glanced at Lizzy and Elena as they waited expectantly. After a few moments passed she said, "All right, all right."

She eased herself down on her left hip and very slowly pushed her black bottoms down until the thick zigzag of her scar was laid bare. We crawled forward to get a better look, our eyes edging along the entire squiggled length of it. I shuddered to imagine bits and pieces of bone floating underneath it like driftwood. Elena must have had the same thought, because she spit out her preztel and buried it underneath the sand.

"Could we touch it?" I whispered. My fingers ached to press down on it, as if in touching it I could heal her wound forever. When Lana nodded, we all crept a little closer, our fingers gently descending until they landed on top of it, where we traced the scar's bumpy relief back and forth, over and over again.

It wasn't long after that that Lana, Elena, Lizzy, and I lay down on the blanket and fell asleep. While Mimi walked Harry up and down the shore looking for seashells, we curled up around Lana, touching her on one side or another, as if it were our job to hold her together. The last thing I heard was Harry's excited squeal before I dropped off into a dead sleep that felt more like a coma than anything. There were no dreams, just a sense of dark empty rooms where nothing floated or drifted. It was as if someone had come in with a broom and swept it clean.

We woke up an hour later to the sound of Mimi's voice yelling, "Lana." We peeled our eyes open, and one by one we came around, propping ourselves up on our elbows, squinting against the sun. I saw Mimi first. She was standing on the porch with a white apron tied around her waist. It was a few more moments before I saw Leo. He was standing in the sand some five or six yards from the porch, his white shirtsleeves rolled up past his elbows, his black pants damp and rumpled from his hot drive. He just stood there, framed against the blue sky, his hands stuffed into his pockets, staring straight ahead at us. He had played that song, I thought, and now that I knew why Lana couldn't bear to hear it, I didn't know what to think of him.

Lana finally saw him and whispered his name. "Leo," she said, as if she had just remembered him. She sat up and brushed the sand off her arms and legs, while Leo remained anchored in the sand, waiting for someone to come and claim him.

"Wait here." She stood up and walked toward him, wrapping a white towel around her waist. Her cane poked into the sand as she strode forward. Leo walked toward her, his hands still stuffed into his pockets. He was too far away for me to see his face, but I somehow knew it lay in a shambles.

When they finally met, they didn't embrace like Elena, Lizzy, and I hoped they would. They stopped as if a line had been drawn between them in the sand, neither of them crossing it. The only thing Leo did was reach up and touch the ends of Lana's short hair. They talked for a few minutes, though of course we couldn't hear them, and instead of coming over to the blanket, they headed down to the shore. Leo peeled off his shoes and socks, and they walked away and so far apart from one another that Elena and I could have easily slipped between them.

Mimi walked down to the blanket and sat down in the sand, where she dug her bare feet into the dampness underneath. We all watched Leo and Lana walking along the shore, growing smaller and smaller, as if they were slipping away from us. Mimi turned to us, burrowing her feet deeper under the sand. "So Lana told you everything last night, huh?"

We nodded, and all that awful, stifling solemnity came back to us on the breeze and crowded our chests again with heavy, gray emotion.

"That's really something that they found them, isn't it?"

"Found who?" Elena said. She sat up, and out of instinct we all moved closer to Mimi—a secret was still a great attraction, and the impulse to prevent it from escaping into the air was still very strong.

"The other men," Mimi whispered. Her head twitched to the right as if the mention of these other men was somehow chilling.

"What men?" Elena said. She dropped the handful of sand she was sifting through her fingers and crept forward on her knees. Lana hadn't told us anything about other men. She'd never even mentioned it.

Mimi dug her feet deeper into the sand and leaned closer to us. "They found out who the white men were. Lana hadn't imagined them like everybody said. 'Course, I believed her all along. Sylvester

Williams was the old man, and the white kid was Matt Bates, a scummy little Bronx hood," she whispered fiercely.

"How did they find them?" Elena asked.

As our eyes widened and our jaws hung open, Mimi glanced nervously up the shoreline. Lana and Leo had turned around. They were not within earshot, but nonetheless they were fast approaching. When she turned back to us, we huddled around her. "The lawyer found out they suppressed the evidence about the white men, and now it's come out."

Mimi paused here and took a breath, fanning herself with her hand. Lana's lawyer had called her a few months back, she said. He wanted to talk to Lana, but he wouldn't tell Mimi what it was about. So Mimi called our old number in Detroit and found out it had been disconnected. She called Grampie in Lansing, but he wouldn't give Mimi our new phone number. I didn't know it, but Lana and Leo hadn't listed our phone numbers since they'd left New York. Mimi told Grampie that it was urgent, so he finally gave her Lana's address. She wrote Lana, telling her that her lawyer wanted to talk to her. That's when Lana called Mimi and told Mimi she didn't want to talk to anybody about anything. Mimi told him what Lana had said, and when he asked for Lana's address so he could write her himself, Mimi wouldn't do it.

"I couldn't, see, because then Lana would never have forgiven me," she said. "So I wrote her again, and when she didn't answer, I told him, and he finally told me they had found out who the white men were. I wrote Lana again and told her what he had told me, and she finally talked to him. He told her that the old man had paid those Negroes to rape her, paid that scummy Bronx hood too. They were prisoners released on parole from Rikers Island. Imagine that!"

The winds blew through my veins just like old times, my nerves straining against them. I suddenly remembered the afternoon Lizzy and I had walked into the kitchen and found Lana heaving a pot cover and a leftover bowl of Harry's chicken noodle soup into the sink. I had suspected something, so I dug down in the garbage and found the tiny ripped-up pieces of Mimi's latest letter. That's when we noticed something really changed in her. She stopped shaking, her voice changed, and her relationship with Leo grew more and more distant. Our stage in the cellar was dismantled, and not long after that she gave us the last installment of the bear and sparrow story, where the man sparrow beat the sparrow over the head with a shovel and left her dead.

Inside my mind another cloud floated away and left in its place a bit more light. They found the two white men. Lana hadn't imagined them after all. The idea that four black men hadn't come in off the street on their own, must have renewed her faith. The knowledge that it had happened the way she saw it, must have given her strength. It must have given her the courage to beat it back, as Leo had often begged her to do. I wondered why she hadn't told us about it last night though. It seemed she would have, considering she told us everything else.

"Why didn't she tell us?" I whispered to Mimi.

Mimi glanced out at the shoreline. Lana and Leo were within ear-shot, so she couldn't answer my question. It disturbed her that she couldn't tell us the rest of the story. You could see it wedged into the deep lines around her eyes and mouth. She leaned back in the sand on her elbows, her face red and tight, her eyes jittering. No wonder Lana had kept us away from her, I couldn't help but think. Ten minutes alone with her, and she would have told us everything.

Leo and Lana drew up to the blanket. I knew immediately from the white, washed-out look on Leo's face that Lana had told him something about it. Leo sank down to his knees in the sand anyway and threw open his arms to me, Elena, and Lizzy. For the moment, we forgot about his part in all of this and felt instead his desperate need to be wanted in the strained air of Mimi's hostility and Lana's indifference. We piled into his big arms, and when he wrapped them around us and breathed us in, I knew he was really hugging Lana, that this warm, tender embrace was meant for her.

We made room for him on our blanket, and after Lana sat down next to Mimi, an awkward silence descended. The idea that those white men had been found seeped into our thoughts and sat between us like a rhinoceros, but even so no one mentioned it. We just sat there staring up at the sky as it slowly whitened, listening to the waves as they crashed on shore, one after another. Had anyone seen us, they would have thought we were a family of deaf-mutes.

Dinner around Mimi's grand dining room table wasn't much better. We mentioned how beautiful her china was, and Elena commented about how similar Mimi's tablecloth was to the one we had on our dining room table. We all complimented Mimi's dinner, and when we took that as far as it could go, we mentioned how lovely it was to hear the ocean and to feel the constant breeze. There wasn't much to say after that. We couldn't talk about Leo's musical, since he had played the jazz, nor could we talk about what Lana was doing. Under normal circumstances, Elena, Lizzy, and I could have talked about what we were planning to do with our summers, but since that led straight back to what Lana and Leo were going to do with theirs, that conversation dried up as well.

By the time dinner was over, my nerves were crawling up the back of my neck, and Leo was almost ready to get into our station wagon and head back to Hamilton. He mentioned something about it, and Mimi was nice enough to tell him to wait until morning. We were all so anxious to break out of our tense gathering that when Mimi suggested we have dessert, we said our stomachs were too full and persuaded her to wait until later.

While Mimi gave Harry a bubble bath, the rest of us went out on the porch and sat on the swings. Elena and Lana sat on one, and Leo, Lizzy, and I sat on the other one. Even without Mimi, it was still uncomfortable. The tension between Lana and Leo was that thick. Something was going to happen between them tonight—that much I could tell. I didn't know where it was going to happen—on the beach, on this porch, in their room—but I knew it was going to. I could feel it as if it had long fingernails that reached out and scratched me.

When it was time to go to bed, Elena took Teddy's old room upstairs, where I'm sure she did her fair share of snooping. Since it had single beds, Lizzy and I were given Lana's old room. As soon as Lana closed the door, we walked around, opening all the drawers, and touching everything. There wasn't much there—a few of Lana's old tap dancing shoes, a scrapbook with old newspaper clippings of jazz musicians, and a whole raft of ticket stubs.

I did find one thing which I kept. On the dresser was a small photograph of Effy and Lana, taken when Lana was no more than ten years old. Effy was dressed in a beautiful, shimmering dress with a white corsage pinned to it. She had her hand on one hip, and her chin was raised ever so slightly. Lana stood in the background, watching Effy with the biggest, moistest, most adoring eyes I had ever seen.

I slipped it out of the frame and pushed it deep under my pillow.

We crawled under the crisp clean sheets in our separate beds, the sound of the waves washing over us, the light from Mimi's beach lamp falling through the opened windows.

"It was really awful what happened to Lana," Lizzy whispered.

The word *awful* sounded so small, so terribly inadequate. It was really the first time we'd been alone since Lana had told us, and now that we were, it seemed it would be impossible to talk about it, to touch it in any way, as if our small words would somehow diminish its profound and wordless horror.

"What's going to happen to me if Leo moves here, Maddie?" Lizzy asked me.

I remembered Lana's third secret to me—that men would never mean that much to me, that I would do something great with my life. I worried that I was somehow going to have to do as she had done, and when I remembered the one and only premonition I had ever had, a chill seized me. It had come to me last summer when I was in the bathroom dousing my nerves with hot water. A cat had cried out in the backyard, and when the bathroom light had flickered on and off, I had the thought that it would be me who saved Lizzy from Garta. I didn't know how, but I sensed it again, as if it had roots which reached down to my stomach.

"Me and Lana won't give you up," I said. Somehow I felt sure about that.

She pulled the sheets up to her chin and stared out the open window at the dark ocean waters as they crept onto the shore with long, smooth fingers and then ran away again.

"Good night," I said.

Lulled by the waves and the thought that Lana wouldn't desert her, Lizzy fell asleep, and I was left alone, as usual, with the strange new shadows. I heard Lana and Leo in the room below me. Their voices drifted up to me, not through a furnace duct or a floor register, but through the opened window. I couldn't make out their words, but I could tell that Lana's voice wasn't the same shrill, lacerating voice I'd always heard at night. No, this voice was different—it was the voice I'd heard in her films.

I didn't listen for very long before I got up and crept down Mimi's creaky stairs to listen. I couldn't stand not knowing what they were saying, especially when their decisions had such a huge bearing on my own small life. I could hear Mimi walking around in her room a few doors down, but I didn't care about Mimi. She'd probably listened at hundreds of doors in her lifetime.

Thankfully, there was a small keyhole underneath the doorknob. It wasn't nearly as good as the broom closet in Detroit or the bathroom grate in Hamilton, but if I closed my right eye and pushed my left eye as close as I could, I could see them inside the room.

The white curtains fluttered at the open window, the ocean curling and uncurling in the hazy distance. Lana was sitting on the edge of the bed, while Leo paced back and forth across the room like a heated tank.

"Why in the hell didn't you tell me?" he whispered loudly. "You've known for months now. Did you have to torture me like this?" he yelled. "Jesus Christ, La." His shirt was halfway untucked, and his hair was sticking up as if he had rammed his thick fingers through it a hundred times already.

"I wanted to find out the details before I told anyone!" she yelled. "I was hoping that I could get both of them, but I can't. They're protected under the statute of limitations." It was a bitter fact to her, and for a moment it looked as if she might cry.

"All this time you've been up here, going over the details, and I didn't know a fucking thing about it. You might have told me, Lana. Jesus Christ—what am I to you?" I could not only see but feel the fit fomenting underneath his seething blue eyes.

She moved to the edge of the bed, her back rigid, her calm vanishing completely. "You made me believe I had imagined those white men, Leo. You made me think I was losing my mind. Do you know what that feels like, goddamn it? Do you have any idea?"

He stopped in front of her, his eyes a scorching blue. "I thought you had imagined them, goddamn it. How many times do I have to tell you that, Lana? Why can't you accept that, for Christ's sake?" He stared at her, his mouth hanging open, his shoulders so tense they were climbing up around his ears.

Lana moved closer to the edge of the bed. There was a red-hot line that ran between their eyes. "Do you know what it's been like all these years to know I had seen them there, and to have you tell me I had imagined them? Do you have any idea? Oh, that idiot," Lana said bitterly, "she's been beaten and raped by three Negroes, and she sees white men."

"La," he whispered fiercely. "Don't."

"You wanted me small, Leo," she yelled. "I sometimes think you were glad it happened. It kept me down, and you wanted that because you don't believe women can be heroes, Leo. You think they can only be fucked."

Those words stopped everything and hung in the air like hooks. Leo stood frozen, a look of shock registering on his face. "You're cruel, Lana," he whispered. Lana stared at him, her eyes hard and bitter, until he walked away from her, over to the window where the breeze blew. I sensed those words had festered in her heart for years, and for whatever reason she felt she could finally utter them.

A long time passed, the roar of the ocean filling the room. Leo stood at the window holding himself up on his arms, while Lana stared blindly down at the floor. He finally took a deep, shuddering breath of air and turned to her. "So how have you been getting by, Lana?" he asked coldly. When she looked away without answering him, he said, "What are you doing—taking Mimi's blood money?"

"I've got a job," she said in disgust.

When she looked away again, his eyes pressed into her like hooks. "Doing what?" he asked. She turned away from him and stared down at the floorboards, a warm flush creeping into her cheeks. *"Doing what?"*

She turned to him then. "I've been singing in a jazz club a few nights a week." She spoke so matter-of-factly, it was shocking.

Both Leo and I were too stunned to move. *"You're singing in a jazz club?"* he yelled. He couldn't believe it. In fact, it was the last thing he expected to hear.

She nodded politely, discreetly even.

I saw a madness possess him. It swept through his eyes like a hailstorm and fell, shaking, to his fists. He looked down at them in horror, as if they didn't quite belong to him, and then slammed them deep into his pockets, where beneath the thin cotton of his pants I saw them clench and unclench, as if they were breathing.

"You left me because I played that fucking song, and you run back here and sing in a jazz club." It was beyond his comprehension. "Every time I play that music now I feel the sickest, fucking guilt, and all this time you've been up here singing. You could have told me, goddamn it. *You could have told me.*"

When Lana didn't say anything, the madness seized him completely. I saw it whirl in the center of his eyes like a hurricane. The veins at his temples popped out in red-hot relief, and the cords at his neck stood out like ropes. He flew at her, his fists clenched at his sides, and for one horrible stark moment I thought he would beat her.

Lana recoiled, and when she opened her mouth I thought that awful scream would come out, but there was no sound other than a strangled gasp. Leo veered off before he reached her and slammed his fist into Mimi's white wall, a small framed photograph of Effy and Lana falling to the floor where it shattered into a dozen pieces. Lana's eyes went swiftly from the shattered glass to Leo's reddened, twisted face.

"I want the children," he yelled. "I don't give a shit what the hell you do with your life, but I want those children."

As if he had leapt ahead of her, had cut through all the other words that were supposed to come before these, she stared at him in shock, her jaw falling open, the red flush in her cheeks vanishing to white. "Is that what you came here for?"

"You're not a good mother to them," he yelled. "You deserted us, and I'm going to take them. You don't deserve them."

It terrified me how quickly they had arrived at this terrible place. There was no talk of them getting back together; there wasn't even any mention of it. They'd bypassed it completely, as if it weren't a possibility at all, and had gone straight to tearing us apart.

Lana stared at him, a strange coldness flashing across her eyes. "You can't have them!" she screamed.

Whatever violence Leo had kept pressed down in his enormous body suddenly rose up, and he wheeled out of control. A Goliath gone mad, he whirled around, and in one bold, outraged movement he overturned Mimi's dresser—it slammed against the wooden floor, all the small bottles of perfumes and hand creams skidding violently across the room. Lana watched in horror as he picked up Mimi's delicate wooden rocker and hurled it against the wall, where it clattered to the floor in a dozen pieces. When he lurched over to a smaller dresser like a tornado gone awry, she regained herself and raced after him. "Leo," she pleaded. "Please stop." She was crying, the tears pouring out of her eyes like rain.

When I heard Mimi's footsteps in the dim hallway, I shot up and raced through the darkened living room, the sound of the breaking waves matching the turbulent crash of my heart. As I fled up Mimi's stairs, I heard the mangled, outraged sound of Leo's voice, his words completely unintelligible to me. I hurried into my room, expecting that Lizzy would be awake, but she wasn't. I dove under the covers and wrapped myself up in the sheets like a mummy, and stared out the window at the dark, rolling ocean. I held my jagged breath and listened for the sound of Lana's and Leo's voices. I couldn't make out a single word. I could only hear a chorus of murmured pitches — Leo's tenor, Lana's soprano, and Mimi's deep alto. I couldn't bring myself to think about what they might be saying either.

My legs and arms were shaking underneath the sheets. It was worse even than when Lizzy and I had opened the door into Minnie Harp's impenetrable darkness. I was terrified, terrified of everything — of Lana, of Leo, of what they were going to do, of the past, of the present, of the future. What horrible things were waiting in the darkness for us all?

I heard the front door slam. I scrambled up to the window just in time to watch Leo storm across the dark sand over to the driveway. I watched, unbreathing, as he yanked open the car door and climbed in. I heard the engine turn over and the sound of him backing recklessly out of the driveway. The car shot forward, the tires screeching on the cold concrete, and then I heard the waves — the unbroken pounding of the waves.

I longed for the distant, enduring sight of the hills, for the smell of the earth and not the sea, for the swell of crickets and insects as they droned in the bushes, and not the sound of the ocean. I wanted to be stretched out in my bed next to Lizzy, while Elena was asleep in the next room and the shadows of the tall windows crept across my walls like old friends. I wanted Lizzy and me to speculate as to what might have happened to Lana, because I realized what I wanted most of all was *not* to know what had really happened to her. In the end, it was too much to know, and it was too awful a thing — worse, I knew, than I could yet imagine.

The doors I had longed to see open, I now wished I could shut. What was behind them was not something I really wanted to know about. It was too painful and ugly, and it filled me with a nameless fear — it told me that terrible things happen to people, things that are unspeakable, unthinkable.

I tried to watch the waves, hoping they would mesmerize me, but all I could think of was what Lana had said about the sea. "It just keeps going back and forth, back and forth," she'd said, "just like the sun and the moon, and it doesn't care who's been born or who's died or who's dying. Everything just keeps going, all the time, all the time."

It scared me to think about it, but I knew somehow it was true. On that night in May when those men had come into Lana's dressing room, I knew the ocean hadn't stopped to gasp. It had kept on rolling back and forth, endlessly.

I squirmed in my bed, my nerves crawling through me like ants, my eyes moving uneasily across the unfamiliar walls. I tried to remember what Lana had told me last night. Right now, someone's been born, I told myself. Just this minute, someone was born somewhere. And right now, someone just died, somewhere, and someone is crying. And now, this very instant, someone somewhere was just beaten, and they're lying on a cold concrete floor all alone. And this moment, someone was stabbed in the back, and someone is pulling the knife out, in Russia or maybe in Spain. Somewhere a man and a woman are fighting bitterly, right now, this minute, about who is right and who is wrong. A man and a woman just kissed, maybe in Hong Kong—they just grasped each other, right now, forgetting everything. And babies are being born all the time. One, two, three of them. They keep being born, one more, two more. And right now, someone was just shot in the head, and this very moment, the blood is pouring all over the floor. And someone is screaming somewhere. In China, in India, in Brazil.

As if an axe fell from the skies above me it severed my life right here, at this moment, at this haphazard juncture, and cut me off from my past completely, relegating that awkward passage to another time, to a previous life almost. It seemed all the sins I had collected in the past year vanished into the roar of the ocean, except for the one against Minnie Harp. I would have to carry that one forward, regardless.

It seemed those hills had only been a stopping point, a brief way station on our way to somewhere else. It had been a safe place where Lana and Leo could come undone, and nothing more. As to what was going to happen now, I couldn't even begin to say. It seemed there was no chance of Lana and Leo coming back together, but I couldn't think about it for very long—it put my heart in such peril.

I crawled into bed with Lizzy and watched the soft rise and fall of her chest as it breathed in time with the push and pull of the sea. I slipped my legs underneath hers and squeezed her hand, as if to hold on. She was like an anchor to me, for just then I had the scariest feeling that we all walked through this life with nothing more than a pocket flashlight to illuminate our steps through the blackness.

22

The first thing I heard when I woke up the next morning was the sound of the ocean. It took me a few moments to recognize what it was and then a few more to remember everything else. It came swimming back to me on a sharp pang, which zipped down to my stomach like a bolt of lightning.

I realized I was clinging to Lizzy; my legs were intertwined in hers, my arm lay under her back, and half my torso was thrown across hers, my head resting heavily on her right shoulder. I pulled my arm out from underneath her and glanced out at the ocean, half expecting to see something like a string of dead bodies washed up on the beach. There was nothing there but the clean, undulating shoreline.

As soon as I heard Mimi downstairs rattling around in the kitchen, I shook Lizzy awake and went across the hall and woke Elena up. Once they were sitting side by side on my bed, the foaming white waves breaking just behind their backs, I told them about last night.

"Lana's singing in a jazz club," I whispered.

They were both shocked.

"Lana told Leo last night," I said. "Then Leo slammed his fist into the wall and put a hole in it. He said he didn't give a shit what she did with her life, but he was going to keep us." An unexpected tear escaped from my eye and rolled down my cheek, sliding into my mouth. "Then Lana said he couldn't have us and Leo threw the dresser over."

"He *threw* the dresser over?" Elena said.

I tried to explain the awful mixture of Leo's seething eyes, the veins which throbbed malignantly at his temples, and the tendons which stood out like ropes on his neck, but I couldn't do it justice. So I took them downstairs and showed them the crescent indentation in the wall and the broken-up pieces of Mimi's rocking chair. They couldn't imagine.

We found Lana sitting down by the water, wearing a white dress, a straw hat, and a pair of dark sunglasses. She looked like a grief-stricken movie star. We sat down in the sand next to her and waited for her to say something. I didn't really know what to think of her anymore—Leo either.

"Leo left last night," she finally said. She straightened her hat and shifted her sunglasses, and though we knew she didn't mean it, she smiled faintly.

"Is he coming back?" Elena asked.

She looked at us, her eyes lingering over us, as if she were feeling our sudden weight in her life. We were no longer three girls for which the truth needed to be forever denied. Whether she liked it or not, we had become a force of our own.

"I don't think so, but we'll see." She drew me and Lizzy under one of her arms and Elena under the other, the four of us digging our feet under the cool, moist sand, our eyes cast out to the restless sea.

Over the course of the next hour, as the sun climbed higher and higher in the sky, Lana told us what had happened to her since she'd come back to New York. She told us everything she could remember, speaking openly and fluidly, almost breathlessly about her ascent back to life. The floodgates, though I could hardly believe it, had finally opened.

She hadn't left because Leo played the jazz. Not really. It had pushed her closer to it, but what had really moved her to act was the knowledge that it had all happened the way she had said—that the white men had really been there. It was the turning point, the juncture at which her road of darkness veered off in the direction of light. Something about it had given her courage.

It took her a while, but she finally visited Mimi. It was not a graceful reunion. Immediately Mimi tried to take control of her life — she talked wildly of Lana singing again, of Lana resuming her career. She'd even made plans which she'd written down and had called some people, but Lana couldn't imagine.

They fought bitterly about it, screaming at each other up in Mimi's apartment on Park Avenue. It seemed to Lana that she'd never left, that she'd never had a life somewhere else. It took a long time, but Mimi finally succeeded in getting her to at least go to the clubs to visit some of her old friends. That was as much as she could possibly do. It had nearly shut her heart down stepping into those smoky places, the sound of the jazz unleashed and swarming in the air. It brought everything back to her in vivid, terrifying detail, but under the panic, under the horror of that one night, lay all the other countless, precious nights she'd spent. The sound of the jazz, she discovered, could unlock those memories as well.

Mimi dragged her to see Sammy first. He was an old man now — he didn't have his own club anymore, but he tended bar in a small one up in Harlem. It was he who first got her up on the stage again. He and Mimi. She was shocked when he first asked her to sing. "How could I?" she gasped.

"Just get up there and open your big mouth," Mimi said.

She couldn't do it that night. It seemed like quite an accomplishment just to sit in the audience and listen to the jazz.

Mimi took her back there again and again, until one night Sammy finally got up on stage and introduced her. "We've got Lana Lamar with us tonight, folks." When the musicians and some of the people in the audience stood up and gave her a thunderous welcome, she found herself walking up there. By the time she took that last step onto the stage, her legs were trembling so much her pant legs shook. Her heart felt like it was coming undone inside her chest, and she was panting so hard she felt like an overheated dog.

The band started playing her favorite song — "Let's Call the Whole Thing Off" — and she was so afraid of what would come out of her mouth that she missed her entrance. She felt like the sparrow who couldn't sing for the bear. Her hands shook like the north wind, and for a few awful moments it seemed she might faint; but the people were so happy to see her up there, she found herself wanting to sing to them.

When she finally opened her mouth, her voice came out. It wasn't as strong as it had once been, but it was still full, and though it surprised her it was still the singing voice of a Negro woman. She hadn't heard it in over nine years. Nine years.

Mimi dragged her to other clubs to more of her old friends, where she almost always ended up on the stage singing one song or another. She slowly got used to it. In fact, she started to like it—she even loved it at times. After a while, it began to seem that with each note, she was taking her life back. Bit by bit, she was regaining it.

When she started singing regularly in a small club in Harlem, her life opened up newly. It was like an awakening after a long, tortuous slumber. People who had once known her came to the club after having read about her return. All kinds of people—black people, white people, people she hardly even remembered, people whom she'd never met, and people who'd heard about her and wanted to see who she was. A lot of nights they stuck around afterward and talked, kicking around ideas, dredging up old ones, thinking up new ones. They wanted to know what she thought after such a long time away.

Her hands still shook every now and then, and her voice wasn't always strong. When we asked her why that happened, she told us that it was something left over from her experience, that she couldn't help it, that whenever fear overtook her she'd lose her voice and her hands would start to shake.

When Elena asked her about Leo, she admitted that she was having a hard time forgiving him. We asked her, "For what?" and she said, "He didn't have enough faith in me." It seemed that Lana had stopped having faith in him too, but I didn't say anything.

We went to hear her sing at the jazz club that night. We drove into the city in Mimi's Cadillac, all of us talking at once, emitting such an energy it seemed the car must have glowed. For the first time in my life, I felt like a normal person, a regular person who was going with her grandmother to hear her mother sing. That meant more to me than I can say.

We drove up to the club sometime after eight o'clock, and while Lana got ready in the dressing room, we sat down at two of the front tables and waited. It was a small, smoke-filled place with black, dusty floors, but it felt safe and homey, like a place a person like Lana could heal. I was surprised, but within an hour it filled up completely—mostly with black people, but there were some white people too.

I wondered where Leo was and what had finally happened between him and Lana last night. In the whirl of our excitement, I had forgotten about him, but now it came back to me on a pang of longing so sharp and pointed I felt it pierce my insides. I wanted him here. I wasn't mad at him, I realized. I knew he wasn't to blame for everything any more than Lana was. It wasn't that simple. I didn't know exactly what it was, but I at least understood that.

When Lana came out on the stage, Lizzy, Elena, and I were surprised. Gone were the glittery dresses and the high heels. There were no flowers in her hair either. She wore a simple black gown and a pair of black pumps. I didn't think she would use her cane to get on and off the stage, but she did.

I wasn't quite prepared to hear her sing. Though I had heard her sing in her films, it wasn't quite the same. It had never really seemed like her exactly. But now the Lana I knew, the woman I had watched over countless afternoons, opened her mouth and sang in a voice so lovely, I was stunned. I felt a love and pride so deep, it crushed me. How she had stifled such a beautiful voice all these years, how she had kept herself so absolutely tuneless, I could not understand.

When she finished her first song, Elena stood up and clapped furiously, her pale white hands a blur in the bluish light. Lizzy and I rose also and clapped until our hands ached. Bravo, Lana, I thought. Bravo.

The rest of the night floated by in a haze of smoke and bluish lights, Lana's torchy voice threading through it all. She had fallen, yes, but I sensed she had risen again—like a phoenix from unbearable, black ashes. "She is my mother," I wanted to cry out. "She is my mother."

When the night was over, when it seemed we might carry Lana home on our shoulders, the old black trumpet player stepped up to the microphone. He squinted his eyes, shielding them from the spotlights. "That you out there, Leo?" he called out.

The sound of Leo's name sent a bolt of lightning down my spine. I spun around in my chair, just as Mimi, Lizzy, and Elena did, and there he was leaning up against the bar. I don't know if it was the sound of Lana's voice after all these years, or if it was the sight of her standing on a stage again, but I could tell by the watery look in his eyes that he had been moved.

"He looks good," Lizzy whispered.

He looked transfixed, but none of us could really put that into words.

We turned around to see what Lana's reaction was. Her eyes snagged on him for a moment, but she looked away from him immediately. A red flush raced up her throat, and though it was only slightly detectable I saw her hands shake. Their eyes caught a few moments later, and they stared at one another across the expanse of heads, something wordless and taut moving between them.

"Come on up, Leo," the trumpet player said. While the audience clapped, Leo hesitated, his eyes moving swiftly between the old man and Lana. When the piano player stood up and gestured to him that the piano was all his, there wasn't much Leo could do but go up there. As he made his way through the crowd, Elena, Lizzy, and I squeezed hands under the tabletop.

After he took his seat, it seemed a shadow fell across Lana's face. Nonetheless, he played the first song they'd ever done together— "Salty Papa Blues." Her hands shook, but by the time she got to the second verse they stopped.

It was almost more than my heart could take—seeing them together, singing and playing the piano. How much better it was to finally let that sound roll out, to fill the room with it, to let it wash over our insides, than it was to forbid it.

Leo played two more songs, the last one being one of those nerve-ticking ones. It wasn't the song he had written for Lana, the one which had played during the worst moments of her life, but it was similar in its foot-stomping, driving rhythm, and it had everyone moving. He played the piano like I'd never seen him play it before—it was as if he'd saved it up all these years just so he could play it like he played it tonight—and Lana couldn't keep her feet still.

It made my heart beat really fast to see them together like that, faster even than when Miss Thomas showed me her birds or took me into her room of perpetual sound and motion. I felt like I could have watched them forever. I couldn't help but think we were witnessing a miracle, a miracle for which I would be unendingly grateful.

When Lana ended the song on her knees with her arms out-stretched to the crowd, it seemed the whole club rose in thundering applause. With each brisk clap, I sensed the heat of their approval driving the illness further and further away. I could almost see it rising from her like a fog.

When the applause died down, a lot of them edged up to the stage. The lights came up, and while the band broke up, Lana walked down to the foot of the stage to speak to them. Leo drifted over to the side curtain where he and the old trumpet player passed a pint bottle of Seagram's Seven back and forth and watched her come to life.

The crowd wanted to know what had happened to her, and when she told them the truth, Lizzy, Elena, and I couldn't believe it. "But I'm back now," she said. "I'm back." When they exploded in applause, I sensed that Lana had never known a finer moment. Somehow through her pain and loss, she belonged to them. She finally belonged to them.

For the next hour, she answered their questions, finally stepping up to the microphone so she could be heard by everyone. They wanted to know what she was going to do now (she said she didn't know), and what she thought after having been away so long. It wasn't anything like the past—there was no tension, no speeches. It made a difference that she'd been raped by three black men and a white man and had come back to them without a single grudge.

As I listened to her, I was struck by the change which had swept through her in one month's time. I wondered what exactly had happened inside of her, what power had reached down and healed her so magnificently. I knew she would never return to the green hills of Hamilton, New York, never again would she sit for weeks, for months in her room. She wasn't really a writer, I realized. She was something else—what, I didn't quite know, but she was something else altogether.

When the crowd finally dispersed and Lana left the stage, Lizzy and I looked around for Leo and discovered that he'd disappeared. We looked all over for him, threading our way through what remained of the crowd, but he wasn't there. Just when it looked like they might actually be capable of speaking, he had vanished.

It hung over me like a heavy blanket all the way back to Long Island Sound. We all sat in the backseat with Lana, talking excitedly, but in the back of my mind was Leo's nagging absence. I kept seeing the empty spot where he'd been standing near the curtain, and it bothered me.

"Where did Leo go?" I finally asked Lana.

"Somebody told me he left." She glanced out the window and watched the darkness roll past for a few minutes.

When we pulled into Mimi's driveway, his car was parked there. The house was completely dark, though.

"What, he's sitting there in the dark?" Mimi said.

"I don't know," Lana answered.

"He used to sit in the dark in our living room after Lana left," Elena whispered.

That felt like light-years ago when Leo and I used to meet in the dark of our living room and not say a word.

Mimi turned the car off, and we all crept quietly across the sand and up the porch steps. The fact that the house was completely dark threw a little dread into our hearts. None of us wanted to meet Leo this way—in the blackness. We found him sitting on the porch swing, perfectly silent and stilled. Mimi swept us into the house before they could even say anything to each other and took us up to bed.

Lizzy fell asleep almost as soon as she lay down, but I couldn't sleep. Not until I knew how it was going to work out between Lana and Leo. I listened to the sound of their bedroom door closing, and waited five minutes before I crept down Mimi's stairs and placed my left eye behind the keyhole. I could see Leo standing at the window again, the white curtains billowing softly around him, while Lana sat on the edge of the bed. It was as if they had never left this room, as if a day had never passed. The tension rode between them again, like a cable they somehow couldn't disconnect.

"You did a nice job tonight," Leo said carefully. He didn't turn around to look at her. "I think I understand how much it means to you to talk to the people. I don't think I ever really knew." His words, so unexpected, bent the air or shifted it somehow, for I sensed a sudden, powerful relief. "I don't know why I never stayed to hear you back then. I don't know what I was thinking."

It took a long time for her to speak, but when she finally spoke, it was to say, "Thank you." She paused for a moment. "I'm sorry I took away your music, Leo," she said. "I don't know what I was thinking either."

He pressed forward on his arms, while she looked down at the floor, her eyes unblinking.

"What should we do now?" he whispered.

"I don't know," Lana answered.

A few more delicate minutes passed, where neither of them moved nor spoke. It seemed the moments were made of glass, that the next words out of their mouths would decide their fate. They feared that, too, if they said the wrong ones, everything would shatter. Doom seemed to hang over them like a hovering bird, until the silence hung for so long the tension began to dissipate. The rise and fall of the waves seemed to pull it from the room, hauling it out to sea.

Leo walked quietly over to Lana and stood in front of her, their bare toes not more than a foot apart. Their eyes met and then shifted away and then met again. When Leo pushed his hands into his pockets, Lana uncrossed her legs and laid her hands in her lap. They looked at one another again, and I sensed in their naked stare a longing to stop, to just stop. As if it floated between them on wings, I understood that there was still something beating and vital between them, that underneath all the years of broken bargains and bitter resentment, there was still something there—something not of the mind, but rather of the heart.

Leo dropped slowly to his knees. He laid his head in her lap and pressed his face against her stomach, embracing her as he had longed to do out on the beach. "La," he choked out, "I only loved you."

She pinched her eyes shut, as if out of all the things he could have said this was the most difficult to hear. She sat there for a while, staring down at his head, until she finally put her arms around him, her hands moving slowly across his back. Her eyes fluttered shut, and he reached up and touched her face with his fingertips, the way he used to before all this had come between them. It seemed to remind her of the Leo she had lost track of, because when she opened her eyes they were soft again. They searched each other's eyes, looking for whatever they'd lost. I sensed that beneath the months of rage and violence, the desperate clawing upward, there was an equally strong need to merge, to join, to reach down past it all to heal.

"What do you want, Lana?" he whispered.

"I need time," she said.

"Do you want me in New York?"

She stared at him for a long time before she spoke. "We'll see, Leo."

"Do the girls like it here?" he whispered.

"Yes, I think so."

"What about Lizzy?" he asked.

"I'm going to keep her."

Leo stared at her for a moment, and when he pressed his lips to her mouth, I took my eye away from the keyhole and walked up Mimi's creaking stairs, to Lana's old bedroom. I crept under the covers and pulled the sheet up to my chin, glancing out the window at the churning ocean. Lizzy was sound asleep, but I told her anyway. "We're going to keep you."

I heard something crackle beneath the pillow and slipped my hand underneath it. It was Elena's pack of Winston cigarettes with a book of matches wedged inside the cellophane. I shook one out and lit it, blowing the smoke out the window where it got lost in the night mist. Up until this moment my whole life had been lived with a man and a woman who had banished their passions and imposed a life of unendurable silence; but now it was finished. The bargain they had struck so long ago was dead.

I didn't know what would happen next, but I took comfort in knowing it would never happen the way it already had. I could only be glad that was over.

I felt the doors and walls that had kept my mind locked in blackness fall away, the dark vapors rushing out, like the smoke from my cigarette escaped out the window, and something deep inside my chest opened and breathed for the first time. I could almost feel life yawning before me — life in all of its magnificence and its horror.

Somewhere someone's been born, I thought. In Poland, in Russia, in Tibet. And right now, this very moment someone died, and someone's crying. And just now someone's been shot, and now someone else. In New York, in China. And this instant, a man and a woman are holding one another in a dark room, beating back loneliness. In Hungary, in Africa, on Long Island Sound. And now, this very second, the sun rose somewhere and fell somewhere else.

I looked out the window again, and I saw the old man and Howard. They were walking quickly across the dark sand, Howard leading the way to the shore. He kept looking over his shoulder, as if he were afraid someone was following him. When his feet hit the water, he forgot about it. He ran in again, flapping his arms up and down clumsily, the water breaking against his skinny, barren chest. The old man stood on the shore and watched him. That was something the Eyes of God would do—take a dying kid down to the water on his last night to let him say good-bye. I only wished that there was a projector room buried deep in the heavens where the Eyes of God could sit and watch us all.

An overweight woman dressed in a white gown came storming down the beach. It must have been his mother, Saracyntia. "HOWARD," she yelled, "GET OUT OF THE WATER RIGHT NOW AND GET UP THERE TO BED." She sounded so much like Garta, I shuddered.

Howard padded up to the shoreline, where he stood looking out at the rolling sea. "I'm King of the Breakers," he yelled over to her. He stretched his arms out in front of him and made like he was pulling the waves in, and when they started to recede, he ran with them, his skinny arms making like they were pushing them away, as if he were all powerful.

"HOWARD," she yelled, stamping her foot in the wet sand. "GET OUT OF THAT WATER NOW. GODDAMN IT, GET OUT."

The old man just stood there watching as Howard staggered back into the water. He stopped when it came up to his waist and turned around. He wrapped his skinny arms around his sunken chest to stave off the cold, while the waves broke over him one after the other. He just stood there shaking, his teeth chattering, while he held his own against those foaming white breakers. "I'm the Pillar in the Tide," he yelled to his mother. "The Pillar in the Tide."

The woman plunged into the water after him, and I turned away. When her shrill voice overpowered Howard's high, squeaky claim to life, I climbed into bed with Lizzy, where I laid my head on her chest and listened to the strong brag of her heart.

I didn't mean to, but I woke her up. "What's wrong, Maddie?" she whispered.

The tears backed up behind my eyes, and my throat pinched off. I couldn't put it into words, but I wanted to tell her how it seemed we were all a little like Howard, like shaky pillars struggling in the tide.